His Promise True

Greta Marlow

Greta Marlow (signature)

EMZ-Piney Publishing
Hagarville, AR

His Promise True
Copyright 2013 by Greta Marlow
All rights reserved.

No part of this publication may be reproduced, stored in a retrieval system or transmitted in any way by any means, electronic, mechanical, photocopy, recording or otherwise without the prior permission of the author except as provided by USA copyright law.

This is a work of fiction. Names, characters, places, and incidents are either the product of the author's imagination or, if real, are used fictitiously.

Published by EMZ-Piney Publishing
Hagarville, AR 72839 USA

ISBN: 978-0-9899597-0-4

*To Jeff, Roger, and Lily
for treating Maggie and John David
like part of our family*

*May the words of my mouth and the meditations of my heart
be pleasing in your sight,
O Lord, my Rock and my Redeemer.
Psalm 19:14*

Chapter 1

September, 1823

I stood for a last minute in the cover of the woods, watching the men with their axes crowd around the whetstone in Charlie Huckett's clearing. Men were come from all over the mountain, here to help Charlie raise a barn and to break it in with drinking and dancing. That's how we did things on the mountain, folks giving help where help was needed. But if my Pa got his way today, one of those men would be helping with something none of them would expect. One of those men—I didn't know which one—was my future husband.

"Get moving," Pa said, jabbing me in the back with the butt of his ax. "Let's get something set up and be out of here before the heavy lifting starts. You know my back ain't any good."

"Who do you aim to promise me to?" I asked, crossing my arms over the bulging bosom Ma had built for me with rags. "What if I don't like him?"

Pa laughed and knocked my arms back to my sides. "Hoping for some fair-faced young lover, are you? That's only in old ballads, girl. You'll like whoever I pick, and you'll make him a willing wife—"

"How will you know whether I'm a willing wife? You plan to live with us?"

I didn't flinch when he grabbed my arm, but no smack came. He leaned close.

"Listen, girl, you'd best tame that tongue. I promise you, if you ain't betrothed to somebody come nightfall, you'll get a lesson you won't soon forget." He pushed me forward, and I stumbled on the hem of Ma's faded best dress. "Lordy, I'll be glad when you're somebody else's trouble! He better be a man with a firm hand, or his life will be

1

pure hell. Now get out there, and don't go hiding so I can't find you. And mind you don't soil your ma's dress."

He started toward the whetstone, but I lingered on the path, pondering how far I could run into the woods before he'd notice I was gone. Somebody giggled, and I whirled around, ready with hot words for whatever boys thought I was so funny. But it was only Martha Handley.

"Maggie Boon! When did you grow that bosom?" she said, coming to link her arm in mine. "You didn't do a very good job stuffing it. The sides don't even match!"

I glanced down at it. "I look like a cow with her udder gone bad."

Martha laughed and patted my tight bun of hair. "If a cow had her tail twisted and pinned up on her head! What are you all fancied up for? You always said you didn't care about getting you a fellow, and now here you are, looking like somebody's wife!"

I sighed. "That's how I'm supposed to look. Pa aims to speak to somebody today about taking me."

The smile faded from Martha's freckled face. "Who?"

"You know my pa. Somebody with something to trade, he says. Somebody settled, I reckon, probably one of the widowers."

She clucked sympathetically. "With a passel of kids, probably."

"I'll be wife and mother in one deal!" I tried to laugh, but it choked off in my throat.

"He wouldn't do that," she said. "You ain't even as old as me."

"I'm old enough, he says." Through the cabin's open door, I saw women and girls stirring around the quilting frame Ellen had set up in her front room. "Don't say anything about it to other folks, Martha," I said. "I don't want folks to know till it's done. Promise?"

"I promise."

"Come on, then," I said, lifting my chin and straightening my false bosom with a quick push. "Let's get a spot at the quilt frame before they're all gone and there's no place to hide this abomination of a bosom."

※ ※ ※

All morning, I had to bear teasing from the curious women, but that didn't bother me near as much as wondering what Pa was doing outside. I must have paid more mind to trying to catch sight of him through the door than to my stitching, because near midday I jabbed the needle into my finger deep enough to draw blood.

"Maggie!" Mrs. Huckabay scolded. "Blood on a new quilt curses it! Quick, go wash yourself."

The water bucket was dry, no doubt because the little boys were too busy chasing around to mind their job of keeping it filled. I snatched up the bucket and hurried into the woods, blessing my good luck for the chance to escape the busy clearing for even a little while. A few steps in, I slowed to listen to the living sounds of the woods. I knew them all, from the plunk of an acorn hitting the ground to the scolding of the squirrel who dropped it. But there was another sound today, a splashing rustle I couldn't quite name. Maybe it's a doe come to drink, I thought, or a fox, even. I held my breath, creeping the last few steps toward the ravine where Charlie's spring pooled under the rocks.

It was something come to drink, all right, but it was no doe. A man squatted by the spring with a dipper in his hand, water running from his dark hair down the sides of his neck. He shook his head like a wet dog would do, and as he wiped water from his face, he saw me. Two bright spots colored his cheeks as he dropped the dipper into the spring and stood. I'd never seen anyone so tall. He had to be at least six feet, maybe more.

"I'm glad you're not a bear," he said.

I couldn't place his face. He had to be somebody from the barn-raising, though, because this was Charlie's spring, not one on any path a traveler might take. He was a young man, lean but strong of build, wearing clothes that were sweat-soaked but well-made. Looking at him, I was sure he wasn't from around here. I knew the men from these mountains and all their sons, and this fellow wasn't one of them.

The red in his face had spread to his throat. "It's a hot day to swing an ax."

His eyes flicked across my false bosom, and one corner of his mouth twisted upward the slightest bit. My face flushed hot and I stepped over the drop-off and edged around him to the spring. Best get out of here quick as I could.

"I'll do that," he said. He squatted by the spring to rinse my bucket and then looked up while water bubbled in. "I can't believe I didn't hear you. Usually I'm better about watching. You walk in the woods quieter than anybody I know." His grin was crooked and just a tad wider than it should've been to look exactly right. "If word gets back to the clearing that I let a girl sneak up on me, I'll never hear the end of it. They're itching for some way to knock me into place, and that would sure do it."

I crossed my arms over that huge bosom. "I won't tell."

He grinned again. "I'm obliged, on behalf of all men from the valley. I've got to keep up our name against these mountain men."

"You're from the valley?" That's why I didn't know him; I'd never been off the mountain.

"I am." He stood, swiping his wet hand against his pants before holding it out to me. "I'm John David McKellar."

I stared at him, probably with my mouth hanging wide open. Even I had heard of the rich McKellars. They weren't like mountain folk, Pa said, not even like other folk in the valley. Old Man McKellar had a deal with the devil, Pa said. That's why their corn prospered so in ground that gave other folks—like us—barely a living.

"What's your name?" He seemed even bigger now that he was right beside me, and I was a little scared of him, though he seemed friendly enough.

"Maggie Boon, from Pine Mountain." I squeezed his fingertips, letting go quickly to reach for the bucket. He got to it first.

"I'll take the buckets if you'll bring the dipper." He offered his hand again to help me over the gully's edge, like he thought I needed his help. I didn't take it, just climbed over the edge and started back to the clearing, quickly. But in two steps he'd caught up with me.

"So you're from Pine Mountain," he said. "I've hunted there before. It has some nice woods to wander in."

He was a strange man. He kept stopping to hold low branches out of my way on the path or to wait for me to catch up to him. Worst of all, he kept talking, like knowing my name made him less a stranger.

"I hope dinner's ready when we get back. My knees may wobble out from under me if I have to cut another notch without something to eat."

"What are you doing here, anyhow?" I asked.

"I heard Charlie needed help, and not to brag, but I'm good with an ax."

I laughed. "You're swinging an ax on a hot day like this, just from kindness?" Pa would've smacked me for such sass, but Mr. McKellar just grinned.

"Well—I also heard Charlie's rolling out a barrel of whiskey once the rafters are up. My pa won't allow whiskey around our place. He's the strictest Presbyterian in the county." He went on, quickly. "They say a fiddler's coming from Glade Spring. I reckon you'll stay for the dancing?"

I looked away. "That depends on my pa."

Just my luck, Pa was one of the men waiting for water. Even across the clearing, I saw his mouth turn down as he caught sight of us.

"You didn't need to carry that," he said as Mr. McKellar set the buckets on the stump. "Maggie's been sitting at that quilt frame all morning while you been working."

"That didn't amount to anything for me," Mr. McKellar said. "It would've been a heavy load for a twig of a girl like her, though." From the corner of my eye, I saw his mouth twist into that crooked smile. "Nice talking to you, Maggie. Maybe you'll get to stay for the dancing."

Soon as he was gone, Pa grabbed my elbow and pulled me away from the men crowding around the water. "Keep clear of that McKellar boy!" he hissed. "I don't know what he's doing here, but you stay away from him. It's hard enough to find somebody who wants you without you slobbering over some rich boy like a hound over a hog's knuckle."

"You ain't found anybody yet?"

He gave me a hard look. "Don't think I won't. You could help me out, you know. Quit hiding that bosom under your elbows. And stick with your own kind, Maggie. A rich valley man don't want a thing from a homely girl like you but what he can lay his hands on. Don't fool yourself he'd stick around once he got it, and there you'd be, ruined."

"I wasn't—"

Pa jerked my arm and pain throbbed in my shoulder.

"Are you backtalking?" I glared at him. His smile was tight. "That's better. Once you're married, your sass is your man's problem. But act right till then, or I'll make you wish you had."

❦ ❦ ❦

The longer we stayed at Charlie's, the more I knew the day wouldn't have a good ending, no matter what. I wondered what would be worse, marrying some old man or going home with Pa mad and full of whiskey. We were still there when the last rafter was raised and Charlie lit a bonfire to brighten the clearing. Martha came to watch with me as the fiddler from Glade Spring called folks together for the first dance set. My throat felt like somebody was squeezing it with a strong hand.

"Your pa spoke to anyone yet?" she asked, pity as clear in her voice as on her face.

"You're sweet on Luther Wiggins, right?" I said, louder than I meant to. "I'll partner with Pete Knight, then, so you can dance with Luther."

She looked doubtful. "Your pa might not like that."

I took her hand. "I don't care. Till he's promised me to somebody, I reckon I'm free to get the good out of my maiden days. Let's dance!"

I'd known Pete Knight all my life, but as we danced, I watched him like I never had before. He was a skinny fellow with big ears, and his folks weren't much better off than mine, but a body would be hard-pressed to find anyone with a sweeter temper than Pete. He'd make a fine husband. If I was only older, I could choose somebody—maybe Pete—for myself instead of having to take whoever Pa found for me. But I couldn't marry yet without Pa's consent, and he wouldn't let me marry Pete Knight, even if I said that's what I wanted. He didn't just want me married; he wanted something in return, and Pete didn't have anything to give.

The song ended with a high squeal, and Pete turned to me again with his hands twisted together.

"Want to go for another?"

I smiled and laid my hand on his arm. "I'll dance every set with you, Pete, if that's what you want. You don't have to keep asking." His grin stretched from one big ear to the other. But as we moved back into line, someone grabbed my shoulder and pulled me away.

"Maggie?" Pete turned, but Phillip Owens was already forcing me toward the barn.

"Let's talk, Maggie Boon." He raised an arm and leaned against the wall like a man trying to hem in a nervous heifer. He smelled of sweat and whiskey, and crumbs of corn pone were caught in his scraggly beard.

He smiled. "Your pa spoke to me."

My heart seemed to stop. Not him. Of all the widowers—

"I reckon you heard my second wife died last spring. That leaves me and the young'uns alone. They sure need a woman's hand. You've seen 'em, I reckon?"

I'd seen them. Six of them, all under ten years old, all with shaggy hair, dirty clothes, their pa's loose mouth.

"I got a pretty nice place," he went on, "better than what you're used to, I'd say. But with a strong, young woman around, a lot more could be done with it." His eyes wandered over my body, lingering on the false bosom. "You're scrawny, but your pa says you're a good worker."

"Mister Owens, I—I got to—" I didn't bother to finish an excuse. I ducked under his arm and slipped through the dancing people, fast so he couldn't catch me, fast so he couldn't keep his piggy eyes on me. I bumped into someone, but I didn't stop to apologize or even to see who it was. I didn't stop until I was under a big tree at the very edge of Charlie's clearing, as far from the dancers as I could get without going into the dark of the woods. In the twilight, a single star winked— or was it blinking back tears, same as me? I leaned against the tree, and thick sobs filled my throat. I knew why Mr. Owens' second wife had died, and his first wife, too. Too many babies. Too many days hoeing corn too soon after those babies. I saw myself grubbing out his cornfields, having his loose-mouthed babies.

"It ain't right!" I stormed. "None of it!" I jerked open Ma's high collar that had been binding me all day and thrust my hand inside the bodice, throwing the wadded rags as hard as I could into the darkness. I pulled the pins from my hair and threw them away, too. Sinking to the ground, I pulled my knees against my chest and buried my face in my arms, letting my hair fall like a curtain to shut out everything as I cried.

So this was how it was going to be. If I refused to marry Phillip Owens—if I even *could* refuse—Pa had promised a beating, and Pa could give a beating that would leave me aching for days. Even worse would be what he'd say, things that would cut to my heart. He'd talk about high and mighty wenches who think they're too good for honest, hard-working men. He'd tell how hard it had been to get any man to look toward a scrawny, homely girl like me and how ungrateful I was to run out on the only one who would. He'd make sure I knew exactly what Mr. Owens had been willing to give for my hand and just how much the family would suffer without it. He'd remind me that every day I stayed unmarried meant less food for my sisters and brothers, my dear little ones, each of them every bit as scrawny as me.

My eyes felt hot and prickly, but they weren't crying anymore. Crying never carried any weight with Pa. I leaned against the tree and took a shuddering breath of the cool air. So this was how it was going to be.

I closed my eyes when I heard footsteps. It was too much to hope for that Pete had come to find me. Likely it was Mr. Owens, or Pa, come to fetch me back.

"Are you all right?" My eyes popped open to see John David McKellar standing a pace away. "You were crying."

"I ain't supposed to talk to you." I struggled to stand in Ma's long dress, and he took my elbow to help me up.

"Why not?" He sounded put off, but I didn't care about coddling his fancy valley feelings at the moment.

"Pa said not to. He says it'll scare off my prospects." I turned toward the dancing, but he caught my elbow and held it, tighter this time.

"Your prospects? What's that mean?"

I hesitated. It was none of his affair. But even valley folks would hear about me and Mr. Owens sometime. "He's trying to find me a husband, and we've got to be careful folks don't think the wrong thing. Now let go of me. I need to get back."

His fingers stayed tight on my arm. "What difference does it make if you talk to me?"

"You sure are interested in other folks' lives!" I snapped. "This don't concern you."

He straightened his shoulders so he looked even taller.

"Is that so? If somebody says I can't have a little confabulation with anybody I please, I say it concerns me. 'Congress shall make no law abridging the freedom of speech.' It's in the constitution of these

United States." He grinned, evidently quite pleased with himself. "Nobody can keep us from talking."

I stared at him, trying to figure if he was serious about the law, or just drunk enough to be making it all up. I could smell whiskey on him, but he didn't really seem drunk—just strange. He grinned again and let go of my elbow. "So. Why can't you talk to me?"

He wasn't going away. I sighed. "Well, for one thing, we ain't the same kind of folks. What you said proves that. I don't know about laws or confabu—what you said. Pa says if my kind of folks sees me mixing with your kind, they'll think I ain't their kind anymore. And no one will want to be my husband then."

He smiled. "You're mighty young to be worrying about a husband."

"I ain't that young. I'll be sixteen come January."

"You're only fifteen? You've got plenty of time, then."

"I don't," I sighed. "Pa wants me married now. He says it's time I'm somebody else's trouble."

He laughed. I glared at him.

"It ain't so all-fired funny!" I started again toward the dancers, but this time he stepped in front of me, and he wasn't smiling anymore.

"I didn't mean to laugh," he said. "Please stay."

His eyes were very dark under strong, straight brows. John David McKellar was a fine-looking man, I noticed, really fine-looking. My heart took to pounding, and I quickly looked at my feet.

"So why's your pa in such a hurry to marry you off?" I looked up again, sharp words ready on my tongue. Fine-looking or not, rich or not, laws or not, he wasn't going to mock me. But there was no trace of mockery in his face. He looked like it mattered to him to know.

"Too many mouths to feed," I told him, straight out. "There's twelve of us, eight girls and four boys. If I go, the corn pone stretches further."

"I guess that's so."

"Pa says the trouble is having so many girls. A man needs sons to work a place. But the new baby was another girl."

"You're the firstborn?" I nodded, and he smiled. "I'm youngest in my family. There are only four of us who lived, all boys."

"So I've heard." I decided not to tell him everything I'd heard about his family. "I thought you'd be dancing."

He had a low, rumbly laugh. "So did I. But that rotgut whiskey of Charlie's is sitting rough on me. Between it and all the noise, I was feeling queasy." He grinned sheepishly. "You won't go telling that, will you? Remember, I've got a name to keep up."

The little laugh in my throat felt queer, and I shook my head.

"I'm not ready to go back to that loud bunch just yet," he said, moving a step closer, "but I believe I could handle some dancing, if you'd like to."

I stared at him. "Out here? Without other folks? I don't—"

"Why not? We can do all the steps." He cocked his ear toward the fiddler. "He's calling *All in a Garden Green*. Do you know that set?"

"I know it."

"Good." He grinned and moved back a few steps to stand facing me.

I stood stone still. He was a strange man, all right. Talking was one thing, but it wasn't right to dance with him, no matter what he said the law said. My good sense told me to just thank him nicely and get back to the crowd, where Pa and my future husband were sure to have noticed by now how long I'd been gone. Looking across at him, though, a foolhardy notion rooted in my heart. I was stuck with Mr. Owens the rest of my days. What was the harm of just one dance with this young and handsome and rich man, a man who seemed to care what I had to say—even if it was just because he was tight on Charlie's whiskey? We were here alone, away from the firelight and the crowd. Pa and Mr. Owens would never even know. I lifted my chin and smiled straight at Mr. McKellar as I stepped forward to fall in with the fiddler's faint call.

Mr. McKellar was a merry partner as well as a handsome one, humming along with the fiddle and adding silly flourishes to the steps that made me laugh. Once he even broke out singing, and I laughed and tipped my head back to look into his face as I turned under his arm.

"Wouldn't you know it? You're a fine singer, too. Are you good at everything?"

He suddenly caught me around the waist with his free arm and pulled me to him, so close I felt his heart thumping through his linen shirt.

"Everything." His lips, eager and warm, were against mine before I could gather my wits enough to understand what was happening.

I don't know that I even heard the snarl that came out of the darkness, but something made me drop Mr. McKellar's hand and pull away from him. Too late, I realized I'd never refastened the buttons on Ma's dress and the bodice was flapping open halfway to my real bosom. I jerked the edges together.

"Too late to start acting the pure maid, you harlot," Pa growled. He slapped me across the face, so hard sparks of light flashed against the darkness. "After I found a decent, hard-working, God-fearing man for you to wed, you sneak off in the dark with some young buck in rut! Get back over there with everyone else!"

"She's not at fault," Mr. McKellar said. "I'm the one—"

"I saw what my eyes saw." Pa's fingernails bit into my wrist as he grabbed my arm. "She sure didn't seem to be fighting you. Jezebel!"

My face was burning. I wished Mr. McKellar would leave. He'd only get Pa more riled if he tried to explain. What was there to explain, anyhow? Pa was right. I'd willfully chosen to stay and talk to a strange man. I'd taken his invitation to dance with no other folk around. I'd let him draw me so close my body had been against his. I hadn't pushed him away, or cried out, or anything.

"She's not at fault," Mr. McKellar repeated. "I lost my good sense for a minute, but she's not to blame for that." Pa turned on him in fury, but suddenly stopped.

"John David McKellar," he said, like the name burned his tongue. "Thought you'd finish what you started earlier, did you?" His laugh was harsh. "You must be drunk, McKellar. Find another skirt to chase around the clearing, and leave my daughter alone. She's naught but quick pleasure to you, but I've got use for her, if Phillip Owens will have the worthless slut after this." Hot pain shot through my elbow as he twisted my arm, and I yelped a little before I could stop myself. "Go tell Owens you're sorry. And make it sound real! I said go!"

My foot caught in Ma's skirt as he pushed me, and I fell. My knees throbbed with the jolt, but I scrambled to get my feet under me before he could jerk me up.

But it was Mr. McKellar who took my arm, helping me to my feet, holding me steady. "Leave her be! She's done no wrong."

"It ain't your affair, boy." Pa jerked me out of Mr. McKellar's grip. "She's my daughter, my property until she's married. I can do with her whatever I please. You've got nothing to say in the matter."

"But he does," I started, like I thought this time would be different. "Just listen to him—"

"What?" Pa sneered. "What will he tell me? That he can't do without you? That he wants you desperately?" He cuffed me on the side of the head with the back of his hand as he pulled me back toward the crowd. "Stupid slut! Even Phillip Owens doesn't really want you! Get back there before he changes his mind and won't marry you."

Mr. McKellar suddenly blocked our path. Pa cursed at him, but he didn't move.

"Owens can't have her," he said. "I'll marry her. Now let her go."

For just a minute, Pa looked dazed, like Mr. McKellar had said something in some strange tongue he couldn't understand. But his eyes suddenly narrowed and his lips clamped together in that way I'd seen when he thought he could pass poor quality hides for top price to some fool of a trader. A hot, sick feeling flooded my belly.

"No!" I cried, but they paid no mind to me.

"Taken a fancy to my Maggie, have you, McKellar?" Pa said.

"Take your hands off her!"

"Certainly!" Pa made a show of backing away. "You say you'll marry her?" The sick feeling was spreading into my chest.

"I will."

"How old did you say you are, boy?"

"Don't worry." Mr. McKellar's voice was cold. "I'm of age."

Pa laughed. "Well, you're a lucky man, McKellar. I heard folks say that fiddler is a magistrate in Glade Spring. Come on. You won't even have to wait."

※ ※ ※

I barely heard Pa's call for the magistrate, only the crowing sound of it. He won't do this, I told myself, even as I stood before the magistrate between him and Mr. McKellar. He thinks he'll humble me so I'll do what he wants without sassing. I saw Martha, her face suddenly gone suspicious, and Pete, too. He looked at me and then up at Mr. McKellar, and his eyes hardened so I would never have guessed him to be the sweet-tempered fellow I'd always known. It's

12

not what you think, I wanted to cry out. Any minute now, somebody will say something, this foolishness will be over, and you'll all have a good laugh.

The magistrate tucked his fiddle under his arm and wiped sweat off his upper lip with a limp handkerchief.

"Do we have to do this tonight, Boon? It's late, and the boy's parents aren't here."

"I'm of age now," Mr. McKellar said. "I don't need their consent."

The fiddler shook his head. "I don't remember the words without my book."

"Say it as you know it," Pa said. "They're so keen to be married, I want it done now."

The man squinted up at Mr. McKellar. "Son, how much did you drink tonight?"

"I'm not drunk," Mr. McKellar said. "Let's get on with it."

The fiddler cleared his throat. "What's your girl's name, Boon?"

"Margaret."

"Are you faint, girl?" the fiddler asked. "You look mighty pale."

"She always looks that way," Pa grumbled. "Quit stalling."

The fiddler stared into the dark sky. Then he took a deep breath and spoke in a solemn voice.

"Folks, John David McKellar and Margaret Boon stand before us to join in matrimony. We are witnesses to their vows." He paused to wipe sweat, so long Pa shifted angrily beside me. "Who gives this girl in marriage?"

"I do!" Pa hooted.

"Marriage is holy," the fiddler said slowly, "set down by God at creation—"

"Since you're worried it's so late," Pa broke in, "just skip all that truck. Get to the part where they pledge their troths." The fiddler sighed again, heavily.

"John David McKellar, do you take this girl as your lawfully wedded wife, to live with her and provide for her all the days that you shall live, to forsake all others—all others—till death do you part?"

"I do." Mr. McKellar's voice was low and steady. If he was having second thoughts, it wasn't showing.

"Do you, Margaret Boon, take John David McKellar as your

husband, to live with him and obey him until death do you part?"

I was the only one with the sense to stop this sham. I took a deep breath and turned to Mr. McKellar, ready to thank him nicely and say I hoped he wouldn't take offense, but I didn't want to live with him, or obey him, or anything with him.

On the other side of Mr. McKellar, I caught Mr. Owens eyeing my now-flat bosom with a smirk, and I read in his look exactly how life would be if I was his wife. He'd be just like Pa, hateful with words and handy with smacks, but worse, because he'd have a husband's rights to me. It would be Ma's life all over, a tumble-down cabin full of babies in too-small clothes, on a rocky hillside with a little patch of corn and a smokehouse, with plenty of nothing but work.

With Mr. McKellar, now—I didn't know what it would mean to be rich, but his shirt was fine linen, not linsey-woolsey. He was well-muscled, not scrawny, so I doubted he ever went to bed with his belly growling. I glanced up at him, but it was impossible to read his nature in his face. Still, there had been something friendly about his crooked grin, something interesting about that kiss—

"The fool girl's too tongue-tied to speak!" Pa said. He poked me hard in the side. "Say you do, Maggie."

"Let the girl make up her own mind, Boon," the fiddler warned. "Your consent or no, I won't perform this marriage if the girl's not willing."

"Oh, she's willing." Pa laughed hoarsely. "Leastwise, she was willing to be his whore out in the dark."

Hatred boiled through my body until I thought I'd scream it at him in front of everybody. Why did he take every little thing I did and make it dirty? He was the one in the wrong, so shiftless he'd rather trade me away than take honest work to feed the little ones. But I was the one who'd bear the brunt of his sloth, forced to give myself for life to some stranger.

A quiet thought suddenly dropped into the swirling heat in my head. *Two words, two simple words.* If I said them right now, I'd be away from Pa forever. Once I married, he had no claim on me; he'd said it himself. I was somebody else's trouble. I nearly laughed aloud. Pa wanted me to be a willing wife, did he? Well, I was willing enough to be a wife, if it meant I was free of him.

"I do," I said, clear and strong.

The fiddler coughed. "Does somebody know of a reason these two should not marry? Anybody?" A rustle of whispers swept the crowd.

"That's long enough," Pa ordered. "Finish it off."

The fiddler pulled at the collar of his shirt. "By the authority given me by the state of Tennessee, but against my better judgment, I pronounce you man and wife. John David, kiss your bride. God be with you when you take her home."

※ ※ ※

Of course, I wasn't free of Pa just yet. He gloated about the union of the Boon and McKellar bloodlines as the fiddler wrote something on the paper Charlie brought for him. Mr. McKellar signed it, but when they handed it to me, I bit my lip.

"Just write your name," Mr. McKellar said.

"She can't," Pa said. "But reading and writing ain't what keep a man warm at night!" He winked broadly at the folks around us.

"Make a mark, girl," the fiddler said. "We'll put your name."

"Get witnesses to sign," Pa added. "I want everybody to know they were joined legal."

We danced a few sets together, like any newly-married couple, but neither of us had our hearts in it. Mr. McKellar hardly glanced at me, and the funny flourishes from before were replaced by a serious look. We were dancing *Peace and Plenty* when Pa threw his arm around Charlie's shoulders and hollered, "It's getting late, boys! Reckon Ellen would give our newlyweds the loan of her fine feather bed?"

Mr. McKellar suddenly stumbled over my foot before he leaned down to speak in my ear.

"You look like you could do with sitting out a time or two. I'll find a place you can rest."

He settled me on a stump in the darkness beside the new barn, brushing the leaves and wood chips away before I sat down. But he didn't sit with me. Firelight fell across his face, and for a moment, he reminded me of how my brother Billy always looked when he knew he was doing something I wouldn't like.

"I'm going for a drink," he said finally. "You'll be all right here." He hesitated and then patted my shoulder awkwardly. "I'll be right back."

I watched him join the men around the barrel. He wouldn't be right back. He might say I looked like I needed rest, but he looked to me like a man desperate for help to face what he'd done. I could see his head, tallest in the group, tip back as he downed a drink in one gulp. So this is how it's going to be, I thought. Best get used to it.

Chapter 2

I spent my first night of married life on the floor of Charlie's new barn, listening to Pa snore and helping Mr. McKellar outside to puke.

I was right; he hadn't come right back. In fact, he'd left me so long on that stump I'd finally tired of waiting and went back to watch the dancing until Joe Towson came to fetch me, not even trying to hide his grin.

"You better check on yore new husband, Maggie," he'd said, loud enough folks could hear over the fiddle. "He's over there puking like a dog. Reckon valley men can't hold liquor like mountain men can. He's cheated us out of a chivaree tonight, boys!"

He wasn't hard to find. A group of the older boys had gathered around him, and I pushed my way through until I could see Mr. McKellar, on his knees and doubled over, heaving so hard I half expected him to cast up his whole stomach. The boys were laughing and jostling each other for a better view. I closed my eyes. I wanted to just walk away and leave the sight of him and his sickening smell far behind me. But he was my husband now, and even though he was so tall and strong, Mr. McKellar looked as pitiful at this moment as one of the babies from home.

"Begone, all of you!" I ordered, and after I'd pushed a couple of them, the boys grudgingly left us. Mr. McKellar was sitting back now, breathing fast and shallow. I squatted beside him. He was shivering.

"Can you move?" I asked, and he nodded. "Let's get you away from this mess."

I helped him to his feet and we stumbled through the darkness toward a tree, where I eased him down to sit.

"It was short-sighted of me to throw away my whole bosom

earlier," I said, lifting the hem of Ma's dress to wipe his mouth.

"My God," he groaned. "I've never been this sick in my life."

I laid my hand against his forehead. His skin was clammy but cool.

"You don't have fever," I said. "It must just be the whiskey."

"Whiskey's never made me sick before. Something's not right—" He suddenly pushed himself away from the tree and crawled a few feet before he was puking again.

He still looked peaky the next morning as we started up the mountain to get my things and, as Pa said, to tell Ma the "good news." He didn't speak at all as we followed Pa up the rocky trail. I wondered what he thought about the mess he'd got himself into, now that he was sobering up. I felt a little sorry for him. He'd come to Charlie's for fun, whiskey and some dancing. I was sure he hadn't planned to leave with a wife. But he had one now, and like it or not, he was going to keep me. I had to get away from Pa and off this hardscrabble mountain, and Mr. McKellar was the only way I saw to do it.

The little ones were playing in the clearing when we got home, and they all stopped stone still when they saw a stranger with us. I felt like a stranger myself, like I was seeing everything with Mr. McKellar's eyes—the one-room cabin, the dirty young'uns in their worn clothes, the overgrown garden, the smokehouse leaning nearly off its foundation. Pa's dog came running from the open doorway of the cabin, with Ma close behind, toting the baby on her hip.

"Thieving rascal!" she screeched. "A curse on you and your ill-begotten pups!" She stopped short when she saw Pa, her face twisted with bad temper. "Look who's finally home! I didn't know it took all night to raise a barn."

"If you'd use your eyes instead of your mouth, you'd notice we got company," Pa answered. "Meet John David McKellar, Maggie's husband."

Ma downright stared at Mr. McKellar before she remembered enough of her Carolina manners to smile brightly and smooth her ragged dress. "Maggie's husband, did you say? Not just her betrothed? Is he one of them valley McKellars?"

"The very same." Pa's glance met Ma's, and I hoped Mr. McKellar hadn't noticed the greedy smile that flickered between them.

The little ones followed us into the cabin, standing with fingers in their mouths or dresses twisted in dirty fists. Betsy waddled to me, and I picked her up, pressing my cheek against her soft curls.

"How did this come about?" Ma crooned, swiping her hand over the bench and pushing Mr. McKellar to sit. "I didn't know Maggie had your acquaintance."

"It was a surprise to me, too," Pa said. "I reckon fine young Mr. McKellar here took a hankering for our girl sometime yesterday. I found them under a tree during the dance, and let's just say I had to act quick to save her purity." My face was burning hot as he winked at Mr. McKellar.

Mary suddenly knocked the lid from the frying pan to the hearth with a loud clatter. Mr. McKellar winced.

"You all want a bite to eat?" Ma asked. "Dinner's just past, but Mary could stir something up."

"We can't stay," I said quickly. "It's a long way down the mountain. I'll get my things." I set Betsy down, and she held up her arms, whimpering. I didn't look at her as I started to the attic.

"Be careful with my good dress!" Ma barked. "Mary, help her. We don't want to keep your brother-in-law waiting."

Mary knelt beside me as I jerked Ma's dress over my head. "Is it true? You're married?" she asked.

"Yep, I'm Missus Margaret McKellar now." My hands were trembling as I stepped into my own dress, but not so bad she'd notice. She leaned closer.

"What did Pa mean about saving your purity?"

"He wants it to seem like something dirty happened," I said. "It didn't. He caught us dancing, that's all. There wasn't any hankering. Pa pushed us into marrying just because he thinks he can get his hands on some of the McKellar riches."

Her eyes were wide. "You know how Pa says McKellars got to be rich."

"That don't seem to fret him now that he thinks he'll get some of those riches himself." I laughed grimly as I folded my only stockings into my second-best dress. "Even if the McKellars invite the devil himself to supper, it's worth it to be free of Pa."

"But you don't even know this man," she whispered.

I shrugged like it was no matter. "He's just a man, like any other. I'll get used to him. What's it matter, anyhow? Pa was set on marrying me to anybody he could get to take me. You know who he chose first? Phillip Owens. At least Mr. McKellar don't have a passel of kids I have to be ma to right away."

"At least he's a sight better-looking than Mr. Owens," she said, and I laughed. Ma pulled herself up the ladder, a little of the familiar sharpness edging out the Carolina manners in her voice.

"Are you girls getting things together or just playing around?"

"I'm coming!" I said, tying back my tangled hair. "Are you in such a rush to rid yourself of me you can't let me tidy my hair?"

She glared at me. "You'll do well to check that sass, Maggie. You don't have charm enough to sass your fine Mr. McKellar."

"Well, my sass is his problem now, not yours." I tucked my bundle under my arm, but she blocked me from starting down the ladder.

"You think you're set up real fine now, don't you?" Her voice was a hoarse whisper. "I tell you, you're lucky your pa was there to get you married before you were fool enough to give yourself to that boy for free."

"I wasn't—" I started, but she wouldn't listen.

"You may satisfy him for a time, Maggie, but you're not what a man like that really wants for a wife. He'll tire of you right quick and find someone better. Just you be smart enough that when you show up here with his baby in your belly, you've got cash money in your pocket, too. As your husband, he'll owe you that much."

I laughed. "And no doubt you'll be plenty glad to take that cash money off my hands. Well, don't count on getting it anytime soon."

"You think he loves you?" she sneered. "Is that what he told you? Well, I've seen plenty of girls forsaken by fellows who swore eternal love. You're a fool if you expect anything different. Abandonment is a hard fate for a woman to face if she lets herself believe everything a man says. Mark my words, you'll beg us to take you back in."

"You're wrong," I said, pushing past her to go down the ladder. "I'm never coming back."

"We'll see," she whispered.

Mr. McKellar raised his eyebrow when he saw my small bundle. "That's all you have?"

Pa snorted. "You want a dowry, do you? Well, Son, you'll have to be satisfied with her maidenhead, if she's still got it to give."

He was making it easy. I marched up to him, sure he wouldn't smack me with big Mr. McKellar so near.

"The joke's on you, Pa," I said. "You may think having me married to a McKellar is your path to a life of ease. But I swear to you, so long as I have any say in it, you'll get nothing, not one ear of corn. And you know what else? There's nothing you can do about it! I'm somebody else's trouble now." I stepped through the door and started as fast as I could across the clearing.

"You got no call to go off with your tail in the air like a dern polecat!" Pa yelled, and that set Betsy to crying. I didn't turn around. Whether Mr. McKellar was behind me or not, I didn't know or much care. Without looking to either side, I crunched through the dry leaves, putting as much space as I could between me and that cabin quick as I could. Curse Pa—Ma too! I meant every word. They'd get nothing more from me. Browns and grays blurred around me until I couldn't tell trunk from leaves, and I had no idea where I was going or how far I'd gone when Mr. McKellar caught up. I was glad he didn't say anything. Every step took me farther from being their daughter, but I wasn't yet ready to be his wife.

Finally, I'd walked off the heat of my anger, and I slowed my pace. Mr. McKellar stopped altogether, putting his hands on either side of his head.

"My head's about to bust," he called. "Let's stop and rest at that creek."

Without thinking, I'd brought us to my hiding spot. The creek was narrow here, forced between jumbled rocks, gurgling as it fell into a small pool before racing on down the mountain. I couldn't count the times the peace of the woods and the water had soothed my troubles. Today, though, I hardly noticed the creek as I sank onto the flat rock beside it. Ma's words, and Mary's, kept whirling in my head. Mary was right—I didn't know a thing about Mr. McKellar. I'd felt sure last night that choosing him was the right thing, but what if it was a bad gamble? For all I knew, Mr. McKellar was a drunkard, or a fool, or even devil's chattel, like Pa said. But my life was tied in with his now, till death did us part. Unless, of course, Ma was right, and Mr. McKellar decided to toss me out. He'd said the vow last night like he meant it, but he'd also told me not a half-hour before that he was queasy from whiskey. Still, drunk or not, he'd promised before a crowd of witnesses to be my husband. I had to see it stayed that way.

Mr. McKellar settled himself on the rock beside me. "At least we have one thing in common," he said. "We both think your pa is a son of a bitch."

What I meant to be a laugh came out sounding more like a strangled sob.

"I'm sorry," he said quickly. "I shouldn't have said that."

"I'm the one who's sorry, Mr. McKellar." I took a deep breath, trying to ease the heaviness in my chest. "I know you don't want to be married to me, and I'm sorry you have to be. But I ain't going back, never."

"There's something else we have in common." His voice was grim. "I wouldn't let you go back even if you wanted to, not when your pa hurts you like that."

My bosom ached like it would split in two, and the tears blurring my eyes spilled over onto my cheeks. I wrapped my arms tight around myself and turned away to stare into the woods, biting my lip hard to keep the sobs inside.

Something warm came to rest on my shoulder, and when I looked, the shock of seeing his big hand there froze the sobs in my throat. I peered at him from the corner of my eyes, wondering if he might be about to force another kiss—or worse—on me, now that I was his wife and alone with him in the woods. Every muscle in my body tightened as I waited for his first move, though I knew, as his wife, I had to let him do whatever he willed.

But he was watching the creek, like he didn't even realize he was touching me. Some of the stiffness slowly eased out of my chest. With another deep breath, I wiped my eyes and scooted over just enough that his hand dropped off my shoulder. He glanced at me then, and I saw his eyes were a rich brown, like chestnuts, not black like I'd thought they were last night. They were more comely than I'd noticed.

"You're all right?" he asked.

I nodded and wiped my eyes with my sleeve. "You might not believe it, but I'm not the weepy type, usually."

He didn't say anything, just smiled a little. We sat for a while in silence, both of us watching the water rushing over the rocks.

"So what do we do?" I asked. "We're really married, with witnesses and that paper—"

"We'll get it annulled." I stared at him, confused. "Like it never happened," he explained.

My heart seemed to drop. "Oh, no!" I protested, but he went on.

"Don't worry, you won't have to go back home. I've got it all planned out. You can stay with my brother's family till I get some money—Zeke will understand, he always does—then we'll go to Jacksborough for an annulment. That'll make everything right in the eyes of the law."

"But what will I do? How will I—"

"I'll do right by you," he said. "I'll find some kind of paid work for you in town so you can stay there instead of going home."

I stared again. "Paid work? With money?"

"Sure," he said. "Some well-off folks pay a girl to do their housekeeping and cooking."

My heart suddenly felt lighter. If folks in Jacksborough would pay enough for cooking and cleaning to keep me there, I'd for sure never have to come back home. I'd be away from Pa and I wouldn't have to marry Phillip Owens. Mr. McKellar said it would be like our marriage never happened, and if I lived in Jacksborough—wherever that was—nobody from the mountain would be there to tell folks any different.

"Like it never happened?" I looked straight into his eyes. "Folks won't think I'm some kind of harlot?"

"They'll have no cause to," he said, quietly. "You might not believe it after how I acted last night, but I'm no rake. I promise I won't dishonor you."

"That sounds fine, then."

"It's too far to get to Zeke's tonight, but I'll take you there tomorrow." His eyes suddenly took on a troubled look. "I'll warn you, Maggie, my folks won't like this, and they're likely to take it out on you as much as me. They'll throw some hard words at us. Just let me handle them."

"Hard words don't bother me."

He studied my face for a minute before he stood. "We'd best be getting down the mountain, then. We'll have to set a fast pace—but not quite as fast as you were going before." He grinned as he offered his hand to help me up. "This just might be the worst headache I've ever had. But don't you go telling that."

I felt a small smile stretch my own lips.

"You set the pace. I'll keep up."

⁂

I couldn't help gawking as I caught my first sight of the McKellars' cabin. It wasn't so much the size, though it was twice again as big as the one at home. It was the two windows on the front, glowing with light. I'd never seen a glass window, but I'd heard women talk about them, and I knew having two meant the McKellars really were rich. My stomach knotted as I followed Mr. McKellar up three steps of solid river rock onto the porch. He sighed, like his stomach was knotted too.

"Remember," he said, "let me do the talking. Just don't say anything."

He pushed the door open, and I stood blinking in the sudden brightness. It seemed like the room was full of people, all of them staring at me. Mr. McKellar nudged me, and I stepped into the room. He moved away to lean his ax against the wall, and without him by me, I felt small and naked to their stares.

"So Bob Dunlop was telling the truth," said a man with a heavy Scots accent.

A tall woman with snow-white hair stood to scoop two more bowls of stew from the pot over the fire. Mr. McKellar motioned me toward the bench by the table, but as I sat down, the woman frowned. Her pale blue eyes seemed to peer right through my skin.

"Wash up first!" was all she said.

Although I was hungry, I could hardly taste the stew. Mr. McKellar acted like it was a natural thing for a man to leave home single and come back wedded, though I did notice his hands trembling as he poured milk for us.

"Let's hear it," the Scotsman said, who I guessed was Mr. McKellar's pa. "Gone two days, leaving nary a word and coming back with a mountain lass Bob claims is your wife—"

"She is my wife," Mr. McKellar broke in. "Bob said the service for us." He pulled the paper from his pocket and laid it on the table. His pa opened it slowly.

"Who is she?" a plump woman across the table asked.

Mr. McKellar laid his hand on my back. "This is Maggie, from Pine Mountain. That's Trisha, my oldest brother's wife. That's Paul there beside her, and Ma, and Pa, and Matthew's beside you." Paul looked very somber, but Matthew was smiling broadly.

"Why didn't you tell us you had a girl?" Trisha asked. Mr. McKellar calmly spooned up some stew.

"Well, I reckon I don't have to tell you what I'm doing anymore, Trisha, since yesterday was my birthday and I'm of age now."

His ma made an angry huffing sound, but Trisha was already asking another question.

"Why the hurry to get married?"

Mr. McKellar shrugged. "Bob was fiddling for the dance. We figured we'd just go ahead with it, since he was already there, and her pa consented—"

"I bet he did," his ma snarled.

"Malinda!" his pa said, and she busied herself at the fire. His pa turned to Mr. McKellar.

"What I'm wondering is why you were at Hucketts' at all. Birthday or no, you left us short-handed for two days in the harvest. We have that biggest field along the creek still to do, and this fine weather won't hold. A man meets his responsibilities, son. A boy seeks pleasure." Mr. McKellar stared into his stew without answering, and his pa leaned back. "I expect you to make up tomorrow what you missed because of that party. Hand me the Bible, Paul. Since we're so tired tonight, I'll do the reading early."

I don't know if we were just unlucky or if Mr. McKellar's pa chose Proverbs 23 specially, but listening to him read the chapter, I felt like crawling under the table. Mr. McKellar sat still and quiet beside me while his pa read, "Withhold not correction from the child, for if thou beatest him with the rod, he shall not die." But his cheeks reddened during the part that said, "For a whore is a deep ditch, and a strange woman is a narrow pit. She also lieth in wait as for a prey." The chapter ended with the evils of drunkenness. As soon as his pa closed the Bible, Mr. McKellar took a candle and started up a set of stairs against the back wall. Though he didn't say to, I quickly followed him. I didn't want to be left alone with his family after a Bible reading about strange women and drink.

By the candlelight, I saw the attic had storage for vegetables at one end and, at the other, two narrow beds with corn shuck mattresses instead of pallets. The roof was so close overhead the only place Mr. McKellar could stand straight was right under the peak. He frowned as he dropped onto one bed.

"Damn Bob Dunlop and his big mouth!" he said. "He probably ran all the way down the mountain so he could get the news to them first." He ran his hand over his hair. "This changes things."

I nodded as the one called Matthew came off the stairs, his grin bigger than before. He slapped Mr. McKellar's back.

"You chose some coming-of-age gift, little brother! Better than the colt I got!" He wadded the quilt from the empty bed into his arms. "I'll sleep by the fire tonight so you can be alone with your bride."

He laughed as Mr. McKellar's face flushed dark. Just then, their pa called up the stairs.

"John David, come down!"

With a deep sigh, Mr. McKellar left, and still grinning, Matthew followed. It was wrong to eavesdrop, but I knew they'd be talking about me. I sat by the top step, careful I couldn't be seen.

"Were you drinking last night?" His pa's voice was stern, but Mr. McKellar's voice was so low I had to lean out over the stairs a little to hear him.

"I wasn't drunk."

"That's not what Bob said. According to him, you were lifting a jug every time he turned around."

"He wouldn't know," Mr. McKellar said. "The whiskey wasn't near where he was fiddling."

His pa's voice exploded in the quiet. "Don't be such a stubborn fool!"

His ma broke in. "Where did you meet that girl?"

"Her name is Maggie, not 'that girl.'"

His pa spoke again, close to the stairs, and I leaned back. "I know what Boon is up to. You'll sleep down here tonight with your brother. Tomorrow I'll ride to Pine Mountain with the girl and some cash and we'll see how much it will take to make him drop this."

"Oh, no!" I whispered. I hadn't considered that anyone but Mr. McKellar would have a say in this. But his pa sounded like a man who expected folks to obey his will, no backtalking. I suddenly saw this was what Pa had in mind all along, and I'd stepped right into his trap. He'd known Mr. McKellar's pa wouldn't let me stay. Pa would get just what he'd wanted out of this marriage in the first place—cash money—and since it would be over so quick, he could still trade me to Mr. Owens. He was probably already talking with Mr. Owens about whether I was worth a hog or some corn.

"No!" I heard Mr. McKellar speak, hot and defiant. "You can't do that!"

"You'll not tell me what I can't do, son!"

"We were married legal! You saw the paper!"

"No one will hold a man to a marriage made when he was out of his mind drunk."

"I wasn't drunk! I knew what I was doing. I made a choice, a sober choice."

"Not according to Bob!" his pa roared. "I'm more inclined to believe him than you! And no doubt there's a barn full of witnesses who saw my son get so drunk he could be duped by a backwoods scoundrel and his daughter. Under the circumstances, the marriage can be annulled easily enough, and no lasting harm's done. You'll sleep down here with your brother tonight, and I'll take the girl home tomorrow."

"Nobody duped me," Mr. McKellar argued. "You're not taking her back to her pa. It's my fault she's in this fix. I'm of age now, and I'll handle it."

There was a long pause, and then his ma spoke in an icy voice.

"Is that girl with child?"

I waited for Mr. McKellar to deny it, but instead there was another pause, longer this time. I leaned out as far as I dared, trying in vain to see why no one was speaking. His pa finally broke the silence.

"John David—no, son—I wanted so much for you—" His voice broke, but then it came back, firm again, and commanding. "We've been too easy on you. I spared the rod of correction too many times when I should've beaten the sinful nature out of you. I warned you specifically about fornication. Fleshly urges lead to naught but sorrow, son. Satisfying a moment's lust has burdened you with responsibility for this lass and, soon enough, her babe. I expect you to honor your obligations like a man, hear?"

I could see Mr. McKellar starting up the stairs, and I hardly had time to clamber back to sit on the bed before he was at the top.

"Why didn't you say something?" I asked. "You know what they'll think about me."

"I'm sorry," he said. "I didn't mean to bring shame on you. But he for sure won't send you back now. He'll want things decent—no blot on the family name. He'd rather have us married than have a misbegotten grandchild in the mountains. It's only for a few days, anyway, until corn harvest is over. Then I'll take you to Zeke's, and I'll tell everyone the truth."

"All right," I said slowly. "I'll go along with it, long as I don't have to go back home. But I don't want to cause trouble between you and your folks."

"You're not causing trouble. It's already there." He gave a bitter laugh as he sat on the empty bed. "Missing two days of corn harvest. I knew he'd be mad. I'm surprised they didn't toss me out before they ever saw you. I'll have to work like a Philistine giant tomorrow to satisfy him." He yawned as he kicked off his moccasins and stretched out on the bed. "Well, that's tomorrow. I don't know about you, but I'm wore out."

I leaned toward him.

"Shouldn't you be over here?" I whispered. He glanced at me with one eyebrow raised. I leaned closer. "Sounds like I'll be here several days. Won't your folks get suspicious if we don't share a bed like married folk? That might be reason enough for your pa to disbelieve you and take me home."

He sat up. "It might, but you don't want—"

"I'll tell you what I don't want. I don't want your pa to pay my pa cash money to take me back, just so I'll be traded to Phillip Owens for a hog or some such."

His eyes on me were steady. "You ever been with a man, Maggie?" he asked, quietly, and though the question was a shock, I didn't look away.

"No, but I saw things, rocking Betsy at night. This is just make-believe, though. Nothing like that would happen." He was shaking his head.

"You're young. You don't know yet what fleshly urges are like. They have powerful force when they're stirred up, mighty hard to resist. They can make a man do things he normally wouldn't do. Like grabbing and kissing you last night—I never meant to do that. It's best we don't risk—"

"But your pa!" I interrupted. "He's so stern, and if he wills it, he'll have me gone! It's only a few times, Mr. McKellar, please—I just can't go back home!"

His dark eyes met mine. "You must really hate your folks."

I reached for his hand. "You made me a promise, and I trust you."

"I don't trust myself," he said, pulling his hand away. "Don't worry about it. He won't take you back."

I still worried on it for a while after he had pinched out the candle. I worried, too, about the little ones back home, with no one there now to watch out for them. But, I couldn't help that. Even if I hadn't come off the mountain with Mr. McKellar, I wouldn't have been there for them much longer; Pa had decided that. All I could do now was watch out for myself. I looked at Mr. McKellar's dark shape in the other bed as the heaviness of sleep crept over me. He'd told his parents he'd made a choice; I'd made my choice too. And whether I was doing the right thing or not, I wasn't sorry.

Chapter 3

I nearly changed my mind the next morning while I sat naked in a tub of water with his ma scrubbing me like she thought dirt had soaked an inch deep into my flesh. When she finally quit, I tingled painfully all over—my pride as well as my skin. She handed me a plain gray dress that must have been Trisha's cast-off, because what bosom I had disappeared completely when I put it on, even after I cinched in the waist with an apron. She yanked a comb through my hair and then twisted it into a tight, heavy ball before looking me over with a frown.

"At least you're clean enough now to sleep on my linens," was all she said.

We spent the rest of the morning washing everything from Mr. McKellar's bed. I wondered, as I wrestled with the wet quilts, if she thought I'd so soiled the bed she'd make me empty the tick and put in fresh corn shucks too. But once the bedding was hanging over the fence, Trisha had dinner waiting for us, and I dropped onto the bench at the table, hot and damp and feeling as cross as ever I could remember.

I'd barely taken a bite before Trisha asked when my baby was due.

"April," I answered, without even thinking. I could see them counting it out, and my heart pounded fast. If they saw through me, I'd be back on the mountain by nightfall.

"So you're two months along," she said, and I nodded. "Where did you meet John David?"

"At the spring, getting water." She looked like she expected more. "He was hunting on Pine Mountain," I added, hoping desperately he'd been away from home sometime two months ago.

"Right after he got back from Nashville," Trisha said to his ma. "I said he'd pick up sinful ways in that town, remember?" She turned back to me. "Did he come hunting on Pine Mountain again?"

She was trying to catch my lie. I'd been lucky so far, but I feared my luck wouldn't last. I shook my head, and Trisha's eyebrows flew up.

"Only the one time? How do you know he's the father, then?"

I flushed hot. "His fleshly urges got the best of him," I muttered. Trisha laughed.

"With a figure like that? You look more like a boy than a woman. There's not enough meat on you to stir up a man's fleshly urges!"

Lucky for me, his ma broke in before I could say what I thought about the amount of meat on Trisha.

"Did he tell you his name? Had you heard of the McKellar family before?" Quickly, I tried to figure what she might be getting at.

"Sure, Pa told me about you all."

Her face hardened, and her lips pressed tight together. "Finish eating," she ordered. "Then strip the last of the beans from the garden and thresh them at the barn. You do know how to thresh beans?"

They hardly said two words to me the rest of the day. I didn't especially care whether they liked me or not. I would only be in their house until corn harvest was over. I did the work his ma laid out for me, and I kept my sass to myself, but that night as I crawled into the clean bed, I felt a naughty pleasure to think how much she hated knowing I was there.

"Our baby's due in April, if anybody asks," I said as Mr. McKellar settled on the pallet I'd made for him on the floor by the bed. He quickly looked at me and then at the quilt his ma had pinned to a rope to separate Matt's bed from ours. I lowered my voice. "They asked me about it today, so I had to make something up. What did you tell your pa? I hope our stories match good enough."

He shrugged. "I didn't tell him anything. Pa's not concerned about details. He's just worried about the family name and my eternal soul. I got a day-long sermon on fornication."

My mean pleasure dimmed. "I'm sorry for all the trouble you're getting for helping me, Mr. McKellar."

"John David," he reminded me. "As for trouble—I'm no angel. It's not the first time I've brought a sermon on myself. Though," he added thoughtfully, "this would be the most serious, if it was true."

"But it's not!" I raised up on my elbow. "When you can take me to Zeke's and tell them the truth, your troubles will be over." He laughed.

"Then I'll get a sermon on bearing false witness."

I laughed too. "You remind me of Billy, my oldest brother."

"I remember him. He glared at me the whole time I was at your folks' place, like he wanted to thrash me for defiling his sister. He didn't seem to care a bit that I'm about two feet taller than he is and nearly twice as old."

"That's Billy, all right." I leaned back against the pillow and stared into the darkness between the rafters. "He'd like you, I think, if he had the chance."

"You miss them pretty bad."

"Oh, sometimes. Not so much."

Truth be told, as the days went on I missed them so much it was like a constant bellyache. Before, I'd often wished for a chance to wipe dishes without someone pulling on my skirt or begging for a drink of water. Now I worked alone most of the time, while Mr. McKellar's ma and Trisha were off working together. Tears came to my eyes when I wondered if the little ones missed me too, but I roughly brushed them away and reminded myself it was better to be a drudge for Mr. McKellar's stern ma for a little while than for Phillip Owens' quarreling children for a lifetime. I wasn't sorry for my choice. I just hadn't expected it to be such a lonely one.

Mr. McKellar, at least, still spoke to me—or listened, more like. No matter how dark my mood got during the day, sitting next to him at supper cheered me, and after the Bible reading I'd rush through my job of getting the chamber pots ready so I could get to the attic and talk to him. I could tell by the slump of his shoulders how weary he was from his day's work, so I wouldn't talk long, maybe just telling how their goose chased me all the way across the yard, or what a wonder it was to have a well so close to the house. He let me talk and he grinned a lot, and by the time he blew out the candle, I always felt like I could stand one more day.

One evening after I'd been in their household for a week, his ma made me restack the firewood before bedtime, and I feared he'd be asleep before she was satisfied. But when I finally got to the attic, he was still awake, sitting on the bed scratching the patchy stubble on his jaw.

"This beard is itching me to death," he said. "I'll sure be glad when we're done and I have time to shave."

"I don't understand what's taking so long," I fretted as I laid out his pallet. I'd had a bad day. His ma had called me an ignorant wench at least three times. "It can't take more than a week to get in a corn crop."

He grinned. "Not in the mountains, maybe. You've probably never seen fields the size of ours."

"Well, how much longer will it be?" I sat by him and loosened the knot of hair that gave me such a headache. "When are we going to Jacksborough for that annulment?"

He hushed me quickly. "It's best if you don't say anything about that," he said in a low voice. "I don't want them to know that's my plan till I have the money."

"Why not? They'll be glad to know I'm leaving."

"I want to do it my way. Sure, Pa would get us an annulment, but he'd just send you back home. Neither of us wants that. I want to see to it you're set up in Jacksborough with people who'll treat you well." He picked up a curl that had fallen over my shoulder, winding it around his finger. "I'll do right by you, Maggie. Just trust me."

So I settled myself for more waiting. But only a couple of days later, he brought in the buckets of milk with news that the first streaks of sunrise were red, a sure sign of rain to come.

"Reckon it will hold off for the day?" his pa said. "There's only a piece of one field left. I surely wish we could finish before rain comes."

I looked up from stirring the corn mush, my heart pounding.

"I could help." They all looked at me.

"Fool girl," his ma started, "a cornfield is no place for a woman carrying a child." But Mr. McKellar broke in.

"Let her help, Pa, if she's willing. It's been such a fine crop, it'd be a shame to have any of it get wet."

"It is a good crop," Old Mr. McKellar admitted. He studied me for a moment. "Pulling corn in a field is harder than pulling corn in a garden patch, lass, and we don't take many rests. Think you can do it?"

I stood as tall as I could. "I'm a good worker. Carrying a child don't affect me."

He studied me for a moment. "You can spare her for the day, Malinda," he said.

So that day, instead of being stuck in the cabin with the women, I rode in the wagon with the men to the field along Stinking Creek. Once I saw it, I understood why the harvest had taken so long to finish. The field stretched along the creek for such a long way that the trees at the other end looked no taller than my thumbnail.

"It's going to be a hot one," my Mr. McKellar said, as he jumped out of the back of the wagon and held out his hand to help me down.

"You'll be in the sun most of the day, lass," Old Mr. McKellar called from the wagon seat. "John David, give her your hat."

Mr. McKellar set the hat on my head, and he laughed when it slipped low on my forehead. My spirits rose higher than they'd been in a long time. Hot work, hard work, I didn't care—it was a good day.

Old Mr. McKellar had me and Paul pulling ears of corn from the stalks and throwing them in the wagon while he drove. My Mr. McKellar and Matthew followed, cutting the naked stalks and binding them into bundles for fodder. They worked fast, and by the time we stopped at midday, sweat had plastered Trisha's dress to my back, and my hands and legs were trembling. I started slowly toward the wagon to fetch the food Mrs. McKellar had packed for dinner, but Old Mr. McKellar stopped me.

"Matthew, fetch the victuals," he called, looking down at me. "Sit and rest, lass."

We ate in the shade of a sweet gum tree near the creek bank, and afterwards, Old Mr. McKellar and Paul lit pipes. My Mr. McKellar slouched against the tree, chewing on a twig, but Matthew wanted to know all about my brothers and sisters. I recited their names and ages, down to the new baby, and he gave a low whistle.

"Twelve children! It would for sure be a struggle to keep food enough on the table for that many." He suddenly grinned. "You plan to sire twelve children, little brother?"

Mr. McKellar threw his half-chewed twig at Matthew and then stood and stretched.

"Maggie, want to walk along the creek?" I jumped to my feet, maybe too eagerly.

"Don't go far," his pa warned. "We'll be back in the field before long."

Mr. McKellar led through the underbrush to the edge of the creek, and we walked along the water in silence. He finally stopped when the bank turned steeper, near a section of the creek broken by several big rocks, with the main channel running deep and green along the opposite bank. But still he didn't say anything, just scratched at the scraggly beard under his chin. I waited, lifting the heavy wad of hair off my sweaty neck and fanning myself with his hat.

"You're hot," he said. "Come over here."

He checked a shady spot for snakes, and then we sat with our bare feet in the water, which was speckled with a few yellow leaves. I had to raise the hem of Trisha's skirt above my knees to keep it from getting wet, but Mr. McKellar politely kept his eyes on the bluff across the creek, kicking his feet a little and making ripples that spread slowly into the deeper water. I dipped my apron in the water, wiping it over my forehead and down my throat.

"It's awful hot for October," I said.

"Those clouds say a big change is coming." He suddenly turned toward me, his face serious. "Maggie, don't push yourself to keep up with Paul. Nobody will think bad of you if you rest once in a while."

"I'm all right. Reckon we'll get done this afternoon?"

"I do. You've been a real good hand out there."

Nobody ever praised my work, and I felt a glow of pleasure as we sat in another friendly silence. He broke a short piece off the branch hanging low above us, and he stripped off the leaves and dropped them in the water one by one. We watched them swirl away on the lazy current.

"I reckon that means you'll be taking me to your brother's house soon," I said. He nodded.

"You'll like Sarah, his wife. She'll treat you better than Ma and Trisha do. You've got a lot in common with her."

"Like what?"

"Ma doesn't like either one of you." He began to peel the bark from the stick with his thumbnail. "You're a mountain girl, and Sarah's a Quaker. Neither one of you is what she would have chosen as wives for her sons."

"She'll be pleased when I'm gone, then."

He studied me with those dark eyes. "I'll get money together quick as I can," he said. "Then we'll get you settled someplace in Jacksborough. I'll find a nice family you can work for, or maybe a kindly widow woman—" He broke the stick into two pieces and threw them in the water, one at a time. "You'll have a regular life, even meet some other fellow to marry."

"Reckon so?"

"Oh, yeah, probably right quick, a pretty girl like you." I looked at him, but he was watching the ripples in the creek.

"Well, if I do, it's thanks to you. You got me away from Pa, and I didn't have to marry Mr. Owens. I won't forget that." He didn't say anything, and on an impulse I reached over and squeezed his hand. He did look up then, and I smiled. "I'll always think kindly of you, Mr. McKellar. Maybe you can visit me sometime."

"We need to head back," he said, getting to his feet. He offered me a hand up, and he watched as I gathered in the waist of Trisha's dress with the apron ties.

"You could wrap that dress around you three times," he joked.

I laughed. "It's all I got, though. I can't find my bundle from home. Your ma must've put it somewhere."

"On the fire," he snorted. "She probably burned it to get rid of the lice. All you mountain folk have lice, you know." I looked up in a huff, but he was grinning, and my huff dissolved as fast as it came.

"So what will I do? I don't want to wear this big old ugly dress of Trisha's all the time! Not that there's anything wrong with it," I added quickly. His laugh echoed against the bluff.

"Well, as Pa would say, take no thought for thy raiment, or wherewithal ye shall be clothed. I'll get you out of Trisha's dress—" His face suddenly went red and he stammered a little as he added, "and into something of your own."

He turned quickly and I watched him move away. He was a strange man, I thought, but it was a nice sort of strange, and I was a little sorry to think we would finish the corn crop in just a few more hours.

⁂

Faraway thunder rumbled as we listened to Old Mr. McKellar reading the Bible, but no rain came till after we'd gone to bed. A chilly fog lingered the next morning, and I wondered if Mr. McKellar would reconsider his plans. But he caught my eye as he was shaving, and when I went to throw scraps to the hogs, he followed me with the basin of soapy water.

"Pa gave me leave to go to Zeke's," he said. "Meet me at the barn in a few minutes."

"What about my chores? Your ma said I'm to clear ashes from the smokehouse today."

He tossed the water over the backs of the tussling hogs. "What does it matter? You won't be coming back."

I slipped away while I was supposed to be sweeping the porch. Mr. McKellar was already in the barn, coaxing a bit into the mouth of a red-speckled gray stallion who didn't seem to favor the notion. I stopped short.

"We're riding?"

"It would take all day to walk," Mr. McKellar said, buckling the bridle straps. "We'll have more time to visit this way. Anyway, I'd like to ride him today while I've got the chance. He gets feisty if I wait too long." He stroked the horse's neck. "What do you think? This is Washington."

The stallion shifted toward me, and I scurried behind the stall wall. "Mr. McKellar, I never rode a horse before," I blurted out. "And this one is so—so tall." He laughed as he threw a blanket and saddle over the horse's back.

"Don't worry," he said. "Just hold on, and you won't fall."

Once I was perched on Washington's hips, though, there seemed to be nothing to hold to except Mr. McKellar himself. I tried to figure what to do, whether to ask Mr. McKellar or just gather up a fistful of his jacket. But Washington started forward with a jump, I swayed backward, and with a yelp, I threw my arms around Mr. McKellar.

"I'm sorry!" I gasped, annoyed by his chuckling but too afraid to let go.

"It's all right," he said. "It doesn't bother me. Do whatever makes you feel steady."

We quickly left the McKellars' clearing and fields behind us. After a while, I felt sure enough of the gentle rocking of Washington's gait to look at something other than Mr. McKellar's back. The trail went through a patch of woods with a few leaves showing brown and red through the pale fog, early signs of the coming fall. It was the first time I'd been in the woods since I'd come off the mountain, and I realized with a pang this might be the last time, too.

"What's Jacksborough like?" I asked.

Mr. McKellar glanced at me over his shoulder. "You'll probably like it. It's like a barn-raising every day, with plenty of folks around."

I sighed. None of those folks would be anyone I knew. Even Mr. McKellar would be gone, and a hollow feeling stirred in my belly as I looked at the strip of sun-browned skin showing above his collar.

"You'll be all right," he said, like he was reading my thoughts. "When I went to Nashville, I was lonesome at first, but it didn't take long to meet folks. You'll be the same."

"Maybe so." I didn't want to think about it just yet. I leaned closer to Mr. McKellar's shoulder. "Why were you in Nashville?"

"To study the law. Ma's brother is a lawyer in Nashville, and she had her heart set on one of her sons going into partnership with him. I was itching to get away from home, so I thought that was my chance. But I had all I could take of it after six months. So I came home. Nashville's a lot bigger than Jacksborough, though."

"You didn't like it?"

He paused. "It was some fun at first."

"Is that when you picked up sinful ways?" He turned again to look at me, his eyebrows raised, and I shrugged. "That's what Trisha said."

He laughed. "Could be. There's plenty of opportunity." He steered Washington onto a bigger trail, and I could barely see a cluster of cabins through the fog. "We'll stop here," he said. "I've got business at the store."

The first thing I noticed when we stepped in the store was the overwhelming smell of tobacco, leather, and vinegar. Then I saw the shelves packed with more things than I had ever known could be in one place. I stared at the tin cups, blankets, kegs of salt pork, wheels of cheese, bullet molds, bags of gunpowder, iron stew pots, stacks of furs—I hardly even knew I was walking as I followed Mr. McKellar back to a counter where two men stood talking.

"Texas is grassland," one man was saying, "no trees to have to clear before you can plant a crop. They say the dirt is so rich and black, corn will jump from seed to six feet high in a fortnight. I've had my fill of breaking my back to make a living in the rocks around here. Best thing is, there's land enough that folks ain't sitting on top of each other like we are here. There's room for everybody. When I get set up, I'll come back for the woman and young'uns, and we'll have a fresh start, free and clear."

The storekeeper looked like he was glad to have an excuse to move away from the talker. "Good day, young McKellar! What can I do for you? Your pa need sacks for his corn?"

"I'm here on my own business," Mr. McKellar said, leaning on the counter. "What do you have in the way of cloth?"

The storekeeper shot a curious glance at me before stepping back to a shelf where woven goods were stacked. "I've got two bolts of cotton calico shipped from England, but it's dear, of course. I have a better price on this nice linen and linsey-woolsey Widow Brooks made."

Mr. McKellar turned to me. "What do you think, Maggie? How much for a skirt and shirt?"

There was no use pretending to turn down his kindness. If, as he said, his ma had burned my clothes, I had to have something to wear in Jacksborough. I guessed at what it would take.

"Three yards for a skirt and two for a shirt, and two more for—" I glanced at the storekeeper and then at Mr. McKellar, who leaned closer. I whispered it in his ear. "A shimmy." He was grinning as he turned back to the counter.

"Six yards of the linsey-woolsey and eight of the linen."

"Mr. McKellar!" I hissed. "That's too much. I said three for a skirt—"

He paid no mind, but leaned across the counter to point at a bolt. "And five of that green calico."

I understood then what he meant to do for me. My throat was tight as the storekeeper cut the lengths of fabric and wrote an account sheet in Mr. McKellar's name.

"You ought not to have done that," I started, as we settled on the edge of the porch with hunks of bread and cheese he'd bought. But before he could answer, the man who'd been talking to the storekeeper walked up with a whiskey jug cradled in his arm.

"Have a swallow?" he asked, sitting down and offering the jug to Mr. McKellar.

"No thanks," Mr. McKellar said. "I've lost my taste for whiskey." The man gave him a strange look before taking a swig.

"Ever hear of Texas?" He didn't wait for an answer. "That's where I'm headed. The Mexicans are giving free land to anyone who'll settle there."

Mr. McKellar smiled. "It's not exactly free. I heard in Nashville that those grants come with conditions."

"It's the same as free," the man insisted. "All you do is swear allegiance to Mexico and the Catholic Church, and the Mexicans give you a parcel of rich land, free and clear. I'm getting to Texas quick as I can to get in on the deal."

He went on for a while about the land that would yield twice the corn for half the effort, and about the water clear and pure as the water of Eden. Mr. McKellar finally stuck the rest of the cheese in his pocket and held out his hand to the man.

"I hope you find Texas is everything you've heard it is."

As he tied the bundle of cloth in front of the saddle, Mr. McKellar watched the man stumble back into the store.

"What a fool," he said. "The land's not free. I heard it's twelve and a half cents an acre. And he's more a fool to think everything they say about Texas is true. I bet not even half of it is true."

"Probably not." But I had other business on my mind. "Mr. McKellar, you ought not to have got all that cloth."

He laughed as he swung into the saddle. "You're as persistent as a cricket under the eaves on a night when a man can't sleep. And when are you going to stop calling me that? It makes me feel like Pa's around somewhere."

"You told me you don't have money right now, not even enough for the annulment. That was a mighty expensive bill."

"It's nothing for you to worry about." He hoisted me up, and I grunted with the effort of pulling myself over Washington's hips.

"You said you'll find me some paid work, right? I can pay you back. How long do you reckon it will take for me to earn enough—"

"You're not paying me back," he interrupted. "I'm repaying you for what Ma took."

"The linen and linsey-woolsey I can see," I said. "But that green calico—that's just a waste."

"No." I looked up, surprised by the sudden hard edge to his voice. "It's not a waste. You need something pretty."

"I don't—" He pulled sharply on the reins, which made Washington bow his head in a little crow hop. I squealed with fear as I pitched forward into Mr. McKellar's back.

"All right, maybe you don't," he said. "But I want you to have it. It matches your eyes." I stared at his back, hardly sure I'd heard right.

"What?"

"It's already cut, so there's no taking it back. Don't worry about the money. I can get means to pay for a few yard goods. Now I don't want to hear any more about it. We need to get to Zeke's." He flipped the reins, and Washington broke into a quick trot that bounced me so I couldn't have said anything else, even if I hadn't been purely dumbfounded.

Chapter 4

It was late afternoon when Washington splashed through a stream crossing the path to a log cabin small as the one I'd grown up in. But size was the only way it was the same. The yard of this cabin was neatly swept and outlined with a split rail fence. A patch of gold flowers clustered around the steps leading to the porch where two people were stacking firewood. They turned and looked at us, shielding their eyes against the sunlight.

"Pa, it's John David!" a small voice cried.

As we dismounted, a little girl ran to Mr. McKellar, and she screamed with laughter as he swept her up in his arms and above his head. As Zeke and Sarah stepped off the porch, my belly clenched tight, just like when I'd first met his family. But it seemed this meeting would be different; Sarah was beaming.

"If Bob Dunlop's been by, I reckon you've already heard about Maggie," Mr. McKellar said as he set the girl down. Sarah seemed to take that as introduction enough, and she hugged me tightly.

"We've been anxious to meet thee, ever since we heard the news!"

Zeke was a huge man, tall like Mr. McKellar but stocky like Paul, and he carried a second girl as easily as if she was a rag doll. His hand swallowed mine. "So Bob was telling the truth for once," he said. "My baby brother is a married man. What did the folks say about it?"

Mr. McKellar grinned as he took the bundle of cloth from the saddle. "What do you think? The same thing you heard when you told them you were going to marry Sarah—Proverbs 23, all those warnings about strange women and wine."

Zeke looked at him intently. "Bob did say you had a lot to drink."

Mr. McKellar's grin faded. "I did most of my drinking after, once

I started thinking about what Pa would say. I wasn't drunk when we said our vows, if that's what you're getting at."

"Then what's the truth?" Zeke asked. "You know what it is folks are saying, and it's not something you want joined to your name."

Mr. McKellar shook his head. "She's not with child."

"I never thought so. But I'd like to know what did happen."

Mr. McKellar went through the whole story, a little heavy on the parts where Pa smacked me and a little light on the part where he himself had pulled me close for a kiss. He made it sound like he'd planned all along to save me from having to marry Phillip Owens.

"She would've been what, his third wife? He's awful hard on women. A girl like Maggie probably wouldn't last six months with him. Pa wanted to pay her pa to forget the whole business, but I wasn't about to let him, not when I know what Boon would've done with her."

"Well, how a marriage starts is not what matters most," Sarah said. "What matters is how thou go on together through thy years as man and wife."

"We're not going on together," I said, and they all looked at me. "We're getting an annulment."

"An annulment?" Sarah asked.

Zeke looked at Mr. McKellar. "Does Pa know that's your plan?"

Red was spreading across Mr. McKellar's cheeks. "No. If he knew, he'd send her back to Boon, you know that. When I get enough money, we're going to Jacksborough. I'll find her some work there with a nice family or an older widow so she won't have to go back home."

"You won't find anything like that in Jacksborough," Zeke said.

"Nashville, then!" Mr. McKellar said. "I'll take her to Nashville if I have to. I'll find something. She's not going back to her pa."

"That's what matters to me," I said. "He says an annulment will make it like nothing happened, in the eyes of the law."

"What about the eyes of the Lord?" Sarah asked.

"Oh, he's done nothing wrong on that account," I said. "He promised to do right by me, and he's kept his word. There's been no fornicating."

Even Mr. McKellar's ears were red by now, and Zeke looked like he was about to bust out laughing.

43

"Well, you're of age now, so I reckon it's your choice," he said. "You'll stay the night?" Mr. McKellar nodded, and Zeke handed the baby to Sarah. "Give Maggie that bundle, then, while we tend to your horse."

※ ※ ※

Nothing else was said about our plans. Sarah marveled over my cloth. She volunteered to cut patterns for me from the paper wrappings, and she took my measurements right then, before the men came back to the house. After supper, I washed dishes at the cupboard in the corner so she could have the table to start drawing the patterns. Zeke was rocking Baby Lily, but Hannah, the other little girl, climbed on Mr. McKellar's lap and looked at him expectantly. They all laughed.

"You know what she wants," Zeke said. "Same as every time you're here."

"What should we start with?" Mr. McKellar asked, tweaking Hannah's nose.

"*The Keeper*!" she squealed, throwing her arms around his neck.

He laughed. "Only if you help on the chorus."

I'd thought Mr. McKellar a fine singer at Charlie's, but Zeke was even better, with a rich tenor voice that filled the little cabin. They sang ballads and play songs and hymns, one after another, as Hannah or Sarah asked for them. I'd never seen anything like it, and it wasn't just the singing. Not a cross word passed anyone's lips the whole evening. They smiled so much and laughed so, I might have believed they were feigning it all just because they knew I was watching, except they seemed to forget I was in the room until Mr. McKellar caught my eye as he stood after tucking Hannah, sound asleep, into the trundle bed.

"You've been mighty quiet, Maggie," he said. "What would you like to hear?"

"Me? Oh, I don't—oh, just anything," I stammered.

"How about *Annie Laurie*?" He grinned just like my little brothers did when they thought they were getting away with something. "Girls always like that one."

He started the song and Zeke joined in, catching Sarah's hand in his and holding it over his heart.

"'*Gave me her promise true,*'" they sang. "*Which ne'er forgot will be, and for bonnie Annie Laurie, I'd lay me doun and dee.*'"

A lump swelled in my throat as I watched Zeke and Sarah. I'd never seen such a tender look on a man's face as the one in Zeke's eyes or such contentment as glowed on Sarah's face. I was embarrassed, like I'd spied them in their marriage bed, yet I couldn't look away. It was one of the old ballads come to life. A lonesome ache I'd never felt before settled in my chest.

"'Her voice is low and sweet, she's a' the world to me, and for bonnie Annie Laurie, I'd lay me doun and dee.'"

Sarah raised Zeke's hand to her lips as the song ended, and then she let go and turned to Mr. McKellar.

"That's plenty for tonight, and fine it was, as always. Clear a spot on the floor, John David, and I'll get quilts for thee and Zeke. Maggie, thou will share the featherbed with me."

"A featherbed?" I gasped, lonesomeness forgotten. Sarah laughed.

"Thou will sleep like an angel floating on a cloud."

※ ※ ※

By breakfast, Mr. McKellar still hadn't mentioned anything about me staying with them, but since they were his folks, I decided to let him be the one to bring it up. He went with Zeke to rebuild a section of fence, which I figured was his way of giving me and Sarah time to get friendly. I was glad of it, because she'd promised to help with cutting my new cloth.

"I'm itching to get my hands on that calico," she said. "But I suppose we should start with something thou can wear right away. Let's spread out this linen first." I held two corners flat while she unfolded the lengths of fabric. "This is good cloth, fine as any thou might find in Jacksborough. That is, if thou go to Jacksborough."

"Oh, I'm going," I said. "Mr. McKellar has it all planned. He'll find me work—"

"As a servant," she interrupted. "Dost thou really want to be a servant?"

"He said I'll be paid."

"Still, a servant is a servant, paid or not." She laid a paper piece against one of the edges of the cloth. "Thou wouldn't have to go, of course. Thou could stay on as John David's wife."

I shook my head. "He don't want to be married."

"That's no matter. He needs to be married." She began to lay spoons on the pattern to hold it still. "I love John David like he's my own brother, but lately he's too restless for his own good. I've been praying, many times a day, that God will provide a good wife who'll settle him down, and thou art the wife God provided."

I couldn't help it. I laughed at her. She smiled.

"I'll admit I'm plenty surprised at times by the means God chooses, but He provided, and I trust Him that thou are the wife John David needs."

I wondered if she might be touched in the head. From what they said about God at the revival meetings on the mountain, He mostly did big things like making the sun stand still or covering the whole world with a flood. It didn't seem to me God would bother with anything as little as getting a wife for John David McKellar.

"You heard him," I said. "The only reason he married me was because he felt sorry for me and wanted to help me out of a bad spot, nothing else. He's a nice enough man, but I'd rather earn my own way in Jacksborough than trap him into something he don't want. I don't think I could stand living with somebody who pities me."

"You think thy mistress in Jacksborough wouldn't pity thee? A young girl going into bond?" She paused in laying out the next paper piece and faced me. "Pity may be where his feelings for thee started, yes, but they don't have to stay there. Tend to him well, and someday thou may find thou are his one, true love."

For a minute, I thought of the look in Zeke's eyes last night as he sang to Sarah, but just as quick, I remembered Ma's parting words. True love? Sarah might have her Zeke, but I knew a girl couldn't count on love. A lucky girl got a husband who was a good provider, not a shiftless man like Pa. If she was really lucky, she got one who was sweet-tempered, who wouldn't smack her when he got angry or drunk. But nobody really expected a husband who'd lay him down and die for her, like *Annie Laurie*'s love.

"True love's only in the old ballads," I scoffed.

She gripped my arm with a look that frightened me a little.

"No, Maggie! True love is real! Sure, the songs don't tell all the truth about love. True love takes work, hard work. It comes from going on together day after day, slogging through thy troubles together, taking some of what thou want and giving a lot of what he needs. It won't come to everybody. It comes to those willing to tend it enough to help it grow." She let go of my arm. "John David's a good man, thou said so. Thou won't find anyone better than him in Jacksborough. But he needs a wife who'll love him and help him grow into an even better man. I believe God means for it to be thee."

I rubbed my arm to wipe away the tight feeling of her fingers. No doubt about it, she was plumb dotty.

"God may want it, but Mr. McKellar don't," I said. "He's set on taking me to Jacksborough."

Smiling, she picked up the scissors and whacked into the cloth with a confidence I knew I'd never muster. "Well, Proverbs says, 'There are many devices in a man's heart; nevertheless, the counsel of the Lord, that shall stand.' Whatever happens, we must have faith it will turn out for the best."

※ ※ ※

Everything that evening was cozier than the one before, mostly because Sarah worked all afternoon to make it that way. When the men came in from the evening chill, the cabin was warm and smelled of what she'd told me were Mr. McKellar's favorite foods. He leaned back in the rocking chair with a contented sigh as we cleared the dishes, a little girl on each of his knees.

"That was a mighty fine meal, Sarah, as always." He sighed. "It's so nice here. At home lately, somebody's always mad about something, mostly about Maggie." He turned to me. "I reckon you two got along all right?"

"We did," I said.

"Maggie is a fine girl," Sarah said. "Like a sister."

"I knew you'd hit it off. That makes me think." He leaned toward Zeke. "You know we're going to Jacksborough for an annulment, once I get some money. But you can imagine how Ma and Trisha treat her—just like they've always treated Sarah. Maybe worse even, with them thinking she's with child. She's not been complaining, but I was thinking it would be better for her if she could stay with you all while I'm getting money together."

"Maggie's going to stay with us?" Hannah said, her face hopeful.

"No," Sarah said from by the cupboard. "She can't stay here, John

David." Both of us turned toward her at once. She kept on calmly wiping a plate. "She can't stay here."

He met my eyes before he turned back to her, disbelief and hurt mingled on his face. "I thought you liked her. Why won't you—"

"There's no room, for one thing," Sarah said. "Where would she sleep?"

"I don't mind the floor," I said quickly. "I always slept on a pallet on the floor at home."

"The cabin's too small," she said. "There's hardly room to walk when the trundle bed's out."

Mr. McKellar turned to Zeke, who only shrugged.

"That's true," he said.

"But it's more than that," Sarah said, coming to stand behind Zeke's chair. "Thou can't keep running from thy responsibilities, John David. Maggie's not like the stray dogs thou used to bring home. Thou can't expect someone else to take care of her because it's inconvenient for thee. Thou have a duty to her."

"I know that! I'm asking for her sake, not mine! I thought you'd be better to her—Ma's so mean—" He looked like one of the little ones back home after a scolding. "What will I do?"

"I don't want to be a burden," I started, but none of them were listening to me.

"You need money, right?" Zeke said. "I can loan you what you need for the annulment. You can take her on to Jacksborough tomorrow." But Mr. McKellar was shaking his head.

"I don't want your money!" he said, and he didn't seem to notice how the girls' faces puckered at the sound of his angry voice, or even that they jumped off his lap to run and hide behind Sarah's skirt. "I don't want to go into debt! I'll get what I need by myself. All I want is a place she can stay while I'm getting it."

He looked from Zeke to Sarah and back again, and then he ran his hand over his hair.

"All right, I'll take her back home! Will that suit you? I don't understand it. What about her good name? You'll send her back, even though everybody believes she's carrying my baby? The longer she stays there with me, the worse it is!"

"She can't stay with us, John David." Sarah's voice was soft but firm. He stared at her for a minute, and then cursed and leaped to his feet, slamming the door as he went outside. Sarah gave us a bright smile.

"The Lord provided," she said.

"With a big push from you," I said, and she laughed.

"We have to make the most of the opportunities He gives when we see them."

"What are you up to?" Zeke asked.

"It's for his own good," she answered. "I thank thee for going along with me. Come, girls, don't cry. Let's get thee ready for bed. There will be no singing tonight."

※ ※ ※

Mr. McKellar ate breakfast the next morning in stony silence, and we left soon after, with hardly a goodbye. Sarah kissed my cheek as she handed me a bundle for dinner later.

"Have faith," she whispered. "The Lord is working."

We rode without speaking for a long while. Even the noises of the woods were hushed, making Washington's hooves echo against the hard dirt path. I held to Mr. McKellar again, but I knew from the tightness of his muscles how angry he was still. I feared his good nature was about to sour and I might've made the wrong choice, after all. Mr. McKellar was a big man, taller than Pa, young, and strong. If he took a notion to smack me, it was likely to hurt a lot.

"It's near midday," he finally said. "Let's eat."

We sat with our backs against a big tree, eating leftover ham and biscuits. Neither of us had much appetite, though, and he soon set his food to the side and sat staring into the woods. He suddenly slapped his hand against the ground and jumped to his feet, pacing back and forth in the little clearing.

"Damn it, I don't understand her! She's never been like this before. And Zeke, going along with her. I just can't see why they'd say no!"

"She thinks I need to stay." I picked at the crumbs on the edge of my biscuit. "She prayed for you to get a wife, so she thinks it was God's will you were at Hucketts' that night we got married."

"She doesn't know what she's talking about. Whiskey had more to do with why I was at Hucketts' than God did!" He snatched up his biscuit and threw it into the woods, hard. "And what she said about you not being a stray dog I expect them to take care of—that goes all over me. Why does everybody make me out to be some young jackass who doesn't realize his responsibilities? I know good and well what I took on by marrying you. I know I'm bound now to take care of you, and I'm doing it, damn it. I've had chances to get out of this if I didn't care about my responsibility to you. I could've just walked off when your pa first found us, or I could've left you alone in the woods coming off the mountain. If I'd slept downstairs that first night and let Pa take you back next morning, I'd be free and clear now. But I couldn't just leave you there, knowing they'd hurt you! I've got a plan for a responsible way to rid myself of you. Why can't they see I'm doing the right thing and help me out?"

The biscuit had fallen off my lap, but I barely noticed. I was shaking, and I felt hot all over.

"You don't have to be responsible on my account," I snapped. "I don't want your pity! I'm not some helpless babe depending on your bountiful generosity. I might not have liked it, but I would've lasted more than six months with Phillip Owens. I would've managed. I always do. Why didn't you find some other way to show everybody what a fine, independent, 'of-age' man you are?"

"It's not like that—" he started, but I cut him off.

"If you're in such a rush to rid yourself of me, why didn't you take Zeke's money so we could get that annulment? You can't lie to me. I know it's not because of the debt. You sure worked up a big enough bill at the store buying all that cloth! You could've been rid of me by tonight, if that's really what you want. But you turned it down, knowing they wouldn't let me stay and I'd have to come back with you. What do you want, Mr. McKellar? Do you want me gone, or not?" He didn't answer, and I turned away. "I just don't know what you want."

There was a long pause.

"Neither do I." His voice was low and miserable. "I thought I did. Coming off the mountain that day, I thought I had it all figured out, and it seemed like the right choice at the time."

His dark eyes met mine, and my belly suddenly made a strange little flop.

"It's still the right thing to do," he said, "but seems like I'm not as happy with it as I was."

We looked at each other in silence for a moment until Washington raised a foot to kick at a fly, rattling the stirrups. Mr. McKellar went to him, but he didn't make any move to get in the saddle, just stroked the horse's neck over and over. I stood and brushed the crumbs from my skirt. He looked up.

"Maggie—" He hesitated. "I—I shouldn't have said that about ridding myself of you. Don't be thinking I think you're a burden. You're not. All right?"

I searched his face, just as I had in front of the magistrate at Charlie's. But this time, I thought I saw an inkling of something to be getting into, and my belly made that strange flop again. I looked away.

"I want to be sure you get in with a good master," he said. "Not just whoever I can find quickest. You understand that, don't you?"

I nodded. He mounted Washington and held out his hand to help me up. I took it, but instead of raising my foot to the stirrup, I looked into his eyes.

"What'll we do now, Mr. McKellar?"

He shook his head. "Go on like before, I reckon. It'll take a while to get some money together. Can you tolerate Ma and Trisha?"

"I'll manage. But I sure wish I'd cleaned those ashes."

※ ※ ※

His ma and Trisha were starting supper when I came through the cabin door, holding the heavy package of cloth against my bosom.

"What's that?" Mrs. McKellar asked. Her lips pinched together as she fingered the calico, already cut into pieces. "Take it upstairs," she ordered. "Then get back down here to fetch water."

Nothing more was said, and I thought that was the end of it. But after the Bible reading, his pa called up for Mr. McKellar. There was no need this time to sit near the stairs to listen—none of them tried to keep their voices down.

"Your ma says Maggie brought in a bundle of yard goods, including a piece of cotton calico."

"She needs clothes." Mr. McKellar's temper was rising already. "Since Ma burned everything she brought from home—"

"They weren't worth keeping," she broke in, "nasty, filthy, hardly better than rags!"

"Still, they were her things! You shouldn't have just taken them!"

His pa's calmer voice rose over theirs. "How did you pay for those yard goods, son?"

"Not with your money, if that's what you mean. I started my own account. I can do that now that I'm—"

His ma's voice exploded into the quiet.

"Of age, of age! I'm sick of hearing that! Being twenty-one years old hasn't changed you! You're the boy you always were, getting into trouble and expecting us to get you out!"

"I don't expect anything of you."

"Except a roof over her head! Except food in her mouth!"

Old Mr. McKellar must have hushed her, because I heard her give a great sniff, and then he spoke.

"Son, I understand the lass needs clothes. You've taken her as your wife, so you have to provide for her. But how do you plan to do that? How will you support her and the babe—" His ma jumped on that idea.

"Oh, yes, you'll have children to support too, and plenty of them! Those mountain people breed like mice. You'll end up with a dozen brats by that little whore!"

"Maggie's no whore." Mr. McKellar's voice was cold. "You do her wrong to say so." I heard the door slam, and then his pa mumbled something in a low, angry voice.

"I don't care!" his ma said. "What else would you call a girl who gets with child by a stranger? I imagine she was plenty eager to do it, too, when she heard he was a McKellar. I bet that child is not even his. She's carrying some mountain boy's bastard and blamed John David just to get money! And he's so besotted all she has to do is flutter those long eyelashes his direction and he'll do whatever she wants. She's already got him to give her a whole wardrobe of new clothes!"

I was trembling all over as I knelt to spread out Mr. McKellar's pallet. Tears gathered on my eyelashes, and I didn't know Matt had come through the quilt curtain until he sat on the foot of the bed.

"Don't take it to heart, Maggie," he said. "It doesn't really matter what she thinks about you. If John David is pleased to be with you, nothing on God's earth will change his mind, surely not Ma."

"I ain't trying to steal from you folks," I whispered. "I don't want to ruin his life. I just want something better for my own."

He sat for a minute longer, watching while I finished making the pallet, and then he squeezed my shoulder before he went back on his side of the curtain. I slowly took off Trisha's dress and folded it. I hated that ugly dress, but the pleasure I'd felt at having something new was tainted now. Every time I wore my new clothes, I'd be reminded they came from Mr. McKellar's charity and that his ma was counting every penny of it. If only I could get to Jacksborough and get wages to pay him back! I pictured myself walking into the cabin with a little bag fat with money. I'd toss the coins to pay for the clothes on the table right in front of Mrs. McKellar, and then I'd pitch one to Trisha.

"For the loan of your ugly gray dress," I'd say, and then I'd stroll right out the door and they'd never see my face again.

Except no telling how long it would be now before I could get to Jacksborough and start earning money. Sarah had stalled that plan, with her daft notion I was God's answer to her prayers. I'd say she was reading the signs wrong. If God wanted me married to Mr. McKellar, everything would be going smoother. It sure wouldn't be a mess like this.

I picked up one of Mr. McKellar's moccasins and ran my fingers over the worn leather. He'd already taken off his shoes before he went downstairs, and now he was out in the cold night, barefoot, because he'd stood up for me, again. I was beginning to lose count of all the times he'd done that. He'd been nothing but kind to me since I'd first seen him at Charlie's spring. And what was I giving him in return? All kinds of trouble with his folks.

Well, that would stop right now. I might have a long stretch of days in his ma's household before he got the money to take me to Jacksborough for that annulment. I'd try harder to get along with her—I'd do anything she told me to do, I'd bow my head to her scolding, I'd swallow a whole bellyful of sass. She'd have no cause to chide him on my account.

I'd gone to bed when Mr. McKellar finally came in, so quiet he might have been a mouse creeping across the floor. He blew out the candle I'd left burning for him, and I heard the rustle of his shirt as he pulled it over his head and a soft thump as he lay on his pallet. I peered over the edge of the bed.

"Mr. McKellar!" I hissed.

"Go to sleep, Maggie."

"Don't worry about what she said. I don't care if they think bad of me or say such things. I don't want to cause any more trouble between you and your folks. So just don't worry about it. It's no different than before." He glanced up at me, but his face was in shadows.

"It's different."

"Why? I don't care." I heard him turn on his side, and I reached down to touch his shoulder with my fingertips. "I'll be gone soon, so just pay it no mind." He shook his head, and I sighed as I rolled onto my back.

"G'night, Mr. McKellar," I whispered. He didn't answer.

Chapter 5

The ashes were still waiting, and as soon as breakfast was cleared, Mrs. McKellar sent me to the smokehouse with a bucket, a broom, and a shovel. I was coming out of the shed with another load of powdery ash when Mr. McKellar and Matt passed on their way from the woodlot. Mr. McKellar handed his ax to Matt and took the heavy bucket from me.

"I don't like the way Ma makes you do all this heavy work while Trisha sits in the house."

"Don't say anything to her about it," I said. "No use riling her up. Trisha couldn't get in under the racks like I can, anyhow. Maybe you can find someplace in Jacksborough where I can work in the house all the time."

His face looked strange, like he'd bit down on something bitter.

"I'll try," was all he said.

Trisha was all a-flutter when we came in for dinner. Seems while I'd been sweeping up ashes, I'd missed the visit from Rafe Henderson, inviting the McKellars to throw in with Hendersons and a couple of other valley families for a corn husking party.

"Henderson thinks it takes whiskey to get men together to work," Old Mr. McKellar scoffed. "It's dissipation. There's always some fight to break up."

"True," Paul said, "but many hands make quick work of a tiresome job."

In the end, Old Mr. McKellar decided the younger McKellars should go with a wagonload of the corn, just to be neighborly. While we were washing the dishes, it was all Trisha wanted to talk about.

"Of course, everybody will want to meet John David's bride," she smirked.

After we were done, I slipped up to the attic and pulled the pieces of calico from the wooden box by the bed and laid them on the quilt. I was afraid to start sewing, afraid of ruining the nicest thing I'd ever been able to call mine. But I had to have something to wear to this corn husking party. Everybody there would know John David McKellar had married a mountain girl; if they didn't, it wouldn't be long before they heard the story. I couldn't change being scrawny and sun-browned, but if there was any way to help it, I wasn't going to show up looking like a beggar in Trisha's cast-offs.

I got up the courage to ask Mrs. McKellar for a needle and some thread, and then I spent every moment when I wasn't doing chores working on my dress. I made sure all my work was done to suit her first, so mostly that meant sewing at night, after the Bible reading. I'd sew by the candlelight until my eyes were so blurred I couldn't see to make another stitch. Once, I woke to find Mr. McKellar was taking the needle from me, and I quickly tightened my fingers around it.

"Not yet," I begged, but he pulled the work away. I covered my face with my hands. "There's so much still to do—"

He laid it across the bed. "It's not that important, Maggie. Don't cry over it."

"It *is* important! I can't be wearing Trisha's ugly old dress when I meet folks."

"Don't worry about that. I don't care what folks think."

"Of course you don't!" I looked into his face, so well-favored. "You're John David McKellar. But I'm Maggie Boon, and folks will be more apt to find fault with me than with you."

"You're Maggie McKellar, far as they know. If anybody finds fault, I'll whip him."

"Not a girl!" I laughed in spite of myself, and he grinned.

"Girls, too." He lay back down. "Get some sleep, Maggie. It won't do you any good to have the prettiest dress at the party if you can't keep your eyes open."

I noticed after that, though, he always seemed to be around to take over one of my chores during the day so I could work on the dress. At night, he'd make up excuses to stay up with me—his moccasins needed mending, or he needed to smooth lumps off the lead balls for his rifle. Sometimes he'd read to me from one of his books, about the wild adventures of some Greek fellow, but mostly we sat on the bed and talked in whispers, and that was enough to keep me awake and working. The night before the husking, we sat up very late so I could finish the buttonholes. Finally, I snipped the thread on the last one and laid down the scissors, tired to the bone.

"See if it fits," he said. Moving into the darkness at the other end of the attic, I stepped out of Trisha's dress and then pulled the yards of calico over my head and poked my arms through the sleeves. I quickly fastened the buttons and stepped back into the circle of candlelight. Holding out my arms, I twirled around once.

"No rips so far. How does it look?" I asked.

It felt wonderful. The fabric was smooth and soft against my skin. For the first time I could remember, my dress wasn't too tight across the shoulders, or too long at the hem, or bunched together at my waist. I twirled around again just for the pleasure of feeling the skirt lift and come swirling in against my legs.

"You're beautiful." I glanced up, certain I'd misunderstood him, but the look on his face told me I hadn't. "You shouldn't worry about what folks will say. You look as fine as any girl in the valley." I quickly looked away.

"Well, I hope so, after all this work." I started back to the dark corner, but he caught my arm and drew me back to him. He reached up to loosen my knot of hair, letting the curls fall free, and then he ran his hands down my aching back to circle my waist. My heart was thumping so hard I saw its flutter under the fabric.

"There was a butterfly in that big old ugly cocoon, after all," he said.

It was the best thing he could have said. I smiled at him, mighty shy but mighty pleased, and he touched my cheek. What might have happened next, I can't say, because Matt suddenly coughed in his sleep, and we both startled, coming back to ourselves. I moved away from Mr. McKellar, back into the shadows, and I waited until I heard him tending the fire downstairs to slip out of the dress and hang it on a peg in the wall.

It was a good while before he came back upstairs and lay down. Tired as I was, I still found it hard to go to sleep, and I knew it was because of him. He was on his pallet on the floor, same as always, but I felt him there as I never had before, closer and bigger—and frightening in a way. He was right. It was different now, and somehow I knew things weren't going back to how they were before.

※ ※ ※

We rode to the husking atop a load of corn on a bright, clear afternoon, and even Trisha couldn't spoil my happiness. She grumbled that my dress was too fine and expensive for a corn husking, which I took as a sign it must look nice on me. Although Matt told me so, Mr. McKellar said nothing. But he sat close enough his arm brushed mine with every bump of the wagon, and I couldn't keep from laughing, as much from the little thrill that ran through me with every touch as from the jaunty traveling songs and bawdy drinking songs I knew they'd never dare sing around home.

I got quiet as we pulled into Hendersons' clearing. Every family in the valley must have come, whether they'd brought corn to husk or not. Mr. McKellar's hand slipped around mine and gave a quick squeeze.

"You're fine," he said in a low voice.

His feet had hardly hit the ground before a young man with a wispy mustache was slapping his back.

"McKellar! I wondered if you'd show up. The tales are that you picked up a little something on a trip to the mountains."

Mr. McKellar helped me down from the wagon and laid his arm across my shoulders.

"Maggie, this is Jed Evans, from the other side of Stinking Creek. Jed, this is my wife—Mrs. McKellar to you."

Jed's grin grew wider. "I guess this just goes to show, even the wary ones can be caught."

"I suppose," Mr. McKellar said mildly. "Henderson got any whiskey tonight?"

Of course, Henderson did, and the men started passing the jug even before two boys from opposite banks of the creek were chosen as captains for the husking contest. I stood with Trisha and watched Mr. McKellar line up with the men and boys on our side of a huge mound of corn. Mr. Henderson and his oldest son laid a rod through the center of the pile, and husks and elbows began to fly.

"That's not a fair match," Trisha grumbled. "Look, the rod was closer to their side than to ours. They don't have to do near as much. They'll win, no doubt about it."

Whether or not she was right about the rod, the other team did finish first, and they hoisted their captain high in the air. I didn't like the way Jed Evans kept taunting Mr. McKellar while our team finished husking the corn and scooping up all the husks for fodder.

"That Jed Evans seems like a rascal," I said to Mr. McKellar as we waited our turn at the food Mrs. Henderson and her daughters had set out. He laughed.

"He doesn't mean anything by it. Jed's like a pesky little dog, always biting at your heels."

Jed was there in the circle of young folk where Mr. McKellar took me to sit while we ate. I ignored him, instead paying mind while Mr. McKellar introduced the others, including one mighty pretty girl with dark red hair hanging loose down her back.

"Come on, now!" Jed said, and his breath already smelled of liquor. "You ought to introduce Bess proper! Every bachelor in this valley has courted Bess Clardy at one time or another, Mrs. McKellar, including your husband. There was a time he was one of her regulars."

Mr. McKellar shrugged. "That's the past, Jed. I reckon coming of age makes a man think more about the choices he makes." Bess' pretty mouth drooped into a pout.

"Well," Matt said, quickly, "I myself don't mind one bit that he's chosen himself right out of the competition for your hand, Bess."

"Me, neither." Jed leaned toward me. "You did all us fellows a favor by catching John David, little Mrs. McKellar. Bess will have to take one of us now." I shifted away from him as Bess laughed.

"Don't be so sure of that, Jed Evans. You fellows aren't the only ones in the world, you know."

There was more husking once we'd eaten. Sunset darkened into twilight, when Mr. Henderson lit a bonfire, though the full moon gave plenty of light to work by. We sat with the young folk again, but this time the fellows clustered together around a jug of whiskey Jed had smuggled over, leaving me alone with the girls. The girls pretended not to care what was going on with the menfolk, but I noticed a lot of eyes cutting over to see if anyone was watching us. It looked like wasted effort to me, for the young men weren't paying us any mind. They were growing louder and more rambunctious as the whiskey took hold. The girls had to console themselves with gossip, and of course, the first thing they wanted to know was about me and Mr. McKellar.

"I heard your pa broke into the dancing so Bob Dunlop could say the ceremony," one girl said. I nodded.

"Thomas Webb said Bob said John David was so drunk a couple of men had to hold him up so he'd be standing to say the vows," said another.

"That's not true!" I scoffed. "I wouldn't have married him if he was that drunk."

"Not even to give your baby a name?" Bess said. I swung around with hot words on my lips, but her little smile made me swallow them. A denial would no doubt get back to Trisha, and then on to Mr. McKellar's pa. There was nothing for it—I had to let them think it of me. I shrugged.

"Maybe Bob Dunlop don't know everything about our business. And maybe folks shouldn't be repeating what they don't know."

That shut them up, but later I caught Bess leaning toward another girl and looking at me, whispering and giggling. Pay it no mind, I told myself, raising my chin a little. You got to expect gossip, things being the way they are.

Most of the gossip was about who was courting who. I'd never been one to care about such things, and since I didn't know the folks they were talking about, I got bored pretty quick with their giggling talk. I kept my mouth shut, only half-listening, working steady and waiting for the dancing, when I'd have a better chance to show off my dress a bit. I'd been studying their dresses, and mine was pretty as any of theirs, I decided, even if it didn't have the tucks and ruffles theirs had. Maybe Mr. McKellar was right. Maybe I did look as fine as any girl from the valley.

But when I stood to stretch my back and legs, Bess gasped.

"You're not wearing shoes!"

I quickly sat back on my feet, hot with shame.

"She probably doesn't have any," someone said. "You know backwoods mountain folk don't wear shoes. Their feet are tough as leather, anyhow, or so folks say."

"Ugh," Bess said. "I never guessed John David would fancy snuggling up to leathery feet every night." They all laughed.

For once, my sass abandoned me. I stared stupidly at the corn in my lap as they went on to talk about somebody else, their giggles ringing in my ears. The worst part was, it was true. I could feel the tough skin of my heels against the back of my legs. I'd been fooling myself. My pretty dress didn't matter one whit. Ma had said it more than once—if you put a pink bonnet on a sow, she's still a sow. I glanced at Bess, with her pretty pale skin and smooth hair. Mr. McKellar had courted her, maybe even right up to the time he'd married me. Probably he was just biding his time with me now, waiting till we had that annulment, and then he'd pick up right where he'd left off with her. His hands around my waist last night? Those brushes of his arm on the ride here? A rich man wanted only one thing from a girl like me, Pa said.

Tears burned in the back of my throat. I looked at the pile of corn. It was nearly done, and I wondered how I'd explain to Mr. McKellar that I didn't want to stay for the dancing after all, even if it meant riding home alone with Paul and Trisha.

"Look!" one of the girls squealed suddenly. "Bess got a red ear!"

Bess was pulling down the last of the husks, and sure enough, the kernels glowed dark red in the bonfire's light.

"Who's it going to be, Bess?" someone called. Bess smiled and flipped the loose ends of her hair over her shoulder. She went over to the young men, and I heard folks laughing as she looked them over, like she was having a hard time choosing.

"Pick me!" Jed cried out, and everybody laughed. Bess laughed too, and then she tossed the red ear into Mr. McKellar's lap.

"For auld lang syne!" she said. She put one hand under his chin and tipped his face up so she could kiss him full on the mouth. I heard girls giggling all around me, though they sounded far away. It seemed like a long time before she straightened, smiled again at the folks around, and flounced back to our group.

"Maybe he'll rethink the wisdom of that choice now," she said, and her eyes cut toward me for just a blink.

I didn't look up at Mr. McKellar, though I could hear the young fellows laughing loud. Folks were talking all around me, and I wondered whether they thought I ought to smack Bess. I wanted to smack her. My hands were trembling as I jerked at the corn husks. He's not my man, I reminded myself, no matter what folks think, no matter about that piece of paper or what Sarah said. Once he got the money, we'd part ways, and he'd be free to kiss—or marry—whoever he wanted. I'd be free, too, to marry any fellow of my own choosing in Jacksborough. Why should the sight of Bess Clardy's lips against his bother me at all?

But when Trisha and Paul left in the wagon, I wasn't in it.

"*Ten Pound Lass,*" Bob Dunlop called. "As many as will, line up, each man opposite the woman of his choice."

I don't think either me or Mr. McKellar took much pleasure from the few sets we danced. After a while, he steered me out of the line and over to a spot behind the crowd around the bonfire. He was going to try to explain, I could tell, and I waited while he worked up his nerve. He brushed one hand across his mouth.

"You having a good time?" he started, but he shook his head impatiently and started again. "You look real pretty."

Before I could answer, Jed Evans joined us, carrying a whiskey jug. In the firelight, his face looked pale and a little twisted, like he was some kind of spook. Mr. McKellar nudged him.

"You all right?"

"Not especially." Jed lifted the jug for a swig. "Nothing's ever enough for you, is it, McKellar? You always had to be a little better than the rest of us—fastest horse in the county, fancy law studies in Nashville, girls practically throwing themselves at you—"

Mr. McKellar snorted. "That's not true. You're drunk." He wrestled the jug away, and Jed pushed him, hard.

"She would've chosen you eventually, we all know that. Then you show up with a wife, and I thought maybe one of us would get a chance, but no!" His voice rose, and people around the fire turned to look. "You'll still dally with Bess, even though that little backwoods wench is carrying your child."

"Shut your mouth," Mr. McKellar said through gritted teeth. More heads were craning to see.

"Pay him no mind," I started, but Jed stepped between us, pushing his face up toward Mr. McKellar's.

"What happened, McKellar? Did you find her in the woods on

62

one of your so-called hunting trips? I bet she was easy for you, wasn't she, an ignorant little lassie like that? You probably didn't even have to bother trying to charm her first. I bet she was all too willing to give herself to the almighty John David McKellar!"

Next thing I knew, the jug of whiskey was spilling out on the ground by my feet and they were pounding on each other. A gasp of excitement rippled through folks as they gathered around, and then Matt came running, pushing through the crowd to tackle Mr. McKellar, and another man grabbed Jed and pinned his arms tight against his back. Fresh blood glistened in the firelight, on both their faces.

Mr. Henderson bustled over and ordered them to leave since they couldn't act decent. Matt took one of Mr. McKellar's arms and led him away, and without another glance at the curious crowd, I followed. When we were a good distance from the sounds of the fiddle, Matt stopped and faced Mr. McKellar. By the moonlight, I could tell Mr. McKellar's left eye was swelling. He was still breathing hard and fast, and he wiped blood from the corner of his lip with his sleeve.

"I'm sick of it, Matt," he said, "the way folks treat her, what they say about her—"

"You're not helping any, fighting with Jed and kissing Bess! Just what do you think Pa will say when he hears about that?" Mr. McKellar swore, and Matt cuffed him on the ear. "Watch your mouth! You don't want folks treating her bad, start by treating her like a lady yourself." Mr. McKellar looked at me sideways and mumbled an apology, and Matt laid one arm across his shoulders. "I know it's hard for you for to hear folks say she's with child when she's not, but you can't—"

Mr. McKellar shot an alarmed look at me. "You told him?"

"I didn't," I said quickly.

"I saw your pallet on the floor," Matt said. "And you know quarters are so close in that attic I can hear what's going on—or not. I won't say anything. You're a man and you can handle your own affairs. But you better master that hot head of yours, brother, or you'll find yourself in real trouble someday." He gave Mr. McKellar a little shake. "Are you cooled down now?" Mr. McKellar nodded, and Matt stepped away. "I'm going back, then. I'm likely to look like a pretty good choice to Bess, now she's seen you and Jed act like a pair of jackasses. Maggie, take him home, but be careful Pa don't see him like this."

We watched until Matt was gone through the dark woods. I looked up at Mr. McKellar. His eye was swollen nearly shut.

"We ought to get something on that eye," I said. "Is there water close by?"

He took me through the woods to a spot where the creek cut in close to the road. Neither of us had any kind of kerchief, so he sat on a piece of fallen tree and gave me one of his wool socks to dip in the water. I squeezed out the sock and laid it over his eye.

"I'm sorry," he muttered. "Jed was mad at me. I don't know why he wanted to shame you."

I gave a short laugh. "Of course they think I'm with child, Mr. McKellar. Why else would someone like me be paired with someone like you?"

He pulled the wet sock away and glared at me as best he could with only the one good eye. "Don't ever say that! You're good as anyone, Maggie, you hear?"

"Sure," I said, to appease him. He settled back, and I laid the sock over his eye again. The woods were quiet. Most trees had dropped their leaves over the past week, and moonlight filtered through the bare branches, making everything a soft silver. Mr. McKellar sat with his face tilted up to me and his eyes closed. With my free hand, I pushed the wavy dark hair off his forehead, away from the wet sock. His hair was soft, and I couldn't help stroking it a few times, just like I used to do with the little ones back home. He was a fine-looking man, awfully fine, even with one eye swollen shut and his lip puffed out around a bloody cut. I touched that puffy lip, and when it curved upward under my fingers, a tenderness so strong it scared me a little stirred inside my bosom.

As good as anyone, he said. But that wasn't true. I was just a mountain girl, a barefoot backwoods wench. He might dress me up in calico, and he might tell me I looked beautiful in it, but that didn't change who I was under that calico, or who he was. We might have fancied each other a bit these last days, but I'd heard Ma say it—a peacock don't nest with a laying hen. I had no right to be touching him like this, like a real wife. I took the sock back to the creek and squatted on the bank, swirling it in the cold water.

"When are you going to get money for that annulment?" I pushed the question past the lump in my throat. He didn't answer for a minute, like I'd caught him by surprise.

"Soon."

"How soon?" I heard leaves rustling and I knew he was getting up. "I don't want to winter over in your home, Mr. McKellar," I said quickly. "Your folks don't want me there, and—well, it's not decent." He stood by me, but I didn't look up.

"Is this because of what he said?"

"No."

"Bess, then, and that blasted kiss! I swear she's nothing." I cut him off.

"Look, we don't have much more time," I said roughly. "In a few days, your ma's going to figure out there's no baby. I won't be able to hide it from her, and then she'll have me out of the house and back home for sure."

He was quiet while he took in what I was saying

"How many days?" he asked.

"A few. Three, four, probably no more than that."

He didn't say anything for a while, but then he squatted beside me and took my hand. His face had a look that was half-hopeful and half-bashful, and I knew he was about to say something he ought not to say, not to me, anyhow.

"Maggie," he started, but I pulled my hand away and gave the sock to him, standing and brushing at my skirt. He stood too, with the wet sock dripping on his bare foot. "Maggie—"

"Please, Mr. McKellar. You promised." I knew he was looking at me, but I kept my eyes on the ripples of moonlight sliding on the creek but going nowhere. Finally I heard him let out a slow breath.

"I reckon I could go tomorrow and see what I can do about it, if that's what you want."

I was trembling, no doubt from the cold of the water. "It's what I want." He stood silently for a moment.

"All right." He went back to where he'd left his moccasin and slipped it on, still holding the damp sock. "My eye's fine. Let's go."

I followed him back toward his home, but the night seemed colder now, and even the bright moonlight couldn't lift the darkness that settled on me.

Chapter 6

The attic was still dark when Mr. McKellar leaned over me.

"I'll be gone a couple of days," he whispered. "Don't tell them anything. As far as you know, I'm hunting." Still dozy, I sat up to see him starting down the stairs, hardly more than a shadow. The door squeaked slightly, and everything was still again.

"Where is he?" Old Mr. McKellar demanded at the breakfast table, in a tone that reminded me of my own pa. That made it easier to tell the half-truth.

"He left before I was really awake. I think he said something about hunting."

"His horse is gone," Paul said. "I'd say he's gone farther than hunting." His pa's eyebrows pulled together at that news, and I feared Mr. McKellar would pay dearly for this trip when he did come home.

Trisha wasted no chance to remind his ma and me of that kiss from Bess Clardy, like she thought that explained everything. For the first few days he was gone, I managed to stay away from Trisha, even if it meant setting myself the worst of chores. I cleared dead plants from the garden, and I scooped dung from the hen coop. I dragged the mattresses down from the attic and refilled them with fresh shucks.

But no matter how hard I worked all day, I found it impossible to sleep once I'd gone to bed. Though my body was tired, I felt too restless to settle down. I told myself it was the change in seasons, and I'd get used to it, just like every year. By this time next week, I told myself, I'll be in some cozy place in Jacksborough, with my own money, and I won't have a thing to worry about.

By the third night, though, I couldn't deny it—I missed Mr. McKellar. I hadn't realized how much it pleased me to meet his eyes as he came in for supper until his pa and brothers came through the door without him. I missed the whispered conversations we had after the rest of the family was sleeping, with his rumbly laugh and the crooked half-smile he always had while I told him about my day. Though I blushed with shame at the thought, I missed the glimpses of his naked shoulders I sometimes sneaked as he took off his shirt before bed. I stared into the darkness, trying to remember the touch of his lips against mine at Charlie's and wondering how it would feel to kiss him the way Bess had. It did no good to chide myself for being foolish or to remind myself I was doing the right thing by leaving. Longing for him spread through me like fever, and I finally gave myself over to it, hugging the pillow and wishing the night done so I could busy myself with work.

The sky threatened rain the next morning, and before I could find some chore for myself, his ma parked me on the porch with a basket of last spring's wool, to pick out burrs and trash while Trisha sat nearby, carding the clean wool. It was the worst job I could've had that morning, given my mood. Burrs pricked the ends of my fingers. Scratchy little bits of trash worked their way up my sleeves against my skin, and I couldn't seem to get rid of them. The worst part, though, was working with Trisha. She seemed to think Mrs. McKellar wanted her to keep an eye on my work, and she complained about it loudly, first that I was so slow, and when I hurried, that I was leaving pieces of trash.

"Look!" She held up a tiny bit of dry leaf. "Just because your folks are too poor to have sheep don't mean you can get by with such a sorry job. Trash like this will catch in the cards and mess up the whole batch."

I snatched the wad of wool off her lap and started picking through it again. She sniffed. "No need to be uppish, missy. If you did it right the first time, there'd be no need to do it over."

I bit back the smart words on my tongue, picking through the entire wad of wool and finding no other trash. She seemed satisfied then, but as she laid it in the basket we heard thunder close by.

"Listen to that!" she grumped. "They won't get much done in the field today. They might have been done before rain moved in if John David hadn't left them short-handed, the lazy oaf."

I don't know why I took her bait, except that a great, empty feeling settled inside me when she said his name.

"He's not lazy," I argued. "He does plenty of work around here."

"What work suits him, sure. But a person can't just pick and choose what work he'll do or when he'll do it. I'm sure Paul would like to take some days to go off hunting."

"Why don't he, then?"

She gave another big sniff. "Paul's got a sense of duty. He knows what's expected of him, and he does it." Rain started to peck against the roof of the porch, and Trisha picked up the basket. "Let's go in."

As we went into the cabin, the rain picked up, drowning out the whirr of Mrs. McKellar's spinning wheel.

"That moved in fast," Trisha said. "They'll be soaked before they can make it in." She picked up the cards and straightened the wool on them. "It's just not right that they'll get all wet and cold while John David is off playing somewhere."

I glared at her. "He's hunting."

"For what kind of game, I wonder?" She laughed. "I'll bet he's hunting like he was when he found you!"

It was simply too much.

"You're wrong!" I said between gritted teeth. "You think you know everything, but you don't."

"You think you know him better than we do?" she shot back. "You've known him how long? Let's see, married for not even a month yet, and not much of a courtship before that, just one quick tryst in the woods. What makes you think you know his nature better than his own family does? He's a lazy, fickle fool."

"He's not!"

She leaned toward me. "Did you think you could change him? Thought that baby would give you some kind of hold on him? Maybe you even think he loves you? Well, girl, listen to me and save yourself some heartache. He'll not stay with a backwoods slut. Why, he's left you behind already."

I leapt to my feet, knocking over the basket of carded wool, spilling her neat little rolls on the floor. "You're wrong! He's a good man, he's going to do right by me, so you just shut your mouth about him, you damned old toad!"

Trisha's face went purple with rage. His ma, on the other hand, was pale. She slapped me as hard as Pa used to, hard enough that my eyes went black for a moment. Her voice was colder than any I'd ever heard. "How dare you talk to her that way? I'll not have her insulted by a nasty little slut who trapped my son into this shameful union so she could get her hands on our property—"

I turned and ran from the cabin, not really knowing where I was going, not really caring that I was running into the rain. I only knew I had to get away from them before I lost all control of myself. My feet carried me to the barn, up the ladder to the far corner of the hayloft. I dropped to my knees, dripping wet from the rain and sobbing with anger, not just at Trisha, but at myself as well, because I couldn't hold my tongue, and now I'd made things worse for him when he did come back.

I heard voices below, and I put both hands over my mouth to stifle the sobs. Metal clinked against metal—it was just the men come from the fields, putting away the tools. I sat still and silent until they'd gone, and then I pulled my knees up and circled them with my arms. I was in trouble, deep trouble, and I hoped Mr. McKellar would be back soon with the money and someplace in Jacksborough for me to go. I sure couldn't stay here.

But instead of my own troubles, my mind worried over what Trisha had said. Was there any truth to it? He *had* been gone a long time. Had he stopped to see Bess on the way, to make things right for when I was gone?

"It don't matter, you goose!" I cried aloud. "He don't have to answer to you for anything!" The rain pounded on the roof, and I lay back in the hay, covering my face with my hands. How long did it take to get to Jacksborough, anyhow?

※ ※ ※

I don't know how long it was before the barn door opened again, just that the rain was only scratching on the roof now and the light was a darker gray. I held my breath, fearful his ma had come to fetch me back to the house. But my heart took a giant leap when a horse snorted. I looked over the edge of the loft to see Mr. McKellar leading Washington into a stall, and I couldn't hold back the cry in my throat.

"You're back!"

Washington spooked at my call, and Mr. McKellar had only just brought him back in control when I hit the bottom of the ladder. Though I was scared to get so close to Washington's heaving bulk, I threw myself against Mr. McKellar. He steadied himself and awkwardly wrapped one arm around me.

"Maggie? What are you doing out here? Is everything all right?"

"No." Tears brimmed up in my eyes again. "I had words with Trisha, and your ma slapped me—I had to get away from them."

His look darkened. "She slapped you? Why?" I leaned toward him, and his arm tightened to bring me closer. I stood for a moment before answering, breathing in the sweet, musky dampness of his buckskin jacket.

"I sassed them, bad. I called Trisha a toad, and I cussed her, but she said you were—she said—" I paused, my heart pounding. "She said you're a lazy oaf, and I couldn't let her do that." His chest rose against my cheek as he laughed.

"You cussed her?" I nodded, and he laughed again as he pulled away to loop the reins over a rail. "I bet Ma liked that." He took my hand. "Come here. I have something for you."

We went back up in the loft, and as I sat down, he laid a small, brown package in my lap.

"You got the money," I said, with a lump rising in my throat, but his eyes were shining.

"Open it."

I tore off the crumpled paper to find a golden heart about the size of a hickory nut, sitting on a pile of fine chain. I stared at it and then at him, and he smiled.

"It's a locket," he said, taking it from me and putting the chain around my neck so the little heart fell against my bosom. "See, you can open it and put a keepsake inside."

Tears were filling my eyes so fast I could hardly see the carved flower raised out of the locket's background.

"Do you like it?" he asked. I nodded, quickly, which sent a tear spilling over. I clutched the locket in my fist and took a deep breath. Waiting wouldn't make this any easier.

"What about the money?"

"I got plenty of money," he said, pulling a small leather bag from his pocket. "I took bets on a couple of races. Washington's a born racer, Maggie. I never saw anything like it. I always thought he was fast, but he's better than I thought. Pa would have a fit of apoplexy if he knew I was gambling, but—"

"Is it enough for the annulment?" My voice wobbled.

"I'm sure it is. But I've been thinking." He was silent for a minute, and I looked at him, trying to learn every line of his face, the serious look of his brown eyes, the little wrinkle in his cheek where his crooked grin always started. I wished I could tuck the sight into this locket as a keepsake to remember forever, even if, like he said, I did find somebody else to marry.

"I asked around town," he was saying, "you know, if anybody might need a girl to help out, and Maggie, there just wasn't anybody I'd feel good about sending you to. So I was thinking on the way back—"

"Will you have to take me to Nashville?"

He paused, shifting the weight of the money bag in his palm. "Did you ever think about what you want your home to be like, your own home, I mean?"

I shook my head. "I never figured I'd have much say about it."

"I thought about it a lot on the way back here." He smiled a little. "Have you ever seen a good pair of mules?"

"Of course. What does that—"

"Each mule has its own nature, but if you've got a good pair, they become a team when you put them in harness, pulling at the same pace, working side by side. I've always thought Zeke and Sarah are like a good team of mules. I decided on the way home that's what I want, what Zeke has with Sarah." He unwrapped my fingers from the locket and held them between his own fingers, meeting my eyes with his. "It makes no sense, with us knowing each other only this little while, and you being so young, but I just have a feeling you could turn out to be a partner like that for me. What I'm saying is, I'd like for you to stay—if you're willing, of course."

My heart suddenly seemed to be swelling to fill my whole bosom. "No annulment?"

"Not now," he said quickly. "But if it turns out bad—if you're not happy—we could still get one later. I read a case once of a couple that had been married for years—they even had children—who got their marriage annulled. So you wouldn't be stuck with me if you were miserable. I promise you that."

I couldn't imagine being miserable ever again. "We'd just keep on like we have been?"

His cheeks reddened. "Not quite like we have been. More like—more like a real husband and wife."

A real husband and wife! My stomach made that strange flop again, but I had to settle something here and now.

"I don't want to live with your folks anymore, Mr. McKellar—"

"John David."

"John David—your ma hates me, and I don't want to stay here. I won't stay here."

"So we'll leave. We'll take this money and get a place of our own, a farm and a cabin. I've got a place in mind." His manner was so like what I'd seen in my little brothers, begging for something but not wanting to be seen as begging. "So. Would you like to be in harness with me? Want to pull together?"

I couldn't keep from laughing. "I do." His grin spread across his whole face.

"That sounded like a wedding vow." His voice was light and teasing, but his eyes were fixed on mine. "I feel like I ought to kiss you."

I quickly looked down, burning with an uncomfortable mix of embarrassment and eagerness.

"I reckon you could," I mumbled.

He moved forward to take me in his arms, and his kiss was just as I remembered, a soft press of his lips on mine. But his arms suddenly tightened, and his mouth pressed harder, almost greedily, as he lowered me to lie beneath him on the hay. I was startled by the heat I felt rising in him. To be truthful, I was a little relieved when the barn door opened again and I heard Matt's voice.

"What the devil?" Washington's bridle jangled and then Matt called out. "John David, are you here?" John David raised on his elbows, breathing fast, his face flushed.

"Go away!" he yelled. But Matt had climbed the ladder to the loft, and he grinned at the sight of us.

"Looks like you're getting a better welcome out here than what's waiting in the house for you, brother. Where have you been, anyway?"

※ ※ ※

Supper was on the table, just as it had been the first night I followed him into the cabin. This time, though, I met their eyes boldly as I walked through the door, my hand wrapped inside John David's. No one spoke during the meal, but sure enough, as I stood to clear the dishes, Old Mr. McKellar motioned for me to sit again. He leaned back in his chair and studied John David for a while before he spoke.

"Where have you been these last days, son?"

"I had business in Jacksborough."

"Such important business you'd shirk your duties here?"

"Yes." There was a long silence. His pa looked at me so intently my very bones seemed to quiver, despite John David's hand around mine.

"Your ma and Trisha had trouble with your wife while you were gone."

"She cursed at us!" Trisha blurted out. "She said foul, unchristian things! She's got no manners or sense of shame!"

"Shame?" John David said, quietly, but I could hear the anger beneath his calm.

"Yes," his pa said. "Shame. Maggie needs to remember she came into our family under shameful circumstances. You may have tried to set right your mistake by marrying her, but there's no way around it, son. The two of you brought dishonor on the McKellar name, and you should act with the humility such guilt calls for. She should keep a civil tongue in her head."

"I'm sure she will if Trisha will," John David said. His grip on my hand was painfully tight.

"You'd do well to remember it too!" his ma suddenly said. "Where would you be if not for the generosity of this family? What if we tossed you out for shaming us, like most folks would? How could you provide for a wife? You can't! No, you won't! You left your pa and brothers to grub out sumac for four days, with no care at all that the corn to grow in that field will put food in that girl's mouth." She leaned across the table toward John David, her eyes narrowed. "You yammer on about being of age but keep acting like a child—"

"That's where I've been," John David interrupted. "I was arranging for our own place."

"Your own place?" Trisha sneered. "Where?"

"We're going to Texas."

I stared at him, open-mouthed, just as they all did. Texas? But he spoke like he'd been making plans for months.

"We'll get one of the land grants the Mexicans are giving out."

Paul recovered first. "You know what they said at the husking," he said. "You'd have to give up your American citizenship and swear allegiance to Mexico, and to the Catholic Church."

"I don't care about citizenship or religion," John David said. "I want the free land. We can't get any land around here."

"There's land to have in the county," his pa started, but his ma broke in.

"He won't listen to you! He wants to go as far away as he can so he can shrug off our authority as his parents. He'll go as far against common sense as he can, to get back at you and me!"

"Ma, I don't think he's doing this to get back at you," Matt said, but she was on her feet, looking down at me.

"It's you! You've beguiled my son, you whore!"

"Be quiet, Malinda!" Old Mr. McKellar ordered, but John David was standing now too.

"I told you not to call her that!" Quick as a flash, she slapped him, and just as quick, I knew she'd gone too far. John David's face was tight with the struggle to keep his temper in control. He touched my shoulder, and I quickly slid off the bench to stand beside him.

"Fine." His voice was grim. "I'll quit abusing your generosity and start providing for my wife on my own, like a man should. We'll leave in the morning. Come on, Maggie."

As soon as we were alone in the attic, I grabbed his arm.

"We're really going to Texas?"

"Texas, the moon, I don't care!" He pulled away and knelt at the wooden box by the bed, jerking things from it. "Tonight's the last night I'll sleep under their roof."

I could hear them arguing downstairs. "It's a different country, for goodness' sake!" Paul said. "They don't even speak English."

"You can't let him go, Jacob!" his ma said. "You're his father—he has to obey you! Make him come down here and listen to reason! He's being a rebellious child!"

"No!" His pa's voice rose. "He's a man, Malinda, older than I was when I left the home country!"

I sat on the bed and watched as John David piled our things beside me—his knives and little bag of bullets, the cloth waiting to be sewn into clothes.

"Where is Texas?" I asked, and he looked up. "I just wondered."

He picked up one of my hands, turning it over and looking at it like he'd never seen such a thing before.

"Such a small hand," he finally said. He closed his hand over mine. "Maybe you'd rather not partner with me if it means leaving. Maybe you'd rather stay in Tennessee."

"I didn't say that. I just wondered where Texas is."

He smiled and laid a heavy book in my lap, flipping it open to a picture with a bunch of lines, some squiggled, some straight.

"This is the United States of America." He pointed to a spot between two straight lines. "Here we are, Campbell County, Tennessee." Keeping that finger in place, he pointed to another spot on the picture, where there were no lines. "This is Texas."

"That's not so far."

He laughed and clapped the book shut. "It's farther than it looks on a map, Maggie."

I was surprised to hear his pa's voice downstairs, reading the Bible like any regular night.

"'So ought men to love their wives as their own bodies. He that loveth his wife loveth himself. For no man ever yet hated his own flesh—'"

"What's that?" I said. "More Proverbs?" John David shook his head.

"Ephesians, chapter 5."

"'For this cause shall a man leave his father and mother, and shall be joined unto his wife, and they two shall be one flesh. This is a great mystery—'" John David turned toward the stairs.

"I'll be damned," he said softly. "He's giving me permission."

His pa's voice was as clear as if he was standing in the attic with us.

"'Nevertheless let every one of you in particular so love his wife even

75

as himself, and the wife see that she reverence her husband.'" I heard the rustle of movement that meant the reading was over. John David took my hand again.

"Maggie, don't worry. I'll take care of you. I promise I'll make things better for you."

"For us," I corrected. He smiled and kissed my hand.

"For us." He knelt again by the box. "Let's get things bundled together tonight so we can get away pretty quick tomorrow."

❦ ❦ ❦

After they'd all gone to bed, we slipped out to the barn, and I held a bag while he filled it with cup after cup of the corn we'd been shelling off the cob every evening. Though I didn't really think his pa would come out to the barn, I peered around at every creak the barn made in the windy night.

"Won't your pa notice this is missing?"

"You're probably right—he's so stingy he probably counts every grain." He lifted the cup to send the shiny, golden kernels sliding into the bag. "But I reckon I earned this. Ever since I was old enough to go to the fields, I've helped with everything from planting to harvest. I'd say Pa owes me a bushel of corn in payment. Anyway, we'll need seed corn for a start." He leaned against the wall, smiling down at me. "Think of it, Maggie, our own place! I'll have my own corn fields. There's nothing in the world prettier than a big field of green corn, ten feet tall, two or three ears to a stalk."

He fell silent, and after a while, I shook the bag to settle the kernels and to remind him of what we were doing. He bent to dip another cupful. "We'll have our own cabin," he went on, "with a bed downstairs near the fire, not in a cold attic where I'm bumping my head every time I stand up. And we'll have glass windows, two of them."

"Let's have flowers," I said. "Like Sarah does."

He laughed. "If you want flowers, we'll have flowers. I'll give you whatever you want."

❦ ❦ ❦

We left the corn by the barn door, ready to be loaded in the morning. It was late when we finally lay down together on his bed as husband and wife. I'd had a chance by then to ready myself for that time, though I found I didn't know so much as I'd thought I did. But he was patient with me, and I was willing for him, and he seemed well-pleased. I lay curled close against him afterward with his arm heavy and warm across my body, marveling that just last night I'd tried to imagine simply kissing him, believing I'd never get to know. Now, I wouldn't be a servant for strangers in Jacksborough—I was truly John David McKellar's wife, and he was taking me to Texas, to make a home there together. I touched the locket lying against my skin, and my heart glowed with triumph. Ma was wrong. John David wouldn't leave me dishonored and desperate; he wanted me for his partner. He wanted me, backwoods wench or not. I fell asleep smiling, and I dreamed of a cabin surrounded by gold flowers and green corn, waving in the breeze.

Chapter 7

We came downstairs very early, when only his pa and ma were stirring, and John David told his pa about the bag of corn.

"I figure it's my inheritance," he said. "Luke, chapter 15."

"The parable of the prodigal son?" his ma said, and I noticed her eyes were pink and swollen. "You know how that turned out—penniless and starving and having to drag himself back home to depend on the mercy of his family."

"I don't intend to waste my substance with riotous living," John David said. "I'd like your blessing, Pa, to take the seed."

"You're welcome to it," his pa said. "But winter is no time for traveling, son. Don't you think you'd be better off to wait till spring?"

"If we wait, we'll get there too late to plant corn."

"What about Maggie?" It was the first time his ma had called me by name, and she said it like a bad taste lingered in her mouth. "You can't mean to make her travel while she's carrying a child. It's too dangerous, for both of them. You ought to wait till after the baby comes."

"There's no baby, Ma," John David said softly. "Forgive me for the lie, Pa, but it was the only way to keep you from taking her back to her pa."

Mrs. McKellar turned on me with a look that felt like a smack, but Old Mr. McKellar cleared his throat and she turned away.

"It's in the past now, son," he said.

"Even if there's no baby now, there will be someday," his ma said. "Then what will you do? What if there's no woman in that wilderness to help her deliver it? A man can't tend a birth, John David."

"We won't be the only people in Texas," John David said. "Lots of folks are heading out there."

"I know plenty about birthing, anyhow," I said. "I helped tend Ma for her last three."

"That may be," his ma spat at me. "But it's different to be the one doing the birthing."

"Your ma has a point, son," Old Mr. McKellar said. "Settling new country is hard enough on a man, but it's much harder on a woman. When you chose Maggie as your wife, you took on the Lord's command to care for her, as 'the weaker vessel.' If you put her through hardship or danger just to satisfy your pride, 'tis sin."

"You tell me to take up a man's responsibility, and that's what I'm trying to do," John David argued. "I can't head up my own household while I'm living as a child in yours."

"But you want to give your household a fair start."

John David looked straight into his pa's eyes. "I have to do it on my own," he said, quietly.

His pa suddenly sighed and shook his head. "A man's past always comes back to haunt him! I said those very words to my own pa when I left Dundee." He slapped John David's shoulder. "Well, if you're set on it, so be it. I won't hinder you. But have something to eat first."

So instead of the hot tongue and cold shoulder I'd feared we'd have as we left the McKellar household, we had help loading our few goods. Old Mr. McKellar brought a dusty packsaddle from the barn and showed John David how to place it on Washington's back and tie bundles to it. He seemed uneasy that we had so little to take. He took me to the cabin, where he tapped Mrs. McKellar on the shoulder as she and Trisha were cleaning up the breakfast dishes without me.

"Malinda, get some bedding they can take along." She frowned, but he frowned back, deeper. "Surely you're not so hard of heart that you won't spare a couple of quilts for your son and his wife."

I kept quiet as we stripped the bed. She folded the stout linen sheets without a word and then rolled them and the quilts into a tight bundle. It was only then that she looked at me.

"I still mean what I said last night," she said in a low voice. "You've stolen another of my children from me. Somehow you beguiled my son into choosing you over his own flesh and blood. Jacob is determined that the boy gets to make his own choice, even if it brings him to ruin." She shoved the bundle against my chest. "See to it his choice is worth what he's giving up."

❧ ❧ ❧

We'd been walking about a half-hour when John David leaned his rifle against a tree and began looking at the ground and kicking through the leaves. He suddenly grinned, put his hands around my waist, and whirled around, lifting me off my feet with a whoop.

"There's the survey marker!" He set me down by a pointed stone jutting out of the ground. "We're not on Pa's land anymore. We've done it, Maggie! We're on our way!"

Whether my giddiness came from the twirling or my excitement was hard to say.

"We're free!" I sang out, and I kissed my hand and patted it on the stone. He laughed.

"Don't be wasting kisses on rocks," he murmured. "I've got better places for them." He pulled me close and I let him kiss me, not caring if a thousand eyes were peering out of the woods.

Our excitement faded, though, during the long day's walk. We soon realized that in our hurry to leave, we'd forgotten to pack anything to eat. Not long after, I felt the heaviness and cramping low in my belly that I knew meant my courses had started. I might have been able to keep my mind off those things by talking, but John David kept such a fast pace I needed all my breath to keep up. As the daylight paled, I was so tired and hungry I followed him without any sense of where we might be, and I wondered why he kept on, why we didn't stop to camp. It wasn't until we waded an icy stream cutting across the road and I saw a square of muted light against the darkness that I knew we had come to Zeke's.

Sarah fussed over me like I was a child, and it suited me fine to just let her do it. She settled me in the rocking chair by the fire and then moved around the room quickly, putting water to warm, mixing batter for corn pone. She spoke in a hushed voice, for the girls were already sleeping.

"Nothing to eat all day and walking from McKellars' house! Thou must be exhausted. I'm sorry thou must wait for pone to cook. Here's a damp rag. Thou can freshen up while thou wait."

But she gasped as I bent to wash my feet. "Thy feet! Surely thou didn't walk all this way with no shoes!" I nodded, too tired to be ashamed. She turned with a hand on each hip as the door opened.

"John David McKellar! What's so important thou made this girl travel all day with no shoes and no food?"

"They've left home," Zeke said. "He says they're getting their own place."

"We're going to Texas," John David said. "We don't want to live at home like Paul and Trisha do." Zeke and Sarah looked at each other.

"I thought thou wanted an annulment," Sarah said, and she didn't look near as happy as I would have thought to find out her plan to keep me as John David's wife had worked so well.

"We changed our minds," John David said.

"So you want your own place," Zeke said. "Why Texas? There's land around here."

"I figure Texas is our best plan," John David said. "The Mexicans are charging twelve and a half cents per acre, and they'll let a man have land on credit. Our government wants a hundred dollars, gold or silver, for eighty acres of land, cash up front. I don't have that much money. But I've got enough to get to Texas and get settled in a household. All I need is a chance at the land."

"You don't have to settle for Mexican land," Zeke said. "I'll help you, and you know Pa would."

John David was shaking his head. "You won't talk me out of this."

"Somebody needs to!" Zeke's voice rose suddenly. "It's a stupid idea! Take a look at your little wife and you can see that. She'll never make it to Texas if she's this worn down after walking just twelve miles from Pa's!"

I quickly sat straighter in the chair. "I'm not so worn down."

"I figured you wrong, Zeke," John David said, jerking up the bundle of bedding he'd set on the table. "I can see we'll get no help here. Come, Maggie, let's go."

"Come, come!" Sarah said, with a meaningful look at Zeke. "The pone is ready. No use wasting it. We can talk more about thy plans tomorrow."

As we ate, the silence between the brothers was solid as a wall, despite Sarah's efforts to chip through it with talk about lighter things.

Finally she gave up and helped me make a pallet of our bedding on the floor in front of the fire. Once we'd all gone to bed, I heard her and Zeke whispering together urgently. I knew John David must hear it too, though he gave no sign. I turned to face him.

"Zeke's wrong about me," I said. "I ain't too worn down from walking today. I can make it to Texas." He reached over me to pull the quilt around my shoulders.

"I kept a man's pace today," he said. "I wanted to get here so bad I didn't think about whether I was pushing you too hard. Especially with your courses starting up." He said it so plain, like it was nothing more than him noticing a scratch on my finger. I flushed hot all over as he went on. "You should've said something."

"That's private. It ain't something a girl talks about with a man."

"But I'm not just any man now, I'm your husband. We're 'one flesh,' as the Bible says. There should be nothing you keep from me." He moved closer, wrapping his leg over mine. "Be patient with me. I've got a lot to learn about a woman's ways. But you'll find I'm an eager pupil."

"Well, I hope you stick with it better than you did with studying the law," I said, and he laughed, so loud I heard the whispering from Sarah and Zeke stop.

"I believe I will. The schoolmaster is much prettier—and I like the lessons better."

※ ※ ※

Right after breakfast the next morning, John David asked Zeke for a piece of buckskin and the use of an awl so he could make me a pair of moccasins. Zeke sipped coffee and watched John David trace a pattern around my foot with the tip of his knife.

"What route do you plan to take to Texas?" he asked. John David didn't look up.

"I'm still figuring on that."

"You're not thinking of taking the Natchez Trace out of Nashville, I hope. Everything I hear says there's still trouble with robbers along the Trace."

"Robbers!" Sarah said. "There's one more thing to worry about!"

"It's our problem, not yours," John David said, and it was obvious, to me at least, that he was working to keep his temper out of his voice.

"You don't need to worry about it."

"But I do," Sarah went on. "So much can go wrong, traveling in wild country. What if one of thee gets sick? What if thy ax slips and cuts thy leg, or Maggie, what if thy skirt catches fire while thou cook over a campfire? What if thou run out of supplies out in the wild?"

"Life's a risk every day," John David said. "My ax could slip any time I'm cutting wood. I could stab my hand with this awl right here at your table."

"The world's full of trouble," I agreed. "As my ma always said, trouble's the one visitor you can count on finding at your door."

"That's where a person just has to be willing to take a gamble," John David said, giving my ankle a quick squeeze before he stood. "Or, if you'd rather, Sarah, that's what faith is for."

"But faith don't have to be blind," Zeke said. "I'm afraid you'll find yourself facing hard times on the way to Texas, and even more once you get there. I just want to feel sure your eyes are fully open to what you might come against."

"You make me sound like a newborn pup." John David slapped the knife onto the table. "I may be young, but I'm no fool! I've thought this through, Zeke."

"Have you, now?" Zeke leaned forward in his chair and turned to look hard at me. "Can you shoot a rifle, Maggie?"

"Well, no," I stammered. "Pa said teaching a girl was a waste of lead."

He turned back to John David. "A woman living in wild country has to know how to handle a rifle. You won't always be with her. Say she's alone when a mad wolf comes, or some fellow with wicked intentions—"

John David laughed. "Good Lord, Zeke, you'll scare the wits out of her!"

"I mean to," Zeke said. John David's face sobered. He stepped across the room to take his rifle from the corner.

"I'll teach her, then," he said. "Come on, Maggie."

I was quick to learn the rhythm of loading ball and powder. But the rifle was so long and heavy I could hardly hold it up, and when the shot fired, I stumbled backward and might have fallen if John David hadn't caught me.

"That's all right," he said. "It takes a few times to get used to the action. Try again."

My hands shook as I poured in the powder. I wanted so much to please him, to show them all he was right to have faith in me. But the force of that rifle was more than I had expected, violent and loud, and to be honest, I dreaded feeling it again. I slowly raised the rifle to my shoulder and tried to aim, but the end of the barrel was wobbling so I couldn't keep it trained on the cracked jug they had set up for a target.

I let the muzzle drop back toward the ground. "I can't."

"It's too big for her," John David said, taking the rifle. "Come on, you can rest it on the fence."

"No." Zeke's voice was hard. "She's got to learn to handle it standing."

John David frowned. "She's too small for it, Zeke. She's only a girl."

"A girl you want to take to Texas. She's got to be able to fire standing, or she's not ready to go. A wolf or Indian won't wait for her to get to some handy fence to steady her rifle." He took the rifle and held it out to me. "Let's see it, Maggie."

I looked up at John David, and he put an arm around my shoulders.

"You don't have to—"

"She does!" Zeke was practically shouting. "If she won't try and you let her get away with it, you two will never get to Texas. You're too weak to go!"

John David cursed at him, and for a minute, I thought they might come to blows. Though I was trembling like a leaf caught in a creek's current, I grabbed the rifle from Zeke. Raising it to my shoulder again, I held my breath and tried to keep it steady while I squeezed the trigger, slowly, like John David had said. The rifle roared and puffed smoke, and when it cleared, I saw John David was grinning.

"I hit it!"

"Not this mark," he said. "Maybe something in the next county. Maggie, you got to keep your eyes open." He laughed and tweaked my nose, just like he always did to the little girls.

Something hot flowed through my body, making my arms and legs feel weak as wet straw. I pushed the rifle hard into his chest.

"The wolves and Indians will just have to take me, then!"

I held my head high as I stalked away from them, and I banged the cabin door shut behind me. The slam startled the girls from their play, and little Lily began to cry.

"I'm not shooting again," I said, jerking up my sewing from where I'd left it.

Sarah didn't say anything, just picked up Lily, and I watched as she comforted the baby, cuddling and rocking her. It was calm and slow, something I was used to, something I was good at—not at all like the terrible power of that rifle. I sank onto the bench by the table.

"I can't do it," I said. She looked up at me.

"So that's it? Thou try only two shots, and then give up?"

"I'm too small. I'm not strong enough—" She cut me off.

"Dost thou really want to go to Texas with him?"

"Of course. We want to have our own cabin and farm, and—"

"Then thou must be strong enough, Maggie. If thou can't shoot, the whole burden of protecting thee falls on John David. If thou want to be a help to him in this venture and not a burden, thou have to be strong enough, even if it's not easy."

I watched as she carried Lily back to the bed where Hannah was playing. How could I ask for another chance, after making such a scene? Yet Sarah was right. I couldn't be a burden that he might tire of carrying.

"He laughed at me," I confessed.

"Ah, he hurt thy feelings, I see." She smiled and sat by me on the bench. "Thou just had one of many lessons about being a wife. That's not easy, either."

"It seems easy enough for you."

She laughed. "Not always. Not at first, especially. A man always seems to change when he goes from being a lover to being a husband, and that takes some getting used to." She patted my knee. "I'll tell thee the wisdom my ma told me the first time Zeke made me cry. She said love is like a creek. If the water's deep enough, thou hardly see a ripple when it goes over a rock. If the water dries up, all thou can see are rocks. What shows, ripples or rocks, depends on thy own eyes. Dost thou understand what I'm saying?"

I heard the men's voices in the yard, coming toward the house. I sighed.

"You mean I have to put some water in the creek."

She laughed. "That lesson will serve thee even better in Texas than knowing how to shoot a rifle."

I met them as they came through the door, and I swallowed hard before looking into John David's eyes. They seemed sorry, not mocking, and that made it easier to ask.

"Can I try again?"

※ ※ ※

It took many tries over the next several days, but I finally learned to steady the rifle well enough to get off a shot that John David and Zeke agreed would at least scare off anyone with evil intentions. I thought that was that, but soon after, John David said I should also learn to manage a horse. Zeke loaned us his old gelding, and so, willing or not, I sat gripping the reins tightly as the gelding plodded along beside Washington.

The gelding was so gentle I quickly got over being afraid of him, and I did learn to ride well enough. But it was soon clear to me John David had planned the lessons mostly for opportunity to satisfy his fleshly urges, taking me to some deserted corner of Zeke's farm where we were sure to be alone. I feared I might conceive a child for real before we ever left for Texas. One afternoon as we rested in a quiet pine grove, I finally told him so. He didn't say anything, just rolled onto his back to stare into the boughs above us.

"Never mind," I said, wishing I hadn't said anything. I moved to get up, but he pulled me back beside him.

"No, you're right. We don't want a baby. That would burden both of us." He was quiet for a minute, picking pine needles from my hair. "Don't worry about it," he finally said. "I'll be careful."

"Be extra careful," I said, raising on my elbow to look into his face. "My folks never had anything because of babies. If I'm anything like my Ma—"

"But I'm nothing like your Pa," he interrupted. "We're not starting out with nothing, the way they did. We'll have a land grant in Texas. And we have a bag of good McKellar seed corn." He touched the locket lying against my bosom. "I gave this as a pledge—I'll take care of you. You can trust me to do that, whatever it takes."

His face was so earnest. How could I doubt him? I leaned down to kiss him, and his arms tightened around me.

"Never doubt it, Maggie," he whispered. "I'll take care of you, always."

❧ ❧ ❧

He was restless. One morning, he rode off alone to buy supplies for the trip and to pay the bill for my new clothes. I was alarmed by how thin the money bag looked when he came back, but he was pleased with the goods he'd bought and said it was money well spent. That night after supper, he brought out his big book with the map in front.

"Maggie, want to see the route we'll take?"

I lifted Hannah on my hip so we could both look over his shoulder as he traced the route with his finger.

"We'll start in Nashville. From there, we'll take the Cumberland River to the Ohio, the Ohio to the Mississippi, down the Mississippi to Natchez. From Natchez, we'll start overland to Texas."

"So you've decided on the river route," Zeke said. "But you don't know anything about boats."

John David clapped the book shut. "I can learn." His jaw tightened as Zeke leaned forward.

"Stop, Zeke," Sarah said suddenly. We all turned to look at her, and her eyes were shiny with tears. "Please stop. Don't spend thy last days together fighting."

"Who says it's our last days?" Zeke started, but Sarah shook her head.

"I've prayed harder this week than ever in my life, that the Lord will change John David's mind and they won't go to Texas. But I'm beginning to believe His answer is no, Zeke. If the Lord wills it, who are we to fight it?"

"I want to spare them hard times," he said.

"Hard times can be good times," she said softly. "Remember?"

Zeke looked up into her face, and then he sighed.

"All right," he said. "I won't go on about it. I still think it's the most harebrained thing you've ever come up with, brother. You're so young, both of you, with hardly two bits' experience in the world between you. I don't see how you can make it. But I won't fight you anymore."

He was good to his word. On the morning we left, not a word passed his lips as he held a lantern so John David could figure out how to load our goods. Washington laid back his ears when the bundles began to jostle against each other, and John David had to spend a good bit of time soothing and stroking him before Washington finally resigned himself to carrying the load, and nothing was left but parting.

The brothers stood still, looking into each other's eyes without speaking until Zeke let out a huge sob and pulled John David into what had to be a bone-crushing hug. John David hid his face in Zeke's broad shoulder, and I heard him mumbling something. I hugged Sarah, who sobbed like she was losing a true sister.

"I hardly got to know thee," she said. "And now we may never see thee again. Take care! I'll be praying for thee, every day."

John David pulled away from Zeke, wiping his eyes with the back of his hand.

"You write and let us know how you're doing," Zeke said gruffly. "If you don't, I'll come find you in Texas and thrash you. You've not got too big and I've not got too old that I can't do it anymore."

"I'll write." John David's laugh was shaky. "Last thing on earth I want is a thrashing from you."

He kissed Sarah and hugged each of the sleepy little girls one last time. Then his long fingers closed around my hand, and I forgot about everything but that we were starting on the path away from Campbell County, toward our own place, our new life in Texas.

Chapter 8

Daylight caught us from behind as we walked on the rough trail away from Zeke's, with the pale sky peeking through the bare branches arched over our heads like the rafters of an unfinished cabin. By early afternoon, the trees were farther apart and the trail joined a true road, where walking was easier. Soon after, we came to a wide creek that sliced across the road, and the ferryman stepped out to meet us. He spit a blob of tobacco juice near John David's feet.

"Two bits each for foot traffic, four bits for the pack animal."

John David paused, his hand halfway in our money bag. "That's twice what it was when I came this way last summer!"

The man shrugged. "That's the price. You can pay it, or you can back up about five miles and take the crossroad to the south to see if you can find a cheaper way around."

John David's mouth was tight as he handed the man our coins. He pulled on Washington's reins to lead him onto the raft, and I followed silently, staring at the deep water. All that stood between me and that water were a few logs lashed together with a rope. My legs trembled as the ferryman pushed away from the bank, and I reached out for a saddle strap, holding so tight my knuckles were pale. The gentle tossing of the raft made me feel sick, and I closed my eyes against it, keeping them closed until I felt a hard bump. John David took my elbow and helped me onto solid ground again.

"Got a little sick, did you? That happens sometimes. Let's rest a minute." I sat on a rock by the roadside, but he paced around, still fuming over the price.

"I know what these ferrymen are doing," he said. "Traffic has picked up because of folk going to Texas, so they're trying to get as much money from us as they can."

"I reckon they've got us," I said. "People have to use the ferry or there's no crossing the creek."

He sighed. "That's business."

It wasn't just the ferryman, though. When we got to Huntsville, John David stopped to have a weak buckle on the packsaddle mended at a blacksmith's shop. The price was twice again what he had expected to pay. Even a slab of bacon for supper took two coins instead of one. John David's good mood of the morning had surely soured as we set up a spot outside of Huntsville to camp for the night.

"Two bits for bacon no better than this?" he grumbled. "I guess I fed the dogs a fortune back home."

We were tired from the day's walking, so we spread our bedding on the grass soon after supper. John David's breathing quickly took on the slow and steady rhythm of sleep, but I lay awake beside him, listening to all the sounds of the woods I hadn't noticed before. The night seemed to be alive with rustling and scratching. I stared into the darkness, trying to see what might be making the sounds, imagining a panther circling the camp, blacker than the black of the woods.

A shriek tore through the air, and I bolted upright with a cry, clutching the covers to my throat. John David was awake at once and reaching for his rifle.

"What is it?" he said. "What is it?"

I couldn't answer. The sound came again, and I grabbed his arm. To my surprise, he put down the rifle and flopped back to the ground.

"It's a screech owl, Maggie." He jerked the quilt back over his shoulder. "A mountain girl ought to know a screech owl's cry."

"What's that other sound?" I whispered. "Over in the brush?"

"Most likely a rat or something. That's probably why the owl is so close. Go to sleep."

I lay down. I couldn't stop shaking.

"I never slept outside before," I murmured. He put his arm around me.

"I'm here, Maggie. Nothing will hurt you. Go to sleep."

He was asleep again within minutes. I tried to sleep, but I kept jerking awake all through the night, reaching for John David just to know he was still there, solid and strong. The next day I forced myself to keep his pace without complaining, thinking surely I'd be so tired

I could sleep with no trouble. But that night was worse, with wind whispering like voices in the trees all night long. By the third night, the weather was turning, and though I huddled close to John David, I couldn't stop shivering, keeping him awake the night through.

My steps were dragging when evening came again, but this time, instead of finding a spot to camp, John David steered off the road into the yard of a cabin with a shabby sign hanging from the front porch. He reached into his pocket for the money bag.

"We'll stay here tonight," he said.

"An inn?" I asked. "But that takes money." He shrugged.

"It's going to be colder tonight than last. Like Pa said, winter's not the best time to travel, so I reckon if we're going to do it, we have to pay the price. Don't worry about the money. Keep an eye on Washington, would you?"

I cursed myself as he disappeared into the tavern. He might blame the cold for the decision to stay here, but I knew he'd sleep out in the weather if he was a man alone. It was my weakness that would cost us this night in an inn.

I barely noticed the man who was stroking Washington's hip. We'd gotten used to people admiring Washington on the road. He was a handsome horse, well-muscled and unusual in his color and markings, so it was to be expected he would catch people's eyes.

"This your pa's horse?" the man asked with a friendly smile. I shook my head. "Your master's?"

"My husband's."

"Begging your pardon, miss!" The man seemed truly embarrassed. "You're so young, I never expected—"

"Expected what?" John David asked, stuffing the money bag into his pocket as he stepped off the porch.

"You're the lady's husband, I reckon? You've got a good-looking horse here." The stranger ran his hand over Washington's haunch. "Not exactly a pack animal. Looks like he might be fast."

"Fast enough," John David said cautiously.

"I thought so. I do appreciate good horseflesh. Don't see much of it around here, not like this, anyway." He picked up one of Washington's feet and studied it. "You ever race him?"

John David paused. "He's raced before." The man straightened and looked John David up and down before leaning back with his hands in his pockets.

"What would you say to a little race right here and now? Against my horse? A little entertainment for the evening, since we hardly ever see a horse like yours."

John David studied the white horse standing behind the man. I thought neither one looked that remarkable. The horse was a little on the thin side, standing there dozing, while the man was a little on the old side. Even after a day of walking and even carrying John David's weight, I figured Washington could easily outrun this pair.

"It might do him good to get out from under the pack," John David said.

"Up the road and back, half mile or so? There's a black gum in the fork of the road. We could circle it." John David nodded, and the man grinned. "All right! Get him unloaded and I'll draw a line here in the road." John David started to unbuckle our packs, but the man grabbed his arm. "I don't suppose you'd be interested in a little wager on the outcome?"

John David looked sideways at me. "I might."

"The price of a night's lodging?" the man asked. I leaned toward Washington's neck to hide my grin. We could make up the money John David had just now paid out for tonight.

"Sounds fair enough," John David said.

"It's a bet!" They shook hands, and the man turned toward the other men who had gathered on the porch and around the yard to watch. "Anybody else want to lay a bet?"

"I won't take any others," John David said quickly. "Only yours."

The start of the race was delayed while John David and I carried our packs into the tavern and the stranger took bets from a few of the men gathered around, including the innkeeper in his dirty apron. John David patted Washington's neck and led him to the line someone had scratched on the ground. The man whistled, and a boy came out of the barn riding a muscular black horse with a shiny coat and long legs.

"Meet Devil's Imp, my horse," the man bragged. "Dark as a demon and twice as fast." The horse reared up a little and tossed its proud head.

A sick feeling swirled in my gut. Even I could tell this horse was a match for Washington. The boy was young and small, and the difference between his weight and John David's could very well mean the difference in the race. I looked at John David and saw good sense and pride struggling in his face. To ride most likely meant handing over a night's lodging, but to call off the race now meant looking like a fool in front of every man in the yard.

"Are you racing?" the man asked. "Or are you giving it up now?"

John David looked down at the reins in his hand, and I was grieved by the droop to his shoulders.

"I reckon—" he started.

"I'm riding," I said, walking over and taking the reins. John David stared at me, too dumbfounded, I reckon, to speak. "I'm riding," I repeated, lifting my foot to the stirrup.

"The other side!" he hissed, as the watching men laughed. I hurried under Washington's neck to the other side and hoisted myself to the saddle. Winning a night's lodging would be the perfect way to make up to him for being too weak to camp. I was glad now for those afternoons riding out to Zeke's fields. Though I'd never been on Washington alone, I'd learned to handle Zeke's gelding just fine and, I reminded myself, John David always praised my riding. He'd said I had a fine seat.

"She's your rider, then?" the man asked. John David's face looked like he had a bad tooth. The man laughed. "Let's add the price of a bottle of whiskey to that wager."

"Good whiskey," John David said. "Not local rotgut."

The boy on the black horse came up beside me, grinning like I was the funniest thing he'd ever seen. "She's riding like a boy," he sneered. "You ought to take bets, Pa, on how much of her leg we'll see when that skirt blows up." I frowned and tucked my skirt tighter under my thighs.

"He'll start fast, Maggie," John David said in a low voice. "Just hang on and make yourself as low to his neck as you can. You won't have to do much to turn him, he knows what to do. He doesn't like jerking on the bit, so don't—" But I didn't hear the rest of his instructions, for the innkeeper was stepping forward to the line with his apron in his hand. John David patted my leg and stepped back. My hands were trembling on the reins. Washington's blood-red ears swiveled backward and then to the front.

The innkeeper flapped his apron, and the black horse darted forward. I don't think I even lifted the reins before Washington leaped after him. I straightened myself in the saddle and then leaned forward, feeling the ends of his mane stinging as they whipped my face. The black horse was a length ahead.

"Come on!" I urged, pushing forward with my knees as if I could catch the black horse myself. Washington answered by springing forward even faster, sending me sliding backward in the saddle, and after a few more strides, we passed the black horse. I caught a glimpse of the boy's surprised face as we whizzed past, but I didn't linger on it. The tree in the fork of the road was just ahead.

I was worried about the turn, but John David was right; Washington obviously knew what I wanted as soon as I moved the rein the least bit. He finished the turn just as the black horse entered it. We were ahead, and all that was left was the straight run back to the clearing. I leaned forward until my cheek nearly touched Washington's neck. My skirt whipped behind me, but I didn't care if my legs did show. We were winning.

"Let's get some money!" I shouted, and he stretched himself out and put even more distance between us and the black horse.

I could see the knot of men in the road now, standing right where I needed to go, right on the line. If they didn't move quick, I'd run them over, at this pace. I quickly glanced back. The black horse was at least three lengths behind us. I could slow down a bit and still win. I leaned back and pulled on the reins gently. Washington kept running. I pulled a little harder.

"Slow down!" I cried, desperately. We had maybe fifty more feet—now only thirty. I yanked the reins back, and Washington suddenly stopped. He gave a quick, hard buck, and then he trotted forward across the line as I landed, hard, on my backside in the dirt with my skirt above my knees. I heard John David yelling, "Somebody get my horse!" and the men were parting, and suddenly I knew why. I scrambled out of the way as the black horse thundered past. John David was running toward me, and I struggled to get to my feet before he could reach me. If he was going to smack me, I wanted to be standing, not cowering in the dirt.

He grabbed my arm. His face was pale, nearly gray.

"My God, Maggie!" he croaked. The black horse's owner was laughing as he came toward us.

"Now that was a bang-up race, for sure! I guess she forgot both horse and rider have to cross the line first to win." Without a word, John David pulled out the money bag, and a lump lodged in my throat as the coins to pay the wager spilled out into his palm. The bag seemed much thinner when he put it back in his pocket.

"That's mighty fine horseflesh you've got, mister," the man said. "But I believe I'd find another rider, one that wears britches." He cackled as he walked away. I kept my eyes on the ground as I waited for John David to do something, or say something, maybe a smack, maybe just a cussing since the yard was still filled with men.

He cleared his throat. "You're all right?" he asked. I didn't raise my eyes from the dirt, just nodded, bracing myself. "You go in, then. I'll tend to Washington."

I watched him through my eyelashes as he took the reins back from some man and went around the corner of the cabin, out of sight. My nerves felt jumpy as a fly on a hot griddle. Why didn't he say something? He had to be mad at me—I was mad at me. Two nights' lodging now, gone! He'd said it before, lots of times, and just now, even—Washington was picky about the bit. It was a stupid mistake, one Pa would've taken out of my hide. I wouldn't blame John David if he did the same. I deserved whatever I got. But I wished he'd get it over with. The waiting was always the worst part. I started toward the tavern, though every step sent pains shooting along my backside and I could hardly see where I was going for the tears fogging my eyes.

*   *   *

He hardly spoke to me the rest of the evening, for the front room of the tavern was loud with folks eating supper and, later, with men drinking whiskey and reliving the race. It was still early when another woman traveler came to me and tapped my shoulder.

"We'd best go on to our room, miss," she said. "A decent woman shouldn't be down here while they're drinking." I looked back at John David, but he was looking into his whiskey, and I turned away, my heart heavy as I followed the woman up the stairs.

I hardly slept that night, and when the darkness began to thin, I crawled over the strange woman and sat on the hearth in the main room by what was left of the fire. I hadn't been there long when John David came out, loaded with our packs. From the looks of him, he hadn't slept much, either. He didn't speak, and I followed him across the yard, clenching my teeth when I saw what was left of the finish line, still scratched in the dirt.

The barn was warm compared to the morning air. I handed bundles to John David as he went about packing the load, but still he didn't say anything. Finally, I couldn't stand it anymore.

"Come on, let's have it!" I snapped. He looked at me blankly. "Give me a smack, or something! Don't tell me you don't want to." He frowned.

"What are you talking about? I'm not going to hit you."

"I should've remembered what you said about the bit. It was a stupid mistake, I know that!"

"Well, I made two mistakes to your one. I shouldn't have taken the bet in the first place, and I never should've let you ride, no matter what you said."

It was worse than a smack. The only thought that had comforted me all the long night was that he'd trusted my riding. Now he said it was a mistake. I swallowed hard as he went on.

"What were you thinking to jump in there like that and say you'd ride? And what in the hell was I thinking to let you race when you've barely been on a horse? Especially when it was obvious they were the kind who'd cheat." He ran his hand through his hair, something I guessed he'd been doing all night, because it was tousled and wild. "There's no telling what that boy could've done, thrown something at you, or bumped Washington—When I think you could've been hurt or killed for a night's lodging—"

"But I'm not hurt," I said quickly. "Just sore. Don't worry, it's going to take more than a toss off a horse to rid you of me now."

He shook his head. "It's not a joke, Maggie."

For a minute, we didn't speak. He turned back to finish the loading, and I stepped in to hold a bundle steady while he tightened the strap.

"I wanted to help," I said. "It's because of me we had to stay here last night."

"You have to watch that your help doesn't cause more harm than good," he said, turning to me. "That was a hard fall you took. You're still limping." He reached around me to press his fingers against my backside. "Where does it hurt? The bony part, here? Or the fleshy part, here?" I winced as he pressed the sorest part, and he rubbed it. "That's it? I was afraid you might have cracked your tailbone, but I guess it's just bruised. At least that's some blessing." He moved away to lead Washington out of the stall.

"You're not mad?" I asked as I followed them out into the yard. "About me losing the money?"

"Don't worry about the money," he said. "I'll manage."

"We can go back to camping tonight." He was shaking his head, and I tried again. "I won't be so skittish, promise."

"Look at the sky. We'll see snow before the day's out."

"We can make a shelter—"

"I said don't worry about it!" he snapped. "I'll handle it. Let's get something for breakfast and see how far we can get before snow falls."

I watched him lead Washington toward the tavern, his shoulders stiff and unyielding. I sighed. I didn't know how far we were from Nashville, and I sure didn't know anything about money, but even I knew what little was in the bag wouldn't last forever. Staying in taverns instead of camping would only speed the day it was all gone. Surely he knew that. Still, he'd vowed to take care of me, and what kind of wife would I be if I already doubted him? We might be partners, but he was lead mule. Best get used to it.

Chapter 9

With the clouds so thick, I couldn't tell the time of day when the first flakes fell, small and hard, stinging my face where they hit. I noticed with relief that the road widened before us, into a clearing around a tavern. But when I pointed it out, John David shook his head.

"I can get a better price a little up the road. It's not much further." And he started to walk faster. I was tired and sore and cold, and I looked with longing at the golden light streaming through the cracks around the door as we passed on by.

It must have been another hour before the road widened again, and I hoped with all my might this was the place he had in mind. The snow was thick enough now that everything looked fuzzy in the growing twilight. The light coating of snow on the road was slick under my wet moccasins, meaning I had to place every step carefully to keep from sliding. To be honest, I didn't care if the price was better here or if it took all the money in the buckskin bag. I just wanted to stretch my cold feet before a fire and sip a cup of tea in drowsy warmth.

John David walked toward the porch and pulled a few coins from the money bag. Then he handed the bag to me, something he'd never done before. I started to follow him up the steps, but he stopped me.

"This might take a little while," he said. "Take Washington to the lee side of the cabin, out of the wind. Make sure he doesn't wander off." He stood before the door, ready to knock but not knocking, watching as I grudgingly tugged on the reins to start Washington around the corner of the cabin.

I leaned close to the cabin wall to keep the cold from blowing down my neck, holding the ends of the reins loosely. Washington wasn't going anywhere. In fact, he looked like he felt as miserable as I did. His normally proud head was drooping, and his hips were dark with melted snow. Poor fellow, I thought. He's used to a warm stall and a bucket of oats in McKellars' barn. Maybe he's more miserable than I am.

"Sure, I remember you!" A woman's voice came through the wall. "You stayed here last summer, coming from Nashville."

I couldn't understand what he was saying, but it wasn't hard to guess, because her voice cut through the snowy stillness like a needle through fine linen.

"Yep, I still take travelers. You're the first to stop in a month or more, though. Not many folk are traveling this time of year."

Something about her voice made me press my ear to the crack between logs to hear better what was going on. John David's voice was low.

"I need shelter for my horse, something warm to eat, and a place to sleep. Trouble is, I've had some hard times and don't have a lot of money to pay for it." I heard the clink of coins on a table. "I know it's not much, but I wondered if you might make—" he paused for the slightest heartbeat, "—an allowance of some kind for me."

"Hard times, eh?" Her voice was warm and sympathetic. "Those seem to be going around. I've had a few myself lately."

"I don't mean to take advantage," John David said. The thought hung in the air, unfinished. The woman was silent for a minute.

"Normally, I'd have to ask for more than that," she said, "but I reckon I could come up with an arrangement. I'd have to charge a couple of bits for your food, and a couple for the horse, to take care of my expenses. As for a place to sleep—" She lowered her voice so I could hardly make out the words, and I strained to hear. "I'll share one with you for free."

My heart seemed to drop and then began thumping like I'd been running. Surely she couldn't mean what I thought—

"That's neighborly of you," John David was saying. "A couple of bits for a meal, you say?" A chill that was not the wind rushed through me. What was he doing? Surely he wasn't—Throwing down the reins, I charged around the cabin and up the steps.

He looked surprised to see me standing on the porch when he came out.

"What's going on?" I demanded. His face reddened, but he ignored my question.

"Tonight's settled. Go on in. I'll tend to Washington."

"This is no inn. Who is that woman?"

He straightened his shoulders and frowned a little. "Go in, Maggie. Get warmed up. I'll be in shortly."

"Go in? After what she said to you? You realize what she's offering, don't you? You have to! You're not exactly an innocent!" My voice was rising, and he grabbed my arm and pulled me toward the edge of the porch.

"Hush!" he hissed. I jerked my arm away, and he leaned toward me, speaking in a low, urgent voice. "She's offering a kindness, so far as I'm concerned, and so far as you're concerned, too. A kindness, that's all. Now get in there and get warm, and don't you say a thing to her. I'll be in shortly." He took a step away and then came back to me, laying his hand on my arm and giving me a pleading look with those pretty brown eyes. I wondered if he'd used the same look on her.

"It's one night, Maggie," he said softly. "Just one night."

I watched him lead Washington to the barn, a pair of shadows only a little darker than the snowy twilight. Even when they were inside and I couldn't tell anymore what was the barn and what was the night, I still stood on the porch. I didn't want to go in. I didn't want to be any part of what he was doing. But it was cold and getting colder as the night fell, and now that I wasn't moving, my feet were nearly numb. I raised my hand to knock on the door.

I'd hoped she'd be a desperate slattern, but she was a handsome woman, pleasingly rounded in the way men seem to like. She looked me over, and I knew she noticed I didn't have any roundness.

"I reckon you're the wife he mentioned," she said. "Why, you're just a girl! You can't be any older than my Jeremy."

That's when I noticed her children sitting around the table, five of them. The oldest was a boy near my own age, sitting stiff in his chair like having me in the room made him uncomfortable. Except for him, the others were all staring at me. I forced a smile at them, but they simply stared.

"You can stand by the fire," the woman said, "but don't get in the way while I stir up something for you all to eat."

I turned my back on the children, standing at the end of the hearth and looking into the flames while the woman put together some supper. It seemed like a long time before John David came in, with a gust of cold air and a shower of snowflakes.

"Don't think the snow will last much longer," he said, setting a couple of our packs in a corner. "I saw a spot in the clouds where the moon might be trying to come through." He came to stand by me at the fire, but I stood stiff and unsmiling as he and the woman babbled on about the cold snap.

Once the food was ready, the woman sent her children to bed, but the boy Jeremy stayed.

"What's your name, mister?" His voice had an unfriendly edge. "Where you traveling to?"

"You don't ask travelers such questions, son!" the woman scolded. "It's none of your business. Lay in a store of firewood, and then get on up to bed." He got up quickly, glancing at John David with dislike as he went past. His ma didn't seem to notice. She called us to the table and brought us plates with ham and beans, and then she set a pan of cornbread and a jug of whiskey between us. She rested her hand on John David's shoulder.

"Anything else I can do for you?" A small, angry growl rumbled in my throat. John David glanced at me.

"Can I get some hot water and a little honey?" he asked.

She brought a kettle from the fireplace and filled the cup, leaning in so her bosom must have brushed his cheek.

"What do you think you're doing?" I snarled, but his sharp look shut me up.

"Making you a toddy," he said. "It'll take the chill out of your bones." The woman moved away to work at her spinning, and he leaned toward me. "Come on, Maggie," he said in a voice low enough she wouldn't hear it over the hum of the wheel. "Just go along with me." He dribbled a little whiskey into the steaming water.

"I don't like it," I said, loud enough she had to be able to hear it. He quickly glanced over his shoulder while he added another splash of whiskey to the cup.

"The first sip *is* pretty awful. But you'll find it gets better." He lowered his voice again as he stirred in a spoonful of honey. "Eat, and drink your toddy. You'll feel better."

He was right. The food was warm and good, and after two or three sips, I could tolerate the taste of his toddy. I took another sip and felt it burn all the way down through my body, warming even my icy toes. Cold air rushed in the room as the boy came in with another armload of wood, so I sipped more toddy, watching through a drowsy haze as he stacked it by the fireplace. The spinning wheel whirred softly, the fire popped, and I leaned my head against my hand.

The next thing I knew, John David was shaking my shoulder in the gray light of early morning. I was on a pallet of our quilts, and the fire was nearly out.

"Let's get going," he whispered. "Washington's ready."

My head was aching, a dull throb deep inside. I tried to clear it with a shake, but the sudden movement made my stomach roil and I nearly retched. He was kneeling in front of me, putting my moccasins on my feet. I noticed I was wearing a pair of his long woolen socks, but I couldn't for the life of me remember when I'd put them on.

"What about breakfast?" I asked. He quickly rolled up our bedding.

"We'll eat on the road this morning."

The air outside was bitterly cold in the pale gray light. Washington stood tied to the corner of the cabin, steam coming in little puffs from his nose. John David secured the bedding bundle over the back of the saddle and we started another day's walk.

It was a miserable morning. Even though he'd wrapped one of the quilts around me, the cold came through quickly, like I didn't have any covering at all. My head ached and my stomach felt empty yet queasy. As the sun rose, the light through the trees was bright and made my eyes burn and water. To top everything off, John David's cheerful whistling was sharp and shrill in the silence. It seemed to pierce my eardrums and to bore straight into the most painful part of the ache in my head. I thought I would lose my mind completely if I had to listen to him one more minute.

"John David! Please, no more whistling!"

He stopped and looked at me in surprise. I laid my hand on my forehead in the blessed silence, and a grin suddenly spread across his face.

"Let's stop for breakfast," he said. "Where's the hardtack?"

He managed to get enough fire going to melt some snow in our tin cups. I brushed the snow off a fallen tree trunk and perched on it, wrapping the quilt tight around me, my eyes closed against the bright sunshine. I felt him sit beside me.

"I'm afraid this is all my fault, Maggie." I opened one eye to look at him. "You must be smaller than I thought. Or it's because you're a woman. I reckon whiskey has a different effect on women than on men."

"What are you talking about?"

"The whiskey. I gave you too much. You're crapulous."

I opened my other eye. "I'm not!"

He laughed. "Maggie, I've been around enough drinking in my life to know a crapulous headache when I see one."

The water was steaming, so he brought the precious package of tea leaves and a few pieces of hardtack from the pack. He handed me a cup of tea and a piece of hardtack, but my appetite was gone. I watched as he dunked his hardtack in the tea and ate half of it in one bite.

"You did it on purpose!" I said. "You gave me that toddy because you knew it would get me drunk and out of the way."

He frowned. "You weren't drunk, not on that little bit. I meant for you to have just enough so you could get a good night of sleep."

"So I wouldn't be any trouble, you mean." I suddenly felt angry beyond reason. "Don't make me out to be a fool! I ain't Pa's daughter for nothing!"

"What are you talking about?"

I jumped to my feet and glared at him. "I don't like what you did, tricking that woman."

"I didn't trick her."

"Don't treat me like a fool!" I shouted, ignoring the pain in my head. "I heard it all! You led her to think you were traveling alone. You didn't say a word about me till the bargain was already struck. Once I had that toddy, you might've shared a cozy spot in her bed instead of sleeping with me on the floor, and I'm none the wiser! "

103

"No! That's not how it was!" He slapped his cup down on the log, sloshing tea on the snow, which melted at once. "All right, I tricked her. When I stayed there last summer, she was giving me the eye, right there in the room with her young'uns. I figured she'd favor me enough that she might lower her prices. But I didn't know that's what her offer would be!"

"You must've guessed at it. You left me outside!"

"Sure I did. I doubt I'd look quite as good to her with a woman hanging on my arm." He looked down at the soggy hardtack in his hand, and then he tossed it into the fire. "I can't believe you think I'd ever take such an offer. I vowed to be faithful to you and I meant it."

"No, you didn't," I said. "You planned to get an annulment."

He was quiet for a minute, looking at me.

"I mean it now," he said. "I'm no angel, Maggie, but I'm not an adulterer, either."

I suddenly wished I hadn't said anything.

"I know," I murmured. For a while, there was no sound but the spitting of the fire. I sat back on the log beside him and handed him my hardtack. He didn't eat it, just turned it over and over in his hand.

"There's other ways to save money," I said. "We can camp." He shook his head.

"We can't camp. Pa was right; this is no season to travel. You didn't complain yesterday, and that's to your credit, but I know you were suffering those last few miles."

"I've been cold plenty of —"

"Well, I'm taking care of you now, not that no-good Boon!" he interrupted. "I won't have you sleeping on the cold ground in the snow, not if I can find some way to get you a place inside a cabin. You may not like how I go about it, but I'm going to take care of you the way a man ought to take care of his woman."

"I don't want you to tarnish your good name so I can sleep in a warm spot. Saving a few bits ain't worth making yourself a cheat."

The muscles in his jaw tightened. He got up and squatted to poke at the fire. "It's not as simple as saving a few bits."

"Why not?" He wouldn't look at me. "It's the money I lost, ain't it?" I said slowly. "We're running short, and you're trying to make up what I lost in that race."

He turned toward me quickly. "I told you, don't worry about it! I'll take care of us."

I don't need taking care of, I wanted to yell out, but my head hurt, and I was weary of fighting.

"Remember what you said when you asked me to stay?" I said. "You said we'd be partners, like a good team of mules, but you sure don't act like I'm a partner. You act like I'm a helpless babe." He was silent, and I leaned forward to take his cheeks, scratchy with several days' growth of beard, between my hands. "John David, nobody binds two mules together and then has only one of them hitched to the wagon. If you got two mules, you use them both. Even if one is young and the older one is better and stronger, you let the young one pull too, to cut down on the burden for either one. Let me help. I want to help. Don't try to pull the whole load alone."

He looked into my eyes without moving for a minute. Then he reached into his pocket and pulled out the money bag. Coming to sit with me again, he poured the coins into my lap and picked out a few.

"Here's how much it takes for a night in an inn." He took my hand and dropped the coins in it before picking up a few more. "Here's how much for Washington. Here's the cost of meals." The pile nearly filled my palm. "That's one day, Maggie, not counting ferry crossings or higher prices as we get closer to Nashville. We still have nearly a week to get there—that's if the weather holds and we don't have to stay an extra day somewhere." He stirred the pile in my lap. "This is all we've got. It should be enough to get us to Nashville. We won't have anything left when we get there, but—" He paused, and the muscles in his throat worked like he was trying to swallow a lump. "But I'll sell Washington in Nashville, and he should bring enough to get us to Texas."

"No," I said softly. "Oh, no!"

"It's for the best." He gathered up the coins and put them back in the bag. "He's a saddle horse, and what I'll need in Texas is a work horse. Much as I hate to lose him, it would be worse to see him hitched to a plow."

I picked up his hand and worked my fingers in between his. We sat in silence for a while.

"We can skip breakfast," I said, "walk an extra hour or so in the morning, have dinner mid-morning. There's the hardtack, not much of it, I know, but it could get us by a couple of days. Maybe you could shoot some small game along the way, though it would take time to cook it. We might as well break into the cornmeal. We can buy more in Nashville."

"It'll be high. Everything's high in Nashville."

"It don't take much to make mush or pone. I can stretch it some by picking up acorns as we go along. I used to grind them up to stretch our meal at home."

"Eating acorns." His face was grim.

"They ain't bad," I said, turning to him eagerly. "It gives a different taste to pone, a pretty good taste."

He looked sideways at me. "Sometimes I wonder which of us is the older mule in this pair."

I laughed. "Well, I can help fill our bellies the rest of the way, but I can't do a thing about that money bag."

"I was thinking about that. I know of another widow on the way—"

I stiffened. "No!"

"Not like last night. This one might let me cut wood or some such job in payment." His eyes suddenly narrowed. "Are you jealous?"

"No," I said quickly, too quickly, maybe, for his grin twisted to one side. "It was the dishonest part I didn't like."

"All right. I'll be an honest man from now on, even if it means eating acorns like a wild hog."

"They ain't bad—"

He laughed as he scattered what was left of the fire with his foot. "Come on, little mule. We've got to put some miles behind us today. It won't help us to save on food if we end up paying for an extra night."

Chapter 10

He didn't like my idea of using acorns to stretch our meal, but I didn't like his plan for saving money, either. When next we saw a ferry crossing on the road ahead, he made a quick turn off the trail into the woods.

"Where are you going?" I asked, scrambling through the underbrush to catch him. "Don't we have to cross here?"

"Not here," he said. "We'll cross upstream."

We cut through the woods until we saw the river again through the trees.

"There's no ferry." I unhooked my skirt from yet another briar. "How will we cross?"

He draped Washington's reins over a low branch and started to undo the bundles. "The old-fashioned way—we'll swim it."

I stopped short. "Swim? I can't—"

"Don't worry. You'll ride. I'll do the swimming."

"You can't swim it!" The river had to be fifty feet across or more, greenish-gray, which I knew meant it was deep. "That don't make sense. It's way too cold to get wet."

"It's not so cold," he said. "The sun's nice. If we keep our clothes dry, we'll be all right. Come on, I'll take you across first."

No matter what I tried, he wouldn't listen to my sense. I ended up sitting behind him with a blanket draped around my neck and with my skirt and shimmy wadded at my waist as he guided Washington into the river. I gritted my teeth as Washington began to swim and the cold water swallowed my bare legs. It took all my will not to drop the rifle I held above my head and throw both arms around John David.

The worst part, though, was the climb up the steep bank on the other side.

"I'm sliding!" I shrieked, letting the arm with the rifle drop enough that the butt whacked him on the side of the head.

"Just hold on!" he said, kicking his heels into Washington's sides to urge him over the lip of the bank.

Once we were back on the ground, he laughed at me.

"I thought I was going to lose you," he teased as he stripped off his shirt and hung it over a low branch. I refused to even smile.

"I thought you were, too." He laughed again and tweaked my chin.

"Little mule has her ears laid back and her foot raised to kick."

He left me on the bank while he rode over and reloaded the packs. I clutched the blanket to my bosom as he stepped into the river to swim across. He was in chest-high before he'd taken more than ten steps.

"Be careful!" My voice echoed strangely across the water. He raised one hand to show he'd heard me, and I held my breath as he began to swim through the middle, his head bobbing above the green water and one hand tight around the reins. He was halfway across, now within twenty feet of the bank, now able to stand again and walk. I had just let out a deep breath when suddenly his head and shoulders jerked forward and he was gone.

"John David!" I screamed, running to the edge of the water as if I could pull him out by the force of my will. "John David!"

He reappeared, several feet downstream from where he'd gone under, swimming hard against the current to catch up to Washington, who was walking the last few feet to the bank. He finally stood, and I splashed through the shallow water to grab his arm and help him up the bank. He was coughing.

"Stepped in a hole," he choked. "Probably ten feet deep."

I snatched up the blanket from where I'd dropped it and wrapped him tight. He was shaking uncontrollably.

"That's it! No more of these crossings!" I said. "I don't care if we don't have enough money! We can save some other way!"

His teeth were chattering, and his lips twitched as he frowned.

"There are at least three or four more crossings, at six bits or more every time—we can't afford that."

I knelt and rubbed his legs to try to bring warmth back to them. "That ain't such a high price."

"Too high for us."

I stood and scrubbed hard on his dripping hair with a corner of the blanket. 'I don't care. I won't do that again! I won't do it, you hear me?"

He pulled the blanket from my hands. "Maggie! No harm's done."

"No harm?" I grabbed the blanket back and began to scrub his chest. "No harm! You could have drowned! You could have been washed downstream, gone, and me left alone out here, with no idea where I am, no idea how to go on to Nashville, or back to home—Did you even think about that? Did you?"

He grabbed me by the arms and gave me a shake that snapped my head back a little. Before I'd even had time to catch my breath, he was pulling me close to his chest.

"I'm all right," he said. "It's going to take more than a dip in a river to rid you of me."

I leaned against him, feeling the ground under me become steady again.

"Better?" he asked, and I nodded. He took the blanket from me and I followed as he went to rub down Washington's dripping sides.

"Can't you at least ride across?" I asked. "Cut down the size of the load and make an extra trip?" He shook his head.

"It's hard on him, too. I've got to keep him in good condition, because he's worth more to us right now than I am. He's already losing some muscle from not being able to graze. If he doesn't bring a good price in Nashville, there's no going on to Texas."

"Now I know you don't have sense! Without you, there's no point going to Texas at all!"

He laughed, and then he leaned toward me with a sly grin. "Would you fetch my britches from that branch over there? Or would you rather I stay as I am?"

I rolled my eyes.

❧ ❧ ❧

I hated every crossing, but with each one, I reminded myself we were that much closer to Nashville. As we closed in on the city, we began to see plenty more folks like us, walking and leading a pack animal loaded with all their earthly goods. None of the horses compared to Washington, though, and that made John David skittish.

"We're an easy target," he told me. "With a two-hundred-dollar horse and you being so young—we've got to be careful who we trust. We come across the wrong sort, it's one quick shot and—" He glanced down at me. "Well, I don't want to think about what would happen then."

He didn't say any more about it, but my mind got busy trying to picture what could happen to us if we ran across the wrong sort of folks. I kept my locket tucked inside my shimmy so it didn't show, and I looked at everyone we met on the road with suspicion, to the point that I spurned any attempt at talk by strangers, even one friendly little girl traveling with her folks.

"You don't have to be so contrary," John David scolded. "Most of these people are just honest folk moving west, like us. You'll know who you need to watch out for."

That night, we stopped at a dingy inn we'd have passed by another time. But the money bag was nearly empty now, and the price advertised on the shingle was the lowest we'd seen all day. We decided we could bear dirty sheets and some lice to save a few bits. As usual, while John David went in to pay, I stayed outside with our packs, and as often happened, a couple of men stopped to admire Washington. Something in their manner, though, reminded me of Pa, and my fingers tightened on the bridle strap. One of them opened Washington's mouth and inspected it. The other turned to me.

"You traveling alone with this fine beast, miss?"

"My husband's inside."

"Going to Nashville, I reckon?"

"I thought folks didn't ask such questions of travelers," I said.

He smiled just the way Pa would have. "Beg your pardon, Missus."

The other man straightened, and I saw a jagged scar running down one side of his face that made his jowl hang a little lower on that side. A shiver ran down my back as his black eyes looked into mine, and I was glad my locket was hidden.

"This ain't no pack horse," he said. "I reckon your husband knows that?" I didn't answer.

"Tight-lipped little wench, ain't she, Hardy?" the first man said with a laugh. Hardy smiled a little, but the scarred side of his face didn't move.

"Let's get a drink," he said. I watched under my eyelashes as they walked away, and only then did I realize how fast my heart was beating.

I was the only woman at supper. That pleased me, for I hoped it meant John David and I would get a bed together, even if some man had to sleep on the floor. John David was talking with a man across the table about Texas and a place called Missouri, and I'm certain he thought me foolish, for I sat so close to his elbow all evening he could hardly move without bumping against me. Hardy and his talkative friend were at the other end of the table, and when I dared sneak a glance at them, Hardy was staring at me with his dark, chilling eyes. But he didn't say anything, and after supper, they took a bottle of whiskey and a pouch of tobacco out to the porch. Shortly afterward, the man John David was talking to left for bed, saying he wanted an early start in the morning. The innkeeper was wiping dishes behind the bar, and the tavern was finally quiet except for the crackle of the fire. I slumped against John David's arm as he finished his drink. We'd walked far that day, and having my belly finally full made me sleepy. But I quickly sat up when Hardy's friend came in and sat across from us, laying a stained deck of cards on the table.

"Could I interest you in a game, my good man?" His voice was friendly—too friendly. "It would be a pleasant way to pass some time before we retire."

"No, thanks," John David said. "I never had much luck with cards."

"Just a friendly game. No betting."

"No thanks."

The man cast a quick glance at me. "You don't mind if he plays, do you, Missus?" I stared at him without speaking, and he turned back to John David. "Come on, one game won't hurt. It's too early yet for bed, and there's no one else to play with."

John David didn't answer, just drained his cup. As he stood, the man banged his fist on the table.

"Damn you, man, sit down! Think you're too good to play cards with the likes of me, do you?"

John David stared as the man came around the table. "What do you want, Mister?"

"I want a game of cards."

"Well, I don't. Come on, Maggie." I stood as John David took a step to get around the man, but with a vile curse, the man stuck out his foot, tripping John David so he hit the floor with a clumsy thud. The man jumped on him, throwing one arm around John David's throat. John David struggled to throw him off, and I ran toward the bar, calling for the innkeeper, who had suddenly disappeared. I whirled back around as the bench fell over. John David had managed to roll onto his back, but the man still straddled him. I saw a quick flash in the candlelight as the man raised his arm—a knife blade. Without thinking, I grabbed John David's rifle from against the wall and swung it as hard as I could. The rifle butt connected with a sickening crack against the side of the man's head, and he fell heavily on top of John David.

"Is he dead?" I gasped. John David pushed the man off his chest and got to his feet.

"He's still breathing." His cheek was bleeding, and he touched his fingertips to the cut. "Just what the hell was that about?"

I stared at the man on the floor, and suddenly I knew.

"Washington!" I shrieked and ran for the door, still holding the rifle.

John David caught up to me halfway across the yard, jerked the rifle from me, and ran with long strides to the barn. I burst in to see him holding the rifle on Hardy, who was in the stall with Washington. Our saddle was hanging halfway on Washington's back, and the stirrups swung dangerously as Washington reared, his ears pinned tight against his head.

"I said, get away from my horse," John David growled. He seemed huge in the low-ceilinged barn, and his eyes were smoldering. One side of his face was dark with blood, and his hair was standing up like a wild man's after the scuffle. I pressed myself against the wall. I'd never seen him like this.

"Maggie!" he ordered. "Fetch a rope from over there." I hurried to the tangled pile of harness, and with trembling hands pawed through it until I found a length of rope.

"No harm meant," Hardy was saying. "I was just going to take a little ride down the road and back. You don't see good horseflesh like him around here too often. I just couldn't resist the temptation, I guess."

"Here's rope," I said in a small voice. "Are you going to hang him?"

"That's usually what happens to horse thieves." John David's voice was grim. Hardy tried to smile again, and his black eyes darted from John David to me and back again.

"You don't really want your woman to see a man hang, do you? Not someone young and sweet as her, not something awful like that." John David glanced at me.

"Get the innkeeper," he ordered.

"He took off soon as the fighting started."

He cursed. "You'll have to tie him, then. Start with his hands."

I could hardly make a slipknot, my hands were shaking so. I stepped next to Hardy and reached for one of his hands, but he slipped it behind him so I'd have to reach around his body to get it. John David moved a step closer, his rifle pointed at Hardy's chin.

"Raise your hands so she can tie them, now!" Hardy brought his wrists together and I looped the rope around them. But as I pulled it tight, he swung his fists up and struck me hard across the face, knocking me back into John David. We both fell, and the end of the rope whipped through my fingers as Hardy ran past. John David shoved me off him and scrambled toward the door, but I never heard his rifle roar, and he was back right away, going straight into the stall with Washington, murmuring something over and over until the horse calmed. I stayed out of the way as he ran his hand over Washington's hips and belly until he could undo the girth strap and lift away the crooked saddle. He didn't speak as he threw the saddle over the short wall. But when he went to pick up the rope from near the door, he seemed to have dwindled back to his regular size, and I wasn't quite so scared of him.

"He got away?" I asked.

He wound the rope into a loose coil. "It's too dark. It wasn't worth wasting the lead." He touched the sore spot on my cheek. "That's already making a bruise." He turned away to drop the rope on a pile of tack.

"I'm sorry I let him get loose." I was surprised when he suddenly took me in his arms and held me tight. He was shaking.

"You've got nothing to be sorry for. But for you, he'd have gotten away with Washington. There'd be no flatboat, no going to Texas." He hugged me tighter. "You saved it all, Maggie. I'm lucky to be partnered with such a contrary little mule."

I looked up at him with a smile, but my pleasure at his words quickly faded at the sight of the dark blood mingled with his beard. "You're cut. Is it still bleeding?"

He touched his fingers to it. "It stings pretty bad."

"Let's take a look." I took his hand and started for the door, but he stood firm.

"I'm staying out here tonight. Because of what he means to us," he added quickly. "He's not just a horse, he's our whole future. I can't risk that someone else might take a notion to ride off with him."

I could see there was no changing his mind. I sighed. "Bring out the packs, then. I'll find a place that ain't got so much muck."

"I don't mean for you to have to stay," he started, but I interrupted.

"You don't think I'd stay in there without you, do you?"

He studied me for a minute. "Of course not—you're a contrary little mule."

The cut was worse than I'd thought. He winced as I washed away the dried blood, and then he turned his face so it caught the candlelight and he could see the cut in his small looking-glass. The cut was about a knuckle's length, just above his beard and gaping open a little. He pinched it shut, but it opened again as soon as he let go.

"We need to close it." His face was somber. "Can you sew it up?"

My stomach flopped. With the little ones back home, I'd seen plenty of scraped elbows and bloody scratches, but I'd never had to do more than clean off the dirt and blood and put on a wrap of some kind.

"Never mind," he said. "Someone in the tavern can do it." He moved to get up, but I took his arm.

"Can you stand for me to do it?"

"I can."

While I searched our packs for the sewing kit, he took a quick swig of the whiskey he'd brought from the tavern.

"That ain't enough to dull the pain," I said. He grimaced.

"If I drink enough to dull the pain, I won't be worth a flitter as a watchdog. Let's just get it over with."

He lay on his back with his head in my lap, holding the candle as close as he could without dripping wax on himself. The inside edges of the cut glistened with fresh blood. I held my breath so I could thread the needle with trembling hands, and then I ran the needle through the candle's flame. I sat for a minute with my hand hovering over his face, trying to get up the nerve to make that first poke into his flesh. His eyes glittered in the candlelight.

"It'll hurt, no matter what," he said softly. "Just do it."

I heard him draw in his breath with the first plunge of the needle and he gripped my ankle tight with his free hand. I quickly pulled the thread through, and it came out dark with blood. I closed my eyes for a moment. Then I opened them and sewed it shut without stopping, twelve pokes with the needle, six small, even stitches. By the time I was tying a knot and snipping off the thread, the candlelight was quivering so I could hardly see what I was doing, and his grip on my ankle had made my foot numb. I put down the scissors and took the candle.

"It's done."

He rolled over and managed to crawl several feet away before he puked. Feeling half-sick myself, I squatted by him and held out the damp rag I'd used to clean the cut. He puked again and then twisted to sit with his back leaning against the wall.

"I shouldn't have had that whiskey," he said weakly, taking the rag. "It wasn't a bit of help, anyhow."

We sat for a minute, trying to gather strength to move away from the mess. Finally, he got unsteadily to his feet and offered me his hand. He inspected my work in the looking-glass.

"Pretty little feather-stitching there, Maggie. That ought to make a fine scar."

"Don't joke about it," I said. "He tried to kill you. He could've cut your throat." I was shaking again, worse now than when I'd been face to face with Hardy. John David laid his arm across my shoulders.

"But he didn't," he said. "You stopped him. All that came of it is a little cut. No real harm's done. Come on, let's find a place to bed down."

He filled the rack in Washington's stall with fresh hay from the measly stack in the loft and threw most of the rest of the stack in the cleanest spot we could find close by. We covered up with every blanket and quilt we had, and John David set his rifle within easy reach before blowing out the candle. I tried to settle down to sleep, leaning on his shoulder, but my mind kept bringing up Hardy's deformed face, or the flash of the knife blade in the candlelight, or the thread dark with blood.

"We ought to get to Nashville tomorrow," he said. "The day after that, we'll be on the river heading to Texas."

At the moment, I didn't care about that one whit. I felt small and weak and scared, every bit a girl, not a woman fit to live in Texas. This had been the shortest leg of the trip, I'd heard John David say so to Zeke, and it was through countryside that was more or less settled, with roads and taverns. Now we would be heading into wilderness, where there wouldn't be any of those things. All I could see ahead of us were more dangers and more hard times to face. I can't do it, I thought. How can I bear more of this?

I was quivering all over, and I pressed closer to John David.

"Tell me about Texas."

"It's a beautiful land, they say," he started, just as he always did. "There are long stretches of land with grass up to a horse's belly. If you pull up that grass, the dirt on the roots is dark and rich. We'll get there just about the time new oak leaves are showing. We'll find a stretch of land with a little swell to it—just enough to remind us of home—and a clear spring that runs through a grove of tall, straight trees. Somewhere along the way, we'll get a mule and a plow, and soon as we have camp set up, I'll plow and get the seed corn in the ground. Once the corn's planted, I'll start on the cabin."

"Tell me about the cabin."

"It'll be only one room at first, but I'll make it so we can add rooms later. We'll have a fireplace made of river rock—I'll not have one of those stick and mud chimneys. The floor will be oak, sturdy enough it won't give when I walk across it and smooth enough so there's no splinters to get in our feet. We'll have a couple of glass windows, not at first, of course, but as soon as the crop comes in. We'll be able to look out on the cornfields, ten feet high, three ears on a stalk."

I let him have a minute with his corn before pressing on. "We'll have a well—"

"I'll put a cistern down by the stream, too, for the milk and butter."

"—because we'll have a cow someday—"

"—a nice, fat one. And I'll break a garden patch so you can grow sweet potatoes to roast in winter—"

"—and there'll be flowers in the yard all summer."

His laugh was low and soft. "Lots of flowers."

As always, when we got to this part, we fell silent. I knew he was still thinking about Texas, but my mind was back on our troubles, the ones we'd been through and the ones still to come. I closed my eyes. One trial at a time, I thought. I may not be strong or brave, but I at least have to try for him. I'm his partner in this. I can't shy away or balk at every shadow on the path.

I sighed, and he kissed the top of my head. At least he's here with me, I told myself. Even a young, ignorant mule can pull through the rough spots if it's hitched with a better, stronger one. And I couldn't think of a better, stronger one to pull with.

Chapter 11

I felt like a very small ant in a big, stirred-up anthill as I followed John David through the tangle of streets in Nashville. People were everywhere, afoot in the streets or riding in wagons, or coming from the buildings along the streets. I was glad when we finally stopped outside a tavern on a street with fewer people. My head was aching from all the noise—or maybe it was just because we hadn't yet eaten anything.

I reached for the bridle to hold Washington as I always did when John David went in to make arrangements, but this time he tied the reins around the porch railing.

"Come in out of the cold," he said, taking my hand. "He'll be all right. I don't see anybody around to steal a loaded horse in broad daylight, even if they had a mind to try it."

The tavern's main room was dim, even at midday. A man with a thin, rusty beard was wiping plates. John David leaned against the counter and waved to catch his eye.

"I'm looking to join up with a party going to Texas. You know where I might find one?"

The man frowned. "If you see three people standing on a street corner, go up and ask. At least one of them is heading to Texas." John David gave me a wide grin as he glanced around the empty room.

"I'd expect to see some of those folk in here."

"Usually you would. But since the river is closed, everybody's going to taverns near the Trace."

John David's grin disappeared. "The river's closed?"

The man turned to put a plate on the shelf behind him. "There's too much ice down river, even though we ain't had any here yet. They say there's a lot on the Ohio. They quit running boats late in October." He looked us over. "I figured everybody knew that, even hicks."

John David was gripping the counter so tight his knuckles were pale. "When do they start running again?" His voice had a strangled sound.

"Depends on the weather. If it's a mild winter, could be February. If it's cold and bad, it's more likely to be late March." The man laid down his rag and leaned toward us. "You gonna buy anything, fellow?"

John David shook his head, and I followed him outside. After the warmth of the tavern, the air seemed even colder, with dampness that promised cold rain or even snow. I looked down the street. A single pair of men staggered along its edges, singing a bawdy song. So we couldn't take the river to Texas. Taking a boat was all we had planned for, all this long way from Campbell County. I recalled how thin the money bag was, and for the first time since I'd know John David, the fear that had been so familiar back home gnawed at my empty belly. What would we eat? Where could we stay? We were only a few coins from broke, and of all these strangers walking around Nashville, there was no one we could turn to, no one.

But that's not true, I reminded myself, pressing my hand over my heart to slow its pounding. John David knows Nashville. He'd lived here. He was bound to know people who would help us. He was probably figuring which of them to go to while I stood worrying. I went to sit with him on the edge of the porch near Washington. He didn't look up.

"What are we going to do?" I asked.

"Hell if I know." He clasped his hands over the top of his head. "I never should have married you. I should've just walked off when I heard you crying, so you would've gone on and married Phillip Owens."

A chill that had nothing to do with the weather gripped my heart. "What?"

"At least with Owens you'd have something to eat and a roof over your head. With me, you've got nothing. Nothing! I swear you're skinnier now than you were when I met you." He leaned forward to rest his elbows on his knees, like a man shielding himself from a blow. "I promised I'd take care of you, give you a better life, but look where that's got us. Sitting on the porch of some second-rate tavern in the cold." He suddenly hit his fists against his knees. "You're no better off with me than you were with your pa!"

The chill in me was spreading, leaving me numb all over. I could see the end of the path his thoughts were taking. Well, I'd get there first.

"Looks like Nashville has plenty of folks," I said. "Somebody's bound to need a serving girl. I reckon we could take what money is left and get that annulment now that we're here."

He turned his head enough to look at me. "Is that what you want to do?"

I should lie to him, I told myself, lie and free him of his burden. But I was too selfish.

"Not especially. But if you want to be rid of me—"

He turned away. "That's not what I meant." He sat for a minute longer with his head in his hands, but then he stood and took my hand. "Let's get something to eat."

We went to a different tavern down the street where the stew was thin and made with stringy mutton, but at least it was hot. Since I figured it might be our last meal for a while, I made myself eat it, though my stomach was tossing like wind through dead leaves. He ate all his stew without talking, and then we nibbled on the stale cornbread while he laid out our choices. None of them included the annulment, and the tossing in my stomach slowly settled. Today, at least, Ma was still wrong.

"It's about three months till the river opens again," he said. "If it winds up being four, we won't get to Texas in time to put in a crop. If we don't raise any corn, I don't know what we'd live on." He paused. "Maybe we shouldn't go on." I looked up quickly, but he kept his eyes down. "We're not so far from home. We could go back. Like Zeke said, Pa would probably help if I asked."

A picture of Trisha's face if we walked back into McKellars' cabin came to mind. To have come all this way—to have made all those hateful creek crossings—to have fought off a horse thief and sewed up a bloody cut—only to end up where we started, with his peevish ma in the next room and pretty Bess Clardy just down the road?

"No," I said. "I won't go back."

"It's the most sensible thing to do," he said, digging his thumbnail into a scratch on the tabletop. "We ought to at least consider it."

"Living in your pa's attic don't get us any closer to our own place."

"Neither does sitting in Nashville for three months. At least there we wouldn't have to worry about having a place to sleep or something to eat."

Now was the time to lie. "I'm not worried. We'll manage."

He looked up then, and something a little hopeful kindled in his face.

"You're sure?"

I nodded. "I want our own cabin in Texas, with flowers and corn ten feet tall."

He sat up, like a load had lifted from his shoulders. "Then we won't go back." He took another piece of cornbread. "We could keep going, take the Natchez Trace from here. But going overland would take nearly as long as waiting for the river to open, and it'd be a lot rougher. If you start out this skinny, you'd be worn down to nothing by the time we got to Texas."

"It's hard on you, too. I notice you're cinching your belt a notch tighter than you did at your pa's." He wasn't listening.

"I'd rather take the river, but we need some way to live while we're waiting for it to open again. I'd need work, and we'd need a place to stay, but it would have to be a place we could afford—"

It struck me suddenly. "Your uncle! You said you studied law in Nashville with your ma's brother. An uncle would take us in."

He shook his head. "You don't know this uncle. I won't go to him."

"Why not?"

"He's arrogant and cruel. I swore I'd never let anyone treat me like that again."

I leaned across the table. "We're desperate, John David."

He slowly crumbled what was left of his cornbread. "I left on bad terms," he confessed. "I can't go back."

"How bad? You wouldn't steal from him, I know that. Did you sass him? Get in a fight? Smack him?" He shook his head. "What?"

He sighed. "I just left, in the middle of the night, without a word to anyone. I couldn't stand it anymore, not even the rest of that night."

"That's all? That's nothing, then." I picked up the limp money bag and tossed it to him. "There can't be more than a couple of coins left, probably not even enough to get us a spot in a barn tonight, much less an inn. You said it yourself—we can't camp in this weather. And think about it. What kind of work will you find in the winter? Who's going to give us a place to stay when we can't pay up front? We're desperate. This uncle is our best chance." He stared into the fire, fingering the cut on his cheek like he hadn't heard me. "As Sarah would say, God provided, John David. You can't be too proud to take this chance."

"I guess not," he said softly. "Pride is a sin." He stared into the fire for a moment longer. Suddenly he stood and went to pound on the bar.

"Hey! Is there some place around here we could get a bath, a warm bath?"

The man stared at him like he was daft. "I reckon you could get one here, if you're willing to pay."

"Is this enough?" John David shook the last of our coins into his palm. The man took them all.

"You can use the room through that door yonder. I'll bring the tub soon as I find it."

John David took my hand and pulled me to my feet. "A bath?" I asked. "An all-over bath?"

His smile was tight. "We need to look respectable. We're going to see Abner Channing."

⁂

Fine snow was spitting in the air as we stood before a neat house of bricks John David said was his uncle's law office. We were dressed in our best clothes, and though I'd managed to smooth out some wrinkles, it was clear we'd been traveling for days. Both of us still had damp hair. It had been no problem to slick down John David's wavy hair with a dab of tallow, but I didn't have the time—or patience—to comb all the tangles from mine. Instead, I twisted it into a bun that hid most of the snarls. I didn't think either of us looked especially respectable, but at least we looked like we were trying, and I hoped that would count for something.

The brass knocker on the door had an animal face with a fierce grimace. John David reached for the door knob instead, and I grabbed his arm.

"Don't sass him," I said. "He has to take you on. We don't have a bit of money left."

He grinned. "He'll take me on, don't fear he won't. Abner Channing has a weakness for pretty young ladies in desperate circumstances. He might be willing to throw me back on the street, but he'd never do it to you." He opened the door without knocking and we stepped in.

The law office was filled with men and big tables covered in paper and books. The chatter of voices stopped as every eye turned to us.

"McKellar?" a man asked.

"Good day, Henry," John David said, as pleasantly as though he'd been away from the office for only a day or two. "I need to speak to Channing."

"I'll say this for you, McKellar, you've got gall if not common sense," another man said, and they all laughed. The laughter died as a man in a gray waistcoat stepped from a doorway in the back wall. Even without an introduction, I knew immediately he was a brother to John David's ma. He had those same piercing blue eyes.

"Did I hear someone say McKellar's here? That foul spawn of a Scotsman has the audacity to walk in this office?" He smiled as he caught sight of us, and his smile curved upward sharply at the corners of his mouth, showing all his teeth, unnaturally white.

"Hello, Uncle," John David said, nudging me forward. "Allow me to introduce my wife, Margaret."

Mr. Channing raised his eyebrows. "Your wife? I knew you were immature, McKellar, but I never suspected you'd pluck a plant before its buds develop. She's what, fourteen?"

"Sixteen," he lied. "I suppose we share a fondness for young wives, Uncle."

"You're still an impudent ass, I see." Mr. Channing crossed the office to take my hand and press his lips to it. "I'm pleased to meet you, young Margaret." He turned to John David, still holding my hand. "I assume you didn't come back simply to introduce your wife. Out with it, McKellar. What do you want?"

"I'd rather talk in your office," John David said.

"I don't care what you'd rather. Out with it."

John David straightened his shoulders. "We're on our way to Texas—"

"Oh, God!" Mr. Channing groaned loudly. "Not another Texas-crazed fool!" John David ignored the interruption.

"—but we had a setback when we got into town. I'd planned to take the river route, but it seems the river is closed for the season. So to pass the time until it re-opens, I'm offering you my service for the next couple of months."

I felt a mad urge to laugh out loud. We were broke and with nowhere to sleep, and he made it sound like he was doing Mr. Channing a favor. Mr. Channing seemed to think the same thing, except he did laugh loudly before he leaned into John David's face.

"What services of yours do you think I would want?" John David didn't blink.

"I have a quick ear, you said so yourself, and I write with a clear hand. I could be a clerk for one of your advanced students."

Mr. Channing's smile always stopped before it could come to a natural rest on his face. He turned to one of the other men in the office.

"What do you think, Giles? Should I trust McKellar as a clerk?"

"I—" Mr. Giles started, but Mr. Channing didn't give him a chance to finish.

"Keep in mind he cost me a good bit of money and the trust of an important client when he disappeared last spring. I've never recovered either." He turned his blue eyes on me. I met those eyes with a steady gaze, hoping my lip wasn't quivering. It felt like it was quivering. "Did your husband put that bruise on your face, Margaret?"

My fingers tightened around John David's arm. "No! He don't hit me. It was a horse thief, on our way from Campbell County."

Mr. Channing stared at me, pursing his lips. "How much money do you have, McKellar?"

John David paused before he answered, quietly, like he hoped none of the others in the office would hear. "Not a pence."

"So you come to me as a beggar." Mr. Channing raised his chin, still staring at me. I didn't know how much longer I could stare back. But he suddenly turned to John David.

"You left me in a bad spot, boy. How can I be sure you won't do the same if I give you another chance?"

"I give you my word."

"A Scotsman's word isn't worth the spit it takes to form it," he sneered. "All right, I'll take you on. I always need someone to handle *fieri facias* cases. But a single unexplained absence or even one afternoon with the slightest whiff of whiskey on your breath, and you won't get another chance to run away. I'll toss your cantankerous Scotch ass on the riverfront and wash my hands of you for good. Understand?"

"I do," John David said slowly. Mr. Channing turned away, obviously finished with us. But John David stepped forward.

"There's one other thing. I need an advance on my pay."

"The first thing you're doing is paying back the money I lost when you deserted me," Mr. Channing snapped. "That's your advance."

"We need something to live on," John David insisted. "Lodging and food, and board for my horse. I told you I don't have any money."

"What do you expect me to do? Take you under my own roof, like last time?"

"I'm not staying in your house." John David's voice was flat and hard. Mr. Channing's eyes narrowed.

"I'm not paying the bill for you to sit in some tavern drinking every night." They stood eye to eye, and I could see neither one would give in. Mr. Giles took a step forward.

"Maybe there's another way," he said. "Isn't there an empty cabin in your slave quarters, sir? Perhaps they could stay there, since it would be only for the winter. You didn't plan to purchase another slave until spring, and you did say you want to know—"

Mr. Channing pursed his lips again. "You have something there, Giles. The overseer says something is going on with my slaves, McKellar. I'd like to know what it is."

"I'm not spying on them for you," John David said. Mr. Channing smiled that strained smile.

"Of course, I forgot. That stubborn Scotch Presbyterian father of yours made a blasted abolitionist of you. Fine. You can stay in the cabin and board your horse in my stable. I'll take it out of your wages. Just keep your blasted Jeffersonian philosophy to yourself. Remember that if you want a warm place to keep your little Margaret." He started away from us. "Be here first thing tomorrow, ready to work, in clothes that don't look like you've slept in them. And find something better than tallow to tame that mess of shaggy hair."

❧ ❧ ❧

125

The snow was thicker now, leaving a layer of white over the countryside as we left the busy town behind. John David led the way down a wide, curving path past a brick house taller than the trees to a row of rough, small cabins. One was dark in the early twilight, and that's where we stopped to peer inside.

Streaks of gray light streamed through at least a dozen holes in the chinking. One wall was mostly taken up by a fireplace with a rough mantel made of a split log. On the opposite wall, a bed frame stood on two legs made of pine saplings, with the end rails crammed into the gaps between the wall logs to hold up the other side. Broken bits of board and sticks cluttered the floor, along with chunks of chinking and what looked to me like a pile of chicken bones beside an old kettle.

"It's crude, but it's some better than I expected, to tell the truth," John David said. "Let's carry in the bundles, and then I'll go for something to build a fire."

Though we had nothing for supper but corn mush and nowhere to sit but the floor, I was content as we soaked up the warmth of the fire.

"Sure beats last night's lodging, don't it?" I said, gathering together the cups and spoons. "With a little fixing up, it'll be a fine place. And it's our first place all to ourselves." I stooped to pick up the kettle from the floor. "Reckon I could use this to wash up?"

"It's rusted through," he said. "Let's get a basin from the kitchen."

I'd seen some Negro folk, as John David called them, as we'd come closer to Nashville, but it was still a shock to see up close the dark skins of the women who looked up when John David opened the kitchen door. The older woman gave a deep gasp, and then she chuckled and came to take his arm and pull him into the room.

"How's the best cook in Tennessee?" he asked. "Maggie, this is Fern."

"Oh, McKella!" she said, patting his arm. "We shore missed you. Ginny!" she called. "Look who it be! McKella! And he's got a girl with him!"

Ginny was thin and lighter brown, with her cheek puckered around a fat pink scar. "You come back? We figured you was gone for good."

"I figured it, too," John David said. "But here I am." He put his arm around my shoulders. "This is Maggie, my wife."

"Yore wife!" Fern had bright, black eyes. "Law, look how skinny she be!" She gave my arm a pat, too. "Well, my vittles can put meat on the bones of a man dead ten years. I'll fatten you up, child. Ginny, go tell Masta Channing McKella's come back."

"Oh, he knows," John David said quickly. "We stopped at the law office before we came here."

"Did you? And you ain't with him for supper?" She tilted her head to the side. "What you doing back here, McKella?"

"We won't be here long. We just need a place to winter over till we can go on to Texas."

"I'm surprised Masta Channing gonna let you stay in the guest room, he was that mad when you took off."

"We're not in the guest room. Channing is letting us stay in the empty cabin on the row." Both Fern and Ginny stared at him and then at each other.

"Folks ain't gonna like having white folk on the row," Ginny said.

"It's only a couple of months," John David said. "You know I won't say anything to Channing about anything that happens down there."

Ginny sniffed loudly. "White folk always make promises, but they ain't too good at keeping them."

"Come on, Fern," John David said. "You always said I made you think of your own boy. You know I won't say a thing."

Fern shot a quick look at me.

"Maybe we know you won't say nothing—"

"Don't worry about Maggie. She's as closemouthed a woman as I ever knew."

"That ain't saying much when you're talking 'bout white women," Ginny said. John David frowned. Fern jerked her head in Ginny's direction.

"They probably done with the cake now," she said. "Go on up and fetch the rest of the dishes." With another big sniff, Ginny stalked out of the room.

"Got something we can do for you, McKella?" Fern asked. "I reckon you didn't come up just to say howdy."

127

John David wrapped his arm around her shoulders. "Now, Fern, you know I'd rather see you than anybody on this place."

"Uh-huh." She crossed her arms over her bosom. "What you want, McKella?"

He grinned. "I need a haircut." She chuckled and ran her hand through the back of his hair.

"That's no lie. You look shaggy as a sheep coming into shearing season. Well, set on that stool yonder."

"I'll help with the dishes in trade," I offered, stepping over to the basin of hot water. She turned to stare at me. "If you don't care," I added faintly.

"Oh, I don't care," Fern said. "I reckon if a white woman want to do work, I ain't gonna tell her no. I just never seen one wanted to before." She laid a dishrag across John David's shoulders. "She one of them Quakers, McKella?"

"No, just a mountain girl."

She watched as I washed one of the strange, slippery, white plates. Then she stretched a swatch of his hair out straight and whacked it off with the scissors.

"Law, you got thick hair, McKella. And it shore is pretty. Look how them little waves just line up there. Seems a shame to cut them off." She snipped off a curl with the tip of the scissors and held it out to me. "There you go, little Miz McKella. Put that in yore pretty locket to remind yoreself of yore true love."

I stared at the curve of the curl as it lay in my damp palm. I didn't want to insult Fern right after meeting her, but it seemed silly to carry a piece of his hair around my neck. But before I could say anything, John David plucked it from my hand and lifted the locket from my bosom.

"You're the most sentimental woman I know, Fern," he said, arranging the hair inside the little heart and snapping it shut. "That reminds me. Can we borrow a sad iron?"

"You ain't got a iron?"

"Oh, and a wash basin, too."

She laughed. "Don't you folks have anything?"

"Not much," he admitted. "We're about as poor as folk get." She patted his shoulder.

"Well, don't you worry. Fern will take care of you. Miz McKella, bundle up what's left of that roast and the bread to take with. You folk can have a good dinner tomorrow, even if you be poor."

Chapter 12

It was long after dark when John David finally came home from his first day of work for Mr. Channing, and he was surely in a sour mood. While I served the roast and potatoes I'd kept warm for him, I tried to find out why.

"What was it Mr. Channing said he wanted you to do, feary-something—"

"*Fieri facias*," he said, like he was cursing. "Collecting debts. Today I rode out into the countryside to serve Mr. Stephen Wilde with a judgment against his property in satisfaction of a debt owed to Abner Channing, Esquire."

Later, as we were getting into bed, I noticed a red welt across his back.

"What's this?" He winced as I touched it.

"Mr. Wilde was most unwilling to part with his fine brood mare," was all he would say, and then he turned his face to the wall.

After that, I didn't ask. He came home in the evenings and ate his supper in silence, barely answering back to anything I said. I wasn't sure he was even listening to me. I knew he didn't want to talk about his day's work, but after spending my days alone in the cabin, I was desperate for talk. I'd done what I could with the little we had to make the slave cabin our home. Within the first week, every crack in the chinking was filled, what clothes we had were hanging on pegs I'd pounded into the wall, the dishes and food supplies were sitting on shelves I'd made from scraps of boards. By the end of the next week, I'd finished sewing together all the fabric Sarah had cut for me. It was a chore then to fill the long days while John David was at Mr.

Channing's office. One afternoon, I fell asleep and let the beans for supper scorch. The cabin still smelled bad when John David finally came home, and it took nothing more than his irked look as he tasted them to bring tears to my eyes.

I was wiping dishes one morning after he left me with a sigh instead of a kiss, and a tear silently dropped on the back of my hand and lay there, glistening in the firelight. I stared at it for a minute, and then I threw the dishrag on the bed and put on my shoes.

"A few minutes, that's all," I muttered as I trudged up the hill toward the brick kitchen. "I'll ask for dab of butter or a couple of eggs, that's all."

Fern looked surprised to find me on the icy back step. "Miz McKella?"

I took a gulp of the cold air. "I wondered if I could get a couple of eggs. I don't mean to be a bother, but—" I couldn't think of anything else to say, and I turned my head so she wouldn't see the tears in my eyes. She smiled and stepped away from the door.

"Shore, honey, you can have some eggs. Come on in and sit a minute while I lay out these loaves."

I felt foolish as I sat at the table and watched her hands, shaping the loaves, patting them smooth, placing them in the pans even while she was looking at me.

"You getting settled good in that cabin?" she asked. I nodded. She covered the pans with a cloth before she sat across the table from me. "I reckon you ain't liking it much that Masta Channing's keeping yore new husband at his law office all the day long."

"I'm glad he's letting John David work."

She gave me a knowing look. "For a place to live, shore you are. But I'm guessing you ain't so glad McKella's gone so much."

I sighed. "I didn't know it would be like this. He don't get home to eat till nearly bedtime, and he's so tired he won't even talk." I suddenly stopped. "But I ain't complaining. I'm just being silly, I know."

"No, yore lonely for him." She smiled and patted my arm. "Don't be ashamed of it, honey. It's sweet. Makes me think of how I felt about my own man when we first jumped the broom. He'd be in the fields, and I'd be in the big house, and all day long, I'd just bide my time working, thinking 'bout when we could be together in our own cabin. A woman can be around folks all the day, but they ain't no company like her own man."

"I ain't used to being alone all the time," I told her. "Back home, there was plenty of young'uns to keep me company."

She chuckled. "Then you tell the Lord Jesus you wants a baby. Babies is sure enough a cure for the lonelies."

"Oh, no, we can't have a baby yet." Her laughter filled the room.

"The way that boy looked at you, you shore can, and I say it won't be long, neither. He won't stay tired forever."

I shook my head. "No, we got to get settled in Texas first. Traveling is mighty rough. I wouldn't want to chance something bad happening while I was carrying a child."

"Well, I reckon not." Her voice dropped low. "Losing a child is pure misery, no matter how it happens. One way or another, I've lost five. My baby Ginny, she's the only one I got left."

"What happened to her face?" I asked, before I could stop myself, but Fern didn't seem to mind.

"She had trouble with Miz Channing a while back." She paused, looking at me with troubled eyes. "They branded her for spreading lies. I tell that girl, don't you say nothing, no matter what you think you see, but she don't listen. I'm scared for her. She's going to get herself sold off someday."

"They branded her?" Her face suddenly stiffened and she left me at the table, going over to a basket sitting on a shelf.

"You say you need some eggs? How many did you want?"

"Just a couple," I started, but a young woman entered the kitchen then, the most beautiful woman I'd ever seen. She was straight-backed and slender, with wings of honey-colored hair framing her smooth, pale face. Her nose was small, her lips were rosy, her eyebrows made lovely arches over her wide eyes. Everything about her seemed to float as she moved, from her hair to the soft blue fabric of her dress.

"Fern, put together a basket for me!" she ordered. "Tell that boy Willie to get the buggy ready. I want to surprise Abner with dinner at the office."

"Again?" Fern said. "Looks like the surprise is gonna wear off if you keep doing it ever' day."

"Fern! I'll have none of your lip." The woman's eyes were surprisingly hard and cold. "There are other girls who cook as well as you, you know." Fern didn't answer for a minute, but when she did, her head was bowed and her voice was quiet.

"Yes'm, Miz Channing." The woman caught a glimpse of me as she turned to go. She laid a small white hand over the top of her bosom, which bulged bounteous and creamy from the low neckline of her bodice. Her eyes were suddenly warm and friendly.

"Who is this, Fern? Is this John David's wife? Why didn't you introduce us?" She took me by the hand and pulled me from the chair. "Margaret, isn't that your name?"

"Maggie," I said, suddenly aware of how very small my bosom was.

"Well, Maggie, you must come with me to the house! I'm far better company than a Negress!"

That's how I came to be standing in a room so fancy I never could've dreamed it. The ceiling was tall, and all along one wall were heavy red curtains that hung to the floor. They were closed against the dreariness of the winter sky, and a fire crackled in the brick fireplace at the far end of the room. Golden lamplight spilled onto furniture like none I'd ever seen—padded chairs with carved wooden arms, walnut tables with feet carved to look like an animal's paw, a long seat that looked something like a bed and something like a chair. I stepped onto the soft, thick carpet and looked at another strange piece of furniture, a sort of cupboard lying on its back atop three spindly legs.

"It's a pianoforte," Mrs. Channing said, lifting a hinged lid to show a number of bone-white pieces. "Abner imported it as a wedding gift for me. It was very expensive. It makes music, see?" She touched one of the bony pieces, and sound wavered in the air. "I can't play it, really, but Abner says someday he'll find a tutor for me. Come, sit." She went to sit on the funny bed-chair, and still staring at the many treasures around the room, I followed to sit on the edge of a padded chair.

"That's a delightful little token of love you're wearing," she said.

"What?"

She smiled. "Your locket. It's lovely."

"Thank you," I said, noticing she was wearing a pendant twice as large. "I guess you could say this was my wedding gift."

"So sweet," she said. "Is it real gold, or plated silver?"

"I—" But she didn't wait for my answer.

"Abner said you're staying in one of the slave cabins," she said. "I was horrified to hear he agreed to that! They're so filthy and dark and small. That's no place for a white woman. It would be no trouble at all for you two to stay in the house with us."

"We like having our own place." But I remembered it wasn't our place, it was theirs. "Well, not really our own," I added quickly, "but a place to ourselves. I reckon we won't have our own place till we get to Texas." She rolled her beautiful honey-brown eyes.

"Texas, Texas! It's all one hears these days! Why is everyone so wild for Texas?"

"The land, I reckon. The Mexicans are giving out land. John David plans to raise corn—"

"Farming?" she scoffed. "You must talk him out of that notion. Farm life is so dreary! It's nothing but hard, never-ending labor. That's fine for dull people with no other choices, but John David is far too clever to waste his mind drudging on a farm."

"It's what he wants," I said. "We'll have a cabin with a well and flowers all around—"

She waved her hand like my words were nothing but a bothersome fly. "You do realize how hard farming would be for you? I see those farm women when they come into town, all brown from being in the sun, some of them nearly as dark as a Negro, with squint marks around their eyes and rough hands and dried-out hair. Ugly and old beyond their years, they are. They work in the fields just like they were men! Why, they might as well be men, for all the womanly charm they have left." She shuddered. "Surely that's not what you want."

"Well, I want what John David wants," I said in a faint voice, "and he wants cornfields."

"Perhaps he thinks so. But I'm sure you could change his mind." She smiled and laid her fingers at the top of the cleft in her bosom. "Men always give a woman what she wants if she uses the weapons God gave her. John David's certainly not immune to such persuasion."

"Yore buggy is ready, Miz Channing." I hadn't noticed Ginny come in. She brought a cloak of fine cherry-red wool to drape over Mrs. Channing's shoulders.

"We must visit again soon, Margaret," Mrs. Channing said, sweeping past with a faint scent of summer lilacs. "My girl will show you out."

I watched through the big window as Willie helped her into a handsome buggy pulled by a matched pair of black horses.

"Miz McKellar?" I turned toward Ginny, and she bobbed her head toward me, same as if I had been Mrs. Channing. "You want I should show you the way out?"

"It's all right. I'll find it myself." She bobbed her head again, but she didn't move. "You can go," I said, more like a question than a command, but she left, same as she would have for Mrs. Channing.

I stood alone in the parlor, surrounded by all that fine furniture. From the corner of my eye, I saw my reflection in a big looking glass on the opposite wall, and I stepped closer for a better look. Young as I was, my skin was already freckled by the sun. In another ten years, I'd probably be as wrinkled and worn-looking as Ma. With one hand, I pushed my bosom higher, and with the other I lifted my hair so it made wings like Mrs. Channing's. But my figure still looked more like a boy's than like Mrs. Channing's, and my fingers, rough from hot dishwater and kindling splinters, snagged on loose hairs.

"You fool!" I said to my reflection, letting my arms drop.

I took the long way toward the back door, peeking into each room along the hallway. There was something new to marvel at in each one—a big, shiny table surrounded by chairs, a clock taller than John David, a cupboard filled with books. When I'd finally seen all the wonders, I made my way back to our dark cabin, where the fire had gone out.

🌿 🌿 🌿

John David was in a better mood that evening, I reckon because it was Saturday and he knew he wouldn't be working on the Lord's Day. After supper, he stretched out on the floor in front of the fireplace, and when I brought him a second cup of tea, he tugged on my skirt.

"Sit with me. Washing up will wait."

Since we didn't have any chairs, I sat on the floor beside him. He held my hand in one of his, against his chest, and stroked my arm with the other.

"You look tired," I said. "Did you have to ride out to the country?"

He shook his head. "Today I loaded bags of milled corn. Abner Channing is now part owner of a gristmill." He sighed.

"I know you hate that *fieri*-whatever work. Just remember, you won't be doing it forever. Only a couple more months." I bent to kiss his forehead. "I met your Aunt Arabella today," I said, hoping to take his mind off his troubles. "She took me to the big brick house."

He sat up quickly, and his look was dark.

"I don't want you going up there anymore."

I stared at him. "Why not?"

"I don't want it, that's why."

"She showed me her furniture, that's all! I didn't do nothing, or say nothing—"

His jaw was set in that way I was learning meant his mind was set too. "Don't go up there no more."

"All right." I stood. "I won't go. But I don't see why it matters. I didn't do nothing to shame you or cause you trouble with them. I just wanted somebody to talk to. There's nobody to talk to down here all day, and you won't say two words to me at night."

"Talk to Fern, if you have to. But I don't want you talking to Arabella."

An ugly thought was twisting through my mind. "Oh, I see how it is. I'm too backward to mingle with high-bred folk, is that it? Plain little Maggie Boon, who's good enough to visit with a Negro slave but don't need to mix with somebody fine like Mrs. Channing!"

He shook his head. "She's not so fine—"

"You don't have to explain," I interrupted. "I promised back at Charlie's to obey you, and I'll keep my promise, like it or not. Even if I ain't done anything wrong. You don't have to say a thing to me."

I turned my back on him and went back to the dishes, and I just managed to hold in my tears until I heard him get up and go outside.

❧ ❧ ❧

Since he'd given me leave to visit with Fern, I made good use of it, going up to the kitchen every day after that. She always chuckled when she saw me on the back step. "We're making pies today," she'd say, or, "I could use a extra pair of hands with this mincemeat." She'd hand me an apron and I followed her around, learning all the tricks of the best cook in Tennessee. She was probably just being kind, but she said I was a help to her, busy as she was in getting ready for Christmas.

"Masta Channing gives me time off working for Christmas," she told me, "but Law, if I don't have to do more'n three days' work in one day to get ready for his parties! He can't have just one, neither. There's the big one for the fancy folk, and then he has another one for the workers from the law office. I reckon you and McKella will be at that one." She laughed. "Miz Channing would shore be surprised if she knew you'll be eating something you made with your own hands at her fancy party."

One morning when I got to the kitchen, she was wrapping a shawl around her shoulders.

"I'm going to market, little Miz McKella. Want to come along?"

The boy Willie drove us into town, and we walked to the different shops where she said the shopkeeper could be trusted. She'd look over the goods carefully, sniffing the meat, shaking the meal to be sure no weevils came to the top. Only when she was satisfied would she tell the shopkeeper how much to put on Mr. Channing's account. Though I didn't say I needed anything, she shopped for me, too.

"How about making a nice pie for McKella tonight? And some potatoes?"

"I ain't got money," I said, and she laughed as she turned back to the shopkeeper.

"Add five pounds of potatoes and two pounds of flour to that account."

The basket on my arm was heavy with good things when we stepped back out in the street.

"Should you have done that?" I asked. "Won't Mr. Channing notice?"

"Not such a little. Anyhow, you folks got to eat." She tapped my arm. "Look at that ruckus yonder! Let's see what's going on."

Fern elbowed through the muttering crowd until we were at the front, and I saw a young woman standing in front of a small cabin, wailing as loud as the baby she held in one arm. As we got closer, I could see two other young'uns hanging on her skirt. A man started to back out the door, slowly, bent like he was dragging something heavy, and the woman rushed forward to beat him on the back with her fist.

"You're not taking it!" she shrieked. "My ma gave that to me, and you have no claim to it!"

Something huge, of a dark walnut, filled the bottom of the door, and the man stooped a little more to lift it over the threshold. He dropped it, though, when the woman began to claw at his neck and face, and as he straightened and whirled to face her, my heart seemed to drop into my belly. I knew that face.

"Step back!" John David ordered the woman, roughly pushing her away. "I already told you I'm here by authority of the law. Your husband owed money to Abner Channing when he died, and that debt has to be paid."

"Not with my wardrobe!" the woman screeched. "My ma gave it to me—me, not my husband!"

John David shuffled his feet quickly to avoid a kick aimed for his shin. He leaned toward her.

"It became your husband's soon as you married," he said. "A married woman's nothing under the law. You can't own property. Now you can step out of the way so I can load this on the wagon, or I can fetch the magistrate to take you to jail."

The woman spat in his face. He cursed, and as he wiped his face on his sleeve, someone in the crowd threw a wad of horse dung that landed in his hair.

"Bastard!" a voice shouted. "Leave her be!"

Other folks took up the call, and more dung flew toward him. He straightened, and as he looked into the crowd, his gaze landed on me. For a minute, I looked right into his eyes, and a pained look passed through them that I saw even across the distance. He quickly turned back to the wardrobe, ignoring the woman's punches and the flying dung as he pulled it across the threshold.

"Come on, Miz McKella," Fern said, and her voice was low. "We got to get some rum for eggnog. Miz Channing, she do love that eggnog. She even wants it for breakfast."

I was quiet all the time she was buying the liquor and all the ride back to the kitchen. She didn't say much, either, as we sorted the goods, and she shook her head as I took up the basket to go back to our cabin.

"It's a hard life," she said. "That's for sure. You all right, Miz McKella?"

Before I could answer, Mrs. Channing came through the door in her fine red cloak.

"I want a plate of gingerbread and a bowl of eggnog brought to my parlor this afternoon," she ordered, and then she noticed me. "Why, hello! Margaret, isn't it? I haven't seen you lately! Why haven't you been back to visit?"

"John David," I stammered. "He—he likes for me to stay close to home."

"Pshaw! I hardly think my parlor could be considered far from that slave cabin you call home!" She linked her arm in mine. "Come help me choose a fabric for my new dress."

"Oh, I can't—John David—" She giggled as she tightened her grip on my arm.

"What a husband doesn't know won't hurt him! Come!"

John David won't find out, I told myself as I walked with her up the hill toward the big brick house. He won't know. Like as not, he wouldn't even talk to me when he finally did come home, not after what I'd seen today. What could it hurt?

The furniture in Mrs. Channing's parlor was draped with lengths of fabric, which she pushed aside to sit on her bed-chair. I carefully lifted the pale blue fabric draped over a chair. It was soft and smooth in my fingers, softer and finer than even my green calico.

"Do you like that one?" Mrs. Channing asked. "It would look pretty on you. I don't want another silk for winter, though. I might save it for spring."

"It looks like spring," I said. "Like a robin's egg."

She laughed. "Like a robin's egg! Such a charming comparison! Just what I would expect from someone from the country. John David always said such amusing things about the mountains when he was here before. I've missed them. Speaking of John David—" She leaned toward me. "Have you persuaded him to stay here in Nashville instead of carrying out that foolish plan for a farm in Texas?"

"No." I laid the silk back against the chair before turning to face her. "To tell the truth, I probably won't try. In Texas, we'll have a farm of our own, but here—" I paused, wondering how much I should say to her, but the look on his face back at the market rose to mind, and the words came tumbling out. "What is there for him here compared to what we can have in Texas? Taking people's livestock? Carrying off their furniture to pay their debts? That's not what he wants to do. I'm grateful your husband's letting him work, I am, but he ain't happy, Mrs. Channing. He'll collect debts for your husband this winter, but what he wants is to be his own master. He can do that in Texas. But not here."

"That's what he's doing? Collecting debts?" I nodded, and she frowned. "Well, I'll put a stop to that!"

"Oh, no! No, you can't," I started, for if she said something, there would be no hiding from John David that I'd disobeyed him. But she laughed.

"I can, and I will. I'll tell Abner to put him to work in the office."

"Please—" But I paused. "In the office? Would he do that?"

She laughed. "Of course! With the right persuasion, Abner will do anything I ask. He'd make John David a partner if I asked." She suddenly sat straight and clapped her hands together with a bright smile. "That's what I'll do! It's perfect! If Abner makes him a partner, John David will have more independence. That should satisfy his desire to be his own master. He'll get a share of all the profits, so the two of you can get a nice house somewhere in town instead of having to stay in that dreadful slave cabin. And I'll take you in hand, introduce you to all the better people in Nashville. When I'm finished with you, no one will ever guess you're from the country. It will be fun!" She got to her feet and dashed over to take my rough, red hands in her soft, slender ones. "Oh, Margaret! It will be perfect! You'll have a much better life than trying to scrape by on a farm in that ridiculous Texas. It's just the thing! Don't you agree?"

I was glad Ginny appeared in the doorway right then to announce the tailor had come. Mrs. Channing gave my hands a quick squeeze.

"You must go now, but I'll speak to Abner about it. Tonight!"

※ ※ ※

All afternoon, while I was working on our supper, I pondered what I should do. The possibility of steady wages and a real place to live seemed so perfect I almost could believe it was an answer to prayer, as Sarah surely would have said. Still I balked at the thought of sharing the news with John David. No doubt it would cheer him to know his days of debt collecting would be over sooner than he'd thought. If I told him, though, he'd know I had gone against his will, and I feared any cheer my news could give him might be overcome by temper. I sure didn't want that. I still hadn't made up my mind whether to say anything when I heard him outside the cabin door, whistling a merry tune. Whistling? And he knocked.

"Is this the home of Mistress Maggie McKellar?" he called through the door. Laying aside the spoon, I hurried to open the door, certain I'd find him half-gone with whiskey. But there was no whiskey smell about him, only a wide and crooked grin. He stood with his hands behind his back.

"Mistress McKellar?"

"You know it's me," I said. "Come in from the cold. Why are you acting so queer? Have you been drinking?" He stepped over the threshold, carefully keeping his back turned away from me as he went to stand by the fire.

"No, no whiskey. These lips want nothing but your sweet kiss." He gripped me tight in one arm and kissed me, a kiss so fiery I was embarrassed, though the cabin had no windows and no one could see.

"John David!" I gasped, gripping his arms and pushing away from him. "What's come over you? I thought you'd be glum because of—"

"That's done with," he said quickly. "No use going back over it." He brought his other arm from behind his back, and he was holding a large package in brown paper. "It's Christmas season. I asked Channing for an advance on this week's pay so I could get you a Christmas present. Here in the city, folks give each other something at Christmas."

He led me to sit on the bed, and he watched with bright eyes as I opened the package. It was a cloak of coarse wool, dark gray. Before I could even lift it from the paper, he had it and was shaking it out and wrapping it around my shoulders.

"Do you like it?" he asked.

"It's warm." But it was plain, too, like a mourning dove's feathers compared to Mrs. Channing's cardinal-red cloak. John David pulled the hood over my hair.

"Even if it's spring once we start for Texas, we're likely to have some cold days," he said. "This should keep chill out of your bones."

"It should. I thank you. John David—" I fell silent. What should I say? Was this the time to tell him what I'd done? Should I tell him he was about to get away from debt collecting and into the law office? That we would have a house in Nashville and plenty of money, that we didn't have to go to Texas for him to be able to take care of me the way he said he wanted to?

He was smiling at me, and I suddenly didn't have the heart to sour his good mood by confessing I'd been to visit Mrs. Channing. Anyhow, what if she forgot to ask what she'd promised? As Ma always said, better to see the berry than the bloom.

"I ain't got anything for you," I said, and his smile grew bigger as he slipped his arms around me, inside the cloak.

"But you do." His kiss was as fiery as before, and this time I didn't resist it. Telling could wait. When he found out everything we'd have, he'd forgive me for going against his will. For the time being, what my husband didn't know wouldn't hurt him.

Chapter 13

I didn't see Mrs. Channing again until Christmas Eve, the night of the party for the working folks. She fluttered among her guests like a beautiful white bird, serving us plates of food with her own hands, since Mr. Channing had given the slaves Christmas Eve for their own celebration. Mr. Channing himself mixed the eggnog, pouring in generous splashes of rum to the approving shouts of the men from the law office, who eagerly jostled to get a cupful. I didn't know any of the other women, and Mrs. Channing was too busy to introduce me, so I sat on a padded couch in the ladies' parlor, waiting for a chance to ask her if she'd said anything about John David to her husband and listening idly to the talk around me.

"Who's even in control of Mexico since they overthrew their emperor last spring?" Mr. Channing's voice carried in from the men's parlor. "I say, nothing will ever come of Texas, in part because the Mexicans won't allow slaves. An economy can't build wealth with nothing but individual farmers. Your father works hard enough, McKellar, I'll grant him that, but a man's single effort can't bring him more than enough to pay taxes and buy what he needs to survive to the next planting season. You'll never have a comfortable house like this one for your little bride if you're an abolitionist farmer."

Through the open door, I saw John David smile stiffly and say something as he backed out of the group. He headed toward the eggnog bowl on the table in the hall, and I left the ladies' parlor to join him.

"What was that name he called you?" I asked in a low voice. "An abo—"

For the first time all evening, John David's smile was a real one. "An abolitionist. It's a person who thinks slavery is wrong and wants to free all the slaves."

"Oh." I ladled up a small cup of eggnog and handed it to him. "Are you one?"

Before he could answer, the music had stopped and Mr. Channing was tapping a spoon against a glass. Mrs. Channing came to take both our arms with a clever smile, and she steered us toward the crowd of people gathered around her husband.

"As you all know," he began, "I've made it a custom to give a token of my favor to those who've served me well each year. It's been another prosperous year, and I want to bestow a share of that prosperity on each of you who've been a part of making it so. James Giles, step forward!"

He gave a small bag of coins and a slap on the back to each of the men who worked in his office. John David was the last one he called forward.

"This reprobate nephew left me in the lurch when he abandoned us last summer. He's most fortunate I'm a generous and forgiving man." I wondered if anyone else noticed the way John David flinched the tiniest bit as Mr. Channing laid one hand on his shoulder. "But for all his fecklessness last spring, he's been wholly dependable this past month. He's proven himself a true asset in closing old debts. Matrimony must agree with him!" A titter of laughter floated about the room as Mr. Channing handed a bag to John David, who nodded his thanks and started to step away. But Mr. Channing tightened his grip, keeping John David beside him.

"I never dreamed I'd say this to a son of that Scotch fool who lured my sister away—" He paused for a long moment, and then he gave us a wide and indulgent smile. "But I'm prepared, McKellar, to offer you a second chance to study with me, perhaps with an eye to turning the practice over to you in a few years if things go well."

John David's face was sober. Mrs. Channing giggled and pinched my arm.

"Quite the Christmas surprise, don't you think?" she whispered, her breath hot against my cheek.

"I know this is sudden," Mr. Channing went on, "and unexpected, no doubt, after last summer's escapade. So I won't ask for your answer tonight. But consider it carefully, McKellar. You won't get such an offer again."

It seemed every man in the room wanted to shake John David's hand and tell him what a lucky offer this was. He had finally got himself free of them and was coming toward me when Mr. Giles threw his arm around John David's shoulders.

"Congratulations! You're most deserving, my friend."

"And most fortunate to have a most persuasive aunt!" Mrs. Channing said, pulling me along to meet them. "Abner put up a bit of resistance to the idea at first, but—" She winked at me as she took John David's hand. "Come, nephew, you dance with me, and Margaret can dance with Mr. Giles." She slid a look at Mr. Giles under her eyelashes, and a tiny smile curved her lips. Mr. Giles cleared his throat.

"I'd be pleased to dance with Mrs. McKellar."

"If anybody's dancing with Mrs. McKellar, it will be me," John David snapped. "Dance with your husband, Arabella."

She laughed. "Abner doesn't dance. He can't leave his guests."

"I don't know this set," I started, and Mrs. Channing laughed again. She gave Mr. Giles another of those veiled smiles.

"Mr. Giles is an excellent dancer. He'll teach you the steps. Come now, John David, don't be so stubborn! You're like one of those country mules. Abner will expect you to be a bit more refined if you're to be a lawyer in the city." John David's jaw tightened as she pulled him toward the center of the floor. Mr. Giles took my hand, and we followed them into the dance set.

I didn't learn the steps from Mr. Giles, and it didn't take long to figure out he wasn't really dancing with me, anyhow. I was only the passing of time between his chances to clasp Mrs. Channing's hand and to gaze into her face. I glanced at John David once when we took hands and turned, but I could tell he was so furious he wasn't even seeing what was happening in front of our noses. As we left the floor, Mrs. Channing laughed breathlessly.

"There, now!" she gushed. "Wasn't that more fun than standing around talking business?"

"I'm afraid Mrs. McKellar might not say the same, thanks to

having a poor teacher," Mr. Giles said. "You must admit, McKellar, with an enchanting partner like Mrs. Channing, it doesn't take long to master the steps."

"I'm sure that's true," someone said, and we all turned to see Mr. Channing's overseer leaning toward us, his face flushed red, probably thanks to the large cup of eggnog in his hand. "The question really is, Giles, have you mastered the dance—or mastered the dancer?" His voice was so loud even people across the room stopped talking and turned to look. Mrs. Channing gasped.

"What a rude thing to say, Mr. Dougan!" she said quickly. Mr. Dougan made a bow so low it was clear he was mocking.

"Begging your pardon, Mistress. It's just that, working with the slaves, I hear things, you know." He staggered a little as he stood. "The way they tell the story, Master Channing's fine little cookie is nibbled by strange lips."

Mrs. Channing's face was pale and her hand was quivering as she laid it over her bosom. But her voice was hard and cold. "You've drunk too deeply of my husband's hospitality, Mr. Dougan. Repeating the idle gossip of slaves! If you wish to keep your position you'll retire for the evening and sleep off your drunkenness. Mr. Giles, will you escort him out of the house, please?"

Mr. Dougan grinned and pretended to tip a hat to Mrs. Channing as Mr. Giles gripped his elbow and pulled him away. Mrs. Channing stared after them for a minute and then turned to the fiddler.

"Come, play something livelier than that dreadful tune! Everyone is far too serious! Merriment! That's what Christmas is about! Abner, dear, more eggnog, please!"

"Let's go," John David said, close to my ear.

The moon was showing through the clouds as we made our way home without speaking. The loud laughter and singing of the slaves' Christmas celebrations drifted around us as we walked and even followed us into our cabin, coming muffled through the walls. I took off my cloak and laid it across the bed.

"He may have been drunk, but I think that fellow was right about Mrs. Channing," I said, and John David laughed as he squatted to stir up the coals.

"No doubt he was."

"That was some party, wasn't it? I never saw the like of it." I waited for him to say something, but he worked at building up the fire without a word. I moved around the room behind him, hanging his jacket and my cloak, turning down the bed, smoothing the covers several times before I finally couldn't stand waiting any more.

"Well," I said, "are you going to take the offer?"

"No," he scoffed.

"You ought to at least consider it, John David." He looked up at me with a frown, and my knees felt a little weak, but it was too late now to stop. "Farming's a life full of hard work, you know it is, and there's never a promise you'll get anything from the work you put into it. I've seen Pa's corn crop fail plenty of times, and I know you've seen crops fail too. Dry years, floods, bugs, frost—there's always something a farmer has to worry about, just to get food on the table. But if you learned to be a lawyer we'd always have plenty, just like your uncle. There'd be no worrying about a thin money bag or a hungry belly, and you could keep Washington for a saddle horse."

He had turned back to the fire.

"Getting to Texas will be hard, too," I went on. "Think about all the troubles we had getting here from Campbell County. And that was in settled territory—just think what it will be like once we're out in the areas where there ain't any folks except Indians. That cut on your face is just now healed up, and that's because Fern gave me the remedies for it. If it had happened on the way to Texas, I wouldn't have had anything to put on it and it might have mortified. And then what would have happened? Folks die from such as that."

"We'll have remedies with us."

"We can't carry everything with us," I argued. "We'll be back to doing without. Well, I'm tired of doing without! I've been doing without my whole life. It's been mighty nice here these last weeks, having plenty to cook for supper and going to bed every night with a full belly. I'd like to live that way, and maybe even have a chance someday to have some of those pretty things like Mrs. Channing has. I don't know that a wild place like Texas can give us that kind of life. We ought to stay with the sure thing."

He looked up at me then. "Is that what you want?" he asked. "To be like Arabella?"

I laughed. "I could never be like her! She's a real lady, like some beautiful flower, and I'm just—"

"Mountain laurel," he said softly. "Hidden back in the shadows among the trees, but so fine and beautiful it takes a man's breath if he takes the time to notice. Mountain laurel, that's what you are, simple, and honest, nothing like her, thank God." He stood and put both hands on my shoulders. "You're right, and Abner's right. If I'm a farmer you'll probably never have a fine brick house or silk dresses like Arabella's. I want to give you fine things. But I can't do what he does to get those things and live with myself. Can you understand that?"

I slipped my arms around him. "I know you ain't happy taking folks' furniture and horses. If you went back to studying the law, you'd be away from all that. You'd be working in the office. Nobody would be spitting on you or cussing you."

His smile was grim. "Not to my face, anyway."

I pressed myself closer to him, resting my chin on his chest so I could look up into his face. "It's a good chance, John David. You ought to at least think about it."

He sighed, but then he leaned down to kiss my forehead. It wasn't a yes, but it wasn't a no, and I felt sure he would see the sense of my thinking before spring came and the rivers opened again. Sarah must be right; the Lord was working, for He had provided.

※ ※ ※

I was still stepping light the next morning when I went to the kitchen for milk. But I stopped short when I saw Fern pouring coffee into cups on a tray, her face streaked with tears.

"What's wrong?" I asked.

"Ginny." Fern wiped her face with her apron. "After what Masta Dougan said last night, Miz Arabella wants Masta Channing to sell Ginny for a field hand. She says she wants him to sell her back East. I told that girl and I told her, it don't matter what Miz Arabella do, just keep yore mouth shut. It ain't our business what the white folk do. I thought that brand would teach her, but now she's gonna be sold—" Her voice broke off in a loud wail.

"Would he do that?" I asked. "Ginny's a good worker."

She sniffled loudly. "He would. If Miz Arabella says to. He'd sell Jesus Christ himself if Miz Arabella said to." She dropped into a chair at the table and laid her head on her arms. "Oh, Jesus! Lord Jesus! She's my last one! I'll never see her no more, just like my boy!"

John David was still in bed, since Mr. Channing had closed the office for Christmas Day. He sat up like a bolt when I burst through the cabin door. I didn't even bother to set down the milk, but went straight to the edge of the bed.

"Mr. Channing is selling Ginny back East because Mrs. Channing says Ginny's who told Mr. Dougan about her and James Giles. But any fool could see it last night! You've got to talk to him! He can't sell her! She's a good worker, and she's the last of Fern's babies—"

"What? Slow down." I repeated the news impatiently, and he leaned back against the pillows.

"Get up!" I pulled back the covers. "Go talk to him!"

He shook his head. "There's nothing I could say to change his mind. We'd best just stay out of it."

"John David! I thought you liked Fern!"

"I do. She's a good woman. But they're slaves, Maggie, his property. I can't tell him what to do with them, and I doubt he'd take it too kindly if I tried."

"So you won't do nothing? You'll just let Fern be grieved without even trying to help?"

"What can I do? I hate to see Fern grieved as much as you do, but the fact of it is, Maggie, he owns them, and he's got the right by law to do whatever he pleases to them or with them. Beat them, brand them, sell them back East—it's his choice, and he's mighty proud of knowing that. I'm telling you, there's nothing I can do without putting us in danger of being back on the streets. And even if I tried and he tossed us out, he'd sell Ginny anyway. That's just how it is."

I could tell no amount of arguing was going to change things. "It ain't right," I fumed.

With a grin, John David reached for his britches. "Is your 'beautiful flower' making an abolitionist out of you?"

He might say there was nothing we could do, but later in the day, he came with me to the kitchen when I took back the empty milk jug. He sat against the table and watched as Fern wrapped a chunk of plum pudding in a cloth for us to take. She wasn't crying anymore, but everything about her seemed to droop. As she handed me the pudding bundle, John David leaned close to speak to her in a low voice.

"I had a long talk with Reverend Winton of the Congregational Church while I was collecting from one of his parishioners the other day. I think he knew more than he was letting on about where the fellow's slaves disappeared to. You ought to have a talk with him yourself." He straightened and took the bundle from me. "We thank you for the pudding."

"What was that about?" I asked as we started back down the hill. He shrugged.

"Best I can do for her without putting us in a bad spot."

※ ※ ※

I stopped in the kitchen a couple of days later, and Fern was acting queer, startling like she'd heard something and looking over her shoulder. I was afraid to hear the overseer had taken Ginny away, so I didn't linger.

"Wait!" she called. "I got some fresh sausage to send." She handed me a bowl, and her eyes were fiercely bright. She dropped her voice low. "You and McKella stay in yore cabin tonight, hear?"

"Why?" I started, but she hushed me.

"Just make McKella stay put tonight. Cook him some nice sausage and biscuits, and then maybe you can work on getting you that baby. Make sure he stays put."

I passed her message to John David as soon as he came home from the law office, and he thought it as queer as I did. He pondered over it all through supper and while I cleaned up afterwards.

"They're planning something," he said. "I wonder—"

"Don't," I said. "She told us to stay put. Whatever it is, she don't want you in on it. So I say let's bank the fire once the dishes are done and go to bed early."

The door suddenly banged open and a black man in a ragged dress coat stepped over the threshold.

"Brothers and sisters, I'm here at last, praise God!" he sang out, but a look of confusion came over his face, and before either of us could move, he was gone, leaving the door open to the cold. John David rushed to the door and peered out into the darkness.

"Who was that?" I asked, pressing my hands over my racing heart. "One of the slaves?"

"He wasn't Channing's. I know all of Channing's slaves." He leaned out the doorway. "They're heading somewhere and they don't seem a bit worried about being heard." He turned to take his jacket from the peg on the wall.

"What are you doing?" I grabbed his sleeve. "You ain't thinking of going after them! Fern said stay put!" He peeled my fingers from his arm. "John David," I pleaded, "just stay out of it. Whatever they're doing don't involve us. Don't be so blasted curious!"

"There might be trouble. Maybe I can head it off." He kissed the top of my head. "Finish your washing and go on to bed. Warm it up for me."

I stood still for a moment after he left, feeling the cold air from the door swirl around my ankles. A chill was settling on my heart, too. Trouble. I pictured all the worst kinds of trouble I'd ever heard folks talk about, and my knees trembled when I thought of John David standing alone to try to stop it. I hesitated for a minute and then grabbed my new cloak and headed out the door. Maybe having a woman there would make folks act right and keep trouble away. But even if trouble came, at least he wouldn't stand alone.

The night was clear, with a bitterly cold wind that lifted the hem of my cloak as I stood in the dark, trying to see which way John David had gone. I heard voices to my left, moving away from me, so I followed them, stumbling over rocks I couldn't see and shivering, from fear as much as from the cold.

I finally found him peering through the cracks between the logs of a small, rough shed. A strange sound of some kind was coming from inside it, a kind of deep moan with a higher sound rising and falling through it. I grabbed his arm tight.

"What is it?"

He startled. "Watch it!" he whispered, and then he frowned. "What happened to obeying me, little mule?"

"What is it?" I pressed my face close to the wall to see between the cracks. We'd found the man who had come to our door, along with what looked to be every slave on Mr. Channing's place. They were standing in a circle, hands on each other's waists, shuffling around and around in a never-ending chain, chanting in low voices, the light of a single lantern highlighting their dark faces. The moans began to form together into a song.

"*I'm a-trouble in de mind, oh, I'm a-trouble in de mind. I ask my Lord what shall I do, I'm a-trouble in de mind....*" In the streak of light coming through the crack, I could see John David was grinning.

"Here's the goings-on Channing has been wondering about," he murmured. "Church."

It wasn't like any church I'd ever been to, even the revival up on the mountain when folks fell to the ground, twitching with the Spirit. I watched as the slaves kept moving in the circle, singing that low song, until one woman raised her hands and swayed back and forth, with a moan that got louder and louder. Others joined her, and soon it seemed like the whole group was making moans and cries, from the lowest bass voice to the little voices of children. The man who had come to our door stepped to the front, with his head tipped back and his hands raised, and he began to speak in a powerful voice that silenced the others.

"Sometimes we look at the world around us, and we don't understand why bad things happen. We know our heavenly Father holds every moment in His big hands, and nothing is done that ain't part of what He has in mind for the world. But sometimes we don't understand what He is doing. We don't see His plan for our sister Ginny—"

"Stay here," John David told me, and he started around the corner of the building. I followed him.

"What are you doing?" I hissed, desperately. "Fern said to stay away!"

He went through the door, bold as could be. With a quick sigh, I plunged after him.

All the slaves turned toward us, a sea of frowning dark faces. A tall man stepped forward, his finger pointing at us.

"You them white folk from the row!"

"We mean you no harm," John David said, but the man stepped closer. I grabbed John David's arm.

"You oughtn't to be here," the man growled.

"Hez!" The preacher man called out. "We ain't got time for that." He turned to John David. "Hez is right, you oughtn't to be here. No white woman has any business here."

"Take her back to yore cabin, McKella!" Fern called. "Quick, too."

"Not until I know what's going on," John David said. The slaves looked at each other, but no one answered. "What's going on?" he demanded. "Tell me!"

The preacher jutted out his chin. "We is here to worship the Lord God, that's all, and we ain't got time to waste."

"Get on with it, then," John David said, and his voice was kinder this time. "I don't aim to stop you." He leaned against the wall, his arms crossed over his chest.

"Yore staying?" the preacher asked, and John David nodded.

"Go on," he said.

The preacher sighed as he lifted a tattered book. Just as he opened his mouth, though, John David spoke again.

"Can you read from that Bible?"

The man shook his head. "My master don't allow his slaves to learn reading. The only Scripture I know is what I learned at meetings when I was a boy."

John David looked at the preacher for a minute, and then he took the book from him and moved to stand under the lantern hanging from a beam. He thumbed through the yellowed pages and cleared his throat. The silence in the barn was like a living thing, waiting.

"I'll read from Romans, chapter 8."

His voice was quiet and low, but every word seemed to ring against the walls of the shed. The preacher stood with his eyes closed, his lips moving slightly as John David read, almost like he was reading the words himself. The other slaves stood quietly, some with their eyes closed, some with their eyes fixed on John David, others staring at the walls or ceiling. I marveled that they were so still and quiet, when I myself felt so jumpy, waiting for the trouble John David had said might come. I knew John David felt the same, for he seemed to have one eye on the Bible and one on the door as he read.

"'And we know that all things work together for good to them that love God, to them who are the called according to his purpose.'"

The door of the shed banged open, and Mr. Channing was standing there with the overseer Dougan, who was holding a lantern and a bullwhip. John David kept reading, but faster.

"'Who shall separate us from the love of Christ? Shall tribulation, or distress, or persecution—'"

"Shut up, you fool!" Mr. Channing bellowed. "I should have known when they were all missing from the row you had something to do with it." He stepped into the shed, followed by Mr. Dougan. "Who got this meeting together? Who?" He grabbed the front of the preacher's shirt. "Who are you? You're not one of mine!"

"Hiram, sir!" The preacher fumbled in his pocket. "From Master Adams' place, sir. I got the papers says I can be here, see?" Mr. Channing snatched the papers away and crumpled them.

"Are you the one who called this meeting?" The slaves' faces were all still as stone. Mr. Channing shook the preacher so his head flopped back. "Did you call this meeting?" he roared. "Did you?"

"I did it," John David said. "I made them come."

Mr. Channing whirled around, and he made me think of a puffball mushroom about to explode.

"I should have known! I warned you to keep your blasted ideals to yourself! You have no right to spread your abolitionist nonsense among my property, you ass!" He struck John David across the face, right on the scar I knew was still tender. "I'll deal with you in the morning. Now get out!"

Chapter 14

"Why'd you say that?" I panted, stumbling along behind him at a trot. "You didn't do nothing but read to them a little."

"Because he won't whip me. But he'd flog them near to death if he thought they were meeting behind his back on their own." He tore open the door of the cabin, went straight to the bed, and ripped the covers from it. I stopped in my tracks.

"What are you doing?"

"We're getting out, like he said." He jerked the mattress from the frame, and with one slice of his knife, severed the knot from the rope that held the bed together. He began to pull it loose from the frame, which collapsed.

"John David!" I grabbed his arm. "Stop! He meant us to leave that shed, not to leave the whole place!"

"It's what he meant. He's going to toss us out. But I'm not giving him the satisfaction of calling me up to the house tomorrow like some naughty little boy, so he can lord it over me before he does."

"Maybe he won't—" He turned and grabbed me by both shoulders.

"You don't understand, Maggie! What I did undermines his authority as their master. He won't let that pass. Tossing us out is the least of what he can do. He can have me taken in on charges if he chooses to—and he might choose to. That could mean a fine, but he'd probably push for time in jail, and he's got friends that would make it happen. Our best bet is to disappear as fast as we can. He won't expect that. Now start bundling things together."

"You're family," I choked. "He wouldn't—" He shook me.

"Damn it, Maggie, don't argue! I'm leaving. If you're coming with me, get things together. But if you'd rather stay here with Arabella in her fancy house and have fancy dresses and three big meals a day, I'm sure Abner could convince a judge I'm an unfit husband and get you that annulment."

I jerked away from him and went to the shelf that held our dishes. They clanked together as I stacked them, and I didn't especially care if they dented. John David finished pulling the rope from the bed frame and tossed it on the pile of bedding.

"I'll get Washington."

I banged the cups into the Dutch oven. "We don't have anywhere to go. Where will we go?"

Before he could answer, there was a knock at the door. John David cursed and swung the door open wide. The preacher man stepped close to the threshold and leaned in a little to look at us. One eye was streaked bloody, and the skin around it looked swollen.

"I ain't staying," he murmured. "Got to get back to my master's place. But Fern said—" He stared at the tumbled bed and the pile of dishes. "What's happening here?"

John David frowned. "It's not your concern."

The preacher's eyes narrowed as he looked up at John David. "You're packing up. You folks is leaving. You is, ain't you? You got some place to go in the middle of a cold night?"

"Not at the moment," John David snapped. "But you do, so I reckon you ought to be getting to it."

The man lowered his head. "Yessir." He turned to go, but before he'd taken more than a step he was back. "I shore liked hearing you read the Word. It may be wrong to tell you this." He scratched the back of his head, and then he looked straight at John David, bold as any white man would do. "You go to old Ford, the tanner on Charlotte Pike. Tell him Hiram sent you. He'll give you a place for the night and won't say nothing. Just say Hiram said so."

"Are we going to do it?" I asked as he watched the preacher disappear into the darkness. "Stay with that tanner?"

"I don't have a better idea," he said. "It's too cold to sleep in the open. I'm going for Washington. Have things ready to load when I get back."

Since Washington was out of practice as a pack horse, and since he wasn't too happy about coming out of a warm barn into the cold night, it took a long while to load our things. I don't know how late it was when we set off into the darkness. The wind had died down, but the cold was bitter. Even with my new cloak, I was numb all over by the time we reached a cluster of cabins with the smell that unmistakably marked them as a tanner's place. John David paused at the door of the cabin closest to the road.

"Let's hope that preacher is right," he muttered as he raised his hand to knock.

A shrill barking started up inside, and a deep voice came through the door. "Who's there?"

"Hiram sent us," John David called. "We need a place for tonight."

"Two in one night? He's shore busy!" The door opened a crack, and I could see the man's face move from sleepy to startled in one glance. "You're white!" He moved to slam the door, but John David threw himself into the crack.

"Hiram said you'd set us up for the night. That's all we need, a place for the night."

The man stopped pushing on the door, but he still glared at us. "How do you know Hiram?"

"From Channing's place, east of here."

"Hiram don't belong to Channing."

"He was preaching!" John David's temper was growing dangerously short. "I was at a prayer meeting he was having on Channing's place. But Channing broke it up, and I don't fancy going to jail for aiding slaves in rebellion. Will you give us a place for the night, like Hiram said, or not?"

"Let me get my clothes on." We stood silently in the cold, listening to the dog inside the cabin barking itself into a frenzy, until the man came out, buttoning a poorly-fitted jacket over his belly.

"The girl got any objection to a bit of a smell?" he asked.

John David shook his head. "Is it snug?"

"It'll keep frost off you."

The tanner took us to a building that smelled so strongly of dung I nearly gagged as I stepped inside. Holding the edge of the cloak over my nose, I watched as he bent to pull a long skin aside from a pit in the ground.

"It's clean," he reassured us. "It just smells like hell. Your fancy slave owner won't be looking for you here."

John David grinned. "Not Channing, that's for sure. What about my horse?"

"Unload him, and I'll put him with the slaughter horses out back."

I waited while they stashed our goods behind barrels of dung, and then the man left with Washington, and John David squatted by the pit, holding out his hand for me. Though I didn't want to, I took it and sat on the edge. Then I scooted off into the darkness.

Something scurried off to the side, and I shrieked, straining to pull myself back up. But John David let go my hand, and I fell the last bit to the ground. I leaped up and pulled my skirts around me, trying in vain to see through the blackness what it was that was in the pit with me. John David dropped to the ground beside me, and I grabbed him.

"Something's here!" I whispered. "A rat or something!"

"Calm down!" He was striking a flint, the tiny sparks useless against the blackness.

"They's rats here, all right," a hoarse voice said, "but they the two-legged kind. What you doing here, McKella? Come to fetch me back for Channing? You double-crossing son of a—"

"Ginny?" he asked, but the only answer was a loud huff. "We're not going back. We don't want to see Channing any more than you do."

I heard a thump that sounded like someone sitting heavily on the ground. John David nudged me, and I sat too.

"Why's she here?" I whispered as he lowered himself to sit by me.

"Someone must have talked to the Reverend Winton."

That was the most miserable night I'd ever lived through. I didn't sleep at all, and I couldn't stop shivering. John David held me close so I could share the heat of his body, but I kept myself stiff in his arms, knowing it was his fault we were in this tanner's pit instead of a warm bed. Worse than that was knowing we didn't have a warm bed to go to for the next night. All my pretty plans for our own house in Nashville were collapsed, just like the bed frame, and here we sat, in the same spot we'd been in when we first got to town. Worse, even, because now Mr. Channing would be looking for John David to put him in jail. Our only hope now was getting to Texas. But how much longer till we could start? Where could we go in the meantime? Did we have enough money to last? The questions whirled through my mind over and over until I longed for sunrise, when the night would be over and we could at least do something, instead of sitting in a tanner's pit, waiting and worrying.

※ ※ ※

The tanner fetched Ginny from the pit while it was still dark. Soon after, John David boosted me out of the pit and I followed him through the empty streets back to the one on the riverfront with all the taverns, where we'd gone when we first came into town. I noticed he avoided the tavern with the rusty-bearded man, going instead to one with a knotted snake on its shingle, far down the street.

"Wait here," he said. I sighed and pulled my cloak tighter around me, and he laid his hand on my shoulder. "You're cold, I know. But I'll have a better chance of getting work if I'm a lone man, not a traveler with a woman along."

It didn't seem to make any difference, though, as we tried all the taverns, even the one with the rusty-bearded man, with no luck. John David brought me some corn pone, still warm from the skillet, as he came out of the last one.

"He's heard the Spotted Hog on Middle Franklin might need a stable boy. It won't pay much, but at least it's work. Let's hurry—it's a bit of a walk from here."

The Spotted Hog reminded me of home, a little dingy and a lot run-down. But when John David came out with a big grin, I thought it looked fine enough. He led Washington to the back of the building, off the street, and tied him to a pole.

"Come in and get warm," he said.

A man with two round chins pushing over his collar looked up as we came in. His eyes were nearly buried in the flesh of his cheeks.

"Who's this, McKellar? Not your wife, I hope. I won't hire a married fellow. I never have luck with married fellows. They only stay till they've scraped together enough money to get to Texas."

"Sister," John David said. I whipped my head around, but he stepped on my foot. He was looking straight into the man's flabby face. "She's my little sister. Our ma died a couple of months back, and we lost our home. Pa left too many debts, you know. I promised I'd take care of Maggie. So we're in Nashville trying to get a start."

"Sister, you say?" The fat man looked at me again. "I guess there's some family resemblance. Can you start today?"

I bit my lip to stop its angry quivering as they went through the arrangements, what John David would do and what he'd be paid. When John David asked about living quarters, the man paused.

"Usually, the stable boy stays in the barn," he said, "but that ain't no place for a girl. I reckon your sister will have to stay here in the tavern."

"I can't," I started, at the same time John David said, "Alone?" But the man didn't seem to hear either of us.

"I don't reckon your sister would be interested in some work?"

"No," John David said flatly. But I was tired of him deciding everything.

"What kind of work?" I asked, shifting sideways to avoid his foot.

"Cooking, serving folk, the like. I lost my serving girl last week to some fast-talking fellow. It's hard for me to keep up with everything. I sure could use a good girl in the kitchen and here with the customers."

John David was shaking his head. "She's not—"

I cut in over him. "I'm pretty good at cooking, long as the food is simple."

The man laughed. "That's all folks expect in a place like this."

"She's not going to cook for you," John David started. I turned on him, my eyes narrowed.

"Listen, Brother, a girl with no husband's got to make her way somehow. She don't know when someone's going to turn the whole world topsy-turvy." I held out my hand to the man. "I'll cook for you, mister."

I felt a hateful pride knowing John David was fuming behind me as the man and I worked out my arrangements. He said I could sleep in the kitchen, and that's when John David finally broke in.

"I'm staying there with her." The man looked surprised, and John David quickly added, "She's young and not used to city living. I don't want fellows coming around pestering her."

"He promised Ma on her deathbed he'd watch out for me," I added. The man shrugged.

"Suit yourself, then. Might keep her from running off with somebody. Well, girl, we'll have a room full of folk come suppertime.

McKellar, the stable is on the back of the lot. You'll need to muck out the stalls first thing. It ain't been done since I lost the last boy."

He went back to the bar and John David clamped my elbow in his fist and steered me out the door to where Washington was tied.

"What the hell were you thinking?" he demanded. "I don't want my wife serving whiskey to a bunch of no-good—"

"It ain't your wife that'll be doing it, it's your sister." His jaw tightened.

"You heard him. He wouldn't have kept me if he knew we're married."

"So you lied to him." I started to untie Washington, and he jerked the reins from my hand. "I ain't happy about that, and you ain't happy about me working. But what makes us unhappy is going to make us some money, and money's what we need."

He took my arm and turned me to face him. "You don't know the kind of fellows who come into places like this, what they're like after a shot or two of whiskey."

I laughed. "You mean the kind who'll grab and kiss a girl he don't even know?"

"That's not fair," he mumbled.

I laughed again and took his hand. "I'm your woman, John David. Cooking and serving for strange men won't change that."

"If any drunk fool so much as lays a finger on you—"

"Nothing will happen! Come on, Brother. Let's see what kind of place we'll be staying in now."

I suppose it was a step up from the slave cabin. At least it had a board floor, instead of dirt. A cupboard stocked with dishes and food took up most of one wall, and a long bench made of a half-log was on the opposite. With a fireplace across one end and a table at the other, I couldn't see where we'd have room enough to make a bed and store our goods. But it was my problem to deal with. John David set our bundles wherever he could find an empty spot, and then he swung up into the saddle.

"Where are you going?" I looked up at him over the last armload of our goods. "The man said the stable needs cleaning."

"I've got business to take care of."

"What business?" He sat for a minute, stroking Washington's neck, before he looked over at me, his mouth set in a tight line.

"Selling Washington."

"Today?"

"We can't pay to keep him, and folks might wonder what a poor stable boy's doing with such a fine horse. It's time for him to do what he came for." He wheeled Washington toward the road with a little dig of his heels.

"Don't be too long!" I called. "You've still got those stables to do!"

I watched until I couldn't see them anymore, and then I looked around at the mess we'd made.

"Clear the table first, I reckon," I said aloud. "There's supper to cook and I need a place to work."

I stayed busy all morning, so I didn't realize until John David came through the door in the middle of the afternoon that I hadn't seen him all day. He laid a little bag fat with coins on the table.

"Find someplace to hide this where nobody would think to look," he told me.

I gasped as I picked up the bag. "So much!"

"He brought top price—two hundred dollars. It's just what I expected. He's a fine horse." His voice was unnaturally dull, and I looked up. But he was already out the door.

I hid the money several different places, only to go back after a few minutes to move it someplace else. Finally, I unlaced the bag of seed corn and stuffed the money deep into the golden kernels. I tied the cord back tight as I could, trying to make it look like the bag had never been opened. There we go, I thought, seed corn and money, the two things our future depends on now, wrapped together in a dirty tow sack.

Although quarters were tight, it was pleasant to cook in a kitchen with plenty of anything I wanted to use close at hand. I liked the idea of adding to our money, doing something I was good at. The tavern owner, Mr. Randall, seemed to think I was good at it, anyhow.

"Tasty, girl, mighty tasty," he said as he tried the fried potatoes. "I reckon you'll work out right well."

Maybe I let his praise go to my head. It wasn't long before I was moving through the tables like I'd been a serving girl all my life, a plate of food in both hands, smiling at strangers. Once while I was clearing a table, I found a coin under an overturned cup.

"They forgot some money," I said to Mr. Randall as he walked past. He laughed.

"They didn't forget it. They left it for you. Sometimes folks do that when they take a fancy to the girl who's serving. You keep it."

I rubbed my thumb over the surface of the coin. It was hard to believe it was my own money, to do with as I pleased. I thought of handing it to John David, of it going with his money to buy our way onto a boat going to Texas, and suddenly I was eager to get more. I wrapped it in a rag and tucked it inside my bodice, so I wouldn't lose it. Then I went back to pouring whiskey and carrying plates of food, with a friendly smile on the side.

John David came in not long after, but I had to finish serving a couple of fellows before I could bring him a plate of hot food and some coffee.

"I have something to show you," I said. "Money! Some folks left it for me." But Mr. Randall came over before I could fetch the bundle from my bodice.

"Sit by the back door, McKellar," he ordered. "That smell will bother the paying folk. Girl, we need another pan of biscuits."

I handed John David his food and hurried off to get the biscuits. It wasn't long, then, till I glanced his way and saw he'd gone.

Most folks cleared out after supper, and I washed dishes between trips serving whiskey to a group of men playing cards. They were so jolly and friendly I couldn't help but grin at their foolishness. One of them in particular, a broad-shouldered fellow with a quick smile, kept calling me over to refill his glass. I saw a likely chance to pick up another coin, so I was sure to smile every time he did.

"New in town, miss?" he asked once. "Need someone to show you around?" I shook my head and leaned to pick up the dirty glasses they had set in the middle of the table. Next thing I knew, his hand was sliding across my rump and squeezing. I jerked straight up, sloshing whiskey on their cards, and they all laughed. I started to give him the sharp edge of my tongue, but the thought of his coins stopped me.

"Do that again, and you'll not have enough cards left for a game," I said instead, and they all laughed again. I went back to the dishes, glad to be able to hide my trembling hands with scrubbing.

They were still playing when I'd washed all the dishes, and I wished they'd leave so I could wipe down their table and go make a pallet on the kitchen floor. Having no sleep the night before was finally catching me, and I leaned against the wall, waiting for them to go.

I must have dozed off, because that's the only way I believe the jolly, broad-shouldered man could have slipped up on me without me knowing it. But his arm was suddenly around me, his hand was scrabbling inside my bodice, and his mouth, foul with whiskey, was hot and sticky against mine. I struggled against him, which only made him laugh and press me hard against the wall with his body.

"She wants to play coy!" he called to his friends.

"Give it up, Brewster," Mr. Randall said, coming over to set bottles of whiskey on the shelf behind the bar. "I reckon this girl ain't that kind. And she's got a watchdog of a brother who's a half-foot taller than you and probably on his way to see why she's still working this late. You've had enough for tonight. Finish up and go on home."

"Another time, then," Brewster whispered into my ear. He pressed a coin into my hand, and then he and his friends left, slapping each other on the back and still laughing.

I turned the coin over between my fingers as I walked to the kitchen. Just the touch of the cold metal made me feel dirty, knowing how I'd come to have it. I surely couldn't tell John David about that. I wanted to throw the coin far into the darkness and be rid of it and of the memory of Brewster's whiskey-soured kiss. But like it or not, it was the biggest coin anyone had given me all evening, a gold one. I had to keep it. We needed all the money we could scrape together.

John David was sitting on the log bench when I got to the kitchen, and he was holding one of Mr. Randall's whiskey bottles.

"I thought you'd be asleep," I said. "It's late."

"Either you did a mighty fine job hiding that money I gave you this afternoon, or somebody already stole it." His voice was deeper than usual and a little slurred. "I've looked all over and can't find a sign of it." I squatted by him to pull the bag of seed corn from under the bench.

"It's safe. I sewed it in here." He brushed his fingers over the bag's rough surface.

"Damn. I never would've thought of that. I reckon that's a fine spot for it, then." He leaned back, slowly. "That's a lot of money. More than I ever had in my life."

"Will it pay for a place on a boat?"

"That and more."

"Well, then, like you said, he did what he needed to do for us." I laid my coins, including Brewster's gold one, in his palm. "Here's what folks left for me tonight. It will help."

"I reckon." He let the coins fall to the floor as he lifted the bottle, but I took it from him. It was light in my hand, like it was nearly empty. He'd probably been sitting down here drinking ever since he'd left the tavern after supper. I'd expected him to have a hard time parting from Washington, but I hadn't thought he'd get drunk over a horse.

"You've had plenty for tonight." I stood to take it to the cupboard, but he grabbed my skirt and pulled me to his lap.

"John David!" I protested. "Don't!"

"I need you, Maggie," he murmured, laying his face against my neck. He smelled as much of whiskey as Brewster had. I stiffened as his fingers slipped inside my bodice.

"Don't! You're drunk."

"Not that much."

I pulled his hand away. "You are! And you smell bad." He sat back then, with a little frown.

"Of course I do. I smell like horse shit. I've been shoveling it all day, remember?"

"Not all day. You didn't get back here till middle of the afternoon, remember?"

He didn't try to hold me as I scrambled off his lap, but his next words stopped me cold.

"I just about kept on riding today."

I turned to stare at him. "What?"

"I was an hour out of town, to the south, headed to Natchez." His eyes were shadowed in the dim firelight, but I looked into them, trying to read just what it was he was telling me. My heart began to pound heavily.

"You were going to Natchez without me?"

Abandonment—Ma had warned me, and I'd scoffed at her.

He slumped forward and crossed his hands over the back of his neck.

"I don't know what came over me," he murmured. "I meant to go straight to Sam Martin to see if he'd buy Washington, but I rode right past his place, just kept going and going. It felt good to ride again." He let out a ragged breath. "Look at us, Maggie. Four months ago I was a son of the most respected folks in the whole Stinking Creek valley, with the best horse in Campbell County. Now he's gone, and here I sit, a damned stable boy. My wife, who I vowed to provide for all the days I live, serves whiskey in a tavern and brings me the coins men leave on the table for her." He laid his hand over his forehead. "This is not how I wanted things to be, not at all!"

It's the whiskey talking, I told myself. He's drunk, and feeling sorry for himself, that's all. But the rub of it was, he'd been sober as a preacher man when he'd left this morning, when he'd been willing to ride off and leave me in the kitchen of this second-rate tavern without so much as a goodbye. Well, maybe I had every reason to feel sorry for myself, too.

"So you were just going to ride off without me?" I kept my voice low, but I couldn't keep it from quivering. "Why? You said you wanted what Zeke and Sarah have. You said we'd be partners, like a good team of mules." I thumped my apron down on the table. "But it felt good to you to ride off on your own and leave me here."

He jostled the table as he edged around it to get to me. "I came back. That's worth something, ain't it?"

"What about next time, though?"

He turned me toward him and tilted my face up with his fingers. "There won't be a next time, I swear it."

"How can you be so sure? Seems like whenever times get hard, you want to toss me off." My throat tightened, and a tear rolled down my cheek before I could blink it away.

He took me in his arms then, and though he did smell bad, a mix of horses and sweat, dung and liquor, I pressed myself against him.

"Don't ever leave me alone," I said.

His arms tightened around me. "I won't. Heck, I don't think I can. I gave it a good try today, but I couldn't do it."

I pulled away to look up at him. "Just don't you do it."

His eyes, dark and suddenly serious, met mine. "I won't, Maggie. I swear it to you."

I looked into his eyes for a minute. He seemed earnest in his promise, though as Ma always said, even an honest-looking apple can hide a worm. But, I reminded myself, one worm don't ruin the whole apple. There's still plenty of good left.

I nodded, and he let me go and bent to pick up the coins from the floor where he'd dropped them. He sighed as he put them in the buckskin bag.

"Times will get better," I said, squatting to spread our pallet on the only clear spot on the floor. "You won't always be a stable boy."

"Maggie—" Something about his voice made me stop to look up at him. "You still want to go to Texas, don't you? Not just because you know that's what I want?"

I looked down at the locket on my bosom that I had thought was the finest thing in the world until I had seen Mrs. Channing's big, jeweled pendants. I looked at the quilts I was spreading out, grown ragged with rough use, and at our two tin cups on the table and at the way the firelight showed every crack in the skin on my hands. Then I looked again at John David, and he looked for all the world like a drowning man clinging to a tree stump in a rushing river current. I smiled and reached for his hand.

"It's a beautiful land," I said, "as fine a place to raise crops as any on this earth. They say in spring it's covered over with wildflowers. We'll find a spot in a meadow, next to a creek with clear, cold water—"

It was all I had a chance to say before he dropped to his knees and kissed me. I knew from that kiss there would never be a fine brick house in Nashville for us, or carved furniture, or silk gowns, and I'd never in my life been so happy to not have something.

Chapter 15

John David spent most of every day for the next month wandering the waterfront, trying to find someone we could throw in with for the trip to Texas. Every evening, he was discouraged because his search wasn't turning up anybody.

"There are plenty of folks willing to take our money," he told me. "But I'd say half of them don't know what they're doing, and the other half I wouldn't trust with a timber rattler."

But one afternoon as I was washing hominy for supper, he rushed in and started pawing through the packs.

"Where's my razor?" he asked when I protested. "I need to clean up. Our luck may be about to change. A man at the boat yard said someone told him there's a guide he knows to be honest saying he's uneasy about his party because there's thirteen folks in it. Maybe I can ease his worry by getting him to add us to the number."

I reckon I sloshed enough whiskey on tables that evening to make a good-sized shot, because I kept looking toward the door every time I heard someone come in. But he never came, and when I'd finished cleaning and got back to the kitchen, he wasn't there, either. I finally went to bed without him, but I lay awake waiting for his footsteps and listening to the town, still busy with the sounds of men's tongues loosened by drink. I startled at a heavy thump against the door, and I reached for the rifle on the floor by the pallet. But it was John David himself who burst through the door, grinning ear to ear.

"We're in, Maggie! We're with the Barnes party, headed for Texas!"

I scrambled to my feet. "Really? We have a spot on a boat?"

"We sure do!" He pulled me into a hug that was so tight it hurt, but I didn't care. "I spent the whole time talking to Griffin—he's the guide—and a couple of the others in the party. They're good people, Maggie, folks we can trust. There are three families besides us, with some children, even. You'll like that. I got to him just in time. The boat will be done in the next couple of weeks. Griffin said we'll be ready to go by mid-February, if the river's ready, and he thinks it will be. Maggie! We're really going!" He did a quick jig step, and I laughed, happy to see him so happy.

"You're jigging? How much did you drink during this talk?"

"Not a bit." He bent and puffed his breath at me. "See? Not a bit. I reckon what swayed them was me having a strong back and being willing to use it. They're trying to find every way they can to keep the cost down, and with me along, they won't need to hire anyone else to man the boat."

I ran my hands up inside his shirt over the solid muscles along his backbone. "Huzzah for your good, strong back!"

His eyes were shining in the firelight. "We're going, Maggie! In less than three weeks." He suddenly pulled away from me and knelt by the goods crammed together under the bench. "We'll need to start getting things together. You got any idea how much meal and salt we still have?"

I knelt beside him and took his face between my hands, turning it so he was looking at me instead of the bundles. "John David! You don't have to tally it up tonight. We ain't leaving in the morning."

He leaned forward to kiss me. "You'll have everything I promised to you, glass windows, a well, a feather bed up off the floor—"

"Flowers," I reminded him. "Don't forget the flowers." He grinned.

"I'll get you every kind of flowers they have in Texas. There'll be so many flowers around that cabin it'll look like it's floating on flowers." He shifted like he meant to get up. "I'll need some money from the seed corn to pay Griffin."

"Tomorrow," I said, pulling him close. "There's time for that tomorrow."

※ ※ ※

The kitchen floor was soon so crowded with supplies that I had to step carefully while I was working. Every night we went through John David's list, and though I couldn't read it, I felt a little thrill every time he marked through a line. We counted the money every night, too. John David taught me the difference between the coins—British shillings and Spanish bits and American dimes. Pride swelled in my chest when he scooped my coins into the bag with his, ready to buy something from the list or to join the money hidden in the seed corn.

One afternoon he convinced me to leave the beans simmering at the edge of the fire so I could see the boat. It didn't look like much to me, just a rough, three-sided cabin perched on the center of a big raft. John David, though, seemed nearly beside himself with pleasure. He'd been that way ever since we'd joined the Barnes party, walking with a bounce in his step and like as not singing a jolly tune. I'd never seen him so carefree, and I wondered sometimes what he must have been like before me, before he had the burden of a wife, when he was just the youngest of the McKellar boys.

A couple of days later, I knew his news as soon as he came into the tavern. He was biting back a grin, and every time I glanced his way, he was watching me with eyes that seemed to glow, even across the room. I finally had a moment to make my way over to him.

"It's done," he said. "Griffin wants to meet with everybody tomorrow, and then we can start loading the boat. It's time, Maggie!"

I laughed. "Don't start jigging!"

He grinned. "I just might." He started to pull me toward him, but I stepped hard on his foot.

"That ain't very brotherly!" I scolded in a low voice.

"What does it matter now?" But he let me go. "Hurry with the washing, hear? We've got a lot to get ready."

Once I'd finished the dishes, though, I went to the table where Mr. Randall was counting the evening's money.

"Me and John David are leaving in a day or two. I figured I ought to tell you."

"Texas fever, I suppose?" I nodded, and he sighed. "Can't say I'm surprised. Every young fellow in Tennessee is taking off for Texas."

My stomach felt knotted the next afternoon as I walked with John David to the tavern where we'd meet Mr. Griffin and the others. John David talked only about Mr. Griffin and the boat, but I didn't care so much about that. I was worried about meeting the other women who'd be on this trip. This wasn't like talking to folks in the Spotted Hog, ones I never expected to see again. No, these folks would be our neighbors, who'd help us raise a cabin and shuck a corn crop. When it came time to birth a baby, it would be one of these women John David would bring to tend me. I knew they'd help, even if they didn't like us—folks had to. But it surely would make life more pleasant if they were like Sarah and not Trisha.

We took seats at the table in the tavern's back room with a stocky man and his wife, who was so fair she looked nearly like a ghost in the dim light. John David introduced them as the Hammonds, Dan and Judith.

"Howdy," I said, and she smiled, but it was a thin smile that faded quickly as she looked away from me toward the door.

John David leaned close, pointing out an older couple at a table with a boy near my age. "That's Barnes and his wife with their oldest boy, Ben. They're the money folks."

A loud clatter behind us broke the quiet. A young man was grinning foolishly and trying to set up a pair of cups, while a girl squatted on the floor, reaching under the table for the silver. She stood awkwardly, and I saw she was round with child. Her dress was several inches too short, pulled high at the waist to make room for the bulk of her belly. She caught my eye, and her face reddened.

"You got to be careful with other folks' things, Luke." She laid the silver on the table and lowered herself into the chair. Luke ducked his head.

"I will, Suzy."

Just then, John David dug his elbow into my side. A well-muscled, sun-browned man was coming through the door.

"It's Griffin," he whispered. "The guide."

The man glanced around the room, frowning. "Where is everybody?" he barked. Mr. Barnes stood.

"We're all here. McKellars just came in."

"You got young'uns, don't you? Where are they? I told you I want to talk to everybody."

Mr. Barnes glanced down at his wife. "The children? I don't think—" Mr. Griffin stepped closer. He was the shorter man, but somehow he seemed to be looking down at Mr. Barnes.

"You're paying me to do your thinking. The young'uns—your slaves, too—will be on that boat. I want them to hear this."

Mr. Barnes's face flushed, but he nodded to his wife, and there was more waiting while she and Judith Hammond went to fetch their children. Once they were back and everyone was settled, Mr. Griffin studied us all with narrowed eyes, rocking slightly on his heels. He didn't seem too pleased with what he was seeing.

"It's a dangerous thing you're doing," he started. "You have no idea how dangerous. I'm going to lay out the dangers today and give you one last chance to back out. If you want to stay behind, I'll give back your money and won't think any worse of you." He paused, like he expected us all to plead to stay behind. "Everyone's in, then? Once we're on the river, there ain't any backing out."

"The rivers we'll be on, the Ohio and the Mississippi, are two of the biggest in this country," he continued. "They're wider and deeper than anything you've ever seen. They have sand bars as long as the street outside and whirlpools bigger across than this room. It's the season for flooding, and that will make the current fast and hard. If you fall off the boat, you'll be swept away before we can get a rope to you. The young'uns are to stay to the middle of the boat—no playing around the edge, hear?" He was glaring at the littlest Barnes boy, who was squirming in his chair. Mrs. Barnes stilled the boy with a pat.

"You folks decided to save money by being your own crew," Mr. Griffin went on. "It ain't too late to change your mind about that, either."

"Now, just a minute!" Mr. Barnes said. "That's why we took on McKellar! You said having another hand gave us enough men to crew for ourselves."

"I did, and I reckon you men can do it. I'm just offering you a last chance not to have to. Not a one of you has experience on a boat."

"You said that didn't make any difference." Mr. Barnes sounded nearly angry. Mr. Griffin gave him a cool look from under raised eyebrows.

"I can teach you enough to get you down the rivers. But you've got to do what I tell you, no arguing and no questions. I've been on flatboats hauling cargo since I was that boy's age, Barnes. I know a hell of a lot more—begging your pardon, ladies—than any of you, and I expect you to remember it. The lives of everyone on the boat may depend on you remembering it."

"We trust you," Dan Hammond said. "We'll do what you say."

"I won't take a piss lest you say so," Luke said. Judith quickly covered her little daughter's ears, but the corners of Mr. Griffin's mouth turned up.

"Good."

He went on about storms and snags and sawyers, river pirates and Indians, sleeping on the ground and cooking over an open fire. I got tired of listening to everything that could go wrong and how hard it was going to be. Instead, I watched Judith's baby girl sleeping in her arms, with her tiny pink mouth drawn in around her thumb. Finally, Mr. Griffin quit talking and we all went for another look at the boat. The other women and I stood on the river's edge while the men followed Mr. Griffin around the boat, listening to him tell how to use the oars. The little Barnes boy climbed onto the roof of the cabin to swing the long pole mounted there.

"What's this?" he called, but no one paid any mind. His mother shook her head.

"We'll be fishing that child out of the water before we leave Nashville. Peter! Get down from there!"

"I hope he'll heed what Mr. Griffin said," Judith murmured. "It would be dreadful to lose him."

"We won't lose anyone," Mrs. Barnes said. "Mr. Barnes says Mr. Griffin is so cautious because this is his first time to guide a group to Texas. Mr. Barnes says he lacks the confidence of experience." She turned to me. "You're Mr. McKellar's wife? Lands, you girls are young! I keep telling Mr. Barnes uprooting oneself to start over in some unsettled place is for the young, but he's never listened to me on that account."

"You've done this before?" Judith asked. Mrs. Barnes nodded.

"Three times on foot from one place in Tennessee to another. I do believe Mr. Barnes was born under a wandering star. Now he says opportunity in Tennessee is too limited, and he wants to be one of the first millers in Texas for all the corn and wheat you folk will grow." She took Judith's squirming baby in her arms. "I say travel is for the young, but I believe I'd rather have Peter to worry about than a little one like this—or to be carrying a babe, like you are, Mrs. Morgan."

"Yes," Judith said. "I would think the travel will be especially hard for you. What if the baby comes before we get to Texas?"

Suzy Morgan shrugged. "It'll come, I reckon."

Mrs. Barnes laughed. "That spirit is why travel is for the young!"

Mr. Barnes and his two sons came over.

"There she is, Lydia! I asked Griffin if we can name her for you, as the queen of the company." She rolled her eyes.

"Howard! Don't be a fool!"

"Come, Lydia, what shall we name her?"

She pondered a minute. "You always say Texas will be our new world. Let's name her Ariel, for the fairy in Shakespeare's *Tempest*."

John David waved to me from the path, and as we started back toward the Spotted Hog, I shook my head.

"What?" he asked, laying an arm across my shoulders.

"Mr. and Mrs. Barnes. They're naming the boat."

He laughed. "They're different kind of folk, for sure. But don't get crosswise with them, Maggie. Naming a boat won't hurt anything."

"I ain't going to say anything. But there's a lot more queer folk in the world than I ever knew about."

❧ ❧ ❧

We counted the money for the last time that night, and then John David put a small amount in his buckskin pouch and we hid the rest in the bag of seed corn. As I bent to sew the top together again, he touched the locket that swung out from my neck.

"Want to put this in here, too? It might be safer that way."

"No!" I clasped it in my own hand. He'd think me foolish, I knew, but serving in the tavern, I liked having it around my neck, inside my bodice where no one could see it. When men got too drunk and slipped an arm around me or were too forward with their words, the locket was a solid reminder better was waiting for me, and somehow that made it easier to smile so they'd leave their coins on the table.

"I'll keep it hid," I promised. "No one will know I've got it."

The seed corn with most of our money inside was in one load he carried to the boat next morning. The weather was unusually warm for February, and his shirt grew damp with sweat as he came back for load after load, since we no longer had a horse to pack our goods. I was sweaty, too, in the stuffy little kitchen, and I left the door open as I cooked supper one last time.

Mr. Randall sighed heavily when I brought him a treat of fried apple pies after all the folk had left the tavern for the night. He raised a pie to his nose for a sniff and smiled. He reached into the box of coins and counted out my pay.

"You've been the best help I've had in a long time," he said. I started to scrape the coins into my apron pocket, but his soft hand suddenly covered mine. "I don't reckon you'd change your mind about going? I could offer you more than that little pile of coins. Marry me, and we'll be partners in this tavern. Don't worry about your brother. A good-looking young fellow like him won't have any trouble finding a Mexican girl. But in this town it's not easy to find good help that will stay more than a few weeks."

I pulled my hand from under his, sweeping the coins into the lap of my apron and wadding it against my bosom as I rushed away. As I stumbled in the dark toward the kitchen, I started to smile, and by the time I got to the kitchen, I was laughing out loud.

"Mr. Randall asked me to marry him!" I said as I burst through the door. "He don't want to have to find someone else to cook. He's desperate enough he said he'd make me a partner in the tavern!"

John David was banking the fire for the night. He didn't look up. "That's quite an offer. You might ought to take him up on it."

I quit laughing. "Is that what you want?"

He turned to me. "I'm teasing, you know that. Though it's true enough I can't give you the easy money of a tavern."

"I don't care about that."

"I know." He took my hand in his, stroking the back of it with his thumb. "Maggie—I was thinking, just now. Maybe it's selfish of me to make you face all those dangers Griffin warned about just because I want to go to Texas so bad. You're so small, and you can't even swim—"

"Stop that!" I pulled my hand away. "I don't plan on getting in the water. You know I want to go, too. Don't worry so much. I bet Mr. Griffin just makes things sound bad as he can so we'll all be extra careful. I used to do that all the time with the little ones back home. Here, let's do something with this money."

He got up and brought the money bag to me. "At least there's only you to worry about. At least we don't have a little one, like Hammonds."

"And I ain't with child, like Suzy Morgan." I poured the coins from my apron into the bag. "What's wrong with her husband? He don't seem right."

"They said he was mule-kicked when he was a boy. Griffin seems to think he'll be all right. I reckon they paid extra to be in the party. They paid for the baby like it was already born, a whole extra portion."

"They don't look like they got the money to pay an extra portion." I pulled the drawstring tight and weighed the bag in my hand a moment before handing it to him.

"That's how we want to look, too," he said. "Like we're the poorest folk in the party. I want folks to think this little bag is all we have."

"I won't say a word otherwise. But I thought you were getting us in with folks we can trust."

"I do trust them." He stuffed the little bag under the pillow, one of the last of our things left in the kitchen. "But temptation has a way of working on folks. Better to not whet an appetite." He suddenly looped one finger inside the chain of my locket and pulled it up to catch the firelight. "Like this pretty little trinket. There won't be many like it once we're out of Nashville. Somebody could be overcome with a desire to see it around a different neck."

"That won't happen!" I snapped. "I told you I ain't going to show it around."

He laughed and let it drop back inside my shimmy.

"I believe I riled up my little mule." He bent to kiss me. "Don't worry, Maggie. Just keep that locket snuggled there safe between your pretty little bosoms, and you'll be putting a Texas wildflower inside it come April."

⁂

The morning dawned clear. I cooked eggs, but my stomach was so queasy with excitement I couldn't eat them, and John David finished my portion. He rolled the bedding while I washed dishes, and then we left the Spotted Hog behind.

Everybody else was already there, having less distance to come. Mr. Griffin was on top of the cabin with Dan Hammond and Ben Barnes, gesturing around the long pole that John David called a sweep. Mr. Barnes and Peter were moving bundles from outside the cabin to in, with Mrs. Barnes and Judith watching. Judith kept looking away, though, to where the Barnes' two girls were walking with her daughter around the raft, each of them holding to one of the baby's hands. Luke Morgan was leading a thin, brown-spotted cow across a pair of narrow planks that served as a bridge to the boat. The cow wasn't too willing to step onto the planks, and Suzy was pushing on her from behind. John David handed the bedding bundle to me.

"That cow will kick her if she doesn't watch out." He hurried to lean his own hip into the cow's rump. Suzy stepped back by me, pushing loose hair behind her ears.

"I do thankee for the help," she called to John David, who grunted as he gave another mighty push. The cow gave in, moving forward so quickly that John David lost his balance and nearly fell into the water. He looked back at us with a sheepish grin and crossed the plank to help coax the cow into stepping on the boat. Still breathless, Suzy offered her hand to me like a man would do. I was surprised to find it was as rough and calloused as a man's.

"Luke said your name's Maggie. I'm Susanna, but everybody calls me Suzy. How old are you?"

I was surprised, too, by her blunt manners. "Sixteen, last month." She nodded.

"A little younger than me, then. Where are you folks from?"

We shared such talk until John David called me to board the boat. I crossed the narrow plank, feeling some sympathy for the cow. Worse than that, the boat swayed as I stepped on. The feeling I was going to fall backward into the water swept over me, and I grabbed for John David's arm.

"I don't know about this," I murmured.

"You'll get used to it." He led me to a stump by the cabin. "Sit here for a while to steady yourself."

I leaned against the cabin wall while the last things were loaded. Ben brought on two sheep and a long-legged mule, and then Dan Hammond and John David helped Mr. Barnes and his slave boy load the heavy millstones. Mrs. Barnes rushed around the cabin, checking and double-checking the piles of goods.

"Look!" Peter shouted. "They're pushing off!"

John David and Mr. Griffin were untying the ropes that bound the boat to land. They tossed the ropes to the body of the raft, and then John David stretched to step from the shore to the boat and hurried to take an oar.

"Heave!" Mr. Griffin shouted, pushing the edge of the boat with one foot while the other men pulled heavily on the side oars. He jumped to the boat, making it pitch sharply, and I closed my eyes against sudden dizziness. But I quickly opened them again to watch us leaving Nashville. The buildings on the shore grew smaller—the size of a woodshed, the size of a washtub, the size of a bucket, the size of a cup. Watching them shrink, I was seized with giddy excitement. After so many months of talking about it, waiting for it, it was finally here. We were started to Texas—for good this time.

Chapter 16

The weather couldn't have been better for our first day on the river, warm with a gentle breeze and fingers of clouds spread across the sky. We camped that night in a grove of hickory and sycamore, and it was mild enough we didn't feel the need for shelter. Mr. Barnes set up a canvas tent for his family, but the rest of us simply spread our bedding on the ground.

I was tired as we sat around the fire after supper, and I leaned against John David's shoulder, watching Judith Hammond stroke her baby's hair and listening to the men talk their way ahead on our route. Mr. Griffin seemed to think the pleasant weather didn't bode well.

"Mackerel skies and mares' tails make lofty ships carry low sails," he quoted. "My pa said he never knew that saying to fail. We're in for bad weather."

It was hard to believe his gloomy predictions, looking up at the soft black sky. I even thought I heard peeper frogs somewhere at the edge of the river when we finally settled into our pallets.

Being new to traveling—and having to take down and pack away Barnes' tent—we got a late start the next morning, the first sign we wouldn't make much progress. And sure enough, by mid-afternoon thunder was rumbling in the distance, and Mr. Griffin ordered the men to steer the boat toward the bank.

"The weather's still far off," Mr. Barnes argued. "I say we keep going." Mr. Griffin gave him a withering look.

"The last place we want to be in a lightning storm is in the middle of a river, Barnes. You folks have a tent, but the rest of us need time to build shelter before it rains."

The wind was picking up a little by the time they'd guided the boat to a suitable place on the bank and secured it so it wouldn't break loose and float away. Mr. Barnes, his sons, and the slave Moses started setting up the canvas tent, and Mr. Griffin began to chop down saplings to build a shelter for himself. John David was looking for the hatchet in our packs when Dan Hammond tapped his shoulder.

"We won't have time to each build a separate shelter. What say you we go together and make one that's a little larger?"

Before John David could answer, Suzy cut in. "Sounds good. Luke, do what they tell you."

Dan looked at John David, who shrugged and turned back to our packs. "All right," Dan said. "Luke, you clear ground between those two cedars. Maybe they'll shield us from the wind."

While the men worked to cut poles and branches, Suzy and I gathered sticks for a fire.

"I know it's forward of me to push in with you all," she said. "But Luke can't build a shelter by himself. He'll do a fine job of whatever they tell him to do, but he can't think of what to do on his own."

"I don't reckon anybody cares."

"That one does." Suzy jerked her head toward Judith, who was talking earnestly to Mrs. Barnes. The baby was clutched in her arms, wriggling and crying to be set down. "Reckon what they're talking about?"

We found out soon enough. Judith came over without the baby, which I figured meant something odd was afoot. She cleared her throat and Dan looked at her over his shoulder while he held two saplings for John David to lash together.

She twisted a corner of her shawl between her fingers. "I asked Lydia if the baby and I can stay in their tent."

Dan looked stunned. "Ain't it too crowded?"

"She told Ben and the slave boy to stay with you all."

"Oh." He turned back to the saplings.

"It will be so much better than a shelter made out of sticks. This shelter is bound to leak, and you know Baby might get sick if she's wet and cold."

"I know. You better get back to her." He walked away from her, following John David to the other end of the frame. She shot a quick glance at me and Suzy before she left for the canvas tent, about the time bright lightning flashed above.

"Get the bedding!" John David called to me over the thunder. "Quick!"

Ben and Moses were helping lay branches across the frame when I came back, and with five men working on the task, the cover went together fast. I'd made three trips bringing bundles of bedding when the rain blew in like a slamming door. All five men tumbled into the lean-to, which wasn't quite as big as Barnes' tent. We were all pushed together, trying to keep as far out of the rain as we could.

The worst was over in just a little while, but steady rain lingered for several hours, finally becoming a drizzle around suppertime. The fire at the entrance to the shelter gave some warmth through a night that grew steadily colder. When we woke in the morning, the ground was white with a thin layer of snow. My fingers were stiff as Suzy and I rolled the bedding, and my belly felt empty and queasy. We'd used all the dry wood during the night, so there was only enough fire to make coffee to soften the cold hardtack. We weren't too far down the river when I felt the soggy, sour mess on its way back up. I didn't make it to the edge of the boat in time.

"Look!" Peter said, jumping to his feet. "She puked right on the boat, Ma!" I glanced over at them. Judith had her nose covered with a handkerchief, looking like she might be sick herself. Mrs. Barnes was holding the back of Peter's jacket to keep him from running over. John David had turned to see what all the ruckus was about, and he called to Mr. Griffin before leaving his oar.

"Are you all right?" he asked, putting his arm around me. I nodded, but then I shook my head as my stomach swirled again. He followed me to the edge of the raft, where I sank to my knees, leaning my cheek against the logs of the short wall. A slight breeze rose off the water, and I sucked in a cool, clean breath of it. John David stood over me, a little frown wrinkling his brow.

"This is better," I said. "I'll stay here a while."

He brought me a dipper full of cold water, which helped a little. I was embarrassed to have him hovering over me while the other men were working.

"I'll be all right." I smiled a little as I handed him the dipper. "I shouldn't have had coffee on an empty stomach. You better get back to your oar. I'll rest a while, and then I'll clean up my mess."

But before I could get to it, I saw Suzy, squatting awkwardly around her big belly, scrubbing the spot with a rag. She staggered a little to find the balance between her belly and her feet so she could stand, and then she came to rinse the rag in the river near where I was sitting.

"I'm much obliged," I called to her. "I was going to do that after a while."

She settled back with a grunt. "You still look mighty green. Anyhow, I cleaned up worse after my master had been out drinking."

"Your master?"

"I was bondservant to a storekeeper in Pikeville before I married Luke." She came and sat heavily next to me. "I might not ought to have done that," she joked. "I may never get back on my feet. Seems like I'm bigger than I ought to be at seven months."

"I always heard travel's hard for a woman with child," I said.

She shrugged. "River travel don't seem near as hard as coming from Bledsoe County on foot. That's why I had to get us on this boat, even though we had to pay extra. I don't think my feet could've held out, walking."

"Why didn't you wait till the baby was born?"

"I reckon it might be worse to travel with a babe in arms than with one in my belly." She reached to rub the ball of her foot between her thumbs. "To be honest, I ain't so sure I had no choice but to go to Texas right now. I had to take the chance I got, whether it was the most comfortable one or not."

"Was Luke that set on going?" She just sat, rubbing her foot, for so long I figured she wasn't going to answer.

"How'd you come by that man of yours?" she said suddenly, her eyes on John David as he pulled on his oar.

Why did my heart take a jump and start to beat faster?

"We met at a barn raising."

"A barn raising." She sighed. "Nice and regular, like decent folk always do. Sometimes I'm jealous of you folk who do things nice and regular." She finally quit rubbing her foot and leaned back to look at me. "If I tell you something, you won't tell anybody, will you? Especially not ol' Barnes." I shook my head, and she gave a deep sigh. "I reckon it won't surprise you none to hear this baby ain't Luke's."

It did surprise me, but she didn't wait for an answer.

"That storekeeper and me, we got into a 'delicate situation'—that's what he called it. 'Trouble' is what I called it. Fellers like him, with standing in town and ambitions, they don't marry girls like me. So I blamed it on Luke, and my master bought out my bond as a wedding present and gave us money for a 'start in Texas,' he said. That's the money we used to buy our way into this party." She crossed her arms over her belly. "Old Barnes might not want me along if he knew that story, bad example for his daughters and all. He wasn't keen on taking lowborn folk like us in the first place, but Griffin talked him into it because he liked our money."

"I won't tell."

She smiled. "Luke's a good boy. He never even asked if the baby was his. He's been so good to me you'd think he's the one chose me out. I'm going to see to it we get everything in Texas that we ought to have. We'll be nice and regular, just like the rest of you folk."

Maybe it was because I felt so sick, or maybe it was that she had spilled out her secret so easily. For whatever reason, I opened my mouth and out fell my own secret.

"We ain't exactly nice and regular," I said. "I'm not a girl John David McKellar would've looked at twice if he hadn't been half-blind with whiskey. I'm a backwoods mountain wench, as his folks said. We got married at that barn raising, the same night we met."

Her eyebrows shot up. "Took advantage of him, did you?"

"You might say that."

Her heavy features cracked into a broad grin. "We ain't so different then, Maggie McKellar." She patted my arm. "Well, don't let it bother you, I say. Luke's happy. And your man seems more content than ol' Dan Hammond does with his nice, regular wife."

"Maybe it's like Ma used to say," I said. "Once the water's in the creek, nobody knows if it came from the spring or the wash tub."

Her laugh was hearty and deep, like a man's. "I reckon that's so."

❧ ❧ ❧

Suzy and I got on real well after that. I was glad, for Mrs. Barnes and Judith didn't seem to have much to say to either of us. Suzy said it was because they thought lowborn girls like us weren't good enough for talking to, but they never said a word to make me think so. I just figured they wanted to sit in the shelter of the cabin, while I spent most of my days close to the edge of the raft. My sick spells lingered on, though we'd been on the boat for several days. Even on the days when I wasn't leaving my meals in the river, I was plagued with a queasy feeling that wouldn't go away. John David blamed the flatboat.

"I figured you might get a little seasick, like you did on the ferry that time," he said. "But I sure didn't think you'd be this bad. Maybe we should have taken the Natchez Trace, after all."

Except for that, the trip was going as smooth as we could've hoped for. The weather was unusually good, Mr. Griffin said—a little cold some days, but mostly clear, and the rain we ran into was mild enough that most times we just kept going. The men learned to pilot the boat quickly, except for Luke. Our biggest scare came the only time he was allowed on the sweep. We were coming to a narrow sandbar, and Griffin called out orders to help Luke steer around it. But I reckon Luke got confused and pushed the sweep the wrong way, which made Griffin yell at him. Luke's hands froze on the pole while he swung his head back and forth, trying to figure what to do. Mr. Barnes, who was manning the oar nearest where Suzy and I were sitting, started to yell too.

"Idiot! You'll run us aground! Listen to Griffin, you halfwit!"

Suzy hopped to her feet, mighty quick for a woman heavy with child. "Don't you call him that!"

Luke heard her yell, and he whipped around toward us, pulling the sweep with him.

"Suzy?" There was a sickening lurch of the boat, and I heard a grinding sound at the same time a heavy jolt pitched me forward. I opened my eyes to see Griffin jumping over the side onto the sand.

"McKellar!" he yelled. "Get up there! Get him away from the sweep and straighten it out. Hammond! Moses! Come help me push off this sand before we're really stuck!"

It didn't take much, really, to free us from the sandbar, just a couple of hard pushes by the men on the bank and a couple of hard pulls by the men on the oars. Soon we were back floating free again, with John David on the sweep and Luke sitting, shamefaced, behind the cabin with his cow. He didn't lift his head, even when Suzy went to him. After a little while, she came back to sit with me.

"He ain't an idiot!" she fumed. "But he sure takes it to heart when somebody says it. Ol' Barnes ain't got the right to be calling him such."

"Anybody could get flustered up there," I agreed. She cut a sharp look at me.

"Not your John David."

I couldn't think of anything to say. It was true—John David had taken to working the boat like he was born to it. Griffin was always calling for him when something needed doing. The two of them took the canoe downriver in the mornings while the rest of us were breaking camp, and if the report came back that there were snags or tricky currents, like as not it would be John David who got the call to run the sweep while Griffin took the gouger to steer us around them. As we left the Cumberland for the Ohio River, John David was spending more and more of his days on the sweep. One night while I was laying out our blankets, Griffin came over and said something to John David, who shook his head. Griffin shrugged and went back to his own little fire.

"What was that about?" I asked.

"Nothing." He glanced at Dan Hammond, who was settling himself against a tree for first turn on guard duty, and then he leaned closer and spoke in a low voice. "Griffin offered to let me off guard duty tonight. He said I probably need a good night's sleep after spending all day on the sweep."

I looked at Dan too, and I thought how cold and lonely guard duty was bound to be, especially in the early hours of the morning, the shift John David always ended up with since he was the youngest of the men.

"Good," I said. "You need a whole night's sleep."

"I told him no," John David went on. "Don't want anybody thinking I'm trying to get special treatment. I already heard grumbling that Griffin favors me."

"Who said that?" He wouldn't tell me, though I figured I knew it, anyhow. I looked toward the canvas tent, but John David tapped my shoulder.

"Don't get crosswise with them," he warned.

"I won't! You don't have to keep telling me!"

I regretted my words right away. We hardly ever had the chance during the day to say anything to each other, and now I'd snapped at him like a peevish dog. But he let it pass. Tears gathered in my eyes as he pulled back the quilts so I could crawl into the pallet with him.

"I'm sorry," I said. He circled me with his arm and drew me to him. The warmth of his body was soothing, and I sighed as the day's tightness slowly dissolved.

"I know you're miserable, being sick all the time," he murmured. "Maybe it will pass soon. Just keep bearing up under it. Before you know it, we'll be off this boat and into our own featherbed in Texas."

His days were busy, but my time passed slowly, watching the trees and cabins on the river banks slide past us, day after day, always the same, whether they were along the Cumberland or the Ohio. Once in a while, we saw other boats like ours on the river, and sometimes at night we'd camp near another party of travelers. We'd all gather around the fire to compare stories and share wisdom about the dangers ahead on the river. Most of the talk, though, was about Texas, and I saw that the dream John David and I treasured wasn't just our dream—there were lots of folks like us, some young and newly married, some worn down from trying to raise families, all hoping for a start with a cabin and fields of corn.

Suzy and I talked about that a lot.

"Only thing is," she said one afternoon, "I ain't quite sure how we'll get set up. Luke's a good boy, and he works harder than anybody I ever saw, but that mule must've kicked the part of his brain that decides things. He can't seem to get two thoughts together for a plan. I don't see how we're going to build a cabin, even."

"Oh, folks will help." I was having a better afternoon. The weather was mild and bright, and I wasn't quite so queasy, so it was easier to be hopeful. Suzy, though, shook her head.

"Folks will be too busy with their own doings to bother with me and Luke."

"You know we'll help. John David's a pretty good hand with an ax."

She laughed. "Seems like your John David's pretty good at whatever he lays his hand to. I'd say you was mighty shrewd when you laid your trap for him at that barn raising."

Coming from anyone else, those words would sting. But not from Suzy. I laughed.

"He'll be pleased to trade off work. That's how it is in new country. Folks got to stick together."

"Well, I reckon." She glanced at Mrs. Barnes and her daughters, sitting with Judith under the shade Mr. Barnes had made from a flap of the canvas tent. "I ain't sure what we'll do for money, either. Luke's folks gave him that cow, and she'll drop a calf in late summer. But a cow and a calf don't make a herd." She sighed. "Oh, I'll think of something. What are you all going to do?"

"Raise corn. We got a bushel of seed corn from his pa, and we've been guarding it like solid gold. He's already planning on a field of corn, ten feet high—" I smiled at the memory. Suzy looked thoughtful.

"It might be a good thing to raise a little corn, for pone and mush. Reckon we'll be able to get seed once we're in Texas?"

"I'm sure the Mexicans would sell some."

"For a pretty penny, I'm sure." She sighed again. "We got to get the most we can out of every one. That money from my master won't hold out forever. We still got a load of supplies to get in Natchez, too. We didn't make the best of plans for this trip. Course, a lot of what's happened ain't stuff I planned on." She patted her belly. "I guess all a feller can do is make the best of what happens and take what chances come up."

※ ※ ※

We'd been on the boat for nearly a month, and there hadn't been any trouble, despite Griffin's warnings. The biggest excitement came when we went from the Ohio River into the Mississippi. Griffin himself ran the sweep at that point, barking orders to the men who were working the oars to keep us in the easiest part of the current as we joined into the brown waters of the bigger river. But though the Mississippi was wide and filled with snags, we didn't have any trouble, just days and days of drifting through the crooked course of the muddy water and nights of camping on banks that showed fewer and fewer signs of people. Sometimes as I sat by the railing I looked into the gray, shadowy woods bordering the river on the west. Arkansas Territory, Griffin said it was, untamed and filled with violence. The way he talked, it had the biggest collection of ruffians, criminals, and Indians this side of hell. I shivered a little as I stared at those bare trees, so silent and dark.

We began to meet boats going upstream as well, keelboats rowed by crews of shirtless men hunched over oars, and sometimes steamboats thrashing the water with big paddles. Peter Barnes kicked me more than once in his eagerness to get to the railing to wave his arms, trying to get the steamboat pilots to toot their whistles. I didn't fault him, though. All of us—except Judith and the slaves—were excited. Every evening now the talk was about the last part of the journey, Natchez and the overland stretch to Texas. We would refresh our supplies in Natchez because, Griffin warned, there would be long stretches with no stores or taverns on the way to Nacogdoches, where the men agreed we would stay while they scouted for a suitable spot to settle.

I noticed John David didn't say much during those talks, but I figured he was just tired from running the sweep all day. One night, though, when we'd gone to bed late because of talking and planning, I found out different.

"Sounds like we'll be in Nacogdoches most of the spring," he grumbled in a low voice. "They want to take time scouting for the perfect spot and applying for the grant. Barnes is a miller and Hammond is a blacksmith, so they're in no hurry. They don't have to worry about getting a crop in the ground, like I do. If I don't find a place quick and raise some corn, we'll be bad off next winter."

Fear twisted my stomach, and I rolled half over to look at him. "Tell them that!"

He sighed. "They wouldn't listen. I'm the youngest man in the party, and the last one they took on. I don't have much influence."

"Griffin would listen. He likes you."

"Soon as we're to Nacogdoches, Griffin's leaving," he told me. "His job will be done."

I stared at the dark sky in silence. I'd known Griffin's only duty was to get us to Texas, but it hadn't really sunk in that the day would come when we would be making our way against the wilderness without him. Somehow, that was more frightening than the thought of not raising a corn crop. I turned my face against John David's chest, and he slid his arm over me.

"Don't let it worry you," he said. "That's still a while off. Let's get there first, and then I'll figure something out."

But neither of us went to sleep for a long time that night.

Maybe it was the lack of sleep or maybe it was the worry, but the next morning I was the sickest I'd been yet, hanging over the side wall again and again. I reckon I was so pitiful Griffin felt sorry for me and gave John David a break from the sweep so he could come sit with me a while. With a knowing look, Suzy handed the damp rag to John David, and then she wandered to the other side of the boat where Luke was rowing. I rested my head back against the railing.

"You don't have to stay with me. I know he needs you up there to get around these snags."

He laid the rag across my forehead. "Hammond's got it. Griffin has us out of the main current so we're not moving so fast and he'll have more time to maneuver around them."

The next thing I remember is hearing a gunshot and feeling a sickening swing of the boat before John David pounced on me and roughly pushed me down on the raft with his body. I peered from under him and saw Dan Hammond slumped across the sweep, and the long pole was all that kept him from falling from the roof of the cabin onto the tent where the other women were sitting. Griffin cursed.

"Pirates!" he shouted. "Everybody get down! Luke! Get up there and get Hammond off the sweep! McKellar! The corner back there's caught a snag! Get over the side and see if you can loose it!"

"Stay down!" John David ordered as he slipped over the railing. I heard a soft splash as he hit the water.

"Luke!" Griffin yelled. "Get Hammond off that sweep!" Luke started to crawl toward the cabin, but Suzy grabbed his arm.

"No!"

"Luke!" Griffin roared. "Damn it, we've got to have that sweep free! They've got a canoe already in the water! They'll come on board and slit every throat! Get up there!" Luke made a jerking move to stand, pulling Suzy with him.

"No!" she screamed. "Somebody else can do it, Luke!"

Griffin swore again, using words I'm sure would've made Judith flinch if she hadn't been screaming and sobbing on the flat of the boat. "Get up there, Luke! Now!"

Another gunshot echoed across the water, and Suzy let go of Luke and fell to the raft. Free from her grasp, Luke sprinted to the roof of the cabin and gave Dan a push, sending him off the cabin and on to the tent, which buckled under his weight. Judith and the Barnes women scrambled from under it, staying low.

"Good boy!" Griffin yelled. "Now reach up and pull the sweep back to be straight!" There was another heavy lurch, and I heard John David call.

"It's free!"

"To the oars!" Griffin bellowed. "Pull like your life depends on it, because it does!" Mr. Barnes, Ben, and Moses all scrambled back to their feet and began to row, pulling hard and fast. Even little Peter jumped up, ready to grab an oar until his mother jerked him down by the back of his shirt. We were moving faster than we ever had, pulling away from the ambush.

"What about John David?" I called to Griffin. "He ain't back!"

Griffin didn't even turn around. "He said he's a good swimmer. We'll see how good."

I crawled along the wall to the back of the boat and pulled myself up on the railing enough to see John David was within a few feet.

"Slow down a little!" I yelled over my shoulder. "Wait for him!" I stretched out my hand to him, but he was still too far away. I leaned out farther, so far I could smell the mustiness of the water below me.

"Come on!" I urged. "Harder. Harder!"

He lowered his head beneath the surface and his arms flashed in and out of the water, and then his hand, wet and slippery, closed around mine. I grabbed it and pulled back with all my weight. His shoulders strained as he pulled himself to the boat and up the side. I clutched him around the waist and helped him roll over the wall, and he lay flat on his back, gulping in air.

"Oh, John David," I whispered, trembling with the fear of what might've happened but hadn't. I heard a deep moan and I quickly touched his face, his hair, his chest. But the moan wasn't coming from him. I swung around to see Suzy lying in a spreading puddle of blood.

"Suzy!" I crawled over and turned her head to me. Her eyes were wide in her pale face.

"I'm hit."

"Where?" She lifted her right arm and waved it toward her left side. I leaned over her and saw the blood was coming from a hole in her upper arm. Best I could tell, the hole went all the way through. Sickness surged through me, and I turned barely in time to keep from puking on her.

"I think we're pulling away!" Griffin yelled. "McKellar, you're back? Get the sweep so Luke can row." John David hurried past, and I caught at his wet pants.

"She's shot," I said stupidly. He leaned close to look.

"In the arm," he said, with a glance up at Luke. "Not life-threatening. Get her to the other side of the boat so Luke won't worry. We've got to put some distance between us and the pirates right now." He laid his hand, cold from the river, against my cheek before he rushed off to the sweep.

"Come on, Suzy." I lifted her shoulders so I could pull her. "Let's get away from this mess I made. You'll be all right. I'm taking care of you."

Chapter 17

Dan Hammond was dead. The bullet had gone into his neck, John David told me later, killing him instantly.

Griffin kept the men rowing hard until we were several miles downriver. When he felt the threat was well behind, he steered us onto a sandbar on the east bank. He took one look at Dan and then pulled the canvas back over him and came to look at Suzy. She was sitting against Luke, who, now that he realized she was hurt, seemed as dumb with shock as Judith was. Griffin undid the rag I'd tied around the wound and turned the arm carefully so he could see it from different views. Suzy was white and biting her lip against the pain.

"A clean shot," he said. "It went all the way through and missed the bone. It should heal all right if we keep it clean and wrapped."

"Aren't you going to cauterize it?" Mr. Barnes asked.

"What you going to do to her eyes?" Luke cried out.

Mr. Barnes gave a disgusted grunt. "Hush, you idiot!" Despite the pain it obviously caused her, Suzy sat up and pointed a finger at Mr. Barnes.

"Don't you call him that!"

Griffin stood. "You ever seen anybody cauterize a gunshot, Barnes?"

"No, but—"

"Well, I have, on hardened soldiers, fighting the Creeks with General Jackson. It's nothing I'd put a woman through, much less a pregnant woman. She'll be all right if we close it." He stalked to the edge of the boat. "Let's raise camp."

"We should bury Hammond first!" Mr. Barnes called after him.

Griffin glanced over his shoulder. "He ain't going nowhere. I'd rather set up before we're all tired from digging a grave."

So Dan's body lay on the boat covered with the canvas flap while the men made camp, but before they went to search out a grave site, Judith insisted they carry him into the Barnes' tent so he could be made proper for burying. The Barnes girls took Judith's baby walking on the river bank to keep her out of the way while I worked with the slave woman to start supper. I welcomed something to do, for it at least gave some escape from the pitiful sound of Judith's weeping. Still, I didn't answer right away when Griffin came back to camp and asked me to close Suzy's wound.

"I know you've been sick today," he said. "I'd ask someone else, but I figured you'd be best." I looked at her, lying against their bedding bundle, her face pale and her eyes closed.

"I'll do it."

It was the first time I'd seen Griffin smile since we left Nashville. "Good girl! I thought you could. McKellar told me you sewed up his face. This shouldn't be any worse. Let's do it before Luke gets back."

Even with a cup of whiskey in her, Suzy twitched so, Griffin could hardly hold her still for me to stitch up the wound. She cursed like a man and cried for me to stop until finally, mercifully, she swooned. I was trembling as I tied off the bandage. Griffin laid her on the ground and sat back on his heels.

"I saw worse in the war that came out all right. If we keep it clean—are you all right, Miz McKellar?"

I scrambled to my feet and stumbled to the edge of the woods, but there was nothing left in my stomach for retching. I took in deep breaths of the cool evening air. It's over, I told myself. The whiskey will make her sleep and in the morning she'll be better.

Footsteps rustled the leaves and I turned to see John David, worry creasing his forehead.

"Griffin said I ought to check on you."

Before I even knew I was going to do it, I'd thrown myself against him. I gave myself over to the trembling I felt outside and in, burying my face in his shirt and drawing in a long breath of him. His heart beat against my cheek, and I listened to the steady thump of it, fearful of how little it would take to make that thumping stop. I pressed closer, choking on a sob. His arms closed tight around me.

"Go on and cry if you need to," he murmured. "Nobody will know but me."

Almost at once, I was ashamed of myself. What did I have to cry about? Judith's husband was dead, and Suzy had a hole in her arm. I pushed away from him and swiped my hand over my eyes.

"I don't. I'm fine." Though every muscle ached to lean against him, taking in his strength, I made myself walk away, back to help finish supper. I couldn't give in to my weakness now, not just yet. I had to be a woman strong enough to get to Texas, for his sake.

❦ ❦ ❦

We buried Dan in a hurry, with no preaching or singing, only a short prayer by Mr. Barnes. The younger men stayed to fill the grave while the rest of us went back to camp and picked at supper. We lingered around the fire, not talking much—at least not until Judith and Mrs. Barnes had taken the children to bed in the tent and I was helping the slave woman wash up. Then the men's talk turned to the question I figured we'd all been turning over in our minds since Dan had fallen with the first gunshot. It was Ben Barnes who said it.

"Can we manage the boat with one less man?"

"We'll find out in the morning," Griffin said.

Mr. Barnes stared at him. "Tomorrow? You don't mean to have us back on the river tomorrow! That's too soon!"

"What would you have us do?" Griffin snorted. "Try to find someplace to hide on this sandbar? You can't let the first spot of trouble make you lose your nerve, Barnes."

Mr. Barnes bristled. "I'm thinking of Mrs. Hammond. She just lost her husband, you know. She needs time to grieve."

"We can't waste time. Mrs. Hammond will understand."

"She shouldn't have to!" Mr. Barnes said. "She's been robbed of her husband and means of support—"

"She wasn't robbed!" Griffin broke in. "Hammond knew the risks, as you all do. I told you back in Nashville this venture is risky."

"But this risk could've—should've—been avoided," Mr. Barnes continued. "If we'd been another fifty feet from the bank—"

"We might've been sucked into an eddy in the main current, and the boat would've gone down. We'd all be dead now, instead of just Hammond," Griffin said.

Mr. Barnes started to say something, but he shut his mouth quick. He glanced over to where Suzy was sleeping.

"What about Mrs. Morgan? Surely you won't make her travel with a fresh wound."

Griffin poured himself more coffee. "It's a straight-through wound, and it's covered. It may cause her pain for a few days, but—"

"I believe if it were my wife," Mr. Barnes said slowly and distinctly, "I'd feel better if she saw a doctor rather than depending on a river guide whose only experience is treating men on a battlefield." Luke jerked his head up to look at Mr. Barnes and then Griffin and back to Mr. Barnes. "Especially since she's with child. I'd feel better if I knew she and the baby suffered no harm."

"Well, yeah," Luke said. "I don't want Suzy to have no harm."

"She don't," Griffin said.

"Still—" Mr. Barnes let the word hang in the air like a puff of smoke.

"I want her to see a doctor," Luke said, getting to his knees.

"Griffin, didn't you say we're a week or less out of Natchez?" John David asked. "You can take her to a doctor there, Luke."

"A lot can happen in a week," Mr. Barnes said. "I've seen perfectly healthy cows die of blackleg in less than a week."

"Jackass!" Griffin spat, but Luke was leaning forward.

"I want her to see a doctor tomorrow!" he cried.

"She can't see one tomorrow," Griffin said. "There ain't a town within floating distance tomorrow."

"The next day, then!" Luke cried. "I don't want to wait no week! I don't want Suzy to die!"

"Where's the nearest town?" Mr. Barnes asked. "As our hired guide, you should know, I should think." Griffin's shoulders suddenly sagged.

"Arkansas Post. But there's no guarantee she'd get to see a doctor. There used to be one, but he may have moved upriver to Little Rock, like most folks have. And it's miles out of our way."

"How close?" Luke demanded. "Could we get her there in a day?"

Griffin shook his head. "We'd have to take her in the canoe up the White River and cross a swampy area on foot. It'd be rough on her, worse than a week riding down the Mississippi on a flatboat."

"How long would it take?" Mr. Barnes asked. Griffin stared into his coffee.

"A couple of days. The White River cutoff is just ahead."

"Let's go there!" In his excitement, Luke had scooted so close to the fire the leather of his shoes smelled hot.

"He said it's miles out of the way," John David started. "Natchez is on the way, and we could—" Mr. Barnes interrupted.

"Would you wait a week to get to Natchez, McKellar, if Mrs. McKellar was wounded?"

"Yeah!" Luke said, swinging around toward John David. "Maggie ain't the one who's shot! It's Suzy!"

"Calm down!" John David said. "You're about to wallow yourself into the fire!"

Luke moved back so he was sitting a little outside the group. "I don't want no harm to come to Suzy." I could swear his voice cracked like he was about to break into tears. For a while, no one spoke.

"What do you think, Luke?" Mr. Barnes said. "Natchez is a week away, and Arkansas Post is two days."

"Two rough days," Griffin added. Mr. Barnes leaned toward Luke.

"What do you want to do, Luke?"

Luke twisted a lock of hair near his temple. "I want—I want—I—"

"What are you asking him for?" Griffin demanded. "He can't make up his own mind. She's the brains of that pair."

"I can too make up my mind," Luke pouted. "I want to take her to the closest place."

Mr. Barnes sat back with a smile. "So, Arkansas Post. I agree with you."

"I don't," Griffin said flatly. "What about you, McKellar?"

John David's voice was low. "I'm for keeping on to Natchez."

"That's two for and two against," Mr. Barnes said. "To break the tie, we ought to look at who's supported most of this trip. I paid for eight folk, and Morgans paid for three. McKellar paid for two. It's only fair to go with what Morgan and I want, since we paid the biggest part."

Griffin suddenly stood and tossed what was left of his coffee on the fire.

"Fine. We'll start for Arkansas Post in the morning." He turned and stalked toward the boat. Mr. Barnes watched him, a smug smile tugging the corners of his mouth. He turned back to look at us the way he always looked at Moses.

"Since Hammond is dead, we'll all take longer turns on guard duty," he said. "I'll take first turn, and Ben will be next. McKellar, you take the early morning shift, and Morgan, you take last shift."

John David jerked at the quilts as we stretched out our pallet.

"Barnes is a blockhead!" he grumbled. "Why waste time going into Arkansas Territory? We'll never get to Texas in time to get a grant and plant some corn."

"What will we do?" I asked.

He sighed. "Wait for them to get back from Arkansas Post, I reckon."

❧ ❧ ❧

Suzy was none too happy to hear the plan.

"I don't need to see no doctor, Luke!" she argued. But for once, there was nothing she could say to sway him. John David and I walked to the water's edge to watch as Luke helped her into the canoe while Griffin held the other end steady. When they were all settled in, John David stepped forward to give them a push into the river.

"Wait!" Suzy turned back toward us, tipping the canoe dangerously. "I'd shore feel better if you was with me, Maggie. Just to have another woman along, you know."

"Oh, I can't—"

She awkwardly shifted to her knees, rolling the canoe even further. "Please? Men don't understand, not like a woman. Come with me, Maggie!"

If I expected John David to give me the excuse not to go, I was disappointed. "It might comfort her to have another woman there," he said. "Why don't you go on? Let's get you a bedroll."

I followed him back to camp.

"I don't want to go!" I argued as he tucked the ends of one blanket into a roll. "Having to camp with two strange men, without you—"

"Don't worry about that. Griffin will watch out for you." He leaned to speak in my ear as he handed me the roll. "Don't you see? He can push them to come back quicker if you're along."

I didn't let go of the sides of the canoe the whole time we were on the Mississippi, though my hands ached from gripping the edges. I'd always thought there was nothing much keeping me out of the water while on the flatboat; I could hardly bear the sight of the water lapping against the sides of the canoe, only inches below my fingertips. When we started across the current to get out of the Mississippi and into the White River, I sucked in a quick breath that ended up sounding a lot like a whimper. Luke grinned.

"What's the matter, Maggie? You scared of falling in? Why, Griffin would pluck you back out of the water like a cat would a kitten."

"Hush up, Luke, and hold steady on the right," Griffin ordered. "We're cutting in just ahead."

The White River was some better than the Mississippi, not nearly so wide or fast. There was a closed-in feeling to it, though, that made the back of my neck prickle. All around us were thick woods, right up to the edge of the water and sometimes even in the water, with spooky little nubs of trunk sticking up all around. I wondered if the silence was cover for the Indians and wild white men Griffin said peopled Arkansas Territory. I half feared another shot would come from the trees, and I more than half hoped if one did, that it would be Luke who was hit and not Griffin. That was especially true the first night, when we camped in those woods. I couldn't sleep. I must have turned over a half-dozen times before I heard Griffin's voice through the dark.

"Get some rest, Mrs. McKellar. You'll need it tomorrow."

The last part of the trip was on foot, through a shallow swamp. Every step was a struggle, sometimes ankle-deep in the muck, sometimes into a hole that swallowed my legs up to the knee. By afternoon, I was so tired I didn't even bother trying anymore to lift the hem of my skirt out of the water. Tired as I was, though, I was more worried about Suzy. Her face was red, and she puffed loudly with every slow step.

"How much farther?" I called to Griffin, who was towing the canoe.

"It don't matter. We ain't stopping now till we get there."

"Can you hold out?" I asked Suzy. She nodded, like she didn't want to waste the effort to speak. I glanced back at Luke, who was sloshing along, whistling. "Here." I moved closer to her. "Lean on me, if you want."

"You're a good girl, Maggie."

I staggered a little under the added weight as she put her arm over my shoulders.

"We'll make it," I mumbled, as much to myself as to her. "We'll get something hot to eat and a place to stretch out, maybe a real bed. How long's it been since you slept in a real bed, Suzy?"

We must've been a pitiful sight walking down the rutted streets of Arkansas Post, leaning on each other, our hair pulling loose and our skirts caked with mud. But nobody much was there to see us, even at the rundown frame hotel where Griffin stopped. The smell of roasted meat was strong, making my belly suddenly ache with hunger.

"Let's eat," Griffin said. "Then we'll see if the doctor's still in town."

Suzy wanted me with her while the doctor checked her wound, so I sat on a small stool in the corner of the dingy room while she sat on the bed. The whole thing was over quickly, just the doctor picking up her bare arm gingerly and looking at both sides of the wound.

"It looks fine," he said. "There's no swelling or red streaks, which would mean taking off the arm. Keep an eye out for those." Suzy shot a nervous glance at me.

"How about the baby? Reckon any harm's come to it?" The doctor cleared his throat as his eyes flicked toward her bulging belly and then back to his bag on the little table by the bed.

"Of course, I can't say for sure, but if you have no pains I'd say everything's fine. I suggest you stay off your feet for a few days to be sure." He fumbled with his bag and went to the door. "If there's nothing else, I'll report your condition to Mr. Morgan."

I reckon the only part of what the doctor said that Luke paid mind to was that part about Suzy staying off her feet, because as soon as we came downstairs to the tavern, he hurried her right back up. He'd hired out the room, he told us, and Suzy should get to bed.

"How much will it cost?" she gasped.

"It don't matter," he said. "You need rest. Goodbye, Maggie." She grabbed his arm.

"Luke! She can't camp with Griffin!"

He looked at me. "Why not?"

Suzy gave a short laugh. "It ain't decent." She gave him a push. "Maggie will stay with me. You'll camp with Griffin."

"Suzy!" he whimpered.

"Go on," she ordered. "It's just for a night. You'll be all right." He gave us one last long-faced look before Suzy shut the door and turned to me. "Well, Maggie, I reckon you'll get your night in a real bed, if you don't mind sharing with me."

The bed was a tad narrow for two grown folk, especially with her belly full of baby, but to tell the truth, it felt so good I didn't care that I was hanging on the edge all night. I woke the next morning more rested than I could remember being since we'd left Nashville. When we came down the stairs, Luke called to us from a table.

"Griffin done went back to the boat," he said.

My good mood faded. "Without us?"

"That doctor said Suzy needs rest," Luke said firmly. "I told Griffin I wasn't going nowhere till she's had some. I hired out the room for the rest of the week."

"No!" Suzy swayed a little and Luke jumped to his feet and helped her to a chair. She turned on him. "We can't afford that!" she hissed.

"We got money," Luke said loudly. "That doctor said you need rest, so that's what you're getting. Have some mush, and then it's back to bed with you."

He hustled her up the stairs before I'd finished my mush, and I sat alone, wondering how I'd pay for it, or for the other meals I'd need till Griffin came back. The decision to send me along had been made so quickly we hadn't thought about money. Of course, we hadn't thought I'd be staying more than overnight, either. I wondered how aggravated John David would be when Griffin showed up at the sandbar alone. I stirred the thin, pale mush, and suddenly bile rose in my throat. I barely got out to the corner of the porch before it came up. Shaking, I leaned back against the tavern. Still sick, too—why was I still sick? I hadn't been on the water for two days now.

A memory flashed into my mind—Ma, bent over the back fence, losing her breakfast just like this. And always not long after, she'd get that swelling in her belly that meant another little one was on the way.

My whole body suddenly felt cold. That can't be, I told myself. John David's been careful this whole time. It must be that the mush was bad, or that I needed more time to adjust back to being on land. It couldn't be anything else.

But the next morning just the smell of the mush sent me rushing outside, and as I leaned my forehead against the rough boards, I wondered if it might be true, if maybe, somehow, John David hadn't been careful enough. How could a girl know for sure? I wondered, laying my hand over my belly. It was flat as ever, giving no sign if anything was different. Still, I'd never been one for a weak stomach.

I determined I'd talk to Suzy about it. But there was no chance to be alone with her, not with Luke hanging around like a loyal hound until bedtime when Suzy ordered him out. Once we were alone, I stood by the wash basin, clutching my hands and trying to get the first word out of my mouth. She grunted as she settled herself.

"You coming to bed?"

"In a minute." My face was burning hot. "Suzy, how did you know—about the baby, I mean?"

She stared at me blankly for a minute, but then her face began to pull together in a wise pucker. I turned away, fiddling with the chipped edge of the basin.

Her voice was soft. "When was the last time you had a monthly?"

I thought back on all that had happened—the trip down the rivers, leaving the Spotted Hog, all of it free of my womanly health. "I ain't sure. Before we left Nashville."

"A month, then? Six weeks?"

"Maybe. I ain't sure." But I was sure. A strange mix of fear and delight flooded through me. My knees felt weak, and I went to sit with her on the bed.

"Course, you can't know for sure till the baby quickens," she was saying, "but between the sickness and your monthly being so late, I'd say there's a chance of it, a real good chance."

My feelings shifted as fast as the shape of a windblown cloud. A baby! John David's child, a true sign of our bond as husband and wife everyone would see as my belly grew over these next months. But even as I glowed with that thought, I feared he'd be angry that I was adding another burden to his load, a mighty heavy burden. Or would he be pleased to hear he was going to have a son? Because it was a boy, I could just feel it—

"Come on, Maggie." Suzy was tapping my arm. "Get some rest. You'll need it. Believe me, I was never so tired in my life as I've been these last months. Griffin ought to be back tomorrow, and we'll go back to the boat. You'll have a little time to think how you want to give your news to John David."

Chapter 18

Griffin didn't return the next day, and it was early evening of the day after when he finally came in the tavern. I knew something was wrong soon as I saw him, and then Mr. Barnes stepped through the door and held it for Judith and her baby. Suzy flashed a quick look at me.

"We're a mite surprised to see you here, Judith," she said. "And you, Mr. Barnes."

"Mrs. Hammond no longer wishes to continue to Texas," Mr. Barnes said. "She has come to Arkansas Post in hopes of catching a steamboat back to Tennessee."

"Yore quitting?" Luke exclaimed.

"This is not healthy land," Judith said. "All this murky water and rot and foul smells! I don't want Baby to get sick from the miasma. We'll be better off back home with family."

The barman brought food, and we ate in silence. Judith picked at her food, and after a while, she asked the barman about getting a room so she could get the baby to bed. Once she was gone, Griffin handed me something wrapped in a rag.

"McKellar sent this," he said.

It was a handful of coins. I smiled as I wrapped them back in the rag and slid it inside my bodice. He was thinking of me.

"Are we going back to the boat tomorrow?" Suzy asked, with a little smile around the corners of her mouth as she looked at me. "I'm plenty rested now."

Mr. Barnes leaned back in his chair. "I believe we shouldn't leave until we're certain Mrs. Hammond has made the arrangements to get back to her family."

"I'm not waiting around for a steamboat," Griffin said. "No telling when one will be through here."

"We won't abandon her in this devilish territory. Not after her husband has been ripped from her."

Griffin slammed his fist on the table. "Barnes! How many times do I have to tell you? Any venture like this has risks—one of those risks is death. I'm sorry for the woman, but you can't hold me responsible for Hammond's death."

Mr. Barnes let his chair fall forward again with a thud.

"You are responsible! We paid you to be our guide! We trusted you to lead us in a way that would be safe, not to have one of us picked off the roof of the boat like a duck on a pond!"

"You make it sound like target practice," Luke grinned.

"Shut up, you nincompoop!" Mr. Barnes snapped. "My point is, Griffin, we contracted with you for expert guidance to Texas, and in my opinion, expert guidance includes safety. I'm wondering how I can be sure we won't have some other mishap."

"You can't," Griffin said sourly. "No expert can get rid of every risk. I can't make your path to Texas smooth and trouble-free, Barnes."

Mr. Barnes sat back and twirled his cup in a little circle.

"Then I am no longer satisfied with your services, Mr. Griffin."

There was a long silence. I glanced at Suzy, who frowned. Griffin's face, though, was expressionless as he stared at Mr. Barnes.

"What are you saying?" he asked.

"I'm saying you've failed us. I'm saying I don't want to take the risk of losing one of my children because of some poor decision you might make. Mrs. Barnes and I talked it over. We aren't going on to Texas with you. We're pulling out of the party."

Griffin cursed. "That leaves just McKellar and Luke. You know I can't run a flatboat with two men."

"That's for you to work out with them. I'm making arrangements in the morning to find means back up river to Chickasaw Bluffs. I'll also expect you to refund my money then, since you didn't get us to Texas." He stood. "Good evening."

No one spoke after he left. Griffin poured himself another whiskey and sat back so that his face was out of the candlelight. Luke laid his chin on his arms, still sulking over the insult from Mr. Barnes. Finally,

Suzy crossed her arms over the top of her belly and sighed.

"Well? You can't work the boat with two men. So what do we do?"

"Maybe you folks need to pull out, too."

"Me and Luke ain't got anyplace else to go. We're counting on one of them land grants."

"John David will want to go on," I said, sure as if he was sitting here. Griffin didn't answer for a long time.

"We'd have to hire help to keep on the river," he said, finally.

"We ain't got the money to hire help," Suzy put in quickly. Griffin leaned forward and set his cup on the table.

"Just as well, I guess. I don't know who in this town could be trusted to come along without cutting our throats. I'll go back and see what McKellar thinks." He left us in silence, with only the candle flame sputtering in its puddle of wax.

"Curse that high and mighty Barnes!" Suzy said. She leaned over to poke Luke. "Go on, Luke. Keep an eye on Griffin tonight. Make sure he don't jump in the river or nothing. We got to have him to get us on to Texas."

※ ※ ※

Griffin said there was no use of us going back to the boat with him since we wouldn't be going on with it, so we stayed in Arkansas Post while he went to talk to John David. Before leaving, he put up a frame for a half-face shelter in a grove of trees on the edge of town and gave us orders to cover it. While Luke cut cedar and cypress branches, Suzy and I laid them over the frame. It wasn't a pleasant morning. I was sick again, Suzy was cross, Luke was still pouting, and the weather was muggy with the threat of rain.

"That doctor must've run up his price since we're strangers," Suzy grumbled. "Don't know why we bothered to see him, anyhow. You done fine sewing it up. And that hotel bill—even with you paying a share, it took more than I expected. If we ain't going on the flatboat, we'll lose the cow. They can't get her across the river in that canoe. We'll have to start out buying cows, and we don't have near as much money as we did have. I don't see how we're going to make it, Maggie, needing something to live on, and with the baby coming soon—" Her voice quivered. "Sometimes I'm just so scared I don't hardly know if I can keep on going."

I laid my hand on her shoulder. "I know what you mean."

"Oh, do you?" Her voice was suddenly harsh. "How could you? You, with that clever man of yours who's so good at everything he lays his hand to, who makes the plans so you don't have to worry about nothing. You got a bag of seed corn that will bring you money come end of summer, but if the market's bad, at least you'll have something to eat. You still got most of the year before you'll be birthing your baby, long enough to be settled someplace, not by the road in some camp. Don't tell me you know how I feel, cause you don't!"

Luke had heard her angry voice and was running back from the edge of the river, hatchet held high.

"It's all right, Luke!" I called. "Don't run with that hatchet!" He stopped and stared at us, and when Suzy waved her hand toward him, he started slowly back, looking over his shoulder at us every few steps.

"Maybe I don't know your troubles," I said, "but you don't know mine, either. We ain't exactly been skipping on a primrose path so far."

She was silent as I went on weaving the branches together.

"I shouldn't take it out on you," she said after a while. I shrugged.

"No hard feelings."

"Luke's a good boy. I ain't ever seen anybody work harder, and I know he was trying to take care of me when he put us in that hotel. But, my God, Maggie—" Her voice broke, and a fat tear slid down her mottled cheek. "How are we gonna make it?"

❧ ❧ ❧

It was early evening of the third day before the men finally got back to town, staggering from the weight of the goods crammed into the canoe. I could hardly control the urge I felt to run to John David. I waited with my hands folded across my belly while Luke helped them settle the canoe along the edge of the shelter, and then John David came toward me. He was sweaty and dirty from the swamp, but I was practically quivering with the desire to throw my arms around him.

"You shaved off your beard," I said instead.

He rubbed his hand over his cheek. "Wasn't much else to do."

"After coming through that swamp, you must be hungry."

He glanced toward the fire, where Suzy was dishing up supper for Luke and Griffin, all of them carefully keeping their backs to us. Luke sneaked a glance at us, but Suzy pulled sharply on his ear and he quickly ducked his head. John David turned back to me, his eyes crinkled in a smile, and slipped his arms around me, pulling me close.

"Did you miss me?" he whispered. I stretched to kiss him, pressing my body against his, but though I could feel he was pleased by my welcome, he laughed softly and pushed me back enough to be decent.

"That's a gratifying answer," he said. "But let's don't forget ourselves, Maggie." Taking my hand, he led me to sit with the others.

"This is all of it," Griffin was saying. "Barnes hired a fellow with a keelboat, so they've already started upstream. There was another boatload of folks camped on the sandbar when I got back, so me and Barnes sold all the livestock to them. Here." He pulled a small bag of coins from his pocket and handed it to Suzy. "It's a fair price."

"What's that?" Luke said.

"He sold the cow," Suzy said. Luke looked stunned.

"She's gone?" His lip trembled. "Pa gave her to me."

"Oh, hush up," Suzy said. She slipped the little bag inside her bodice. "So, what's the plan now, Griffin?"

They had decided we'd take the Southwest Trail to cut across Arkansas Territory to Texas. We'd have to go upriver to Little Rock, and Griffin reckoned the best way was to hire another canoe if we could find one, since the swamp was so thick we'd never get there afoot. In Little Rock, we'd buy mules to pack our goods, and we ought to be able, he said, to lay in supplies of food there.

I leaned against John David, only halfway listening to Griffin's plans. I was trying to work out a plan of my own. Though I'd thought of little else in the days since I'd found out I was with child, now that the time was come, I couldn't think of a good way to put such a private thing into words, even to the man who had fathered that child. I sure didn't want anybody else around to hear it, in case I was clumsy in the telling—or in case he didn't take the news so well. Maybe I could ask him to help me haul some water—

"The thing that worries me most," John David said, "is the women having to walk all the way. Especially you, Suzy. Going overland will be awful rough for you and the baby. No offense meant, but you're likely to slow us down, too. If the choice was mine to make, Luke, I'd have her go back up river with Judith and then fetch her and the baby once I had things settled."

My heart jumped into my throat as Suzy gave me a sideways glance. "It ain't your choice, though, is it?" she said.

"I didn't mean any offense—just saying what I would do. A trail through the wilderness is no place for a woman with child."

"No two ways about it," Griffin agreed. "It'll be rough. Maybe we can find a cart or wagon of some kind in Little Rock. Might be we could get by with only two mules, instead of three or four."

"How much would a cart cost, though?" Suzy asked. Griffin shrugged.

"I don't know. We'll have to see when we get there."

※ ※ ※

They went into town early the next morning to see about a second canoe. Luke wandered down to the river to fish, and I was glad, because I could hardly move without bringing the taste of bile to my mouth. Suzy brought a damp cloth to lay across my forehead.

"You ain't told him yet, have you?" she asked.

"He'll send me up river with Judith," I moaned. She clucked her tongue.

"You ain't going to be able to keep it from him much longer. Even Luke's starting to notice you're always sick. Your man's got eyes, and clever as he is, he'll put it together sooner or later."

For some stupid reason, tears rolled down my cheeks. "I want to stay with you all. I don't want to go back with Judith."

"I know." She squatted beside me and wiped my face gently. "I wonder if chamomile tea would settle your stomach. Ma always used it for sick stomach. Course, it ain't the same kind of sickness, but it might help."

"Reckon so?"

She smiled as she wiped my forehead again, and I loved her more than I'd ever loved my own ma.

"It's worth a try, ain't it?" she said. "At least it might help you keep it hid till we're on the road and it's too late for him to send you back."

"What a husband don't know won't hurt him," I said slowly.

She laughed. "What's that?"

"Just something somebody told me once. But where will I get chamomile around here?"

She pondered for a while, and then she grinned.

"Judith Hammond! I'll wager she's got some. The way she's always worrying over that baby, it wouldn't surprise me none. Surely she'd share if you told her your news."

I wasn't quite so sure as I started to town later that morning, alone, for Suzy said her feet were achy and she didn't want to make the trip. It was breezy and chilly, as March can be early on, and threatening yet another storm. I pulled my cloak close and wondered how to ask Judith for the chamomile. Probably only ten words had passed between us on the whole trip down the rivers. And I was sure she remembered, same as I did, that it was John David that Dan replaced on the sweep the day he was killed.

She looked surprised when she peered out the door at me, but she let me in. Her baby was sitting on a blanket she had spread on the rough wooden floor.

"Baby looks well," I said. She motioned for me to sit on the bed. "Any word on when you'll be able to catch a steamboat?"

"They say the *Eagle* should be coming from Little Rock any time." She jumped up as the baby started to crawl off the blanket. "No, no, Baby! This floor is filthy! Stay on the blanket!" The baby started to fuss, and Judith picked her up and rocked her back and forth. She looked at me over the baby's head. "Why are you here?"

I stared at my hands in my lap. "I wondered—Suzy said you might have some chamomile I could have. I'll pay for it," I added quickly.

"Chamomile?"

"For my stomach. Suzy thought it might help. I'm—I—" I clenched my hands together and took a steadying breath. "I'm going to have a baby, myself, see."

She stared at me, still rocking her baby. "Your troubles are just beginning, then," she murmured.

She gave me the chamomile and wouldn't take any money for it, though I offered more than once. I finally took it and left without paying, just to be away from that dark, cheerless room. Stepping outside was little relief, though. The wind had picked up and thick clouds hung low in the sky. I hurried along the road, trying to get back to camp before the rain came in. I couldn't shake the gloom that had settled over me in Judith's room. 'Your troubles are just beginning,' she'd said. Of course a woman had troubles carrying a baby. Just look at this sickness, and Suzy's swollen feet, and most surely the pain that gripped a woman's body during the birthing itself. Somehow, though, I was sure none of that was what she meant. Her face, pale and sad, floated through my mind like some kind of ghost, and I actually let out a little shriek when thunder boomed close by.

"Maggie! Watch where you're going!" John David was laughing as he grabbed my shoulders and steered me around a muddy spot in the field. I looked up, and a fat raindrop hit the side of my nose. "Here it comes!" he called. "Come on, we can beat it!"

We ran the last bit to the shelter, and John David jerked up the blanket flap to let me go through. But I'd barely taken a step inside before I stopped. He bumped against me as he tried to come in.

"Move—" But he stopped dead still too.

The ground was littered with golden kernels, spilling from the wide open mouth of our bag of seed corn.

"Oh, my God." John David's voice was faint. He stepped around me and dropped to his knees by the bag, digging frantically through the kernels. "It's not here!"

I suddenly felt light-headed and I grabbed the frame of the shelter to steady myself. Nothing else of our goods seemed to be bothered, but it looked like a windstorm had gone through everything belonging to Luke and Suzy. Cold rain hit my cheek as Griffin pulled the blanket aside to come in. John David had picked up the bag of corn and dumped it, scattering it with his hands.

"It's not here!" he croaked. Griffin took a quick look at the place. "Money?"

"Everything we had." John David clasped his hands together over the back of his head. "The money from selling my horse, our wages—oh, God—"

"Morgans are gone?" Griffin turned and went back out in the rain. John David stood and turned to me. His face was pale.

"Why did you tell her?"

"I—I didn't."

"You did! How would she have known where to look?"

"I didn't tell her!"

His grip on my arm was tight. "Damn it, Maggie! How could you be so stupid?"

Griffin came back in. "The canoe's gone. They're trying to get away on the river. They must've gone down river, because she can't row with that arm and I don't think one man could push against the current. They can't be too far. We might be able to catch them."

John David pushed past me to follow Griffin outside, and their voices quickly grew fainter. I stood stone still, holding to the frame of the shelter, feeling sick and knowing it had nothing to do with the baby. How could she? After everything we'd been through together—I sank to the ground by the pile of scattered corn. All of it, gone. All that was left were the three coins in my pocket and whatever John David had left in the little bag. There couldn't be much. He hadn't kept out much in the first place. We didn't want folks thinking we had much of anything—

I scooped up a handful of the bright kernels and sifted them between my fingers. His precious seed corn. The stuff of our dreams, ready to go in the ground, and there was ground waiting to cover it, rich ground that grew grass up to a horse's belly. But how were we going to get there? A lump rose in my throat, but I forced myself to swallow it. I would not cry—I wouldn't. Slowly, I scooped up the handful of corn again and let it trickle back into the bag. Then, quickly, with purpose, I scooped and scraped and picked until every kernel was back in place, and then I sewed the bag shut.

?► ?► ?►

It rained the rest of the day. John David and Griffin didn't come back until after dark, and I could tell by their silence and the sag of John David's shoulders the search had been for nothing. I didn't speak, either. It would do no good. I handed them each a bowl of hot beans over corn cakes, and while Griffin dived in on his with appetite, John David only pushed his around some with the spoon before setting it down and leaning forward to rest his head in his hands. I put another chunk of wood on the fire, and then I moved to sit in the darkness at the back of the shelter.

"Eat something, McKellar," Griffin said softly. "We done the best we could."

John David didn't raise his head. "We can't go to Texas. Thirty bucks for a mule—I don't have it."

"I'll loan you money for a mule. Pay me back once you get a crop."

"A mule's just the beginning. We've got to have something to live on while we're waiting for the crop."

"I know you're good for it," Griffin started, but John David finally looked up.

"I don't want to start out in debt." Griffin silently poured himself some coffee and sat looking at John David while he blew across the top to cool it.

"What will you do, then?"

It was a long time before John David answered. "Find work, I reckon. There's always somebody willing to pay for a strong back."

They didn't talk anymore, and after a while Griffin drained his coffee cup and took his bedroll to the far side of the shelter, where Suzy and Luke should have been. I came out of the shadows to tend the fire and pick up John David's untouched bowl of food. He was still staring into the fire when I crawled between our blankets.

"You coming to bed?" I called, softly, so as not to bother Griffin.

"In a while."

I lay down, flat on my back, looking at the shadows of the firelight on the roof of the shelter, my hands resting on my belly. Sighing, I closed my eyes and settled myself for what I knew would be the longest night of my life.

※ ※ ※

Griffin left the next morning after breakfast. He stood for a while with his hands in his pockets, watching as John David finished eating.

"Sorry I didn't get you to Texas, McKellar," he said, finally. "I like you. Barnes said you were too young to be reliable, but you never shirked in anything I asked you to do." He paused. "I wondered if you might be interested in working as a guide with me. We could pick up another party easy enough, there's so many people crazy to get to Texas. You could make a good bit of money."

I looked up from the basin where I was washing dishes. John David was shaking his head.

"What would I do with Maggie?"

"Send her upriver with Hammond's wife."

"Oh, no!" I said, before I could stop myself. They both looked at me, and I quickly ducked my head again.

"It wouldn't be for long," Griffin said. "You could work the season with me until next winter, get a nice little sum together, and then go back for her."

My heart grew heavier with every word. It made good sense for him to go. And angry as he was, it would be easy for him to go.

"We don't have money for the fare, or anybody she could stay with," John David said. I looked up, a tiny twig of hope sprouting in my bosom. "We'll just stay and see what I can get here. We got this far. It might not take me so long to get enough to go on from here."

Griffin was looking at me. "Maybe not." He pulled his hand from his pocket and dumped a pile of coins on the seat of the saddle. "I'm giving back this part of what you paid me."

"No, you don't," John David started, but Griffin wouldn't listen.

"It's fair. I gave money back to Barnes. I'll keep the portion for getting you this far. But I didn't get you all the way there, so I ain't keeping your money." He stuffed his hat on his head, low over his eyes. "Good luck, McKellar."

Neither of us said anything for a while after he'd left. John David sat slumped over his cup of coffee. But when I went to pick up his empty bowl, his hand closed over mine. I knelt beside him.

"I didn't tell Suzy about the money," I said. "I swear I didn't. She must have been trying to take some corn. She said once it might be a good idea to raise some."

"Such a small hand," he said softly. But that was all. I studied his face as we sat in silence. He was still a handsome man, even with that scar across his cheek, but there was a worn look to him that hadn't been there the first time I'd looked into his face at Charlie Huckett's spring. I gently pushed the hair back from his forehead.

"Thank you for not sending me back with Judith."

"You'd be better off, instead of being stuck in a half-face camp in the wretched middle of nowhere." His eyes met mine for the first time since we'd discovered the money was gone. "But I couldn't lose everything."

My throat tightened. "We won't get corn planted this year, will we?"

He shook his head. "If wages are the same here as in Nashville—which is not for sure—it'll be well into summer before we have enough to get a mule. And we have to have money to pay for some place to live. We can't stay in this camp."

"We can. It don't bother me—" But he cut me off.

"It's not what I want for you." He sighed, like a man twice his age, and got to his feet. "I'll go see what kind of work needs doing in Arkansas Post. You might go through that stuff Morgans left and see if anything's worth keeping."

I stood for a long time after he left, staring at the tumbled packs. She'd been in such a hurry to get away with our money that she hadn't cared to leave behind most of what they'd brought from Tennessee. I finally opened one of the bundles, and tears burned in my eyes as I drew out a soft blanket, meant for swaddling a baby. The softness caught against my calloused fingers as I held it to my face, and I couldn't say whether my tears were from hating her or mourning her.

"Why'd you do it, Suzy?" I whispered. "Why did you have to take away our chance when your chance came up? We could've helped each other. You know we would have."

But now we wouldn't. I laid the little blanket aside to keep. Its softness would wrap my baby, not hers.

Chapter 19

John David's news wasn't encouraging when he came back from town. Most business had moved upriver to Little Rock when the capital of Arkansas Territory moved there a couple of years back. For what work he could find, the pay wasn't much. Just as he'd thought, it would take most of the summer to get enough to outfit us with a mule and the supplies we'd need. I counted it up in my mind. By the end of summer, I'd be getting heavy with the child—not in a good way to take off walking to Texas.

"Ain't there anything better?" I asked.

He shrugged. "The best pay I heard about was on a keelboat. The captain's looking to fill out his crew. He's taking supplies to a place called Fort Smith, in the middle of the territory. I could make as much in one trip up and back as I could working all summer here. But that's mighty hard work."

I nodded, remembering the keelboat crews we'd seen on the Mississippi, straining to push the boat against the current at hardly more than a crawl.

"I heard they need a cook, too." He gave a short laugh. "If I could cook worth a flitter, I'd sign for that. It's not nearly so hard on the back." He chewed his cornpone in thoughtful silence. "Like I said, the money's good, and I'm not afraid of the work, but what would you do while I'm going to Fort Smith and back?"

"Maybe I could work in the hotel."

He shook his head. "They don't get enough business to need a serving girl."

"Well, you said the boat needs a cook. I could do that."

He snorted. "A keelboat's no place for a woman."

"Then I won't be a woman." I was as surprised to hear the words as he was, but somehow I knew they were right. "I'll be a boy," I said, a little faster as the idea caught hold, "your younger brother—"

"Maggie!"

"No, listen!" I leaned toward him. "We could save the money you'd have to pay to keep me someplace, and we could earn two wages instead of one. We'd earn enough to maybe get to Texas in time to put in a late crop!"

"You're not a boy," he said flatly. "Nobody would believe it."

"I bet they would." I got up to find the looking glass. I studied my face, and I was pleased to see how much my features resembled Pa's. "I could pass for a boy."

He shook his head. "Not with a bosom, you won't."

I laughed. "Well, there's the blessing in a small bosom! It won't take much to hide it. Trisha always said my figure looked more like a boy's than a woman's. Here's some good fortune, too!" I dug into the pile of the Morgans' things. "Suzy left Luke's extra clothes—look! I can alter them to fit. We can cut my hair to look like yours."

Disbelief spread across his face as he began to realize I was serious.

"Cut your hair like a man's? Maggie! The Bible says it's a shame for a woman to be shorn. I don't want you to dishonor yourself just so we can have money!" I came back to kneel in front of him.

"Who else would know? It won't shame me. I want to help. What's the shame in that?"

He shook his head, but I wasn't giving in this time. It was our last chance.

"We could be together, John David. I don't want to stay some strange place without you, with no word of you for weeks."

"What about your courses?" he said. "You can't hide that on a keelboat in such close quarters with a bunch of men." I smiled and caressed his face, answering in the sweetest voice I could manage in my excitement.

"I can. It won't be a problem. Nobody will know, I promise you that. Let's do it, John David, please? We've had troubles before, but we've always been together. Let's stay together this time."

His face was still disbelieving, so I moved close to kiss him.

"I want to be with you," I whispered against his lips. "Always."

His sudden sigh and the way his mouth yielded to mine told me, beyond any doubt, I'd get my way.

❧ ❧ ❧

The boat was leaving at dawn in two days. John David went straight back to town and got us hired on. He spent most of the money left in the bag on a room in the hotel, and then we hauled all our goods back to town. The plan was for me to go to the captain as a girl wanting to ship goods to an uncle in Fort Smith, using Griffin's money to pay the charges. Once all our goods were safely on the boat, we'd come back to the hotel and turn me into a boy. The next morning, we'd report for work as John David and Matthew McKellar.

Once John David left for work the next morning, I ironed my green dress on the bed and washed myself as best I could in the dingy basin. Around the middle of the morning, just as we'd planned, I picked my way through the muddy streets to the river bank where the boat was tied. John David and another man were straining to push a barrel up a ramp onto the boat.

"Yoo-hoo!" I called, waving to them. "Can you help me?" They both looked up, but of course it was the other man who hopped down from the ramp.

"Hold that, McKellar," he called over his shoulder as he came toward me. He was sweaty and breathing heavily from the effort of pushing the barrel. He swept the limp hat off his head and held it with both hands. "You called, Miss?"

I hoped my smile was a good imitation of Arabella Channing's.

"I'm looking for the captain. I was told at the hotel you're going to Fort Smith."

"Yes'm," the fellow panted. He had to be as old as my pa, with his thinning hair damp with sweat and clinging to his head. His face was red, but it was hard to say whether that was from working or from being flustered. He offered me his dirty arm. "This way, Miss."

He stepped aside to let me go first up the ramp where John David was braced against the barrel, grinning. As we passed, John David tipped his hat and spoke in a low voice.

"Careful, Kirby, she might be somebody's wife."

"Shut your maw, you mangy excuse for a man-child," Kirby muttered behind me. "I saw her first. I'll see to it you get a nasty surprise in your bedroll first night on the river if you don't butt out."

He took me straight to the captain, who was barely taller than I was, but whose bright blue eyes and stick-straight posture made him seem bigger. The arrangements were made quick enough, and I was pleased to have a couple of coins left as the captain led me back out of his cabin. John David and Kirby had finally managed to get the barrel on deck and were rolling it toward the center of the boat. The captain barked at them, and they both turned, Kirby snapping to attention, John David more slowly, holding his hand against the small of his back.

"You two!" the captain ordered. "When that barrel's in place, accompany this lady to the hotel and see that her goods are loaded."

John David came to the tavern with the crew from the boat that evening, so I finished my solitary supper quickly and went upstairs. Their laughter came up through the floor, and they were still drinking and singing bawdy songs downstairs when moonlight streamed through the cracks in the shutters over the window opening. How long John David would be, I didn't know. I combed through my hair a half dozen times, until every tangle was gone, and I was settling back in the bed when the shutters rattled heavily. I sat up quickly, pulling the covers to my throat. A hoarse whisper came through the crack.

"Maggie! It's me! Let me in, quick!"

"John David?" I hurried to unlock the shutters and swing them open, carefully, so I wouldn't knock him off his perch on the windowsill. "Why are you out there? Why didn't you just come up the stairs?"

He crawled through the window and clumsily got to his feet, leaning to peer out the window before he pulled the shutters closed. Then he turned and grinned.

"Come up the stairs? With Kirby watching them like a hawk for another sight of you?"

My face flushed. "He was not."

He laughed. "He was. He'd break that door down and tear me limb from limb if he had any notion I was up here with you instead of heading to a camp on the river."

I couldn't think of anything to say, and I fingered the locket at my bosom. John David lifted the little heart in his own hand.

"You'll have to take this off sometime. Matt wouldn't wear it, you know."

"I got a place planned for it. Once we're on board, I'll hide it good." I went to the table where I'd set out the tools we'd need to turn me to a boy. Picking up the scissors, I turned to him.

"How much did you have to drink? Can I trust you to do the cutting?"

"Of course." But instead of cutting, he stroked the back of my hair, over and over, lifting it off my neck, twisting it between his fingers.

"Come on," I said. "Just cut it. It's getting late."

"It's so beautiful," he murmured. "Always makes me remember how you looked in the moonlight that night at Charlie Huckett's, the prettiest girl I'd ever seen—"

"What I remember is you were drunk that night, about as bad as you are tonight." I reached around to take the scissors from him. "I'll do it, if you're going to go all soppy on me."

But he caught my hand before I could lift it to snip off the section I'd pulled up.

"Not yet." He pulled the scissors off my fingers and let them drop with a clatter to the floor. "We'll have time in the morning, plenty of time. But before we turn you into my brother, I want one more night with my wife."

❧ ❧ ❧

My head felt strangely light and cold once the hair was off and lying in a big pile on the floor. I ran my fingers through what was left, as I'd seen John David do so many times, and it seemed to me it was nearly as thin as Kirby's. I picked up the looking glass and peered at myself.

"It's ugly," I said. John David looked up from where he was scooping together the pile of hair.

"The uglier, the better. Maybe Kirby won't be throwing any glances your way."

While he dropped my hair down the hole of the privy behind the tavern, I cut wide strips from one of the sheets Suzy had left and wrapped them around my body tight enough to flatten my bosom so I felt sure no one would notice it. I was tucking the shirt into my britches when he came back, carrying two cups of hot tea and a wedge of cornpone. He stopped short in the doorway, a slow grin spreading over his face.

"Well, pitch me naked in a briar patch." He circled around, looking me up and down. "You'll pass. I'd bet my life on it."

He wasn't so cocky later, when we were standing together in front of Captain Russell.

"Your brother, is he?" the captain asked, peering at me with those bright eyes.

"Yes, sir. Matthew," John David answered.

"How old did you say he is?"

"Sixteen." The captain suddenly reached out and rubbed his hand along the smooth skin of my cheek and jaw. I hardly dared to breathe, and John David shifted nervously as the captain pulled his hand back.

"You're lying to me, McKellar." He took a long draw on his pipe. "There's no way this boy is sixteen – he barely has peach fuzz. He's what, thirteen?"

"Y—Yes, sir." Color was creeping across John David's cheeks. The captain laughed.

"Oh, think nothing of it, McKellar! I suppose you thought I wouldn't take on a boy so young."

"No, sir."

"You say he's a good cook."

"Better than our own ma, sir."

"Then I don't care if the boy is thirteen or thirty-one. The last cook left everybody with pain gnawing in their guts. It's hard to move a boat on sick stomachs. I had to doctor the whole crew before that mess was purged out of their bellies. You, Matthew!"

"Yes, sir?" I tried to make my voice deeper.

"You know how to cook a good beef steak?"

"Yes, sir!"

※ ※ ※

That was the start of my life as a boy. It wasn't as hard as I'd thought it might be, not even the sickness, thanks to Judith's chamomile. At first, I stayed out of sight as much as I could, back in the cabin so the men wouldn't notice me. But as the days went on, I realized nobody was paying mind to me anyhow, and I thought it might really be possible to fool them, after all. I began to feel easier around them, and

I liked the freedoms that came with being a boy that I'd never known as a girl, like wearing britches. I'd never noticed before how a skirt was always twisting around my legs or getting caught on something. I liked the keelers, too, even though they had no modesty and I had to pretend I was used to seeing things no woman ought to see. They cursed all the time, but there was something friendly in even the insults they laid on each other, and the first time Kirby said I was a mighty fine hand at the skillet for an ill-favored weanling, I felt as pleased as I could ever remember.

Progress up the river was slow. On a good day, we'd make twelve miles, and that was a day that began as soon as the sun was high enough to see the river banks and that didn't end until the light was starting to gray again. That's when my work started. It was my job, with the help of the old man they had on board as fiddler, to set up camp, gather firewood, lay out bed rolls, and cook a big supper. The keelers would sit around and wait, resting their backs, drinking the only whiskey Captain Russell allowed for the day, and talking, always talking. Kirby, I thought, was worst of them all to talk.

The third night out, Kirby tried to provoke John David into a fight. John David let out a little groan as he eased himself to the ground after getting up to fill his cup, and Kirby laughed at him.

"Sore, are you, McKellar? Why, I bet tomorrow you won't even be able to move! Pretty young fellow like yourself probably never did an honest day's work in your life. These past two days are a taste of a real man's work, little lady. If your delicate back can't take it, maybe you better go back to your needlework or whatever it is you types do."

"Lay off him, Kirby," said Barclay. "We all had a rough time when we started."

"Not me," Kirby bragged. "I started on a boat when I was younger than baby McKellar over there—" he waved my direction—"and I ain't never had a sore back any day yet. I'm strong! Got a backbone of cast iron and a set of muscles tougher than alligator hide. Look at these arms!" He whipped off his shirt to show the bulging muscle in his upper arm. "Big as an ordinary man's thigh, that is!" He strutted over to the jug and tipped it up with a graceful swing while the other men laughed. "Yes, siree," he continued, wiping his mouth on his forearm. "I've wrestled men taller than me and had 'em pinned to the ground, begging for mercy like a woman. I tore a wildcat apart jaw from jaw when it jumped out on me from the woods, and I lifted a fully-loaded boat off a sandbar once while everybody else stood on deck fretting about what to do. I'm the strongest, meanest, smartest, rip-snortingest roarer on this boat, and that includes you, Captain Russell, no offense meant, sir, but it's true." He turned and smiled triumphantly at John David. "What have you done, McKellar?"

John David slowly leaned back on his elbows and stretched out his long legs. "Well," he said quietly, "you ever wonder how I got this scar on my face? I'd best not give the details, not even in a lawless place like Arkansas Territory. I'll just say if you mention my name back in Nashville, there's a pretty lady—a widow, she is now—who recalls me as the fellow who 'removed her wardrobe.' You ever used that muscle, Kirby?"

The other men whooped with laughter as Kirby's face went deep red. He took another swig on the jug, and John David grinned as he caught my eye.

He didn't complain, but I knew he ached from the strain of the work. Whether he was bending his back to push on an oar or throwing his shoulder against a pole and slowly walking it forward in line with the other men, it was cruel work, repeated time after time, all day long. The worst part, I thought, was the cordelling, when the water was too deep for poling and they had to pull the boat along by rope from the shore. One evening when he took his plate, I caught a glimpse of his palm, blistered and bloody, and I barely bit back the cry on my lips. There must've been something of it in my eyes, though, because he quickly set the plate on his lap and closed his fist.

"They'll make calluses," he said in a low voice, and I nodded, moving on to give a plate to the next fellow. But every time we stopped after that, I searched in the woods, and one evening, I finally found the heart-shaped Balm of Gilead leaves I wanted. I stripped off a handful of buds, and the next day while the men were wrestling through the mud and brush on the river's edge to drag the boat along, I mixed the buds into lard to make a salve. When we stopped that evening, I watched for John David to make his solitary trip into the woods, and I followed, glancing around to be sure nobody noticed.

He startled when he turned and saw me.

"Nobody saw," I said quickly. "I made sure of it. Here, this is for you. It's balm for your hands." I shoved the bowl toward him. Instead of taking it, he closed his hand over mine.

"You shouldn't be here," he said, pulling off my hat and letting it drop to the ground. "It's an awful risk."

I closed my eyes as he pulled me toward him, his fingers ruffling my hair. "I know. I'm going."

"Captain Russell would have us off the boat quick as lightning if he knew." His whiskers were scratchy against my cheek.

"Then we'd sure be in a fix," I whispered, "stuck here in nowhere, Arkansas Territory—" His lips touched mine, and I threw my free arm around his neck as we kissed, for all the world like a pair of starving folk tearing into fresh cornbread.

I didn't hear anything, but he suddenly stiffened and pulled away.

"What?" He hushed me with a fingertip and turned to stare into the woods. There was no sound or movement that I could tell.

"No one there," he said. "Probably just some critter. Still, I reckon we better watch the brotherly love." He let go of my hand, taking the salve. "What's this?"

I doctored his hands with all the tender, womanly care I wanted to give his whole sore body. He didn't say anything else, but when I finished, he raised my hand to his lips and set my hat back over my rumpled hair. We took different routes back to camp, him coming from the woods, me skirting around to come up from the river with an armload of driftwood, like I'd been out gathering it the whole time.

It was the only time we slipped, for I made myself stay away from him after that, fearing something in my face would tell everyone I was no brother. Our stop a couple of days later in Little Rock, with its port busy from the traffic of a steamboat, might have given us a chance to steal some time together, but I stayed in the keelboat's cabin, watching through a crack in the siding while John David left with the rest of the crew to find a tavern. Then I went with the old fiddle man, Stewpot, to the shops, looking for supplies to replace what we'd used so far.

Stewpot was my best friend on the keelboat, I suppose. He'd been the cook with the crew for so many years Captain Russell didn't have the heart to fire him, even when he couldn't cook anymore, and now Stewpot played the fiddle to take the men's minds off the slow pace they were making up river. I wasn't sure how well Stewpot could see—his pale eyes seemed clouded over—and that made me feel easier around him. He didn't ask questions, either.

He wasn't the best fiddler I'd ever heard, but his music always seemed to reach inside me and stir my thoughts. I took to sitting on the roof of the cabin with him as we made our way up the river, listening to his music and daydreaming. Some of the time, I'd go over the same familiar dream of the cabin and cornfields, but more and more I was thinking about the baby and about the time when I'd finally get to tell John David he was a pa. My belly was still flat, but I imagined I could feel our son inside me, and I wondered what he'd be like. He'd have dark hair like the both of us, no doubt, and I hoped he'd have John David's dark eyes. Maybe he'd be tall like his pa, too, and just as strong. I watched the muscles in John David's sunburned arms and shoulders bulge with the effort of pushing the pole against the mud on the river bottom, and my belly suddenly made that now-familiar flop. I shook my head forcefully, trying to clear away such thoughts, and Stewpot looked up from his fiddle.

"A bee," I mumbled. "Nearly got me."

After that, I kept my eyes off of John David and on the landscape we were passing through. As we went farther west, the swamps were replaced by regular woods, their trees fuzzy with spring greens and rusty browns and sometimes the pink limbs of a redbud. For all its wildness, Arkansas Territory was pretty, I thought, a lot like home. The creeks were rushing with spring rain, just like they would be back in Campbell County. I wondered how the little ones on Pine Mountain had made it through the winter. It would be time to try again with a garden soon, and I wondered if anyone would see that one was planted, with me gone. Thinking of a garden always made me wonder if we'd get our own corn planted in time. But worries, no matter what they were, seemed far away as the warm sunshine rested on my shoulders.

It was at the close of one of those warm, sunny days that we reached a spot on the river that Captain Russell said was the halfway point on the trip. We camped in the shadow of a big mountain with rocky bluffs showing through the budding trees. This night, there wasn't the usual joking and talking around the fire as I cleaned the dishes. Instead, the men sat quietly, drinking whiskey or chewing on the ends of their pipes. Kirby finally made a loud snort and stood to shake himself.

"Anybody up for a couple rounds of Sweat?" No one answered, and he kicked the foot of the man nearest him. "Come on, Glover! No betting, let's just play."

"Naw."

Kirby turned to others. "Johnson? Ashe?" But when no one took him up on the offer, he dropped back down by the fire, grumbling. "Don't know what's wrong with everybody. Acting like they're wore out or something."

"It's the spirit," Stewpot said, which made everyone look up. Stewpot never said anything.

"What spirit?" Kirby's voice sounded lost somewhere between scoffing and scared.

"The girl who died here." We waited, but he didn't say anything else, just sucked on his pipe.

"Well?" Kirby demanded. "Let's hear it, you miserable fleabite!"

Stewpot took a long draw on his pipe and let out a puff of smoke that caught the firelight for a moment. "It's an Indian tale. They say there was a French fellow, long ago, coming to the New World to explore. He was betrothed to a beautiful girl, who wanted to marry him right away and come with him. But he said no, he'd do the exploring on his own, and then come back for her. She didn't want to part from him, though. So she dressed herself like a cabin boy and got a job on the ship. Called herself Jean, and the crew took to calling her Petty Jean, since she was so little. Fooled them all, she did. Even her own man didn't recognize her."

My face was growing hot, and I was thankful to be kneeling by the tub of water, where no one would notice me.

"They got to this very mountain and stayed all summer with the Indians. But the night before they were to start back to France, Petty Jean fell ill of fever, so ill they couldn't leave. Of course, while they were tending her, they found out her secret. She knew she was dying, so she asked to be buried on the mountain overlooking the river. At sundown, she died, and they did as she wished. She's buried somewhere on this mountain. So the Indians say."

There was silence after Stewpot finished his story. Then Kirby snorted again.

"Indian tales! Indian rubbish is more like it. Ain't no woman fool enough to dress like a man and work on a boat just so she can be around her beloved." I held my breath to try to calm my racing heart.

"Who knows?" Stewpot murmured. Kirby laughed loudly.

"Well, if there was a woman fool enough to try it, there ain't a man couldn't spot it in two winks. Your eyes may be going bad, Stewpot, but I believe I could see the difference between a man and a woman no matter what she was wearing." He drew a female figure in the air, which set the men laughing, and I glanced around at them under my eyelashes. John David was leaning against a boulder with his arms resting on his knees. He was looking straight at me with that crooked grin.

"What're you grinning about, McKellar?" Kirby asked peevishly. I quickly looked away.

"I agree with you for a change," John David said. "I believe I'd be able to spot the difference myself. Not that I'm getting a chance anytime soon, by the look of things."

"Not now, no," Kirby said, his enthusiasm growing, "but you wait till we get to Fort Smith. I've heard there's Indian women there willing to trade their favors for little of nothing—a handful of buttons, maybe, or a couple of ribbons. Start saving your pennies now, McKellar. The captain gives us a week of leave in Fort Smith."

I looked up. A week of leave! I hadn't thought past the day-to-day on this trip up the river, but suddenly I saw before me a bright ending I hadn't expected. A week of leave, a week when there would surely be time to get John David away from them all and finally share my news.

"How long till we get there?" I asked. "To Fort Smith?"

"Two or three weeks, if the weather's good," Kirby said, turning toward me. "What you got up your sleeve, Baby McKellar? You saving pennies for an Indian woman?"

They all laughed like it was the funniest thing they'd ever heard, but I didn't care. Two or three more weeks—I could wait that long.

Chapter 20

A couple of days later, the chamomile was finally gone, despite my efforts to be sparing with it. I'd barely put eggs in the skillet before the smell set me off, and there was nothing for it. I puked in front of them all.

"Good God, Matt!" Kirby roared. "What are you trying to do, ruin our appetites so you don't have to cook?"

"Sorry," I mumbled, kicking sand over the mess. "Them eggs must be bad. Probably better throw 'em out."

"You all right, brother?" John David called from where he and Ashe were washing themselves in the river. I waved to him and, wiping my mouth on my sleeve, went back to the eggs, hoping that one time would be all for this morning.

But we'd barely shoved off before I had to lean over the side of the boat. This time, there were no eggs to blame it on. Captain Russell ordered John David to fetch me to his cabin.

"He don't have any fever," John David said, laying his hand on my forehead.

"Stomach ailments don't always have a fever." Captain Russell laid a large, wooden box on the table and began to sort through it. "Obviously, the boy ate something that disagreed with him. A dose of calomel will purge his system and set him right again."

Purge! I looked up at John David in alarm. How would I manage to keep our secret if I had to spend the day running to the bucket?

"Nothing's wrong with me," I said quickly. "It was just them eggs, sir."

But Captain Russell had found what he was looking for, a box of big, white pills. He handed one to me. "Rush's Thunderbolts, they're called. They'll clean you out right away." I looked up at John David again, begging him without words to help, but he shook his head the tiniest bit.

"I'm—I'm all right," I stammered. "It won't happen again, I swear it won't!"

"Come along, Matthew," Captain Russell said sternly. "I know purging ain't the most pleasant experience, but I also know nothing clears up these little complaints quicker. Tell him, McKellar."

"You'll be all right," John David said.

"I've doctored my crew for years," Captain Russell boasted. "Never lost a one. You ain't that different from any other boater I've had, just younger. Come now, take the medicine."

There was nothing to do but take it. I nearly gagged trying to swallow it, but John David led me outside and fetched a dipper of water for me. The men were casting curious glances our way as they trudged forward with their poles.

"They'll find out!" I said in a hoarse whisper. "How can I hide it, hitching my britches up and down all day?"

"They won't find out. They'll steer clear of you, most likely. Who wants to watch someone sitting on the bucket?" He glanced over his shoulder and then leaned closer. "It was the eggs, right? You're not getting that seasickness again, are you?"

I looked out across the water to the wild river bank, with no sign of a human hand. Though we'd seen a few clusters of houses along the way, Captain Russell said they belonged to Indians. Surely it was safe to tell John David about the baby now. He wouldn't put me off the boat in an Indian town. It wasn't the cozy scene I'd daydreamed about, but I needed his help.

"John David," I murmured urgently, "I've got something to tell you."

"McKellar!" Captain Russell barked. "He'll be fine! Back to work!"

"Don't worry," he said, backing away. "They won't find out."

※ ※ ※

It was a miserable day. The pill cramped my gut hard every half-hour or so all day long, forcing me to the bucket again and again. Even when there was nothing left in me, the medicine kept working, leaving me aching and weak. But John David was right—no one found us out. They all stayed clear of me, even once we'd camped. Captain Russell let me have the evening to rest, so Stewpot cooked supper, which made the men grumble. I lay on my back in my bedroll, too weak to even raise my head when John David brought me some water. He lifted my shoulders and held the cup to my lips.

"I know today's been rough," he said in a low voice. "But tomorrow ought to be better. Captain Russell said it's a day of purging and then things are set right."

I didn't feel like talking. I closed my eyes and he laid me back on the ground, sneaking in an awkward little caress to the back of my neck. I tried to rest, but the same question kept gnawing at my mind. What would happen tomorrow or the next day or the next when I was sick again? Purging wasn't going to help this sickness, but I couldn't tell Captain Russell that without giving myself away, and that would cost us our last good chance to be able to go on to Texas. But I couldn't take another day like this one. Somehow, I had to find a way to bear up under the sickness, to hide it better. Surely it couldn't go on much longer. Even for Ma, it had been a temporary thing. I slowly rubbed my hand over my sore belly. Come on, little one, I thought, help me. I can't be sick no more.

I was enough better the next morning to stir up the fire and put on a pot of coffee. As I fried the salt pork, though, my gut began to ache again, and I feared I was in for another day of purging. Nothing ever came, though, and the ache wasn't so bad that I couldn't get things readied for us to shove off for another day on the river.

I'd been too sick the night before to notice the strange outcropping of rock above the bank where they'd made camp, and I climbed on the roof with Stewpot to look at it as we slowly pulled away. It was a huge, slanted bluff, sticking out alone toward the sandy beach.

"Dardanelle Rock," Stewpot told me. "The Indians tell that a young chief waited here for a sign from his love to say she would run away and marry him. He stood on that rock, they say, waiting for her to wave her mantle, but though he waited for hours, he never saw the sign. They say he jumped off the rock into the river at sunset and died."

The pain in my belly was deeper now, and I shifted, trying to find a way to ease it.

"Don't you know any happy stories?" I asked. "Seems like somebody dies in every story you tell."

"I tell the ones I know," he said, raising the fiddle to his chin. The pain was spreading, and I bent into it, hoping it would pass without a trip to the bucket. "What would you like to hear?"

"Don't care," I grunted. I decided I needed the bucket, after all. But as I stood and took a step, my britches clung to my leg, and I looked down. A stain was soaking the britches, a stain dark like blood—

"Something's wrong," I heard myself moan. The stain was growing, and I wrapped my hands low around my belly like I could somehow stop it. "I need John David, Stewpot, get him for me, please. Please!"

It wasn't John David who was first up the ladder. Captain Russell stood with his mouth hanging open, and I saw John David craning to see around him, his face going pale as he caught sight of me. They both just stared, without moving. It was Stewpot who pushed past them, put an arm around me, and guided me to a chair. The stain had spread to my knee on one side.

"What in blazes is wrong with him?" Captain Russell bellowed. Stewpot laid a gentle hand on my back.

"It ain't a him, Captain, it's a her. And unless I miss my guess, the poor girl's losing a babe."

※ ※ ※

They put me in the captain's quarters, on his narrow bed with a straw tick and a scratchy wool blanket. Captain Russell and Stewpot left soon after, and I could hear the captain shouting orders to the men to get back to work. There was a jerk followed by the slow, forward glide of the boat. John David sat on the edge of the bunk, his face still pale, holding my hand.

"Good Lord, Maggie," he said. "Are you all right?" I nodded, which sent tears rolling down my face and into my hair.

"The baby ain't."

He brushed the hair away from my forehead. "A baby. I never thought about that happening."

"How did it happen? You were always careful." My voice wobbled. "We wanted to wait until we were settled somewhere."

"Don't worry about that. I guess it happens when it happens. We can't say when that will be." He stroked my hand with his fingertips. "When did it happen, reckon? How far along were you, I wonder?"

"I ain't sure. It must've happened while we were in Nashville. I didn't know, though, till we got to Arkansas Post—"

He stiffened. "You knew? In Arkansas Post?"

"I was still sick while we were staying there, when I wasn't on the boat, and Suzy said—"

"She knew?" he exploded, suddenly getting to his feet. "You told that thieving slut, but you didn't tell me?"

"I wanted to," I said quickly.

He was pacing the tiny room. "You knew, all that time we were planning to go on the Southwest Trail, when you talked me in to getting you work on this boat. You knew." He stood still, with his back to me. "You lied to me."

"I never lied," I started, but he turned to look at me, and his eyes were wet.

"Why didn't you tell me? I was that baby's father, for God's sake." His voice broke. He sat back down, in the chair across the room, as far from me as he could get.

"We wanted to wait—"

He suddenly leaned forward, and his dark eyes seemed to bore into me. "I can't believe you'd keep it from me, something that important. You should have let me know. Why didn't you tell me?"

I looked up at the rough boards on the ceiling, away from those intense eyes. "I never had a chance. Somebody was always around."

"Not after Griffin left. Not those nights in the hotel. You could've said something then. Why didn't you tell me then?"

"I don't know."

"Damn it, you do know!" he growled. "Why didn't you tell me?"

He wasn't going to give up. "I was afraid you'd make me go back upriver with Judith," I whispered. He sat back, hard.

"Of course I would have sent you with her! Or found some way to keep you in that hotel. Or found some other work I could do in Arkansas Post. I would've taken care of you and the baby. You sure wouldn't be on a keelboat, living like a man! But you decided it was better to lie to me—"

"I wanted to stay with you!" I cried. "Don't you see? You told Suzy if it was up to you, you'd send her away. I didn't want that, to go back and be alone, to lose track of you! I wanted to stay with you—"

"At the cost of our baby's life?" The cold anger in his voice scared me. "Was earning a few dollars so important to you it was worth killing our baby?"

His words hit me like a smack, harder than one of Pa's, harder than the smack his ma gave me. I stared at him, and he stood and took a step toward the door.

"Don't leave," I managed to say, but he turned his back on me.

"I'm going back to work. We've got to have that money, you know."

The door banged behind him. The tiny room suddenly seemed as silent as the hole they'd put Dan Hammond in, and the chill of John David's anger filled it, pressing down on me till I could hardly breathe. How could he think I had chosen money over my baby? I hadn't meant harm—how could he even think I would? Yet he had said so. I wished desperately that he had smacked me, or cussed me, something with a heat that would burn itself out quickly and be gone, anything but leaving me alone, going back to his keelboat pole without even a look my way, with that cold, hard anger that would fester. He wasn't even trying to understand, to see I'd done what I'd believed was best for us all—for the baby, too.

I heard him answer Captain Russell, and though I couldn't make out the words, I knew by the sound of their voices the captain wasn't pleased and that I'd added more to our troubles. My throat ached, and I stared at the mildew stains on the boards above me. Our whole life together has been nothing but troubles, I thought, starting with that first kiss under Hucketts' oak tree. Troubles and worry, all distilled down into this pain inside me. I laid my hands across my belly, still flat, never to grow round and heavy. Already I could feel emptiness spreading, where only yesterday there had been life. How could it happen like that? What had I done that was so wrong? Why should this little one have to pay for my wrongs, this little one whose life was ending now before it had even started?

"It ain't right, none of it!" I groaned. I pulled the wool blanket higher over my shoulders, but I couldn't stop shivering, while my dark-eyed boy left me, slowly, steadily, surely.

Stewpot came in later with news of their plans for me. I couldn't stay on the boat, Captain Russell said, now that my deception was found out. Fortunately, he said, the Presbyterians had an Indian mission school only a few miles upriver. I could stay there, he said, and be cared for by the missionaries and their wives. I listened with a heavy, dull feeling, keeping my face pressed into the pillow. I could imagine the welcome missionaries and the wives of missionaries would give me, coming to them in these circumstances, dressed like a boy with my hair cropped short, clearly a dire sinner.

I was startled to feel Stewpot's gnarled hand on my shoulder.

"Poor child," he said, "I know your pain. My own wife suffered loss of three unborn babes." I didn't answer, but he went on in a low voice. "It's hard to say which is worse—the pain of loss or the pain of guilt. Or maybe it's the pain of secrets uncovered before their time." Something in his voice made me turn to him.

"You knew I wasn't a boy."

He smiled. "I once nearly stumbled into a tender scene in the woods not meant for the captain or crew." I stared at his strangely clouded eyes.

"Was I wrong to do it, to keep it secret?" I tried to swallow the lump in my throat. "It seemed like the best thing at the time, but now—John David, he's awful mad."

"I know his pain, too."

I pressed my fists against my eyes. "Everything's gone so wrong, everything! Nothing's turned out like it ought to have done. It's all just trouble and hurt, and I can't make the pain go away—"

"This is big pain."

I grabbed his hand. "What should I do? What can I do to fix this?"

He patted the back of my hand. "Some things can't be fixed, child. Some pain won't go away. Some pain you simply must bear. But is this pain that bonds, or pain that shatters?"

I wasn't in the mood for one of his riddles. I pulled my hand away and turned my back on him, pressing my face into the pillow again. I heard him shuffling toward the door, and after some time I heard the fiddle start up, not a jaunty work tune, but a ballad, slow and sad. It took a bit for the tune to settle in, but then I recognized it—*Annie Laurie*, the song the brothers sang to Sarah on that night that seemed so long ago now, the night I'd seen such tenderness in Zeke's eyes. I had hoped that night to see tenderness in my own true love's eyes someday—not anger, not blame, not such complete coldness. The sobs I'd been holding down all morning finally broke free, coming faster and harder, until I couldn't muffle them in the captain's pillow.

I heard Kirby's voice, harsh and angry.

"Stewpot! Cut it out! Look at McKellar! Have some pity on the man, for God's sake!" The music stopped.

Some things can't be fixed, I repeated. It had never been right, not from the start. I'd been fooling myself. Though he hadn't wanted to be married to me, he'd tried to make it right—we'd both tried. But the differences between us were too many and too great. A square peg couldn't fit a round hole unless part of it was shaved off or splintered off by pounding, and then it was not what it had been before. It was something less, something scarred and worn and sad. It was wrong to try to force it to fit. I took a deep, quivering breath and wiped the tears from my eyes. I knew what I had to do, what I should've done long before. The thing now was to find the way to do it.

* * *

As it turned out, the way came quicker and easier than I'd thought it would.

It was early afternoon when Glover jumped out of the first canoe and pulled it up on the gravel of an opening in the trees along the creek we'd taken off the Arkansas River.

"It's just ahead," Captain Russell said. "Help her onto the litter." He turned to the men who were getting out of the second canoe, the one with all our goods. "Try to get it all in one trip. We don't want to lose too much time."

Dwight Mission was bigger than I'd expected it to be in this wilderness, a cluster of cabins surrounded by fresh-plowed fields waiting for corn. I could hear the drone of young voices chanting together from one building. Chickens squawked as Kirby kicked at them to clear his path. A woman followed by two girls with shiny black hair came from one of the buildings but stopped short when she saw our company.

"What's this?" she called. "Is the boy ill?"

"Begging your pardon, ma'am," Captain Russell said, "but this ain't a boy, it's a girl, and yes, ma'am, she's ill. We wondered if you folks would be kind enough to tend to her."

The woman handed something to one of the girls and sent them on across the yard. I could see them turning back, craning to see, as the woman came toward us. Her belly was big with child, just as Suzy's had been, and I bit my lip as I turned my face away.

"Nothing that will spread to the children, I hope?" She laid her hand against my cheek. "She doesn't seem to have fever."

"It won't spread—it's—well—it's—" The captain's face was fiery red and he seemed unable to finish. John David cleared his throat, but his voice was still husky as he spoke.

"She's lost a baby, ma'am." I heard her gasp.

"Oh! Oh, I'm so sorry. Certainly, she's welcome to stay. Come, bring her to my cabin."

She said her name was Abigail Washburn, the wife of one of the men who started the mission. She fussed around getting me into her bed, bringing me fresh water, going in and out to tell the men where they could store our things. It made me tired to see her fluttering like a moth between the flames of two candles, waddling along behind her big, round belly, and I closed my eyes as she pulled blankets over my shoulders.

"You poor dear," she murmured. "Was there an accident? Did you fall?"

"No." I didn't want to talk about it, not to her, not to anyone. I heard the door swing open.

"I need a few words with her," John David said. "She's my wife."

"Oh, of course!" I heard the swish of her skirts and the closing of the door. The bed dipped to one side, and I knew he was sitting on the edge. But I didn't open my eyes, and he didn't speak.

"You said you needed to talk to me," I said, finally.

"Maggie—" His voice choked, and it was a moment before he tried again. "Are you resting easy?"

A bitter laugh forced its way through my lips. "Sure, I reckon. What did you want to say? I need some sleep." He still didn't say anything. I opened my eyes. "Well?"

"This is for you." He laid a small bag on the blanket, and I could tell by sight it held money. "It's your wages. Captain Russell gave it to me just now. Hide it someplace safe." His face was troubled.

"Did he fire you too?"

"He's not happy with me." He paused. "But he wants me to stay and help them get to Fort Smith. He was short-handed, anyway." He paused again, fingering the cord of the little bag. "I know I promised I wouldn't leave you alone, but I'm going on with them, Maggie. We need the money too bad not to. You'll be cared for here till I get back."

My stomach clenched as I realized my chance.

"About that." I was surprised how calm my voice was, since my heart was pounding so. "You don't have to come back."

He looked up. "What?"

"I know it ain't been easy for you all this time, carrying the burden of a wife you didn't even want. It's a blessing this baby died, I reckon, so you don't have obligation to provide for a child, too." He looked like someone had punched him hard, straight in the face.

"Maggie—"

"It was good of you to get me away from Pa, and I'll always be grateful to you for that. But us together, it's been one trouble after another, you know it has," I said, faster, so he couldn't break in. "It ain't fair to ask you to go on with this. You wanted to leave me that day in Nashville, but you felt honor-bound to come back. Well, this time you don't have to."

"I thought you said—" he started, but I cut in over him.

"I took advantage of you being drunk at Charlie's barn raising, and that was wrong of me. It never should've come to this. You promised me we'd get an annulment if ever I wanted it. Well, I want it now." He closed his eyes. "I'm going to make things right, John David. I'm setting you free. You can shake off your bond to me and do whatever you wish."

"I don't want to—"

"Don't be a fool," I said. "Of course you want to. The whole world's open to you once you're rid of me."

"You don't mean that," he said, "you're just upset about the baby."

I sat up, quick.

"This ain't about the baby!" I was quivering all over. "It's gone! What I'm telling you is I want you gone, too!"

"You don't mean that," he repeated, like he was as half-witted as Luke. A great ball of fury lit in my chest and burned its way through my whole body, exploding in my head. My hand flew up and I smacked him, hard, across the face.

"Don't tell me what I mean!" I snarled. "You don't know nothing about me! You never have! I'm tired of it, you hear? I want that annulment, like you promised!"

He sat stone still with the mark of my hand on his face. "That's what you want?" His voice was quiet, but I could hear anger building again behind the quiet. "After telling me not to toss you off when times get hard, this is what you want? To just throw away everything? Like it never happened?"

I clenched my trembling fists against the white-hot fury. "It is! How many times do I have to say it?"

"McKellar!" Captain Russell's voice was muffled by the door, but he was clearly impatient. "We're starting back. Are you coming or not?"

I saw his hand shaking as he slowly wiped it across his mouth. He rose from the bed and took a step, but then he looked back like he was about to say something.

"Goodbye," I said, dropping back to the pillow and closing my eyes tight.

"That's it?" he said, but I turned my head away from him. "Fine, then, you contrary little—"

The door opened and closed, and I heard Captain Russell speak and John David answer. Then there was silence, and I knew he was gone and I'd never see him again. Tears burned my eyes, but I rubbed at them roughly. Some pain won't go away, I thought, but at least now we won't cause each other more pain. It's the right thing to do. Best get used to it.

Chapter 21

They were kind to me at the mission. For the first couple of days, Mrs. Washburn insisted I stay in their bed, saying my body had been through an ordeal and needed rest. But once the pain and bleeding stopped, I asked if there was someplace else I could stay. I said it was because I didn't want to be a bother to them, but truly it was because I couldn't stand to be around her and Reverend Washburn, with their two little ones and their contented looks for each other, especially not around her, with her belly full of baby.

They moved me into a cabin with the Cherokee girls, who stared at my short hair and bare neck and giggled a lot, whispering in a tongue I didn't understand. Finally, I asked if I could stay someplace by myself, and though Reverend Washburn looked stern, Mrs. Washburn suggested the timber house behind the dining hall. It didn't seem to have any purpose other than storing things, including our things, and I made myself a pallet from our quilts and was suited well enough with no company but the mice.

Mrs. Washburn also finally gave in to my arguments that I should repay them for my keep, and she set me the task of helping in the kitchen. It was good work, as there were so many people to feed, and all day I kept my mind bent on peeling potatoes, kneading bread, and washing dishes.

Come evening, though, when I was alone in the dark of the timber house, it was harder not to think about all that had happened. The first few nights, I thought about the baby, and the aching emptiness felt like a crouching panther, waiting to swallow me whole and leave my mind in darkness. I held the panther at bay by thinking about other things, keeping them close like a glowing torch I could wave when I felt the darkness creeping in. I went over and over the things

John David had said to me in the captain's cabin on the keelboat, and I decided I had been right to send him away. He'd walked away from me, I reminded myself, when I'd done what I did so we could stay together. He should have understood that, or at least tried to.

Instead, he'd left me a lone woman, in wild and lawless county, with hardly any money and nothing planned for my future. I couldn't stay at the mission forever, not that I'd want to. The Washburns were kind, but I knew they were just biding time, and someday, when John David didn't come back, they'd want to know why. I didn't fancy having to confess to strict Reverend Washburn the twists of fortune that led me to be dumped at the mission. No, I had to leave, and soon. But where could I go?

Not home—that was the one thing I was sure of. I could just imagine how Pa and Ma would gloat that my fancy McKellar husband had finally tired of me and tossed me out, and I vowed I would never give them that satisfaction. I might be abandoned, but I would never be desperate enough to go home.

That left Nashville and the Spotted Hog. Mr. Randall would probably be pleased enough to take me back to cook and serve. I'd make it clear I had no interest in marrying him or, for that matter, any other man, which I figured would suit him just fine.

One night I took my little bag of wages to supper and asked Reverend Finney, who handled the mission's money, if there was enough for passage back to Nashville.

He counted the coins with ink-stained fingers. "I don't know current rates for travel, but this would seem to be plenty."

"I've heard there's steamboats that bring goods to the mission. When does the next one come?" I asked. He and Reverend Washburn looked at each other.

"We can't be sure," Reverend Washburn said. "I'm sure we'll have one soon, before the river gets too low, perhaps within the month." He gave a meaningful look to Mrs. Washburn, who was rocking little Corrine. She nodded.

"What about Mr. McKellar, dear?" she asked. "When do you expect his return? He was going to Fort Smith, right?"

I didn't answer, just scooped up my coins, and she, being a true lady, didn't press me.

※ ※ ※

Jane Hicks, though, wasn't old enough to be polite. Jane was one of the Cherokee girls, the only one who was friendly. She didn't giggle at my hair, so I tolerated her constant talk about God. One afternoon we were planting potatoes with the other girls, and she was telling me, again, the story of how she found Jesus, thanks to Reverend Washburn.

"Eyes turned to Heaven," she said as she dropped a piece of potato into the hole I'd made. "Just as ours should be. Reverend Washburn says we should turn our eyes to the Lord for protection. He says there's nothing to fear from demons or witches as long as we trust our hearts to the Lord Jesus."

"You ain't afraid of witches, are you?" I asked. "There ain't even such a thing, is there?"

She looked up, her black eyes wide. "Oh, yes! The elders of the tribe tell horrible stories about the wicked things witches do to children. Sickness, pain, bad behavior—oh, yes, there are witches and they walk among us! But the Lord won't let them touch us if we put our faith in Him. Reverend Washburn says it's in the Bible." She dropped another potato piece. "It's not just children they torture, though. The elders say grown people can be touched, too. Like that man from the boat."

"What man?" I stepped away to make another hole, and she crawled along, dragging the basket of potato pieces behind.

"That man from the boat a couple of weeks ago. I know you know who I mean, because he came out of Reverend Washburn's cabin after they took you in. He was very pale, even for a white man, and he looked so sad, like he carried great pain in his heart. I know a witch was tormenting him." She looked up. "That hole is too deep."

"I reckon it is. Sorry." I pushed a bit of dirt back into the hole.

"Who was that man?" she asked. I sighed, leaning on the hoe handle and looking across the garden patch where other pairs of girls were working.

"My husband."

"Oh." She paused. "Ain't you going to cover this one?"

"Sorry."

"You must miss him." She was crawling ahead to the next spot. "How long till he'll be back?"

"He ain't coming back."

She sat on her knees. "How do you know?"

"I told him not to."

"Oh." That seemed to satisfy her, because we planted several hills without speaking. But then she paused again with a knowing look.

"He's a bad man, ain't he? I saw a devil's mark on his cheek. He hurt you, didn't he? That's why you look so sad all the time. Demons must be working through him."

"No," I said quickly. "He ain't a bad man. He's a good man, a kind man." She looked confused, but she suddenly smiled.

"I see! You put out the deerskin." I stared at her, and she got to her knees eagerly. "With our people, if a husband don't please his wife, she puts all his things on a deerskin outside the door. Then he must leave. What did he do as your husband to displease you?"

I pawed at the ground with the point of the hoe. "Nothing," I said softly. "I wasn't displeased with him. He was a good husband to me."

She frowned. "I don't understand. You say he's a good man and a good husband. Why would you send him away?"

I didn't answer, and she soon seemed to forget it and went on to talk more about the love of Jesus. But once we'd finished with the potatoes and I'd taken the hoe to the shed, I felt too restless to stand by a fire in the kitchen. The day was mild, with a few clouds along the edges of the sky and a breeze ruffling my hair. I started toward the creek with intentions of washing the garden dirt from my feet. But when I came to the creek's edge, I turned instead and followed it through the border of trees the men had left between it and the fields. I walked until I could no longer hear the voices of the children around the mission and until the border of trees grew wider, and even after the border had turned to uncut woods. I walked to where the woods ended, until I was standing on the very edge of the river, its gray-blue water sliding past, wide and silent.

Why would you send him away? Jane's question echoed in my mind, and I still didn't have an answer, except maybe that I'd wanted him to hurt as much as I did. Seems I'd got what I wanted, if a young girl could see it on his face. 'Like he carried great pain in his heart,' she had said. I tried quickly to clutch the familiar torch of blame, but it had lost its power, and I had to admit it—as much as I might blame him for my hurt, knowing he was hurt too didn't make my pain any less. And much as I might like to blame it on witches, I knew I was the one who'd caused him that hurt. I winced as I recalled the things I'd said to him, the smack I'd put across his face, just like his ma had done.

Why would you send him away? It had never been right, I'd told myself in the keelboat's cabin. But thinking back, I remembered plenty of times it was right, probably as right as any man and woman could be together. We'd had plenty of troubles, yes, but we'd always faced them together, like a good team of mules—until I'd decided to cut him from the traces and pull the whole load of our baby on my own. What a husband don't know won't hurt him, I'd said, but I knew now that was wrong. My deception had hurt him—it hurt us all.

The worst of it was, there was nothing I could do now to turn back the damage I'd done. I couldn't bear to think how I'd wounded him—taking the tender feelings we'd shared and making them out to be a sham on my part all this time. I'd made it seem he meant nothing more to me than a convenient way to get away from Pa, only a means to a nice cabin and farm. How could I do that to him—a good man, a kind man, the man I loved?

"It's true," I whispered. "I love you, John David. Oh, I do!"

But now my life stretched out in front of me, my time flowing past as empty and silent as this river. There would be no cabin or cornfields, no babies with his brown eyes. I could almost hear his voice asking, *'That's what you want?'* With a cry, I crumpled to the gravel on the bank, covering my face with my hands, seeing before me nothing but despair, bottomless and black like the hell I deserved.

⁂ ⁂ ⁂

The sunlight was slanting along the water when I finally raised my head and slowly pushed myself up from the gravel. It was past suppertime; they'd miss me helping to clean up. I was brushing sand from my skirt when something caught my eye—a flat stone the size of a small hickory nut, touched with gold by the setting sun. I picked it up and turned it over between my fingers. Suddenly I clenched it in my fist and started into the woods, half-walking, half-running back toward the mission.

Mrs. Washburn seemed taken aback when I crossed the yard in front of her at a trot.

"Maggie? Jane said you weren't in the kitchen."

"I'll be there in a minute," I panted.

I threw open the door of the timber house and rushed to our packs, tossing them aside until I found the one I wanted, pawing through it until I felt the softness of Suzy's baby wrap. I carefully unfolded it, letting out my breath slowly as the block of light from the doorway caught the soft gleam of the locket, just where I'd put it when we left Arkansas Post. I pulled it up by the chain and slipped it around my neck. With trembling fingers, I opened it and touched the lock of soft, dark hair curled around its edge.

"A token of love," I whispered. A man could easily walk away from an obligation if he was freed from it by the one he was beholden to. Love, though—that would be harder to leave behind, and easier to come back to. I closed the locket and slipped it inside my shirt, feeling the cool metal come to rest between my breasts.

"Please let him come back." I heard the words, so I knew I'd said them out loud, and suddenly more were tumbling out, a prayer, when I'd never prayed in my whole life. "Please let him love me. Please let his love be bigger than the hurt I caused him. Oh, please, let him come back!"

❧ ❧ ❧

I wore the locket all the time after that, tucked inside my shirt so it could rest against my skin, a constant reminder of the hope I was clinging to. As if I needed a reminder—it was all I could think about. Even the kitchen work couldn't keep my mind distracted. I remembered what Sarah had said about praying for John David, and I prayed too, so often I wondered if God thought I was as talky as Jane Hicks. I started taking a walk every afternoon, and no matter what path I started on, every walk ended the same—down on the river bank, gazing west, toward Fort Smith.

Still, the days passed with no sign of the keelboat. One afternoon, a pirogue loaded with supplies landed at the mission; the steamboat was docked on the river. All the next day, the men and boys were busy making trips back and forth to unload the boat, but in the evening Reverend Finney took a moment to speak with me.

"The boat will leave in the morning," he said. "Shall I speak to the captain about booking passage for you?"

I told him I'd think about it, and I did, all night long in the dark timber house. It had been nearly a month since I'd sent John David away, and I was beginning to fear I'd missed the keelboat's passing, that I'd been so mean he really wouldn't come back. The sensible thing to do would be to gather a few things and start back to Nashville, where I had at least some guarantee of a future. But I fancied the locket felt heavy on my chest, and I clutched it tight, leaning back against John David's bag of seed corn.

"A little longer, God," I murmured. "I'll wait a little longer."

🙟 🙟 🙟

More days passed. We were well into April now, and the Cherokee boys planted corn in the waiting fields. The girls begged Mrs. Washburn to allow them to do their sewing outside, and one beautiful afternoon, she gave in. I sat mending clothes with Jane and some other girls. As usual, Jane was talking about God and His mercy, but today I was only half-listening. My hope had dwindled to a single bubble of flame at the end of my wick.

"Look," one of the girls said. "Somebody's coming." We all raised our heads to see, and my heart took a giant leap and began to pound madly. The figure was still too far away to tell much about it, but clearly it was a man, a tall man, taller than most—

I dropped my sewing and started toward him, resisting the urge to break into a run, just in case it wasn't him, after all. The closer he came, though, the more certain I was. The way he walked and the set of his shoulders were so familiar it brought an ache inside me. We met in front of a half-built cabin, and for a minute, we looked at each other without speaking. His hat shadowed his face, but it looked to me like the skin around one eye was a tad greenish, and a deep scratch mark ran down the side of his face and onto his neck. He took off the hat, and I could see it was true—he was only partly healed from another fight.

"Will you walk with me, please, Maggie?" His manner was polite, more like he was talking to Mrs. Washburn than to me. I nodded, and we started off side by side, back down the path toward the creek.

He didn't look at me, and I felt a shyness had come between us, more like folks who were courting than folks who'd been married. We turned to follow the creek toward the river. The mission was behind us now, hidden by the border of trees. He glanced at me.

"You're looking well," he said. "Better than last time I saw you."

"You sure look worse than last time I saw you." He laughed, and it was a pleasant sound, not angry or bitter. My heart made another grateful leap.

"My face is not the worst of it." He stopped and took off his hat again, bending closer and parting the hair around his ear with one hand. I gasped. A chunk was missing from the ear, leaving an edge black with dried blood. He grinned as he straightened. "I guess I should've listened to Matt."

He started walking again, and I hurried to catch him.

"What happened?"

"I got in a fight the first night in Fort Smith." He didn't sound at all concerned that a chunk of his ear was gone. I half-wondered if my cruelty had made him go mad.

"I reckon what started it was those Indian women Kirby told about," he said, and some of the brightness seemed to go out of the sunshine.

"Oh."

He looked sideways at me and stopped. "I didn't go in to them, Maggie. At first, I was determined I would—you said I was free to do as I wanted. Barclay wanted to give me first go at them, but Kirby insisted on drawing straws, and I lost. I lost on the second draw, too, and the longer I waited, the more I thought about you." He paused, and I swear I could hear my heart pounding in the quiet as his eyes met mine.

"I know you said things weren't right with us," he said softly, "but I thought they were. The way I felt—the way I feel—it's not being honor-bound to some obligation. You said you were a burden to me, and I'm sorry you saw it that way. I never felt like you were a burden." He touched my hand, lightly, like he wasn't sure I'd allow it. "I thought we had something good, Maggie, something that meant something, and I didn't want to spoil the memory of it by visiting some whore. So I left."

Tears were creeping down my cheeks. "I didn't mean that," I said. "I didn't mean any of it. I just said whatever I thought would hurt you most. I don't know why I wanted to hurt you." His hand, still rough from the ropes, slipped around mine.

"I hurt you, too. I know you didn't set out to do things to harm the baby. It was hateful of me to accuse you, and I'm sorry for it. Things just happen, I reckon. It probably wouldn't have made any difference if you'd been in the hotel instead of on the boat."

"I should've told you I was with child, no matter what. It was wrong of me not to. I will, next time, soon as I know myself." I searched his face, holding my breath, hoping—

He smiled and tucked the curly ends of my hair behind my ear. "Next time? Does that mean you're willing to have me back?"

My breath came back in a rush. "More than willing! I ain't too proud to say it. I'm begging you to come back!"

He was grinning. "That saves me considerable trouble, then. All the way down the river I've been trying to think of how to tell you I'm going to break my promise about that annulment. I don't care what kind of scene it makes for the missionaries and the Indians to see. I'm not ever leaving you again. We're staying married, no matter what the little mule says."

My laugh was shaky, and more tears spilled from my eyes. Somewhere in the back of my mind, Ma's voice was whispering, telling me I couldn't believe what he was saying. But I was tired of listening to her, tired of holding back a piece of myself to go on without him, just in case. I might be a fool, but I was going to believe him this time, with my whole heart.

I laid my head against the familiar spot on his chest, and he wrapped his arms around me. It felt better than I had remembered.

"I'm so sorry," I murmured. "I was afraid you'd never come back, after that smack and hose hateful things I said. Can you forgive me?"

"There is one thing I want from you," he said, drawing back to look at me. "I don't want to hear you say ever again that I married you because I was drunk. For one thing, it's not true, but for another, I don't care how we started. I'm choosing to partner with you, here and now." He took my chin in his hand and tipped it up, and his fingers were gentle but firm. I couldn't have looked away, even if I'd been of a mind to try. "I love you, Maggie. That's all that matters. You got that?"

I smiled up at him. "It took a while to get it through my contrary head," I said. "But I reckon your little mule is finally broke to harness."

※ ※ ※

"You still ain't told me what happened to your ear," I said, as we walked on toward the river.

He laughed. "You may put me back on the boat once you hear that story."

"Never!" I linked my arm in his, and he laughed again.

"Well, I was pretty miserable when I left the other fellows, so I found a place I could get whiskey, and I drank a lot of it, a whole lot. It didn't help, though. It just made me feel worse, in fact. I kept thinking about never seeing you again, and I got to feeling lower and lower. All the time, this cocky little fellow kept pestering me, and finally, I just swung around and punched him right in the mouth."

"You started the fight?" I gasped, and he nodded.

"Knocked him flat on his back. But he had friends, and I didn't. I tell you, they don't fight according to any rules out here. They were doing just about anything, gouging, kicking—one of them bit a notch out of my ear before someone pulled him off me."

I stopped. "That's from a bite?"

He nodded. "I'm lucky, though. I could've lost an eye if one of them had been able to get his thumb up in the socket, according to the soldier at the jail."

"The jail?"

He laughed again, though I couldn't see why.

"They took me to the blockhouse at the fort for public drunkenness and assault. I spent most of the week there before the magistrate came around to hear my case." He looked down at me. "Between the whiskey and the fine I had to pay, not much is left of my wages."

"John David!" I started to scold, but then I remembered that when he'd lost the money he'd thought I wanted nothing more to do with him. There hadn't been any reason to save. I softened my voice. "What'll we do about getting to Texas? It's time to plant corn."

"We're not going to Texas."

I stared at him. All these months, all the trouble we'd been through, trying to reach that dream of our own cabin and cornfields, and now he said we were giving it up?

He was pulling on my arm, leading me toward the creek bank. He dropped to the ground and patted a spot beside him, and I sat, still not believing what he'd said.

"I had a lot of time to think in jail," he started. "It took a couple of days to quit feeling sorry for myself, but then I started thinking straight again, and I decided two things. First, I would set things right with you, no matter what. The other was, that field of corn and the cabin we want can be anywhere. We don't have to be in Texas. All I wanted, anyway, was a place to call my own. Why not Arkansas Territory? At least it's part of the United States and folks speak English. The soldiers said it's just a matter of time before the government moves the Indians on to the west, since more and more white folk are coming to settle here."

"But the price of land," I reminded him. "That's why we were going to Texas, for the free land. How can we get land here? We ain't exactly prospered enough to buy any. All we've got is my wages and what's left of yours. Our supplies won't last long, and we'll have to spend what money we have to get more. We'll be lucky to make it through summer, much less to buy land."

"That's true enough."

"Why, then? What's changed your mind?"

He didn't answer for a minute, just picked a blade of grass and smoothed it between his fingers. When he spoke, his voice was quiet.

"You told me once that Sarah said it was God's will for us to get married. I laughed it off at the time, but sitting in jail, I started seeing things differently. Maybe Sarah's right. Maybe God's hand has been at work in everything that's happened to us." I stared at him, and he smiled. "Think about it, Maggie. There were plenty of times when things could have turned out worse than they did, like that time Washington threw you off or when that thief attacked me with a knife. Remember when we got to Nashville and the river was closed? I thought I had the worst luck of any man alive, but now I see the river being closed was a good thing. We'd have been a lot worse off if I'd tried to sell Washington right then. He had lost enough muscle on the trip he wouldn't have brought near as much money as he did after a month of eating oats in Channing's barn. What we got from him would have been all the money we had, and it wouldn't have lasted any time. We'd have been completely broke when we got to Natchez, with no way to go on and no one to turn to—"

"It didn't turn out any better since we stayed," I interrupted. "Now we're in Arkansas Territory with nowhere to go, and we're the same as broke—" My throat tightened. "If we'd been able to leave when we first got to Nashville, we might've got to Texas before there was a baby, and it wouldn't have died."

"We can't know that." He twisted the grass around one finger. "God gave us enough to get to Arkansas Territory. Maybe losing the baby was part of His plan, a way to get us to stop here instead of keeping on to Texas."

I quickly wiped my eyes. "That's a mighty harsh plan."

"It is." He put his arm around me. "I'm not saying I understand it. But if we're stronger as man and wife because of the loss, maybe there's some good in it."

I leaned against his shoulder, and he drew me closer. We sat in silence for a while before he spoke again, softly.

"Look around, Maggie. It's beautiful here, a lot like home with the mountains and timber. There's plenty of clean water, and the weather's pleasant. I reckon there couldn't be a nicer place to settle, not even Texas. You know how folks are, anyway. Probably half of what they say about Texas is not even true."

"But what about the seed corn? What will we do with nowhere to plant it? Eat it? Then we'd not have seed next year." I shook my head. "It'd be some awful hard times. I just don't see how we could make it."

"I don't see how, either. But it reminds me of some verses Pa made us read every time there was a dry spell and the corn looked poor." He closed his eyes and recited. "'Although the fig tree shall not blossom, neither shall fruit be in the vines; the labor of the olive shall fail, and the fields shall yield no meat; the flock shall be cut off from the fold, and there shall be no herd in the stalls; Yet I will rejoice in the Lord, I will joy in the God of my salvation. The Lord God is my strength, and he will make my feet like hinds' feet, and he will make me to walk upon mine high places.'" He opened his eyes and smiled at me. "I don't see how we can make it, but I know we'll be all right. I don't have to know how it will all work out. It's like Sarah said—there may be hard times, but they can be our good times, too. We'll make them our good times."

I looked into his eyes, and what I saw there was what I'd been praying for, the hope that had kept me off the steamboat heading for

Nashville, a love just like in the old ballads. No, I told myself, better than the old ballads, for this was what Sarah had promised I'd find with him, all those months ago—true love born of going on together, day by day.

When had it happened? I wondered. There was no clear path we had taken to get here. Our life together had been a tangle of troubles, one after another. Looking back at it now, though, maybe I understood what he meant. There was a pattern in the weaving together of all the tangles—all the good moments, the bad things that could have happened but didn't, and even the worst things that did happen, like losing our baby. Every strand made for a stronger weave, our bond as husband and wife, reflected now as this promise in his eyes and stretching out in ways I couldn't predict. Did it really matter if our cabin was in Texas or Arkansas Territory? John David was back, and we would be in that cabin together. Maybe I didn't need to know just how things would turn out for us, so long as I trusted there was a Master at the weaving.

He had taken my hand in his. "Captain Russell is waiting at the mouth of this creek. If you really would rather go on to Texas, we'll go. He said he'd drop us off at Little Rock. We could catch the Southwest Trail, just like we planned. But, Maggie, I believe we can have everything we thought we'd have in Texas right here—the cabin with glass windows, the cornfields, the babies—"

He suddenly reached around me and came back holding a tiny blue flower between his fingers. It was plain and simple, only four small petals on a bare stem, but there was something lovely about it, all the same.

"You'll have flowers," he said.

Smiling, I pulled the locket from inside my shirt. He opened it and laid the tiny flower inside, next to the lock of his hair. I snapped it shut, pressed it to my lips and then pushed myself up from the ground.

"Come on," I said, pulling on his hand. "Let's tell Captain Russell they're going on without you."

Author's Note

Americans have always been a restless people. Even before the thirteen colonies declared their independence from Great Britain, people like Daniel Boone were pushing past the Appalachian Mountains, into the interior of the continent. The Oregon Trail is probably the most familiar pioneering story in American history, but before there was an Oregon Trail, people flocked to Mexican Texas in search of a better life.

Maggie and John David were not real people, but they represent those early Texas pioneers. During the 1820s and 1830s, many people abandoned their homes in Tennessee and other settled areas, leaving only the notation "GTT," meaning "Gone to Texas," scrawled across their door. Of all the reasons people had for leaving, John David's reason was probably most common—a desire for land and a new start. Mexican Texas was especially attractive to Americans during the 1820s, thanks to two factors: the Land Act of 1820, in which the U.S. Congress set the price of public land at $1.25 per acre, gold or silver, with a minimum purchase of 80 acres, meaning anyone wanting land had to have at least $100 in hard cash; and a generous immigration policy by the newly independent republic of Mexico, which was feeling the impact of a decade-long war against Spanish colonial rule. The Mexicans hoped to use controlled colonization by Americans to help secure Texas from Indians and encroachment by the United States. Ironically, what was meant to be a defensive policy instead opened the floodgates to immigrants, with approximately 30,000 Americans settled in Texas by 1830.

Most of the other characters in this story are also fictional but represent some of the different groups of people who made up the

American South of that time: slaves and slave owners, merchants and poor people, outlaws and keelboat workers, among others. Not everyone in the book is fictional, however. All the characters mentioned in association with Dwight Mission in Arkansas Territory were real people, although they are used fictitiously in this story. Dwight Mission was founded in 1820 by the American Board of Commissioners for Foreign Missions (ABCFM) of the Presbyterian Church as a mission school for the children of the Cherokee Indians who had moved to Arkansas from their homes in the East. Cephas Washburn and Alfred Finney were the two missionaries who braved the Arkansas wilderness with their families to establish the mission. Jane Hicks was also a real person, although all we know about her is what is recorded in Washburn's *Reminiscences of the Indians*—that she was one of the mission's earliest converts to Christianity, at age 12, and that prior to her conversion, she had a special fear of witches. Washburn also noted that Jane died of typhoid fever less than a year after her conversion, "to be forever with Jesus and her little brother in heaven."

If most of the people in the book are fictional, all the specific places mentioned are real. I've made an effort to portray the places in Maggie's and John David's world as they would have been. One thing writing this book has made me aware of is that the world that seems so permanent to us is actually a very changeable one. For example, all the rivers Maggie and John David used as their "highways" to Texas—the Cumberland, the Ohio, the Arkansas, even the Mississippi—have been dammed to regulate the flow of water for flood control and to make them more consistent for navigation. The Arkansas River one sees today is nothing like the river John David would have struggled against with his keelboat pole.

Also, communities that were once thriving centers of commerce, like Arkansas Post, dried up and disappeared for various reasons. In the case of Arkansas Post, the death blow came with the relocation of the territorial capital to Little Rock; although the town lingered through the 1850s, it never recovered its original stature. Today, nothing remains but an Arkansas state museum park with five exhibit buildings. The original Dwight Mission suffered a less honorable fate. At its peak, the school had approximately one hundred Cherokee students. In 1828, when a treaty forced the Cherokee to relocate to present-day Oklahoma, the mission went with them. The original site for the school, one of the first west of the Mississippi, is now at the bottom of Lake Dardanelle, with only a highway historical marker to note it ever existed.

To find out more about the history and lifestyles of *His Promise True*, visit www.emzpineypublishing.com.

About the Author

Greta Marlow teaches communication, speech, and public relations courses at a small, private college in Arkansas. This is her first novel (unless you count the one about the Razorback basketball team she wrote when she was 14). She lives with her husband and two nearly-grown children at the foot of the Ozarks Mountains. Although chances don't come very often, she loves to hike through the woods and along the creeks in the mountains and imagine she's following the footsteps of people like Maggie and John David along the rocky paths.

Acknowledgments

As the saying goes (with slight paraphrase), "Behind every successful writer is a great community." I want to thank everyone who gave encouragement through the process of bringing this book to life, but there are four people in particular who deserve special thanks: Cara Flinn, for being the best "first reader" ever and a profoundly patient listener; Christopher Hawthorne Moss, for reading and commenting on early drafts and for unfailing encouragement; Janet Reid, the literary agent who, although this book is not in a genre she represents, renewed my faith in it with her comments; and Nancy Dane, for a final, firm push out of the nest.

Coming in 2014.....

A Permanent Home

    John David McKellar dreams of building a home for Maggie and his growing family in the mountains of Arkansas Territory, despite a government treaty that gives the land he wants to the Western Cherokees. He tries to get around the treaty, first by squatting illegally on the land and later by going with other white settlers in an effort to stake an early claim in the disputed area called Lovely's Purchase. Nothing works, though, and he blames his failures on the Cherokees, especially Elwin Root, a young warrior who seems intent on stealing even Maggie's affections, the one thing John David thought he could be sure of.
    Desperate to feed his family, John David takes work with the federal agent for the Cherokees, even though he views the Indians as his enemy. But by the time another government treaty moves the Cherokees farther to the west, it's not so easy for John David to say who the real enemy is. When a former ally threatens to once again deny him a chance at the land he wants, he'll have to swallow his pride and rebuild some long-neglected bridges to get what he wants—a permanent home.